At the Sign of ¡. ¸ ⸗.. ₐₙₐ Racket

A painter's greatest masterpiece is inspired by a young girl of angelic beauty, but their resulting marriage only serves to reveal the deep divide between their true natures . . .

The Ball at Sceaux

. . . a haughty young demoiselle, the last child to marry from an old noble family, is raised to be all too discerning in her choice of a future husband, with tragic consequences . . .

Letters of Two Brides

. . . a lifelong correspondence between two young women illustrates their different ideas about love and marriage—one valuing romance and excitement, the other marital duty—but as they begin to live out their philosophies of love and life, one thrives and prospers as a wife and mother while the other is slowly consumed by jealousy . . .

These three works form the first volume of Balzac's monumental *Comédie Humaine*. Left unfinished at the time of the writer's death, it is a vast literary undertaking composed of some hundred short stories, novellas, and novels set in the shadow of the Napoleonic Wars during the Bourbon Restoration and the July Monarchy. Throughout, Balzac utilizes nineteenth century French society to examine humanity and the human experience with all its attendant virtues, vices, and peculiarities. The works in this volume are preceded by an introduction in which the author sets forth the history of the project and explains his principles of composition.

Following the authoritative French Pléiade edition in the ordering of the stories, Noumena Press plans to release Balzac's complete magnum opus in a set of forty-five matching volumes, each one newly annotated, edited, and with the original illustrations from the Furne edition of 1842.

Honoré de Balzac (1799-1850), considered by many to be one of the principal founders of realism in literature, was one of France's most prolific and influential writers.

De Balzac

THE HUMAN COMEDY, VOL. I
At the Sign of the Cat and Racket
and Other Works
by Honoré de Balzac

Translated from the French by Clara Bell and R.S. Scott
with Illustrations from the Furne Edition

Noumena Press
Baltimore
www.noumenapress.com

Noumena Classics are published by Noumena Press.
This edition © 2008 Noumena Press. All rights reserved.
www.noumenapress.com

Version 1.1

ISBN-13   978-0-9767062-0-5 (paperback)
LCCN   2008943784

Printed on acid-free paper

Edited and annotated by R.J. Allinson, BA, MLIS

Cover: Detail of *Monsieur Guillaume* (1846) by Jean Louis
Ernest Meissonier. Cover Design by Rachel Thern.

Noumena Press makes every effort to publish books of the
highest possible quality. However, despite our best efforts,
errors or omissions are sometimes unavoidable. Please help
us to improve our editions by reporting any problems to
editor@noumenapress.com. Suggestions as to how we can
make our books better are also welcome. Relevant changes
will be incorporated into future versions.

Table of Contents

The Human Comedy

Studies of Manners
Scenes From Private Life

Addenda that follow each story provide cross-references to character appearances in other works of the *Human Comedy*.

List of Plates

Author's Introduction
(*Avant-Propos*)

In giving the general title of "The Human Comedy" to a work begun nearly thirteen years since, it is necessary to explain its motive, to relate its origin, and briefly sketch its plan, while endeavoring to speak of these matters as though I had no personal interest in them. This is not so difficult as the public might imagine. Few works conduce to much vanity; much labor conduces to great diffidence. This observation accounts for the study of their own works made by Corneille, Molière, and other great writers; if it is impossible to equal them in their fine conceptions, we may try to imitate them in this feeling.

The idea of *The Human Comedy* was at first as a dream to me, one of those impossible projects which we caress and then let fly; a chimera that gives us a glimpse of its smiling woman's face, and forthwith spreads its wings and returns to a heavenly realm of phantasy. But this chimera, like many another, has become a reality; has its behests, its tyranny, which must be obeyed.

The idea originated in a comparison between Humanity and Animality.

It is a mistake to suppose that the great dispute which has lately made a stir, between Cuvier and Geoffroi Saint-Hilaire, arose from a scientific innovation. *Unity of structure*,* under other names, had occupied the greatest minds during the two previous centuries. As we read the extraordinary writings of the mystics who studied the sciences in their relation to infinity, such as Swedenborg, Saint-Martin,* and others, and the works of the greatest authors on Natural History—Leibnitz, Buffon, Charles Bonnet, etc., we detect in the *monads* of Leibnitz, in the *organic molecules* of Buffon, in the *vegetative force* of Needham,* in the correlation of similar organs of Charles Bonnet—who in 1760 was so bold as to write, "Animals vegetate as plants do"—we detect, I say, the rudiments of the great law of Self for Self, which lies at the root of *Unity of Plan*. There is but one Animal. The Creator works on a single model for every organized being. "The Animal" is elementary, and takes its external form, or, to be accurate, the differences in its form, from the environment in which it is obliged to develop. Zoological species are the result of these differences. The announcement and defence of this system, which is indeed in harmony with our preconceived ideas of Divine Power, will be the eternal glory of Geoffroi Saint-Hilaire, Cuvier's victorious opponent on this point of higher science, whose triumph was hailed by Goethe in the last article he wrote.

I, for my part, convinced of this scheme of nature long before the discussion to which it has given rise, perceived that in this respect society resembled nature. For does not society modify Man, according to the conditions in which he lives and acts, into men as manifold as the species in Zoology? The differences between a soldier, an artisan, a man of business, a lawyer, an idler, a student, a statesman, a merchant, a sailor, a poet, a beggar, a priest, are as great, though not so easy to define, as those between the wolf, the lion, the ass, the crow, the shark, the seal, the sheep, etc. Thus social species have always existed, and will always exist, just as there are zoological species. If Buffon could produce a magnificent work by attempting to represent in a book the whole realm of zoology, was there not room for a work of the same kind on society? But the limits set by nature to the variations of animals have no existence in society. When Buffon describes the lion, he dismisses the lioness with a few phrases; but in society a wife is not always the female of the male. There may be two perfectly dissimilar beings in one household. The wife of a shopkeeper is sometimes worthy of a prince, and the wife of a prince is often worthless compared with the wife of an artisan. The social state has freaks which Nature does not allow herself; it is nature *plus* society. The description of social species would thus be at least double that of animal species, merely in view of the two sexes. Then, among animals the drama is limited; there is scarcely any confusion; they turn and rend each other—that is all. Men, too, rend each other; but their greater or less intelligence makes the struggle far more complicated. Though some savants do not yet admit that the animal nature flows into human nature through an immense tide of life, the grocer certainly becomes a peer, and the noble sometimes sinks to the lowest social grade. Again, Buffon found that life was extremely simple among animals. Animals have little property, and neither arts nor sciences; while man, by a law that has yet to be sought, has a tendency to express his culture, his thoughts, and his life in everything he appropriates to his use. Though Leuwenhoek, Swammerdam, Spallanzani, Réaumur, Charles Bonnet, Müller, Haller and other patient investigators have shown us how interesting are the habits of animals, those of each kind, are, at least to our eyes, always and in every age alike; whereas the dress, the manners, the speech, the dwelling of a prince, a banker, an artist, a citizen, a priest, and a pauper are absolutely unlike, and change with every phase of civilization.

Hence the work to be written needed a threefold form—men, women, and things; that is to say, persons and the material expression of their minds; man, in short, and life.

As we read the dry and discouraging list of events called History, who can have failed to note that the writers of all periods, in Egypt, Persia, Greece, and Rome, have forgotten to give us a history of manners? The fragment of Petronius on the private life of the Romans excites rather than satisfies our curiosity. It was from observing this great void in the field of history that the Abbé Barthélemy devoted his life to a reconstruction of Greek manners in *Le Jeune Anacharsis*.*

But how could such a drama, with the four or five thousand persons which society offers, be made interesting? How, at the same time, please the poet, the philosopher, and the masses who want both poetry and philosophy under striking imagery? Though I could conceive of the importance and of the poetry of such a history of the human heart, I saw no way of writing it; for hitherto the most famous story-tellers had spent their talent in creating two or three typical actors, in depicting one aspect of life. It was with this idea that I read the works of Walter Scott. Walter Scott, the modern troubadour, or finder (*trouvère=trouveur*), had just then given an aspect of grandeur to a class of composition unjustly regarded as of the second rank. Is it not really more difficult to compete with personal and parochial interests by writing of Daphnis and Chloe, Roland, Amadis, Panurge, Don Quixote, Manon Lescaut, Clarissa, Lovelace, Robinson Crusoe, Gil Blas, Ossian, Julie d'Etanges, My Uncle Toby, Werther, René, Corinne, Adolphe, Paul and Virginia, Jeanie Deans, Claverhouse, Ivanhoe, Manfred, Mignon,* than to set forth in order facts more or less similar in every country, to investigate the spirit of laws that have fallen into desuetude, to review the theories which mislead nations, or, like some metaphysicians, to explain what *Is*? In the first place, these actors, whose existence becomes more prolonged and more authentic than that of the generations which saw their birth, almost always live solely on condition of their being a vast reflection of the present. Conceived in the womb of their own period, the whole heart of humanity stirs within their frame, which often covers a complete system of philosophy. Thus Walter Scott raised to the dignity of the philosophy of History the literature which, from age to age, sets perennial gems in the poetic crown of every nation where letters are cultivated. He vivified it with the spirit of the past; he combined drama, dialogue, portrait, scenery, and description; he fused the marvelous with truth—the two elements of the times; and he brought poetry into close contact with the familiarity of the humblest speech. But as he had not so much devised a system as hit upon a manner in the ardor of his work, or as its logical outcome, he never thought of connecting his compositions in such a way as to form a complete history of which each chapter was a novel, and each novel the picture of a period.

It was by discerning this lack of unity, which in no way detracts from the Scottish writer's greatness, that I perceived at once the scheme which would favor the execution of my purpose, and the possibility of executing it. Though dazzled, so to speak, by Walter Scott's amazing fertility, always himself and always original, I did not despair, for I found the source of his genius in the infinite variety of human nature. Chance is the greatest romancer in the world; we have only to study it. French society would be the real author; I should only be the secretary. By drawing up an inventory of vices and virtues, by collecting the chief facts of the passions, by depicting characters, by choosing the principal incidents of social life, by composing types out of a combination of homogeneous characteristics, I might perhaps succeed in writing the history which so many historians have neglected: that of Manners. By patience and perseverance I might produce for France in the nineteenth century the book which we must all regret that Rome, Athens, Tyre, Memphis, Persia, and India have not bequeathed to us; that history of their social life which, prompted by the Abbé Barthélemy, Monteil* patiently and steadily tried to write for the Middle Ages, but in an unattractive form.

This work, so far, was nothing. By adhering to the strict lines of a reproduction a writer might be a more or less faithful, and more or less successful, painter of types of humanity, a narrator of the dramas of private life, an archaeologist of social furniture, a cataloguer of professions, a registrar of good and evil; but to deserve the praise of which every artist must be ambitious, must I not also investigate the reasons or the cause of these social effects, detect the hidden sense of this vast assembly of figures, passions, and incidents? And finally, having sought—I will not say having found—this reason, this motive power, must I not reflect on first principles, and discover in what particulars societies approach or deviate from the eternal law of truth and beauty? In spite of the wide scope of the preliminaries, which might of themselves constitute a book, the work, to be complete, would need a conclusion. Thus depicted, society ought to bear in itself the reason of its working.

The law of the writer, in virtue of which he is a writer, and which I do not hesitate to say makes him the equal, or perhaps the superior, of the statesman, is his judgment, whatever it may be, on human affairs, and his absolute devotion to certain principles. Machiavelli, Hobbes, Bossuet, Leibnitz, Kant, Montesquieu, *are* the science which statesmen apply. "A writer ought to have settled opinions on morals and politics; he should regard himself as a tutor of men; for men need no masters to teach them to doubt," says Bonald.* I took these noble words as my guide long ago; they are the written law of the monarchical writer. And those who would confute me by my own words will find that they have misinterpreted some ironical phrase, or that they have turned against me a speech given to one of my actors—a trick peculiar to calumniators.

As to the intimate purpose, the soul of this work, these are the principles on which it is based.

Man is neither good nor bad; he is born with instincts and capabilities; society, far from depraving him, as Rousseau asserts, improves him, makes him better; but self-interest also develops his evil tendencies. Christianity, above all, Catholicism, being—as I have pointed out in the Country Doctor (*Le Médecin de Campagne*)—a complete system for the repression of the depraved tendencies of man, is the most powerful element of social order.

In reading attentively the presentment of society cast, as it were, from the life, with all that is good and all that is bad in it, we learn this lesson—if thought, or if passion, which combines thought and feeling, is the vital social element, it is also its destructive element. In this respect social life is like the life of man. Nations live long only by moderating their vital energy. Teaching, or rather education, by religious bodies is the grand principle of life for nations, the only means of diminishing the sum of evil and increasing the sum of good in all society. Thought, the living principle of good and ill, can only be trained, quelled, and guided by religion. The only possible religion is Christianity (see the letter from Paris in *Louis Lambert*, in which the young mystic explains, *à propos* to Swedenborg's doctrines, how there has never been but one religion since the world began). Christianity created modern nationalities, and it will preserve them. Hence, no doubt, the necessity for the monarchical principle. Catholicism and Royalty are twin principles.

As to the limits within which these two principles should be confined by various institutions, so that they may not become absolute, every one will feel that a brief preface ought not to be a political treatise. I cannot, therefore, enter on religious discussions, nor on the political discussions of the day. I write under the light of two eternal truths—Religion and Monarchy; two necessities, as they are shown to be by contemporary events, towards which every writer of sound sense ought to try to guide the country back. Without being an enemy to election, which is an excellent principle as a basis of legislation, I reject election regarded as *the only social instrument*, especially so badly organized as it now is (1842); for it fails to represent imposing minorities, whose ideas and interests would occupy the attention of a monarchical government. Elective power extended to all gives us government by the masses, the only irresponsible form of government, under which tyranny is unlimited, for it calls itself law. Besides, I regard the family and not the individual as the true social unit. In this respect, at the risk of being thought retrograde, I side with Bossuet and Bonald instead of going with modern innovators. Since election has become the only social instrument, if I myself were to exercise it no contradiction between my acts and my words should be inferred. An engineer points out that a bridge is about to fall, that it is dangerous for any one to cross it; but he crosses it himself when it is the only road to the town. Napoleon adapted election to the spirit of the French nation with wonderful skill. The least important members of his Legislative Body became the most famous orators of the Chamber after the Restoration. No Chamber has ever been the equal of the *Corps Législatif,** comparing them man for man. The elective system of the Empire was, then, indisputably the best.

Some persons may, perhaps, think that this declaration is somewhat autocratic and self-assertive. They will quarrel with the novelist for wanting to be an historian, and will call him to account for writing politics. I am simply fulfilling an obligation—that is my reply. The work I have undertaken will be as long as a history; I was compelled to explain the logic of it, hitherto unrevealed, and its principles and moral purpose.

Having been obliged to withdraw the prefaces formerly published, in response to essentially ephemeral criticisms, I will retain only one remark.

Writers who have a purpose in view, were it only a reversion to principles familiar in the past because they are eternal, should always clear the ground. Now every one who, in the domain of ideas, brings his stone by pointing out an abuse, or setting a mark on some evil that it may be removed—every such man is stigmatized as immoral. The accusation of immorality, which has never failed to be cast at the courageous writer, is, after all, the last that can be brought when nothing else remains to be said to a romancer. If you are truthful in your pictures; if by dint of daily and nightly toil you succeed in writing the most difficult language in the world, the word *immoral* is flung in your teeth. Socrates was immoral; Jesus Christ was immoral; they both were persecuted in the name of the society they overset or reformed. When a man is to be killed he is taxed with immorality. These tactics, familiar in party warfare, are a disgrace to those who use them. Luther and Calvin knew well what they were about when they shielded themselves behind damaged worldly interests! And they lived all the days of their life.

When depicting all society, sketching it in the immensity of its turmoil, it happened—it could not but happen—that the picture displayed more of evil than of good; that some part of the fresco represented a guilty couple; and the critics at once raised a cry of immorality, without pointing out the morality of another position intended to be a perfect contrast. As the critic knew nothing of the general plan I could forgive him, all the more because one can no more hinder criticism than the use of eyes, tongues, and judgment. Also the time for an impartial verdict is not yet come for me. And, after all, the author who cannot make up his mind to face the fire of criticism should no more think of writing than a traveler should start on his journey counting on a perpetually clear sky. On this point it remains to be said that the most conscientious moralists doubt greatly whether society can show as many good actions as bad ones; and in the picture I have painted of it there are more virtuous figures than reprehensible ones. Blameworthy actions, faults and crimes, from the lightest to the most atrocious, always meet with punishment, human or divine, signal or secret. I have done better than the historian, for I am free. Cromwell here on earth escaped all punishment but that inflicted by thoughtful men. And on this point there have been divided schools. Bossuet even showed some consideration for great regicide. William of Orange, the usurper, Hugues Capet, another usurper, lived to old age with no more qualms or fears than Henri IV or Charles I. The lives of Catherine II and of Frederick of Prussia would be conclusive against any kind of moral law, if they were judged by the twofold aspect of the morality which guides ordinary mortals, and that which is in use by crowned heads; for, as Napoleon said, for kings and statesmen there are the lesser and the higher morality. My *Scenes of Political Life* are founded on this profound observation. It is not a law to history, as it is to romance, to make for a beautiful ideal. History is, or ought to be, what it was; while romance ought to be "the better world," as was said by Madame Necker,* one of the most distinguished thinkers of the last century.

Still, with this noble falsity, romance would be nothing if it were not true in detail. Walter Scott, obliged as he was to conform to the ideas of an essentially hypocritical nation, was false to humanity in his picture of woman, because his models were schismatics. The Protestant woman has no ideal. She may be chaste, pure, virtuous; but her unexpansive love will always be as calm and methodical as the fulfilment of a duty. It might seem as though the Virgin Mary had chilled the hearts of those sophists who have banished her from heaven with her treasures of loving kindness. In Protestantism there is no possible future for the woman who has sinned; while, in the Catholic Church, the hope of forgiveness makes her sublime. Hence, for the Protestant writer there is but one Woman, while the Catholic writer finds a new woman in each new situation. If Walter Scott had been a Catholic, if he had set himself the task of describing truly the various phases of society which have successively existed in Scotland, perhaps the painter of Effie and Alice*—the two figures for which he blamed himself in his later years—might have admitted passion with its sins and punishments, and the virtues revealed by repentance. Passion is the sum-total of humanity. Without passion, religion, history, romance, art, would all be useless.

Some persons, seeing me collect such a mass of facts and paint them as they are, with passion for their motive power, have supposed, but wrongly, that I must belong to the school of Sensualism and Materialism—two aspects of the same thing—Pantheism. But their misapprehension was perhaps justified—or inevitable. I do not share the belief in indefinite progress for society as a whole; I believe in man's improvement in himself. Those who insist on reading in me the intention to consider man as a finished creation are strangely mistaken. *Séraphita*, the doctrine in action of the Christian Buddha, seems to me an ample answer to this rather heedless accusation.

In certain fragments of this long work I have tried to popularize the amazing facts, I may say the marvels, of electricity, which in man is metamorphosed into an incalculable force; but in what way do the phenomena of brain and nerves, which prove the existence of an undiscovered world of psychology, modify the necessary and undoubted relations of the worlds to God? In what way can they shake the Catholic dogma? Though irrefutable facts should some day place thought in the class of fluids which are discerned only by their effects while their substance evades our senses, even when aided by so many mechanical means, the result will be the same as when Christopher Columbus detected that the earth is a sphere, and Galileo demonstrated its rotation. Our future will be unchanged. The wonders of animal magnetism, with which I have been familiar since 1820; the beautiful experiments of Gall,* Lavater's successor; all the men who have studied mind as opticians have studied light—two not dissimilar things—point to a conclusion in favor of the mystics, the disciples of St. John, and of those great thinkers who have established the spiritual world—the sphere in which are revealed the relations of God and man.

A sure grasp of the purport of this work will make it clear that I attach to common, daily facts, hidden or patent to the eye, to the acts of individual lives, and to their causes and principles, the importance which historians have hitherto ascribed to the events of public national life. The unknown struggle which goes on in a valley of the Indre between Madame de Mortsauf and her passion is perhaps as great as the most famous of battles (*Le Lys dans la Vallée*). In one the glory of the victor is at stake; in the other it is heaven. The misfortunes of the two Birotteaus, the priest and the perfumer, to me are those of mankind. La Fosseuse (*Le Médecin de Campagne*) and Madame Graslin (*Le Curé de Village*) are almost the sum-total of woman. We all suffer thus every day. I have had to do a hundred times what Richardson did but once. Lovelace has a thousand forms, for social corruption takes the hues of the medium in which it lives. Clarissa, on the contrary, the lovely image of impassioned virtue, is drawn in lines of distracting purity. To create a variety of Virgins it needs a Raphael. In this respect, perhaps literature must yield to painting.

Still, I may be allowed to point out how many

irreproachable figures—as regards their virtue—are to be found in the portions of this work already published: Pierrette Lorrain, Ursule Mirouët, Constance Birotteau, La Fosseuse, Eugénie Grandet, Marguerite Claës, Pauline de Villenoix, Madame Jules, Madame de la Chanterie, Eve Chardon, Mademoiselle d'Esgrignon, Madame Firmiani, Agathe Rouget, Renée de Maucombe; besides several figures in the middle-distance, who, though less conspicuous than these, nevertheless, offer the reader an example of domestic virtue: Joseph Lebas, Genestas, Benassis, Bonnet the curé, Minoret the doctor, Pillerault, David Séchard, the two Birotteaus, Chaperon the priest, Judge Popinot, Bourgeat, the Sauviats, the Tascherons, and many more. Do not all these solve the difficult literary problem which consists in making a virtuous person interesting?

It was no small task to depict the two or three thousand conspicuous types of a period; for this is, in fact, the number presented to us by each generation, and which the *Human Comedy* will require. This crowd of actors, of characters, this multitude of lives, needed a setting—if I may be pardoned the expression, a gallery. Hence the very natural division, as already known, into the *Scenes of Private Life*, of *Provincial Life*, of *Parisian*, *Political*, *Military*, and *Country Life*. Under these six heads are classified all the studies of manners which form the history of society at large, of all its *faits et gestes*,* as our ancestors would have said. These six classes correspond, indeed, to familiar conceptions. Each has its own sense and meaning, and answers to an epoch in the life of man. I may repeat here, but very briefly, what was written by Félix Davin*—a young genius snatched from literature by an early death. After being informed of my plan, he said that the *Scenes of Private Life* represented childhood and youth and their errors, as the *Scenes of Provincial Life* represented the age of passion, scheming, self-interest, and ambition. Then the *Scenes of Parisian Life* give a picture of the tastes and vice and unbridled powers which conduce to the habits peculiar to great cities, where the extremes of good and evil meet. Each of these divisions has its local color—Paris and the Provinces—a great social antithesis which held for me immense resources.

And not man alone, but the principal events of life, fall into classes by types. There are situations which occur in every life, typical phases, and this is one of the details I most sought after. I have tried to give an idea of the different districts of our fine country. My work has its geography, as it has its genealogy and its families, its places and things, its persons and their deeds; as it has its heraldry, its nobles and commonalty, its artisans and peasants, its politicians and dandies, its army—in short, a whole world of its own.

After describing social life in these three portions, I had to delineate certain exceptional lives, which comprehend the interests of many people, or of everybody, and are in a degree outside the general law. Hence we have *Scenes of Political Life*. This vast picture of society being finished and complete, was it not needful to display it in its most violent phase, beside itself, as it were, either in self-defence or for the sake of conquest? Hence the *Scenes of Military Life*, as yet the most incomplete portion of my work, but for which room will be allowed in this edition, that it may form part of it when done. Finally, the *Scenes of Country Life* are, in a way, the evening of this long day, if I may so call the social drama. In that part are to be found the purest natures, and the application of the great principles of order, politics, and morality.

Such is the foundation, full of actors, full of comedies and tragedies, on which are raised the *Philosophical Studies*—the second part of my work, in which the social instrument of all these effects is displayed, and the ravages of the mind are painted, feeling after feeling; the first of the series, *The Magic Skin*, to some extent forms a link between the *Philosophical Studies* and *Studies of Manners*, by a work of almost Oriental fancy, in which life itself is shown in a mortal struggle with the very element of all passion.

Besides these, there will be a series of *Analytical Studies*, of which I will say nothing, for one only is published as yet — *The Physiology of Marriage*.

In the course of time I purpose writing two more works of this class. First the *Pathology of Social Life*, then an *Anatomy of Educational Bodies*, and a *Monograph on Virtue*.*

In looking forward to what remains to be done, my readers will perhaps echo what my publishers say, "Please God to spare you!" I only ask to be less tormented by men and things than I have hitherto been since I began this terrific labor. I have had this in my favor, and I thank God for it, that the talents of the time, the finest characters and the truest friends, as noble in their private lives as the former are in public life, have wrung my hand and said, Courage!

And why should I not confess that this friendship, and the testimony here and there of persons unknown to me, have upheld me in my career, both against myself and against unjust attacks; against the calumny which has often persecuted me, against discouragement, and against the too eager hopefulness whose utterances are misinterpreted as those of overwhelming conceit? I had resolved to display stolid stoicism in the face of abuse and insults; but on two occasions base slanders have necessitated a reply. Though the advocates of forgiveness of injuries may regret that I should have displayed my skill in literary fence, there are many Christians who are of opinion that we live in times when it is as well to show sometimes that silence springs from generosity.

The vastness of a plan which includes both a history

and a criticism of society, an analysis of its evils, and a discussion of its principles, authorizes me, I think, in giving to my work the title under which it now appears—*The Human Comedy*. Is this too ambitious? Is it not exact? That, when it is complete, the public must pronounce.

Paris, July 1842

At the Sign of the Cat and Racket
(*La Maison du Chat-Qui Pelote*)
Translated by Clara Bell

*To Mademoiselle Marie de Montheau**

La figure de monsieur GUILLAUME annonçait la patience, la sagesse commerciale, et l'espèce de cupidité rusée que réclament les affaires.

LA MAISON DU CHAT-QUI-PELOTE.

Plate I: *Monsieur Guillaume*
Illustration by Jean Louis Ernest Meissonier

Half-way down the Rue Saint-Denis, almost at the corner of the Rue du Petit-Lion,* there stood formerly one of those delightful houses which enable historians to reconstruct old Paris by analogy. The threatening walls of this tumbledown abode seemed to have been decorated with hieroglyphics. For what other name could the passer-by give to the Xs and Vs which the horizontal or diagonal timbers traced on the front, outlined by little parallel cracks in the plaster? It was evident that every beam quivered in its mortices at the passing of the lightest vehicle. This venerable structure was crowned by a triangular roof of which no example will, ere long, be seen in Paris. This covering, warped by the extremes of the Paris climate, projected three feet over the roadway, as much to protect the threshold from the rainfall as to shelter the wall of a loft and its sill-less dormer-window. This upper story was built of planks, overlapping each other like slates, in order, no doubt, not to overweight the frail house.

One rainy morning in the month of March, a young man, carefully wrapped in his cloak, stood under the awning of a shop opposite this old house, which he was studying with the enthusiasm of an antiquary. In point of fact, this relic of the civic life of the sixteenth century offered more than one problem to the consideration of an observer. Each story presented some singularity; on the first floor four tall, narrow windows, close together, were filled as to the lower panes with boards, so as to produce the doubtful light by which a clever

3

salesman can ascribe to his goods the color his customers inquire for. The young man seemed very scornful of
this part of the house; his eyes had not yet rested on it.
The windows of the second floor, where the Venetian
blinds were drawn up, revealing little dingy muslin
curtains behind the large Bohemian glass panes, did
not interest him either. His attention was attracted to
the third floor, to the modest sash-frames of wood, so
clumsily wrought that they might have found a place
in the Museum of Arts and Crafts to illustrate the early efforts of French carpentry. These windows were
glazed with small squares of glass so green that, but for
his good eyes, the young man could not have seen the
blue-checked cotton curtains which screened the mysteries of the room from profane eyes. Now and then the
watcher, weary of his fruitless contemplation, or of the
silence in which the house was buried, like the whole
neighborhood, dropped his eyes towards the lower regions. An involuntary smile parted his lips each time
he looked at the shop, where, in fact, there were some
laughable details.

A formidable wooden beam, resting on four pillars,
which appeared to have bent under the weight of the
decrepit house, had been encrusted with as many coats
of different paint as there are of rouge on an old duchess's cheek. In the middle of this broad and fantastically
carved joist there was an old painting representing a
cat playing rackets. This picture was what moved the
young man to mirth. But it must be said that the wittiest of modern painters could not invent so comical
a caricature. The animal held in one of its forepaws
a racket as big as itself, and stood on its hind legs to
aim at hitting an enormous ball, returned by a man in
a fine embroidered coat. Drawing, color, and accessories, all were treated in such a way as to suggest that
the artist had meant to make game of the shop-own-
er and of the passing observer. Time, while impairing

this artless painting, had made it yet more grotesque by introducing some uncertain features which must have puzzled the conscientious idler. For instance, the cat's tail had been eaten into in such a way that it might now have been taken for the figure of a spectator—so long, and thick, and furry were the tails of our forefathers' cats. To the right of the picture, on an azure field which ill-disguised the decay of the wood, might be read the name "Guillaume," and to the left, "Successor to Master Chevrel." Sun and rain had worn away most of the gilding parsimoniously applied to the letters of this superscription, in which the Us and Vs had changed places in obedience to the laws of old-world orthography.

To quench the pride of those who believe that the world is growing cleverer day by day, and that modern humbug surpasses everything, it may be observed that these signs, of which the origin seems so whimsical to many Paris merchants, are the dead pictures of once living pictures by which our roguish ancestors contrived to tempt customers into their houses. Thus the Spinning Sow, the Green Monkey, and others, were animals in cages whose skills astonished the passer-by, and whose accomplishments prove the patience of the fifteenth-century artisan. Such curiosities did more to enrich their fortunate owners than the signs of "Providence," "Good-faith," "Grace of God," and "Decapitation of John the Baptist," which may still be seen in the Rue Saint-Denis.

However, our stranger was certainly not standing there to admire the cat, which a minute's attention sufficed to stamp on his memory. The young man himself had his peculiarities. His cloak, folded after the manner of an antique drapery, showed a smart pair of shoes, all the more remarkable in the midst of the Paris mud, because he wore white silk stockings, on which the splashes betrayed his impatience. He had just come, no doubt, from a wedding or a ball; for at this early hour he had in his hand a pair of white gloves, and his black hair, now out of curl, and flowing over his shoulders, showed that it had been dressed *à la Caracalla*, a fashion introduced as much by David's school of painting as by the mania for Greek and Roman styles which characterized the early years of this century.

In spite of the noise made by a few market gardeners, who, being late, rattled past towards the great market-place at a gallop, the busy street lay in a stillness of which the magic charm is known only to those who have wandered through deserted Paris at the hours when its roar, hushed for a moment, rises and spreads in the distance like the great voice of the sea. This strange young man must have seemed as curious to the shopkeeping folk of the "Cat and Racket" as the "Cat and Racket" was to him. A dazzlingly white cravat made his anxious face look even paler than it really was. The fire that flashed in his black eyes, gloomy and sparkling by turns, was in harmony with the singular outline of his features, with his wide, flexible mouth, hardened into a smile. His forehead, knit with violent annoyance, had a stamp of doom. Is not the forehead the most prophetic feature of a man? When the stranger's brow expressed passion the furrows formed in it were terrible in their strength and energy; but when he recovered his calmness, so easily upset, it beamed with a luminous grace which gave great attractiveness to a countenance in which joy, grief, love, anger, or scorn blazed out so contagiously that the coldest man could not fail to be impressed.

He was so thoroughly vexed by the time when the dormer-window of the loft was suddenly flung open, that he did not observe the apparition of three laughing faces, pink and white and chubby, but as vulgar as the face of Commerce as it is seen in sculpture on certain monuments. These three faces, framed by the window, recalled the puffy cherubs floating among the clouds that surround God the Father. The apprentices snuffed up the exhalations of the street with an eagerness that showed how hot and poisonous the atmosphere of their garret must be. After pointing to the singular sentinel, the most jovial, as he seemed, of the apprentices retired and came back holding an instrument whose hard metal pipe is now superseded by a leather tube; and they all grinned with mischief as they looked down on the loiterer, and sprinkled him with a fine white shower of which the scent proved that three chins had just been shaved. Standing on tiptoe, in the farthest corner of their loft, to enjoy their victim's rage, the lads ceased laughing on seeing the haughty indifference with which the young man shook his cloak, and the intense contempt expressed by his face as he glanced up at the empty window-frame.

At this moment a slender white hand threw up the lower half of one of the clumsy windows on the third floor by the aid of the sash runners, of which the pulley so often suddenly gives way and releases the heavy panes it ought to hold up. The watcher was then rewarded for his long waiting. The face of a young girl appeared, as fresh as one of the white cups that bloom on the bosom of the waters, crowned by a frill of tumbled muslin, which gave her head a look of exquisite innocence. Though wrapped in brown stuff, her neck and shoulders gleamed here and there through little openings left by her movements in sleep. No expression of embarrassment detracted from the candor of her face, or the calm look of eyes immortalized long since in the sublime works of Raphael; here were the same grace, the same repose as in those Virgins, and now proverbial. There was a delightful contrast between the cheeks of that face on which sleep had, as it were, given high relief to a superabundance of life, and the antiquity of the heavy window with its clumsy shape and black sill. Like those day-blowing flowers, which in the early morning have not yet unfurled their cups, twisted by the chills of night, the girl, as yet hardly awake, let her blue eyes wander beyond the neighboring roofs to look at the sky; then, from habit, she cast them down on the gloomy depths of the street, where they immediately met those of her adorer. Vanity, no doubt, distressed her at being seen in undress; she started back, the worn pulley gave way, and the sash fell with the rapid run, which in our day has earned for this artless invention of our forefathers an odious name, *Fenêtre à la Guillotine.* The vision had disappeared. To the young man the most radiant star of morning seemed to be hidden by a cloud.

During these little incidents the heavy inside shutters that protected the slight windows of the shop of the "Cat and Racket" had been removed as if by magic. The old door with its knocker was opened back against the wall of the entry by a man-servant, apparently coeval with the sign, who, with a shaking hand, hung upon it a square of cloth, on which were embroidered in yellow silk the words: "Guillaume, successor to Chevrel." Many a passer-by would have found it difficult to guess the class of trade carried on by Monsieur Guillaume. Between the strong iron bars which protected his shop windows on the outside, certain packages, wrapped in brown linen, were hardly visible, though as numerous as herrings swimming in a shoal. Notwithstanding the primitive aspect of the Gothic front, Monsieur Guillaume, of all the merchant clothiers in Paris, was the one whose stores were always the best provided, whose connections were the most extensive, and whose commercial honesty never lay under the slightest suspicion. If some of his brethren in business made a contract with the Government, and had not the required quantity of cloth, he was always ready to deliver it, however large the number of pieces tendered for. The wily dealer knew a thousand ways of extracting the largest profits without being obliged, like them, to court patrons, cringing to them, or making them costly presents. When his fellow-tradesmen could only pay in good bills of long date, he would mention his notary as an accommodating man, and managed to get a second profit out of the bargain, thanks to this arrangement, which had made it a proverb among the traders of the Rue Saint-Denis: "Heaven preserve you from Monsieur Guillaume's notary!" to signify a heavy discount.

The old merchant was to be seen standing on the threshold of his shop, as if by a miracle, the instant the servant withdrew. Monsieur Guillaume looked at the Rue Saint-Denis, at the neighboring shops, and at the weather, like a man disembarking at Havre, and seeing France once more after a long voyage. Having convinced himself that nothing had changed while he was asleep, he presently perceived the stranger on guard, and he, on his part, gazed at the patriarchal draper as Humboldt may have scrutinized the first electric eel he saw in America. Monsieur Guillaume wore loose black velvet breeches, pepper-and-salt stockings, and square toed shoes with silver buckles. His coat, with square-cut fronts, square-cut tails, and square-cut collar clothed his slightly bent figure in greenish cloth, finished with white metal buttons, tawny from wear. His gray hair was so accurately combed and flattened over his yellow pate that it made it look like a furrowed field. His little green eyes, that might have been pierced with a gimlet, flashed beneath arches faintly tinged with red in the place of eyebrows. Anxieties had wrinkled his forehead with as many horizontal lines as there were creases in his coat. This colorless face expressed patience, commercial shrewdness, and the sort of wily cupidity which is needful in business. At that time these old families were less rare than they are now, in which the characteristic habits and costume of their calling, surviving in the midst of more recent civilization, were preserved as cherished traditions, like the antediluvian remains found by Cuvier in the quarries.

The head of the Guillaume family was a notable upholder of ancient practices; he might be heard to regret the Provost of Merchants, and never did he mention a decision of the Tribunal of Commerce without calling it the *Sentence of the Consuls*.* Up and dressed the first of the household, in obedience, no doubt, to these old customs, he stood sternly awaiting the appearance of his three assistants, ready to scold them in case they were late. These young disciples of Mercury knew nothing more terrible than the wordless assiduity with which the master scrutinized their faces and their movements on Monday in search of evidence or traces of their pranks. But at this moment the old clothier paid no heed to his apprentices; he was absorbed in trying to divine the motive of the anxious looks which the young man in silk stockings and a cloak cast alternately at his sign-board and into the depths of his shop. The daylight was now brighter, and enabled the stranger to discern the cashier's corner enclosed by a railing and screened by old green silk curtains, where were kept the immense ledgers, the silent oracles of the house. The too inquisitive gazer seemed to covet this little nook, and to be taking the plan of a dining-room at one side, lighted by a skylight, whence the family at meals could easily see the smallest incident that might occur at the shop-door. So much affection for his dwelling seemed suspicious to a trader who had lived long enough to remember the law of maximum prices;* Monsieur Guillaume naturally thought that this sinister personage had an eye to the till of the Cat and Racket. After quietly observing the mute duel which was going on between his master and the stranger, the eldest of the apprentices, having seen that the young man was stealthily watching the windows of the third floor, ventured to place himself on the stone flag where Monsieur Guillaume was standing. He took two steps out into the street, raised his head, and fancied that he caught sight of Mademoiselle Augustine Guillaume in hasty retreat. The draper, annoyed by his assistant's perspicacity, shot a side glance at him; but the draper and his amorous apprentice were suddenly relieved from the fears which the young man's presence had excited in their minds. He hailed a hackney cab on its way to a neighboring stand, and jumped into it with an air of affected indifference. This departure was a balm to the hearts of the other two lads, who had been somewhat uneasy as to meeting the victim of their practical joke.

"Well, gentlemen, what ails you that you are standing there with your arms folded?" said Monsieur Guillaume to his three neophytes. "In former days, bless you, when I was in Master Chevrel's service, I should have overhauled more than two pieces of cloth by this time."

"Then it was daylight earlier," said the second assistant, whose duty this was.

The old shopkeeper could not help smiling. Though two of these young fellows, who were confided to his care by their fathers, rich manufacturers at Louviers* and at Sedan, had only to ask and to have a hundred thousand francs the day when they were old enough to settle in life, Guillaume regarded it as his duty to keep them under the rod of an old-world despotism, unknown nowadays in the showy modern shops, where the apprentices expect to be rich men at thirty. He made them work like Negroes. These three assistants were equal to a business which would harry ten such clerks as those whose sybaritical tastes now swell the columns of the budget. Not a sound disturbed the peace of this solemn house, where the hinges were always oiled, and where the meanest article of furniture showed the respectable cleanliness which reveals strict order and economy. The most waggish of the three youths often amused himself by writing the date of its first appearance on the Gruyère cheese which was left to their tender mercies at breakfast, and which it was their pleasure to leave untouched. This bit of mischief, and a few others of the same stamp, would sometimes bring a smile on the face of the younger of Guillaume's daughters, the pretty maiden who has just now appeared to the bewitched man in the street.

Though each of these apprentices, even the eldest, paid a round sum for his board, not one of them would have been bold enough to remain at the master's table when dessert was served. When Madame Guillaume talked of dressing the salad, the hapless youths trembled as they thought of the thrift with which her prudent hand dispensed the oil. They could never think of spending a night away from the house without having given, long before, a plausible reason for such an irregularity. Every Sunday, each in his turn, two of them accompanied the Guillaume family to Mass at Saint-Leu,* and to vespers. Mesdemoiselles Virginie and Augustine, simply attired in cotton print, each took the arm of an apprentice and walked in front, under the piercing eye of their mother, who closed the little family procession with her husband, accustomed by her to carry two large prayer-books, bound in black morocco. The second apprentice received no salary. As for the eldest, whose twelve years of perseverance and discretion had initiated him into the secrets of the house, he was paid eight hundred francs a year as the reward of his labors. On certain family festivals he received as a gratuity some little gift, to which Madame Guillaume's dry and wrinkled hand alone gave value—netted purses, which she took care to stuff with cotton wool, to show off the fancy stitches, braces of the strongest make, or heavy silk stockings. Sometimes, but rarely, this prime minister was admitted to share the pleasures of the family when they went into the country, or when, after waiting for months, they made up their mind to exert the right acquired by taking a box at the theatre to command a piece which Paris had already forgotten.

As to the other assistants, the barrier of respect which formerly divided a master draper from his apprentices was that they would have been more likely to steal a piece of cloth than to infringe this time-honored etiquette. Such reserve may now appear ridiculous; but these old houses were a school of honesty and sound morals. The masters adopted their apprentices. The young man's linen was cared for, mended, and often replaced by the mistress of the house. If an apprentice fell ill, he was the object of truly maternal attention. In a case of danger the master lavished his money in calling in the most celebrated physicians, for he was not answerable to their parents merely for the good conduct and training of the lads. If one of them, whose character was unimpeachable, suffered misfortune, these old tradesmen knew how to value the intelligence he had displayed, and they did not hesitate to entrust the happiness of their daughters to men whom they had long trusted with their fortunes. Guillaume was one of these men of the old school, and if he had their ridiculous side, he had all their good qualities; and Joseph Lebas, the chief assistant, an orphan without any fortune, was in his mind destined to be the husband of Virginie, his elder daughter. But Joseph did not share the symmetrical ideas of his master, who would not for an empire have given his second daughter in marriage before the elder. The unhappy assistant felt that his heart was wholly given to Mademoiselle Augustine, the younger. In order to justify this passion, which had grown up in secret, it is necessary to inquire a little further into the springs of the absolute government which ruled the old cloth-merchant's household.

Guillaume had two daughters. The elder, Mademoiselle Virginie, was the very image of her mother. Madame Guillaume, daughter of the Sieur Chevrel, sat so upright in the stool behind her desk, that more than once she had heard some wag bet that she was a stuffed figure. Her long, thin face betrayed exaggerated piety. Devoid of attractions or of amiable manners, Madame Guillaume commonly decorated her head—that of a woman near on sixty—with a cap of a particular and unvarying shape, with long lappets, like that of a widow. In all the neighborhood she was known as the "portress nun." Her speech was curt, and her movements had the stiff precision of a semaphore. Her eye, with a gleam in it like a cat's, seemed to spite the world because she was so ugly. Mademoiselle Virginie, brought up, like her younger sister, under the domestic rule of her mother, had reached the age of eight-and-twenty. Youth mitigated the graceless effect which her likeness to her mother sometimes gave to her features, but maternal austerity had endowed her with two great qualities which made up for everything. She was patient and gentle. Mademoiselle Augustine, who was but just eighteen, was not like either her father or her mother. She was one of those daughters whose total absence of any physical affinity with their parents makes one believe in the adage: "God gives children." Augustine was little, or, to describe her more truly, delicately made. Full of gracious candor, a man of the world could have found no fault in the charming girl beyond a certain meanness of gesture or vulgarity of attitude, and sometimes a want of ease. Her silent and placid face was full of the transient melancholy which comes over all young girls who are too weak to dare to resist their mother's will.

The two sisters, always plainly dressed, could not gratify the innate vanity of womanhood but by a luxury of cleanliness which became them wonderfully, and made them harmonize with the polished counters and the shining shelves, on which the old man-servant never

left a speck of dust, and with the old-world simplicity of all they saw about them. As their style of living
compelled them to find the elements of happiness in
persistent work, Augustine and Virginie had hitherto
always satisfied their mother, who secretly prided herself on the perfect characters of her two daughters. It
is easy to imagine the results of the training they had
received. Brought up to a commercial life, accustomed
to hear nothing but dreary arguments and calculations
about trade, having studied nothing but grammar,
book-keeping, a little Bible-history, and the history of
France in Le Ragois,* and never reading any book but
what their mother would sanction, their ideas had not
acquired much scope. They knew perfectly how to keep
house; they were familiar with the prices of things; they
understood the difficulty of amassing money; they
were economical, and had a great respect for the qualities that make a man of business. Although their father
was rich, they were as skilled in darning as in embroidery; their mother often talked of having them taught
to cook, so that they might know how to order a dinner
and scold a cook with due knowledge. They knew nothing of the pleasures of the world; and, seeing how their
parents spent their exemplary lives, they very rarely
suffered their eyes to wander beyond the walls of their
hereditary home, which to their mother was the whole
universe. The meetings to which family anniversaries
gave rise filled in the future of earthly joy to them.

When the great drawing-room on the second floor
was to be prepared to receive company — Madame
Roguin, a Demoiselle Chevrel, fifteen months younger
than her cousin, and bedecked with diamonds; young
Rabourdin, employed in the Finance Office; Monsieur
César Birotteau, the rich perfumer, and his wife, known
as Madame César; Monsieur Camusot, the richest silk
mercer in the Rue des Bourdonnais, with his father-in-
law, Monsieur Cardot, two or three old bankers, and

some immaculate ladies—the arrangements, made necessary by the way in which everything was packed away—the plate, the Dresden china, the candlesticks, and the glass—made a variety in the monotonous lives of the three women, who came and went and exerted themselves as nuns would to receive their bishop. Then, in the evening, when all three were tired out with having wiped, rubbed, unpacked, and arranged all the gauds of the festival, as the girls helped their mother to undress, Madame Guillaume would say to them, "Children, we have done nothing today."

When, on very great occasions, "the portress nun" allowed dancing, restricting the games of boston, whist, and backgammon within the limits of her bedroom, such a concession was accounted as the most unhoped felicity, and made them happier than going to the great balls, to two or three of which Guillaume would take the girls at the time of the Carnival.

And once a year the worthy draper gave an entertainment, when he spared no expense. However rich and fashionable the persons invited might be, they were careful not to be absent; for the most important houses on the exchange had recourse to the immense credit, the fortune, or the time-honored experience of Monsieur Guillaume. Still, the excellent merchant's daughters did not benefit as much as might be supposed by the lessons the world has to offer to young spirits. At these parties, which were indeed set down in the ledger to the credit of the house, they wore dresses the shabbiness of which made them blush. Their style of dancing was not in any way remarkable, and their mother's surveillance did not allow of their holding any conversation with their partners beyond Yes and No. Also, the law of the old sign of the Cat and Racket commanded that they should be home by eleven o'clock, the hour when balls and fêtes begin to be lively. Thus their pleasures, which seemed to conform very fairly to their father's position, were often made insipid by circumstances which were part of the family habits and principles.

As to their usual life, one remark will sufficiently paint it. Madame Guillaume required her daughters to be dressed very early in the morning, to come down every day at the same hour, and she ordered their employments with monastic regularity. Augustine, however, had been gifted by chance with a spirit lofty enough to feel the emptiness of such a life. Her blue eyes would sometimes be raised as if to pierce the depths of that gloomy staircase and those damp store-rooms. After sounding the profound cloistral silence, she seemed to be listening to remote, inarticulate revelations of the life of passion, which accounts feelings as of higher value than things. And at such moments her cheek would flush, her idle hands would lay the muslin sewing on the polished oak counter, and presently her mother would say in a voice, of which even the softest tones were sour, "Augustine, my treasure, what are you thinking about?" It is possible that two romances discovered by Augustine in the cupboard of a cook Madame Guillaume had lately discharged—*Hippolyte Comte de Douglas* and *Le Comte de Comminges**—may have contributed to develop the ideas of the young girl, who had devoured them in secret, during the long nights of the past winter.

And so Augustine's expression of vague longing, her gentle voice, her jasmine skin, and her blue eyes had lighted in poor Lebas's soul a flame as ardent as it was reverent. From an easily understood caprice, Augustine felt no affection for the orphan; perhaps she did not know that he loved her. On the other hand, the senior apprentice, with his long legs, his chestnut hair, his big hands and powerful frame, had found a secret admirer in Mademoiselle Virginie, who, in spite of her dower of fifty thousand crowns, had as yet no suitor. Nothing could be more natural than these two passions at cross-purposes, born in the silence of the dingy shop, as violets bloom in the depths of a wood. The mute and constant looks which made the young people's eyes meet by sheer need of change in the midst of persistent work and cloistered peace, was sure, sooner or later, to give rise to feelings of love. The habit of seeing always the same face leads insensibly to our reading there the qualities of the soul, and at last effaces all its defects.

"At the pace at which that man goes, our girls will soon have to go on their knees to a suitor!" said Monsieur Guillaume to himself, as he read the first decree by which Napoleon drew in advance on the conscript classes.*

From that day the old merchant, grieved at seeing his eldest daughter fade, remembered how he had married Mademoiselle Chevrel under much the same circumstances as those of Joseph Lebas and Virginie. A good bit of business, to marry off his daughter, and discharge a sacred debt by repaying to an orphan the benefit he had formerly received from his predecessor under similar conditions! Joseph Lebas, who was now three-and-thirty, was aware of the obstacle which a difference of fifteen years placed between Augustine and himself. Being also too clear-sighted not to understand Monsieur Guillaume's purpose, he knew his inexorable principles well enough to feel sure that the second would never marry before the elder. So the hapless assistant, whose heart was as warm as his legs were long and his chest deep, suffered in silence.

This was the state of the affairs in the tiny republic which, in the heart of the Rue Saint-Denis, was not unlike a dependency of La Trappe. But to give a full account of events as well as of feelings, it is needful to go back to some months before the scene with which this story opens. At dusk one evening, a young man passing the darkened shop of the Cat and Racket, had paused for a moment to gaze at a picture which might have arrested every painter in the world. The shop was not yet lighted, and was as a dark cave beyond which the dining-room was visible. A hanging lamp shed the yellow light which lends such charm to pictures of the Dutch school. The white linen, the silver, the cut glass, were brilliant accessories, and made more picturesque by strong contrasts of light and shade. The figures of the head of the family and his wife, the faces of the apprentices, and the pure form of Augustine, near whom a fat chubby-cheeked maid was standing, composed so strange a group; the heads were so singular, and every face had so candid an expression; it was so easy to read the peace, the silence, the modest way of life in this family, that to an artist accustomed to render nature, there was something hopeless in any attempt to depict this scene, come upon by chance. The stranger was a young painter, who, seven years before, had gained the first prize for painting. He had now just come back from Rome. His soul, full-fed with poetry; his eyes, satiated with Raphael and Michelangelo, thirsted for real nature after long dwelling in the pompous land where art has everywhere left something grandiose. Right or wrong, this was his personal feeling. His heart, which had long been a prey to the fire of Italian passion, craved one of those modest and meditative maidens whom in Rome he had unfortunately seen only in painting. From the enthusiasm produced in his excited fancy by the living picture before him, he naturally passed to a profound admiration for the principal figure; Augustine seemed to be pensive, and did not eat; by the arrangement of the lamp the light fell full on her face, and her bust seemed to move in a circle of fire, which threw up the shape of her head and illuminated it with almost supernatural effect. The artist involuntarily compared her to an exiled angel dreaming of heaven. An almost unknown emotion, a limpid, seething love flooded his heart. After remaining a minute, overwhelmed by the weight of his ideas, he tore himself from his bliss, went home, ate nothing, and could not sleep.

The next day he went to his studio, and did not come out of it till he had placed on canvas the magic of the scene of which the memory had, in a sense, made him a devotee; his happiness was incomplete till he should possess a faithful portrait of his idol. He went many times past the house of the Cat and Racket; he even ventured in once or twice, under a disguise, to get a closer view of the bewitching creature that Madame Guillaume covered with her wing. For eight whole months, devoted to his love and to his brush, he was lost to the sight of his most intimate friends forgetting the world, the theatre, poetry, music, and all his dearest habits. One morning Girodet* broke through all the barriers with which artists are familiar, and which they know how to evade, went into his room, and woke him by asking, "What are you going to send to the Salon?" The artist grasped his friend's hand, dragged him off to the studio, uncovered a small easel picture and a portrait. After a long and eager study of the two masterpieces, Girodet threw himself on his comrade's neck and hugged him, without speaking a word. His feelings could only be expressed as he felt them—soul to soul.

"You are in love?" said Girodet.

They both knew that the finest portraits by Titian, Raphael, and Leonardo da Vinci, were the outcome of the enthusiastic sentiments by which, indeed, under various conditions, every masterpiece is engendered. The artist only bent his head in reply.

"How happy are you to be able to be in love, here, after coming back from Italy! But I do not advise you to send such works as these to the Salon," the great painter went on. "You see, these two works will not be appreciated. Such true coloring, such prodigious work, cannot yet be understood; the public is not accustomed to such depths. The pictures we paint, my dear fellow, are mere screens. We should do better to turn rhymes, and translate the antique poets! There is more glory to be looked for there than from our luckless canvases!"

Notwithstanding this charitable advice, the two pictures were exhibited. The *Interior* made a revolution in painting. It gave birth to the pictures of genre which pour into all our exhibitions in such prodigious quantity that they might be supposed to be produced by machinery. As to the portrait, few artists have forgotten that lifelike work; and the public, which as a body is sometimes discerning, awarded it the crown which Girodet himself had hung over it. The two pictures were surrounded by a vast throng. They fought for places, as women say. Speculators and moneyed men would have covered the canvas with double napoleons, but the artist obstinately refused to sell or to make replicas. An enormous sum was offered him for the right of engraving them, and the print-sellers were not more favored than the amateurs.

Though these incidents occupied the world, they were not of a nature to penetrate the recesses of the monastic solitude in the Rue Saint-Denis. However, when paying a visit to Madame Guillaume, the notary's wife spoke of the exhibition before Augustine, of whom she was very fond, and explained its purpose. Madame Roguin's gossip naturally inspired Augustine with a wish to see the pictures, and with courage enough to ask her cousin secretly to take her to the Louvre. Her cousin succeeded in the negotiations she opened with Madame Guillaume for permission to release the young girl for two hours from her dull labors. Augustine was thus able to make her way through the crowd to see the crowned work. A fit of trembling shook her like an aspen leaf as she recognized herself. She was terrified, and looked about her to find Madame Roguin, from whom she had been separated by a tide of people. At that moment her frightened eyes fell on the impassioned face of the young painter.

She at once recalled the figure of a loiterer whom, being curious, she had frequently observed, believing him to be a new neighbor.

"You see how love has inspired me," said the artist in the timid creature's ear, and she stood in dismay at the words.

She found supernatural courage to enable her to push through the crowd and join her cousin, who was still struggling with the mass of people that hindered her from getting to the picture.

"You will be stifled!" cried Augustine. "Let us go."

But there are moments, at the Salon, when two women are not always free to direct their steps through the galleries. By the irregular course to which they were compelled by the press, Mademoiselle Guillaume and her cousin were pushed to within a few steps of the second picture. Chance thus brought them, both together, to where they could easily see the canvas made famous by fashion, for once in agreement with talent. Madame Roguin's exclamation of surprise was lost in the hubbub and buzz of the crowd; Augustine involuntarily shed tears at the sight of this wonderful study. Then, by an almost unaccountable impulse, she laid her finger on her lips, as she perceived quite near her the ecstatic face of the young painter. The stranger replied by a nod, and pointed to Madame Roguin, as a spoil-sport, to show Augustine that he had understood. This pantomime struck the young girl like hot coals on her flesh; she felt quite guilty as she perceived that there was a compact between herself and the artist. The suffocating heat, the dazzling sight of beautiful dresses, the bewilderment produced in Augustine's brain by the truth of coloring, the multitude of living or painted figures, the profusion of gilt frames, gave her a sense of intoxication which doubled her alarms. She would perhaps have fainted if an unknown rapture had not surged up in her heart to vivify her whole being, in spite of this chaos of sensations. She nevertheless believed herself to be under the power of the Devil, of whose awful snares she had been warned of by the thundering words of preachers. This moment was to her like a moment of madness. She found herself accompanied to her cousin's carriage by the young man, radiant with joy and love. Augustine, a prey to an agitation new to her experience, an intoxication which seemed to abandon her to nature, listened to the eloquent voice of her heart, and looked again and again at the young painter, betraying the emotion that came over her. Never had the bright rose of her cheeks shown in stronger contrast with the whiteness of her skin. The artist saw her beauty in all its bloom, her maiden modesty in all its glory. She herself felt a sort of rapture mingled with terror at thinking that her presence had brought happiness to him whose name was on every lip, and whose talent lent immortality to transient scenes. She was loved! It was impossible to doubt it. When she no longer saw the artist, these simple words still echoed in her ear, "You see how love has inspired me!" And the throbs of her heart, as they grew deeper, seemed a pain, her heated blood revealed so many unknown forces in her being. She affected a severe headache to avoid replying to her cousin's questions concerning the pictures; but on their return Madame Roguin could not forbear from speaking to Madame Guillaume of the fame that had fallen on the house of the Cat and Racket, and Augustine quaked in every limb as she heard her mother say that she should go to the Salon to see her house there. The young girl again declared herself suffering, and obtained leave to go to bed.

"That is what comes of sight-seeing," exclaimed Monsieur Guillaume—"a headache. And is it so very amusing to see in a picture what you can see any day in your own street? Don't talk to me of your artists! Like writers, they are a starveling crew. Why the devil need they choose my house to flout it in their pictures?"

"It may help to sell a few ells more of cloth," said Joseph Lebas.

This remark did not protect art and thought from being condemned once again before the judgment-seat of trade. As may be supposed, these speeches did not infuse much hope into Augustine, who, during the night, gave herself up to the first meditations of love. The events of the day were like a dream, which it was a joy to recall to her mind. She was initiated into the fears, the hopes, the remorse, all the ebb and flow of feeling which could not fail to toss a heart so simple and timid as hers. What a void she perceived in this gloomy house! What a treasure she found in her soul! To be the wife of a genius, to share his glory! What ravages must such a vision make in the heart of a girl brought up among such a family! What hopes must it raise in a young creature who, in the midst of sordid elements, had pined for a life of elegance! A sunbeam had fallen into the prison. Augustine was suddenly in love. So many of her feelings were soothed that she succumbed without reflection. At eighteen does not love hold a prism between the world and the eyes of a young girl? She was incapable of suspecting the hard facts which result from the union of a loving woman with a man of imagination, and she believed herself called to make him happy, not seeing any disparity between herself and him. To her the future would be as the present. When, next day, her father and mother returned from the Salon, their dejected faces proclaimed some disappointment. In the first place, the painter had removed the two pictures; and then Madame Guillaume had lost her cashmere shawl. But the news that the pictures had disappeared from the walls since her visit revealed to Augustine a delicacy of sentiment which a woman can always appreciate, even by instinct.

On the morning when, on his way home from a ball,

Théodore de Sommervieux—for this was the name which fame had stamped on Augustine's heart—had been squirted on by the apprentices while awaiting the appearance of his artless little friend, who certainly did not know that he was there, the lovers had seen each other for the fourth time only since their meeting at the Salon. The difficulties which the rule of the house placed in the way of the painter's ardent nature gave added violence to his passion for Augustine.

How could he get near to a young girl seated in a counting-house between two such women as Mademoiselle Virginie and Madame Guillaume? How could he correspond with her when her mother never left her side? Ingenious, as lovers are, to imagine woes, Théodore saw a rival in one of the assistants, to whose interests he supposed the others to be devoted. If he should evade these sons of Argus, he would yet be wrecked under the stern eye of the old draper or of Madame Guillaume. The very vehemence of his passion hindered the young painter from hitting on the ingenious expedients which, in prisoners and in lovers, seem to be the last effort of intelligence spurred by a wild craving for liberty, or by the fire of love. Théodore wandered about the neighborhood with the restlessness of a madman, as though movement might inspire him with some device. After racking his imagination, it occurred to him to bribe the blowsy waiting-maid with gold. Thus a few notes were exchanged at long intervals during the fortnight following the ill-starred morning when Monsieur Guillaume and Théodore had so scrutinized one another. At the present moment the young couple had agreed to see each other at a certain hour of the day, and on Sunday, at Saint-Leu, during Mass and vespers. Augustine had sent her dear Théodore a list of the relations and friends of the family, to whom the young painter tried to get access, in the hope of interesting, if it were possible, in his love affairs, one of these souls absorbed in money and trade, to whom a genuine passion must appear a quite monstrous speculation, a thing unheard-of. Nothing meanwhile, was altered at the sign of the Cat and Racket. If Augustine was absent-minded, if, against all obedience to the domestic code, she stole up to her room to make signals by means of a jar of flowers, if she sighed, if she were lost in thought, no one observed it, not even her mother. This will cause some surprise to those who have entered into the spirit of the household, where an idea tainted with poetry would be in startling contrast to persons and things, where no one could venture on a gesture or a look which would not be seen and analyzed. Nothing, however, could be more natural: the quiet barque that navigated the stormy waters of the Paris Exchange, under the flag of the Cat and Racket, was just now in the toils of one of these tempests which, returning periodically, might be termed equinoctial. For the last fortnight the five men forming the crew, with Madame Guillaume and Mademoiselle Virginie, had been devoting themselves to the hard labor, known as stock-taking.

Every bale was turned over, and the length verified to ascertain the exact value of the remnant. The ticket attached to each parcel was carefully examined to see at what time the piece had been bought. The retail price was fixed. Monsieur Guillaume, always on his feet, his pen behind his ear, was like a captain commanding the working of the ship. His sharp tones, spoken through a trap-door, to inquire into the depths of the hold in the cellar-store, gave utterance to the barbarous formulas of trade-jargon, which find expression only in cipher. "How much H.N.Z.?" — "All sold." — "What is left of Q.X.?" — "Two ells." — "At what price?" — "Fifty-five three." — "Set down A. at three, with all of J.J., all of M.P., and what is left of V.D.O." — A hundred other injunctions equally intelligible were spouted over the counters like verses of modern poetry, quoted by romantic spirits, to excite each other's enthusiasm for one of their poets. In the evening Guillaume, shut up with his assistant and his wife, balanced his accounts, carried on the balance, wrote to debtors in arrears, and made out bills. All three were busy over this enormous labor, of which the result could be stated on a sheet of foolscap, proving to the head of the house that there was so much to the good in hard cash, so much in goods, so much in bills and notes; that he did not owe a sou; that a hundred or two hundred thousand francs were owing to him; that the capital had been increased; that the farmlands, the houses, or the investments were extended, or repaired, or doubled. Whence it became necessary to begin again with increased ardor, to accumulate more crown-pieces, without its ever entering the brain of these laborious ants to ask—"To what end?"

Favored by this annual turmoil, the happy Augustine escaped the investigations of her Argus-eyed relations. At last, one Saturday evening, the stock-taking was finished. The figures of the sum-total showed a row of Os long enough to allow Guillaume for once to relax the stern rule as to dessert which reigned throughout the year. The shrewd old draper rubbed his hands, and allowed his assistants to remain at table. The members of the crew had hardly swallowed their thimbleful of some home-made liqueur, when the rumble of a carriage was heard. The family party were going to see *Cendrillon* at the Variétés,* while the two younger apprentices each received a crown of six francs, with permission to go wherever they chose, provided they were in by midnight.

Notwithstanding this debauch, the old cloth-merchant was shaving himself at six next morning, put on his maroon-colored coat, of which the glowing lights afforded him perennial enjoyment, fastened a pair of gold buckles on the knee-straps of his ample satin breeches;

and then, at about seven o'clock, while all were still sleeping in the house, he made his way to the little office adjoining the shop on the first floor. Daylight came in through a window, fortified by iron bars, and looking out on a small yard surrounded by such black walls that it was very like a well. The old merchant opened the iron-lined shutters, which were so familiar to him, and threw up the lower half of the sash window. The icy air of the courtyard came in to cool the hot atmosphere of the little room, full of the odor peculiar to offices.

The merchant remained standing, his hand resting on the greasy arm of a large cane chair lined with morocco, of which the original hue had disappeared; he seemed to hesitate as to seating himself. He looked with affection at the double desk, where his wife's seat, opposite his own, was fitted into a little niche in the wall. He contemplated the numbered boxes, the files, the implements, the cash box—objects all of immemorial origin, and fancied himself in the room with the shade of Master Chevrel. He even pulled out the high stool on which he had once sat in the presence of his departed master. This stool, covered with black leather, the horse-hair showing at every corner—as it had long done, without, however, coming out—he placed with a shaking hand on the very spot where his predecessor had put it, and then, with an emotion difficult to describe, he pulled a bell, which rang at the head of Joseph Lebas's bed. When this decisive blow had been struck, the old man, for whom, no doubt, these reminiscences were too much, took up three or four bills of exchange, and looked at them without seeing them.

Suddenly Joseph Lebas stood before him.

"Sit down there," said Guillaume, pointing to the stool.

As the old master draper had never yet bid his assistant be seated in his presence, Joseph Lebas was startled.

"What do you think of these notes?" asked Guillaume.

"They will never be paid."

"Why?"

"Well, I heard the day before yesterday Etienne and Co. had made their payments in gold."

"Oh, oh!" said the draper. "Well, one must be very ill to show one's bile. Let us speak of something else. — Joseph, the stock-taking is done."

"Yes, monsieur, and the dividend is one of the best you have ever made."

"Do not use new-fangled words. Say the profits, Joseph. Do you know, my boy, that this result is partly owing to you? And I do not intend to pay you a salary any longer. Madame Guillaume has suggested to me to take you into partnership. — 'Guillaume and Lebas;' will not that make a good business name? We might add, 'and Co.' to round off the firm's signature."

Tears rose to the eyes of Joseph Lebas, who tried to hide them.

"Oh, Monsieur Guillaume, how have I deserved such kindness? I only do my duty. It was so much already that you should take an interest in a poor orph— —"

He was brushing the cuff of his left sleeve with his right hand, and dared not look at the old man, who smiled as he thought that this modest young fellow no doubt needed, as he had needed once on a time, some encouragement to complete his explanation.

"To be sure," said Virginie's father, "you do not altogether deserve this favor, Joseph. You have not so much confidence in me as I have in you." (The young man looked up quickly.) "You know all the secrets of the cash-box. For the last two years I have told you almost all my concerns. I have sent you to travel in our goods. In short, I have nothing on my conscience as regards you. But you — you have a soft place, and you have never breathed a word of it." Joseph Lebas blushed. "Ah, ha!" cried Guillaume, "so you thought you could deceive an old fox like me? When you knew that I had scented the Lecocq bankruptcy?"

"What, monsieur?" replied Joseph Lebas, looking at his master as keenly as his master looked at him, "you knew that I was in love?"

"I know everything, you rascal," said the worthy and cunning old merchant, pulling the assistant's ear. "And I forgive you—I did the same myself."

"And you will give her to me?"

"Yes—with fifty thousand crowns; and I will leave you as much by will, and we will start on our new career under the name of a new firm. We will do good business yet, my boy!" added the old man, getting up and flourishing his arms. "I tell you, son-in-law, there is nothing like trade. Those who ask what pleasure is to be found in it are simpletons. To be on the scent of a good bargain, to hold your own on 'Change, to watch as anxiously as at the gaming-table whether Etienne and Co. will fail or no, to see a regiment of Guards march past all dressed in your cloth, to trip your neighbor up— honestly of course!—to make the goods cheaper than others can; then to carry out an undertaking which you have planned, which begins, grows, totters, and succeeds! to know the workings of every house of business as well as a minister of police, so as never to make a mistake; to hold up your head in the midst of wrecks, to have friends by correspondence in every manufacturing town; is not that a perpetual game, Joseph? That is life, that is! I shall die in that harness, like old Chevrel, but taking it easy now, all the same."

In the heat of his eager rhetoric, old Guillaume had scarcely looked at his assistant, who was weeping copiously. "Why, Joseph, my poor boy, what is the matter?"

"Oh, I love her so! Monsieur Guillaume, that my heart fails me; I believe——"

"Well, well, boy," said the old man, touched, "you are happier than you know, by God! For she loves you. I know it."

And he blinked his little green eyes as he looked at the young man.

"Mademoiselle Augustine! Mademoiselle Augustine!" exclaimed Joseph Lebas in his rapture.

He was about to rush out of the room when he felt himself clutched by a hand of iron, and his astonished master spun him round in front of him once more.

"What has Augustine to do with this matter?" he asked, in a voice which instantly froze the luckless Joseph.

"Is it not she that—that—I love?" stammered the assistant.

Much put out by his own want of perspicacity, Guillaume sat down again, and rested his long head in his hands to consider the perplexing situation in which he found himself. Joseph Lebas, shamefaced and in despair, remained standing.

"Joseph," the draper said with frigid dignity, "I was speaking of Virginie. Love cannot be made to order, I know. I know, too, that you can be trusted. We will forget all this. I will not let Augustine marry before Virginie.—Your interest will be ten per cent."

The young man, to whom love gave I know not what power of courage and eloquence, clasped his hand, and spoke in his turn—spoke for a quarter of an hour, with so much warmth and feeling, that he altered the situation. If the question had been a matter of business the old tradesman would have had fixed principles to guide his decision; but, tossed a thousand miles from commerce, on the ocean of sentiment, without a compass, he floated, as he told himself, undecided in the face of such an unexpected event. Carried away by his fatherly kindness, he began to beat about the bush.

"Deuce take it, Joseph, you must know that there

are ten years between my two children. Mademoiselle Chevrel was no beauty, still she has had nothing to complain of in me. Do as I did. Come, come, don't cry. Can you be so silly? What is to be done? It can be managed perhaps. There is always some way out of a scrape. And we men are not always devoted Céladons* to our wives—you understand? Madame Guillaume is very pious. . . . Come. By Gad, boy, give your arm to Augustine this morning as we go to Mass."

These were the phrases spoken at random by the old draper, and their conclusion made the lover happy. He was already thinking of a friend of his as a match for Mademoiselle Virginie, as he went out of the smoky office, pressing his future father-in-law's hand, after saying with a knowing look that all would turn out for the best.

"What will Madame Guillaume say to it?" was the idea that greatly troubled the worthy merchant when he found himself alone.

At breakfast Madame Guillaume and Virginie, to whom the draper had not yet confided his disappointment, cast meaning glances at Joseph Lebas, who was extremely embarrassed. The young assistant's bashfulness commended him to his mother-in-law's good graces. The matron became so cheerful that she smiled as she looked at her husband, and allowed herself some little pleasantries of time-honored acceptance in such simple families. She wondered whether Joseph or Virginie were the taller, to ask them to compare their height. This preliminary fooling brought a cloud to the master's brow, and he even made such a point of decorum that he desired Augustine to take the assistant's arm on their way to Saint-Leu. Madame Guillaume, surprised at this manly delicacy, honored her husband with a nod of approval. So the procession left the house in such order as to suggest no suspicious meaning to the neighbors.

"Does it not seem to you, Mademoiselle Augustine," said the assistant, and he trembled, "that the wife of a merchant whose credit is as good as Monsieur Guillaume's, for instance, might enjoy herself a little more than madame your mother does? Might wear diamonds—or keep a carriage? For my part, if I were to marry, I should be glad to take all the work, and see my wife happy. I would not put her into the counting-house. In the drapery business, you see, a woman is not so necessary now as formerly. Monsieur Guillaume was quite right to act as he did—and besides, his wife liked it. But so long as a woman knows how to turn her hand to the book-keeping, the correspondence, the retail business, the orders, and her housekeeping, so as not to sit idle, that is enough. At seven o'clock, when the shop is shut, I shall take my pleasures, go to the play, and into company.—But you are not listening to me."

"Yes, indeed, Monsieur Joseph. What do you think of painting? That is a fine calling."

"Yes. I know a master house-painter, Monsieur Lourdois. He is well-to-do."

Thus conversing, the family reached the Church of Saint-Leu. There Madame Guillaume reasserted her rights, and, for the first time, placed Augustine next herself, Virginie taking her place on the fourth chair, next to Lebas. During the sermon all went well between Augustine and Théodore, who, standing behind a pillar, worshiped his Madonna with fervent devotion; but at the elevation of the Host, Madame Guillaume discovered, rather late, that her daughter Augustine was holding her prayer-book upside down. She was about to speak to her strongly, when, lowering her veil, she interrupted her own devotions to look in the direction where her daughter's eyes found attraction. By the help of her spectacles she saw the young artist, whose fashionable elegance seemed to proclaim him a cavalry officer on leave rather than a tradesman of the neighborhood. It is difficult to conceive of the state of violent agitation in which Madame Guillaume found herself—she, who flattered herself on having brought up her daughters to perfection—on discovering in Augustine a clandestine passion of which her prudery and ignorance exaggerated the perils. She believed her daughter to be cankered to the core.

"Hold your book right way up, mademoiselle," she muttered in a low voice, tremulous with wrath. She snatched away the tell-tale prayer-book and returned it with the letter-press right way up. "Do not allow your eyes to look anywhere but at your prayers," she added, "or I shall have something to say to you. Your father and I will talk to you after church."

These words came like a thunderbolt on poor Augustine. She felt faint; but, torn between the distress she felt and the dread of causing a commotion in church she bravely concealed her anguish. It was, however, easy to discern the stormy state of her soul from the trembling of her prayer-book, and the tears which dropped on every page she turned. From the furious glare shot at him by Madame Guillaume the artist saw the peril into which his love affair had fallen; he went out, with a raging soul, determined to venture all.

"Go to your room, mademoiselle!" said Madame Guillaume, on their return home; "we will send for you, but take care not to quit it."

The conference between the husband and wife was conducted so secretly that at first nothing was heard of it. Virginie, however, who had tried to give her sister courage by a variety of gentle remonstrances, carried her good nature so far as to listen at the door of her mother's bedroom where the discussion was held, to catch a word or two. The first time she went down to the lower floor she heard her father exclaim, "Then, madame, do you wish to kill your daughter?"

"My poor dear!" said Virginie, in tears, "papa takes

your part."

"And what do they want to do to Théodore?" asked the innocent girl.

Virginie, inquisitive, went down again; but this time she stayed longer; she learned that Joseph Lebas loved Augustine. It was written that on this memorable day, this house, generally so peaceful, should be a hell. Monsieur Guillaume brought Joseph Lebas to despair by telling him of Augustine's love for a stranger. Lebas, who had advised his friend to become a suitor for Mademoiselle Virginie, saw all his hopes wrecked. Mademoiselle Virginie, overcome by hearing that Joseph had, in a way, refused her, had a sick headache. The dispute that had arisen from the discussion between Monsieur and Madame Guillaume, when, for the third time in their lives, they had been of antagonistic opinions, had shown itself in a terrible form. Finally, at half-past four in the afternoon, Augustine, pale, trembling, and with red eyes, was haled before her father and mother. The poor child artlessly related the too brief tale of her love. Reassured by a speech from her father, who promised to listen to her in silence, she gathered courage as she pronounced to her parents the name of Théodore de Sommervieux, with a mischievous little emphasis on the aristocratic *de*. And yielding to the unknown charm of talking of her feelings, she was brave enough to declare with innocent decision that she loved Monsieur de Sommervieux, that she had written to him, and she added, with tears in her eyes: "To sacrifice me to another man would make me wretched."

"But, Augustine, you cannot surely know what a painter is?" cried her mother with horror.

"Madame Guillaume!" said the old man, compelling her to silence.—"Augustine," he went on, "artists are generally little better than beggars. They are too extravagant not to be always a bad sort. I served the late Monsieur Joseph Vernet, the late Monsieur Lekain, and the late Monsieur Noverre. Oh, if you could only know the tricks played on poor Father Chevrel by that Monsieur Noverre, by the Chevalier de Saint-Georges, and especially by Monsieur Philidor!* They are a set of rascals; I know them well! They all have a gab and nice manners. Ah, your Monsieur Sumer—, Somm——"

"De Sommervieux, papa."

"Well, well, de Sommervieux, well and good. He can never have been half so sweet to you as Monsieur le Chevalier de Saint-Georges was to me the day I got a verdict of the consuls against him. And in those days they were gentlemen of quality."

"But, father, Monsieur Théodore is of good family, and he wrote me that he is rich; his father was called Chevalier de Sommervieux before the Revolution."

At these words Monsieur Guillaume looked at his terrible better half, who, like an angry woman, sat tapping the floor with her foot while keeping sullen silence; she avoided even casting wrathful looks at Augustine, appearing to leave to Monsieur Guillaume the whole responsibility in so grave a matter, since her opinion was not listened to. Nevertheless, in spite of her apparent self-control, when she saw her husband giving way so mildly under a catastrophe which had no concern with business, she exclaimed:

"Really, monsieur, you are so weak with your daughters! However——"

The sound of a carriage, which stopped at the door, interrupted the rating which the old draper already quaked at. In a minute Madame Roguin was standing in the middle of the room, and looking at the actors in this domestic scene: "I know all, my dear cousin," said she, with a patronizing air.

Madame Roguin made the great mistake of supposing that a Paris notary's wife could play the part of a favorite of fashion.

"I know all," she repeated, "and I have come into

Noah's Ark, like the dove, with the olive-branch. I read that allegory in the *Génie du Christianisme*,"* she added, turning to Madame Guillaume; "the allusion ought to please you, cousin. Do you know," she went on, smiling at Augustine, "that Monsieur de Sommervieux is a charming man? He gave me my portrait this morning, painted by a master's hand. It is worth at least six thousand francs." And at these words she patted Monsieur Guillaume on the arm. The old draper could not help making a grimace with his lips, which was peculiar to him.

"I know Monsieur de Sommervieux very well," the dove ran on. "He has come to my evenings this fortnight past, and made them delightful. He has told me all his woes, and commissioned me to plead for him. I know since this morning that he adores Augustine, and he shall have her. Ah, cousin, do not shake your head in refusal. He will be created Baron, I can tell you, and has just been made Chevalier of the Legion of Honor,* by the Emperor himself, at the Salon. Roguin is now his lawyer, and knows all his affairs. Well! Monsieur de Sommervieux has twelve thousand francs a year in good landed estate. Do you know that the father-in-law of such a man may get a rise in life—be mayor of his *arrondissement*, for instance. Have we not seen Monsieur Dupont become a Comte of the Empire, and a senator, all because he went as mayor to congratulate the Emperor on his entry into Vienna?* Oh, this marriage must take place! For my part, I adore the dear young man. His behavior to Augustine is only met with in romances. Be easy, little one, you shall be happy, and every girl will wish she were in your place. Madame la Duchesse de Carigliano, who comes to my 'At Homes,' raves about Monsieur de Sommervieux. Some spiteful people say she only comes to me to meet him; as if a duchess of yesterday was doing too much honor to a Chevrel, whose family have been respected citizens these hundred years!

"Augustine," Madame Roguin went on, after a short pause, "I have seen the portrait. Heavens! How lovely it is! Do you know that the Emperor wanted to have it? He laughed, and said to the Deputy High Constable that if there were many women like that in his court while all the kings visited it, he should have no difficulty about preserving the peace of Europe. Is not that a compliment?"

The tempests with which the day had begun were to resemble those of nature, by ending in clear and serene weather. Madame Roguin displayed so much address in her harangue, she was able to touch so many strings in the dry hearts of Monsieur and Madame Guillaume, that at last she hit on one which she could work upon. At this strange period commerce and finance were more than ever possessed by the crazy mania for seeking alliance with rank; and the generals of the Empire took full advantage of this desire. Monsieur Guillaume, as a singular exception, opposed this deplorable craving. His favorite axioms were that, to secure happiness, a woman must marry a man of her own class; that every one was punished sooner or later for having climbed too high; that love could so little endure under the worries of a household, that both husband and wife needed sound good qualities to be happy, that it would not do for one to be far in advance of the other, because, above everything, they must understand each other; if a man spoke Greek and his wife Latin, they might come to die of hunger. He had himself invented this sort of adage. And he compared such marriages to old-fashioned materials of mixed silk and wool. Still, there is so much vanity at the bottom of man's heart that the prudence of the pilot who steered the Cat and Racket so wisely gave way before Madame Roguin's aggressive volubility. Austere Madame Guillaume was the first to see in her daughter's affection a reason for abdicating her principles and for consenting to receive Monsieur de Sommervieux, whom she promised herself she would put under severe inquisition.

The old draper went to look for Joseph Lebas, and inform him of the state of affairs. At half-past six, the dining-room immortalized by the artist saw, united under its skylight, Monsieur and Madame Roguin, the young painter and his charming Augustine, Joseph Lebas, who found his happiness in patience, and Mademoiselle Virginie, convalescent from her headache. Monsieur and Madame Guillaume saw in perspective both their children married, and the fortunes of the Cat and Racket once more in skilful hands. Their satisfaction was at its height when, at dessert, Théodore made them a present of the wonderful picture which they had failed to see, representing the interior of the old shop, and to which they all owed so much happiness.

"Isn't it pretty!" cried Guillaume. "And to think that any one would pay thirty thousand francs for that!"

"Because you can see my lappets in it," said Madame Guillaume.

"And the cloth unrolled!" added Lebas; "you might take it up in your hand."

"Drapery always comes out well," replied the painter. "We should be only too happy, we modern artists, if we could touch the perfection of antique drapery."

"So you like drapery!" cried old Guillaume. "Well, then, by Gad! shake hands on that, my young friend. Since you can respect trade, we shall understand each other. And why should it be despised? The world began with trade, since Adam sold Paradise for an apple. He did not strike a good bargain though!" And the old man roared with honest laughter, encouraged by the champagne, which he sent round with a liberal hand. The band that covered the young artist's eyes was so thick that he thought his future parents amiable. He was not above enlivening them by a few jests in the best taste. So he too pleased every one. In the evening, when the drawing-room, furnished with what Madame Guillaume called "everything handsome," was deserted, and while she flitted from the table to the chimney-piece, from the candelabra to the tall candlesticks, hastily blowing out the wax-lights, the worthy draper, who was always clear-sighted when money was in question, called Augustine to him, and seating her on his knee, spoke as follows:—

"My dear child, you shall marry your Sommervieux since you insist; you may, if you like, risk your capital in happiness. But I am not going to be hoodwinked by the thirty thousand francs to be made by spoiling good canvas. Money that is lightly earned is lightly spent. Did I not hear that hare-brained youngster declare this evening that money was made round that it might roll. If it is round for spendthrifts, it is flat for saving folks who pile it up. Now, my child, that fine gentleman talks of giving you carriages and diamonds! He has money, let him spend it on you; so be it. It is no concern of mine. But as to what I can give you, I will not have the crown-pieces I have picked up with so much toil wasted in carriages and frippery. Those who spend too fast never grow rich. A hundred thousand crowns, which is your fortune, will not buy up Paris. It is all very well to look forward to a few hundred thousand francs to be yours some day; I shall keep you waiting for them as long as possible, by Gad! So I took your lover aside, and a man who managed the Lecocq bankruptcy had not much difficulty in persuading the artist to marry under a settlement of his wife's money on herself. I will keep an eye on the marriage contract to see that what he is to settle on you is safely tied up. So now, my child, I hope to be a grandfather, by Gad! I will begin at once to lay up for my grandchildren; but swear to me, here and now, never to sign any papers relating to money without my advice; and if I go soon to join old

Father Chevrel, promise to consult young Lebas, your brother-in-law."

"Yes, father, I swear it."

At these words, spoken in a gentle voice, the old man kissed his daughter on both cheeks. That night the lovers slept as soundly as Monsieur and Madame Guillaume.

Some few months after this memorable Sunday the high altar of Saint-Leu was the scene of two very different weddings. Augustine and Théodore appeared in all the radiance of happiness, their eyes beaming with love, dressed with elegance, while a fine carriage waited for them. Virginie, who had come in a good hired fly with the rest of the family, humbly followed her younger sister, dressed in the simplest fashion like a shadow necessary to the harmony of the picture. Monsieur Guillaume had exerted himself to the utmost in the church to get Virginie married before Augustine, but the priests, high and low, persisted in addressing the more elegant of the two brides. He heard some of his neighbors highly approving the good sense of Mademoiselle Virginie, who was making, as they said, the more substantial match, and remaining faithful to the neighborhood; while they fired a few taunts, prompted by envy of Augustine, who was marrying an artist and a man of rank; adding, with a sort of dismay, that if the Guillaumes were ambitious, there was an end to the business. An old fan-maker having remarked that such a prodigal would soon bring his wife to beggary, father Guillaume prided himself *in petto* for his prudence in the matter of marriage settlements. In the evening, after a splendid ball, followed by one of those substantial suppers of which the memory is dying out in the present generation, Monsieur and Madame Guillaume remained in a fine house belonging to them in the Rue du Colombier,* where the wedding had been held; Monsieur and Madame Lebas returned in their fly to the old home in the Rue Saint-Denis, to steer the good ship Cat and Racket. The artist, intoxicated with happiness, carried off his beloved Augustine, and eagerly lifting her out of their carriage when it reached the Rue des Trois-Frères,* led her to an apartment embellished by all the arts.

The fever of passion which possessed Théodore made a year fly over the young couple without a single cloud to dim the blue sky under which they lived. Life did not hang heavy on the lovers' hands. Théodore lavished on every day inexhaustible *fioriture* of enjoyment, and he delighted to vary the transports of passion by the soft languor of those hours of repose when souls soar so high that they seem to have forgotten all bodily union. Augustine was too happy for reflection; she floated on an undulating tide of rapture; she thought she could not do enough by abandoning herself to sanctioned and sacred married love; simple and artless, she had no coquetry, no reserves, none of the dominion which a worldly-minded girl acquires over her husband by ingenious caprice; she loved too well to calculate for the future, and never imagined that so exquisite a life could come to an end. Happy in being her husband's sole delight, she believed that her inextinguishable love would always be her greatest grace in his eyes, as her devotion and obedience would be a perennial charm. And, indeed, the ecstasy of love had made her so brilliantly lovely that her beauty filled her with pride, and gave her confidence that she could always reign over a man so easy to kindle as Monsieur de Sommervieux. Thus her position as a wife brought her no knowledge but the lessons of love.

In the midst of her happiness, she was still the simple child who had lived in obscurity in the Rue Saint-Denis, and who never thought of acquiring the manners, the information, the tone of the world she had to live in.

Her words being the words of love, she revealed in them, no doubt, a certain pliancy of mind and a certain refinement of speech; but she used the language common to all women when they find themselves plunged in passion, which seems to be their element. When, by chance, Augustine expressed an idea that did not harmonize with Théodore's, the young artist laughed, as we laugh at the first mistakes of a foreigner, though they end by annoying us if they are not corrected.

In spite of all this love-making, by the end of this year, as delightful as it was swift, Sommervieux felt one morning the need for resuming his work and his old habits. His wife was expecting their first child. He saw some friends again. During the tedious discomforts of the year when a young wife is nursing an infant for the first time, he worked, no doubt, with zeal, but he occasionally sought diversion in the fashionable world. The house which he was best pleased to frequent was that of the Duchesse de Carigliano, who had at last attracted the celebrated artist to her parties. When Augustine was quite well again, and her boy no longer required the assiduous care which debars a mother from social pleasures, Théodore had come to the stage of wishing to know the joys of satisfied vanity to be found in society by a man who shows himself with a handsome woman, the object of envy and admiration.

To figure in drawing-rooms with the reflected lustre of her husband's fame, and to find other women envious of her, was to Augustine a new harvest of pleasures; but it was the last gleam of conjugal happiness. She first wounded her husband's vanity when, in spite of vain efforts, she betrayed her ignorance, the inelegance of her language, and the narrowness of her ideas. Sommervieux's nature, subjugated for nearly two years and a half by the first transports of love, now, in the calm of less new possession, recovered its bent and habits, for a while diverted from their channel. Poetry, painting, and the subtle joys of imagination have inalienable rights over a lofty spirit. These cravings of a powerful soul had not been starved in Théodore during these two years; they had only found fresh pasture. As soon as the meadows of love had been ransacked, and the artist had gathered roses and cornflowers as the children do, so greedily that he did not see that his hands could hold no more, the scene changed. When the painter showed his wife the sketches for his finest compositions he heard her exclaim, as her father had done, "How pretty!" This tepid admiration was not the outcome of conscientious feeling, but of her faith on the strength of love.

Augustine cared more for a look than for the finest picture. The only sublime she knew was that of the heart. At last Théodore could not resist the evidence of the cruel fact—his wife was insensible to poetry, she did not dwell in his sphere, she could not follow him in all his vagaries, his inventions, his joys and his sorrows; she walked groveling in the world of reality, while his head was in the skies. Common minds cannot appreciate the perennial sufferings of a being who, while bound to another by the most intimate affections, is obliged constantly to suppress the dearest flights of his soul, and to thrust down into the void those images which a magic power compels him to create. To him the torture is all the more intolerable because his feeling towards his companion enjoins, as its first law, that they should have no concealments, but mingle the aspirations of their thought as perfectly as the effusions of their soul. The demands of nature are not to be cheated. She is as inexorable as necessity, which is, indeed, a sort of social nature. Sommervieux took refuge in the peace and silence of his studio, hoping that the habit of living with artists might mould his wife and develop in her the dormant germs of lofty intelligence which some superior minds suppose must exist in every being.

But Augustine was too sincerely religious not to take fright at the tone of artists. At the first dinner Théodore gave, she heard a young painter say, with the childlike lightness, which to her was unintelligible, and which redeems a jest from the taint of profanity, "But, madame, your Paradise cannot be more beautiful than Raphael's *Transfiguration!** — Well, and I got tired of looking at that."

Thus Augustine came among this sparkling set in a spirit of distrust which no one could fail to see. She was a restraint on their freedom. Now an artist who feels restraint is pitiless; he stays away, or laughs it to scorn. Madame Guillaume, among other absurdities, had an excessive notion of the dignity she considered the prerogative of a married woman; and Augustine, though she had often made fun of it, could not help a slight imitation of her mother's primness. This extreme propriety, which virtuous wives do not always avoid, suggested a few epigrams in the form of sketches, in which the harmless jest was in such good taste that Sommervieux could not take offence; and even if they had been more severe, these pleasantries were after all only reprisals from his friends. Still, nothing could seem a trifle to a spirit so open as Théodore's to impressions from without. A coldness insensibly crept over him, and inevitably spread. To attain conjugal happiness we must climb a hill whose summit is a narrow ridge, close to a steep and slippery descent: the painter's love was falling down it. He regarded his wife as incapable of appreciating the moral considerations which justified him in his own eyes for his singular behavior to her, and believed himself quite innocent in hiding from her thoughts she could not enter into, and peccadilloes outside the jurisdiction of a *bourgeois* conscience. Augustine wrapped herself in sullen and silent grief. These unconfessed feelings placed a shroud between the husband and wife which could not fail to grow thicker day by day.

Though her husband never failed in consideration for her, Augustine could not help trembling as she saw that he kept for the outer world those treasures of wit and grace that he formerly would lay at her feet. She soon began to find sinister meaning in the jocular speeches that are current in the world as to the inconstancy of men. She made no complaints, but her demeanor conveyed reproach.

Three years after her marriage this pretty young woman, who dashed past in her handsome carriage, and lived in a sphere of glory and riches to the envy of heedless folk incapable of taking a just view of the situations of life, was a prey to intense grief. She lost her color; she reflected; she made comparisons; then sorrow unfolded to her the first lessons of experience. She determined to restrict herself bravely within the round of duty, hoping that by this generous conduct she might sooner or later win back her husband's love. But it was not so. When Sommervieux, fired with work, came in from his studio, Augustine did not put away her work so quickly but that the painter might find his wife mending the household linen, and his own, with all the care of a good housewife. She supplied generously and without a murmur the money needed for his lavishness; but in her anxiety to husband her dear Théodore's fortune, she was strictly economical for herself and in certain details of domestic management. Such conduct is incompatible with the easy-going habits of artists, who, at the end of their life, have enjoyed it so keenly that they never inquire into the causes of their ruin.

It is useless to note every tint of shadow by which the brilliant hues of their honeymoon were overcast till they were lost in utter blackness. One evening poor Augustine, who had for some time heard her husband speak with enthusiasm of the Duchesse de Carigliano, received from a friend certain malignantly charitable warnings as to the nature of the attachment which

Sommervieux had formed for this celebrated flirt of the Imperial Court. At one-and-twenty, in all the splendor of youth and beauty, Augustine saw herself deserted for a woman of six-and-thirty. Feeling herself so wretched in the midst of a world of festivity which to her was a blank, the poor little thing could no longer understand the admiration she excited, or the envy of which she was the object. Her face assumed a different expression. Melancholy, tinged her features with the sweetness of resignation and the pallor of scorned love. Ere long she too was courted by the most fascinating men; but she remained lonely and virtuous. Some contemptuous words which escaped her husband filled her with incredible despair. A sinister flash showed her the breaches which, as a result of her sordid education, hindered the perfect union of her soul with Théodore's; she loved him well enough to absolve him and condemn herself. She shed tears of blood, and perceived, too late, that there are *mésalliances* of the spirit as well as of rank and habits. As she recalled the early raptures of their union, she understood the full extent of that lost happiness, and accepted the conclusion that so rich a harvest of love was in itself a whole life, which only sorrow could pay for. At the same time, she loved too truly to lose all hope. At one-and-twenty she dared undertake to educate herself, and make her imagination, at least, worthy of that she admired. "If I am not a poet," thought she, "at any rate, I will understand poetry."

Then, with all the strength of will, all the energy which every woman can display when she loves, Madame de Sommervieux tried to alter her character, her manners, and her habits; but by dint of devouring books and learning undauntedly, she only succeeded in becoming less ignorant. Lightness of wit and the graces of conversation are a gift of nature, or the fruit of education begun in the cradle. She could appreciate music and enjoy it, but she could not sing with taste.

She understood literature and the beauties of poetry, but it was too late to cultivate her refractory memory. She listened with pleasure to social conversation, but she could contribute nothing brilliant. Her religious notions and home-grown prejudices were antagonistic to the complete emancipation of her intelligence. Finally, a foregone conclusion against her had stolen into Théodore's mind, and this she could not conquer. The artist would laugh, at those who flattered him about his wife, and his irony had some foundation; he so over-awed the pathetic young creature that, in his presence, or alone with him, she trembled. Hampered by her too eager desire to please, her wits and her knowledge vanished in one absorbing feeling. Even her fidelity vexed the unfaithful husband, who seemed to bid her do wrong by stigmatizing her virtue as insensibility. Augustine tried in vain to abdicate her reason, to yield to her husband's caprices and whims, to devote herself to the selfishness of his vanity. Her sacrifices bore no fruit. Perhaps they had both let the moment slip when souls may meet in comprehension. One day the young wife's too sensitive heart received one of those blows which so strain the bonds of feeling that they seem to be broken. She withdrew into solitude. But before long a fatal idea suggested to her to seek counsel and comfort in the bosom of her family.

So one morning she made her way towards the grotesque façade of the humble, silent home where she had spent her childhood. She sighed as she looked up at the sash-window, whence one day she had sent her first kiss to him who now shed as much sorrow as glory on her life. Nothing was changed in the cavern, where the drapery business had, however, started on a new life. Augustine's sister filled her mother's old place at the desk. The unhappy young woman met her brother-in-law with his pen behind his ear; he hardly listened to her, he was so full of business. The formidable symptoms of stock-taking were visible all round him; he begged her to excuse him. She was received coldly enough by her sister, who owed her a grudge. In fact, Augustine, in her finery, and stepping out of a handsome carriage, had never been to see her but when passing by. The wife of the prudent Lebas, imagining that want of money was the prime cause of this early call, tried to keep up a tone of reserve which more than once made Augustine smile. The painter's wife perceived that, apart from the cap and lappets, her mother had found in Virginie a successor who could uphold the ancient honor of the Cat and Racket. At breakfast she observed certain changes in the management of the house which did honor to Lebas's good sense; the assistants did not rise before dessert; they were allowed to talk, and the abundant meal spoke of ease without luxury. The fashionable woman found some tickets for a box at the Français,* where she remembered having seen her sister from time to time. Madame Lebas had a cashmere shawl over her shoulders, of which the value bore witness to her husband's generosity to her. In short, the couple were keeping pace with the times. During the two-thirds of the day she spent there, Augustine was touched to the heart by the equable happiness, devoid, to be sure, of all emotion, but equally free from storms, enjoyed by this well-matched couple. They had accepted life as a commercial enterprise, in which, above all, they must do credit to the business. Not finding any great love in her husband, Virginie had set to work to create it. Having by degrees learned to esteem and care for his wife, the time that his happiness had taken to germinate was to Joseph Lebas a guarantee of its durability. Hence, when Augustine plaintively set forth her painful position, she had to face the deluge of commonplace morality which the traditions of the Rue Saint-Denis furnished to her sister.

"The mischief is done, wife," said Joseph Lebas; "we

must try to give our sister good advice." Then the clever tradesman ponderously analyzed the resources which law and custom might offer Augustine as a means of escape at this crisis; he ticketed every argument, so to speak, and arranged them in their degrees of weight under various categories, as though they were articles of merchandise of different qualities; then he put them in the scale, weighed them, and ended by showing the necessity for his sister-in-law's taking violent steps which could not satisfy the love she still had for her husband; and, indeed, the feeling had revived in all its strength when she heard Joseph Lebas speak of legal proceedings. Augustine thanked them, and returned home even more undecided than she had been before consulting them. She now ventured to go to the house in the Rue du Colombier, intending to confide her troubles to her father and mother; for she was like a sick man who, in his desperate plight, tries every prescription, and even puts faith in old wives' remedies.

The old people received their daughter with an effusiveness that touched her deeply. Her visit brought them some little change, and that to them was worth a fortune. For the last four years they had gone their way like navigators without a goal or a compass. Sitting by the chimney corner, they would talk over their disasters under the old law of the *maximum*, of their great investments in cloth, of the way they had weathered bankruptcies, and, above all, the famous failure of Lecocq, Monsieur Guillaume's battle of Marengo. Then, when they had exhausted the tale of lawsuits, they recapitulated the sum total of their most profitable stock-takings, and told each other old stories of the Saint-Denis quarter. At two o'clock old Guillaume went to cast an eye on the business at the Cat and Racket; on his way back he called at all the shops, formerly the rivals of his own, where the young proprietors hoped to inveigle the old draper into some risky discount, which, as was his wont, he never refused point-blank. Two good Normandy horses were dying of their own fat in the stables of the big house; Madame Guillaume never used them but to drag her on Sundays to high Mass at the parish church. Three times a week the worthy couple kept open house. By the influence of his son-in-law Sommervieux, Monsieur Guillaume had been named a member of the consulting board for the clothing of the Army. Since her husband had stood so high in office, Madame Guillaume had decided that she must receive; her rooms were so crammed with gold and silver ornaments, and furniture, tasteless but of undoubted value, that the simplest room in the house looked like a chapel. Economy and expense seemed to be struggling for the upper hand in every accessory. It was as though Monsieur Guillaume had looked to a good investment, even in the purchase of a candlestick. In the midst of this bazaar, where splendor revealed the owner's want of occupation, Sommervieux's famous picture filled the place of honor, and in it Monsieur and Madame Guillaume found their chief consolation, turning their eyes, harnessed with eye-glasses, twenty times a day on this presentment of their past life, to them so active and amusing. The appearance of this mansion and these rooms, where everything had an aroma of staleness and mediocrity, the spectacle offered by these two beings, cast away, as it were, on a rock far from the world and the ideas which are life, startled Augustine; she could here contemplate the sequel of the scene of which the first part had struck her at the house of Lebas—a life of stir without movement, a mechanical and instinctive existence like that of the beaver; and then she felt an indefinable pride in her troubles, as she reflected that they had their source in eighteen months of such happiness as, in her eyes, was worth a thousand lives like this; its vacuity seemed to her horrible. However, she concealed this not very charitable feeling, and displayed for her parents her newly-acquired accomplishments of mind, and the ingratiating tenderness that love had revealed to her, disposing them to listen to her matrimonial grievances. Old people have a weakness for this kind of confidence. Madame Guillaume wanted to know the most trivial details of that alien life, which to her seemed almost fabulous. The travels of Baron de la Hontan, which she began again and again and never finished, told her nothing more unheard-of concerning the Canadian savages.

"What, child, your husband shuts himself into a room with naked women! And you are so simple as to believe that he draws them?"

As she uttered this exclamation, the grandmother laid her spectacles on a little work-table, shook her skirts, and clasped her hands on her knees, raised by a foot-warmer, her favorite pedestal.

"But, mother, all artists are obliged to have models."

"He took good care not to tell us that when he asked leave to marry you. If I had known it, I would never had given my daughter to a man who followed such a trade. Religion forbids such horrors; they are immoral. And at what time of night do you say he comes home?"

"At one o'clock—two——"

The old folks looked at each other in utter amazement.

"Then he gambles?" said Monsieur Guillaume. "In my day only gamblers stayed out so late."

Augustine made a face that scorned the accusation.

"He must keep you up through dreadful nights waiting for him," said Madame Guillaume. "But you go to bed, don't you? And when he has lost, the wretch wakes you."

"No, mamma, on the contrary, he is sometimes in very good spirits. Not infrequently, indeed, when it is fine, he suggests that I should get up and go into the woods."

"The woods! At that hour? Then have you such a small set of rooms that his bedroom and his sitting-room are not enough, and that he must run about? But it is just to give you cold that the wretch proposes such expeditions. He wants to get rid of you. Did one ever hear of a man settled in life, a well-behaved, quiet man galloping about like a warlock?"

"But, my dear mother, you do not understand that he must have excitement to fire his genius. He is fond of scenes which— —"

"I would make scenes for him, fine scenes!" cried Madame Guillaume, interrupting her daughter. "How can you show any consideration to such a man? In the first place, I don't like his drinking water only; it is not wholesome. Why does he object to see a woman eating? What queer notion is that! But he is mad. All you tell us about him is impossible. A man cannot leave his home without a word, and never come back for ten days. And then he tells you he has been to Dieppe to paint the sea. As if any one painted the sea! He crams you with a pack of tales that are too absurd."

Augustine opened her lips to defend her husband; but Madame Guillaume enjoined silence with a wave of her hand, which she obeyed by a survival of habit, and her mother went on in harsh tones: "Don't talk to me about the man! He never set foot in church excepting to see you and to be married. People without religion are capable of anything. Did Guillaume ever dream of hiding anything from me, of spending three days without saying a word to me, and of chattering afterwards like a blind magpie?"

"My dear mother, you judge superior people too severely. If their ideas were the same as other folks', they would not be men of genius."

"Very well, then let men of genius stop at home and not get married. What! A man of genius is to make his wife miserable? And because he is a genius it is all right!

Genius, genius! It is not so very clever to say black one minute and white the next, as he does, to interrupt other people, to dance such rigs at home, never to let you know which foot you are to stand on, to compel his wife never to be amused unless my lord is in gay spirits, and to be dull when he is dull."

"But, mother, the very nature of such imaginations—"

"What are such 'imaginations'?" Madame Guillaume went on, interrupting her daughter again. "Fine ones his are, my word! What possesses a man that all on a sudden, without consulting a doctor, he takes it into his head to eat nothing but vegetables? If indeed it were from religious motives, it might do him some good—but he has no more religion than a Huguenot. Was there ever a man known who, like him, loved horses better than his fellow-creatures, had his hair curled like a heathen, laid statues under muslin coverlets, shut his shutters in broad day to work by lamp-light? There, get along; if he were not so grossly immoral, he would be fit to shut up in a lunatic asylum. Consult Monsieur Loraux, the priest at Saint Sulpice, ask his opinion about it all, and he will tell you that your husband, does not behave like a Christian."

"Oh, mother, can you believe——?"

"Yes, I do believe. You loved him, and you can see none of these things. But I can remember in the early days after your marriage. I met him in the Champs-Élysées. He was on horseback. Well, at one minute he was galloping as hard as he could tear, and then pulled up to a walk. I said to myself at that moment, 'There is a man devoid of judgement.'"

"Ah, ha!" cried Monsieur Guillaume, "how wise I was to have your money settled on yourself with such a queer fellow for a husband!"

When Augustine was so imprudent as to set forth her serious grievances against her husband, the two old people were speechless with indignation. But the word "divorce" was ere long spoken by Madame Guillaume. At the sound of the word divorce the apathetic old draper seemed to wake up. Prompted by his love for his daughter, and also by the excitement which the proceedings would bring into his uneventful life, father Guillaume took up the matter. He made himself the leader of the application for a divorce, laid down the lines of it, almost argued the case; he offered to be at all the charges, to see the lawyers, the pleaders, the judges, to move heaven and earth. Madame de Sommervieux was frightened, she refused her father's services, said she would not be separated from her husband even if she were ten times as unhappy, and talked no more about her sorrows. After being overwhelmed by her parents with all the little wordless and consoling kindnesses by which the old couple tried in vain to make up to her for her distress of heart, Augustine went away, feeling the impossibility of making a superior mind intelligible to weak intellects. She had learned that a wife must hide from every one, even from her parents, woes for which it is so difficult to find sympathy. The storms and sufferings of the upper spheres are appreciated only by the lofty spirits who inhabit there. In any circumstance we can only be judged by our equals.

Thus poor Augustine found herself thrown back on the horror of her meditations, in the cold atmosphere of her home. Study was indifferent to her, since study had not brought her back her husband's heart. Initiated into the secret of these souls of fire, but bereft of their resources, she was compelled to share their sorrows without sharing their pleasures. She was disgusted with the world, which to her seemed mean and small as compared with the incidents of passion. In short, her life was a failure.

One evening an idea flashed upon her that lighted up her dark grief like a beam from heaven. Such an idea

could never have smiled on a heart less pure, less virtuous than hers. She determined to go to the Duchesse de
Carigliano, not to ask her to give her back her husband's
heart, but to learn the arts by which it had been captured; to engage the interest of this haughty fine lady for
the mother of her lover's children; to appeal to her and
make her the instrument of her future happiness, since
she was the cause of her present wretchedness.

So one day Augustine, timid as she was, but armed
with supernatural courage, got into her carriage at two
in the afternoon to try for admittance to the boudoir
of the famous coquette, who was never visible till that
hour. Madame de Sommervieux had not yet seen any of
the ancient and magnificent mansions of the Faubourg
Saint-Germain.* As she made her way through the
stately corridors, the handsome staircases, the vast
drawing-rooms—full of flowers, though it was in the
depth of winter, and decorated with the taste peculiar to
women born to opulence or to the elegant habits of the
aristocracy, Augustine felt a terrible clutch at her heart;
she coveted the secrets of an elegance of which she had
never had an idea; she breathed in an air of grandeur
which explained the attraction of the house for her
husband. When she reached the private rooms of the
duchesse she was filled with jealousy and a sort of despair, as she admired the luxurious arrangement of the
furniture, the draperies and the hangings. Here disorder was a grace, here luxury affected a certain contempt
of splendor. The fragrance that floated in the warm air
flattered the sense of smell without offending it. The
accessories of the rooms were in harmony with a view,
through plate-glass windows, of the lawns in a garden
planted with evergreen trees. It was all bewitching, and
the art of it was not perceptible. The whole spirit of the
mistress of these rooms pervaded the drawing-room
where Augustine awaited her. She tried to divine her
rival's character from the aspect of the scattered objects;

but there was here something as impenetrable in the disorder as in the symmetry, and to the simple-minded young wife all was a sealed letter. All that she could discern was that, as a woman, the duchesse was a superior person. Then a painful thought came over her.

"Alas! And is it true," she wondered, "that a simple and loving heart is not all-sufficient to an artist; that to balance the weight of these powerful souls they need a union with feminine souls of a strength equal to their own? If I had been brought up like this siren, our weapons at least might have been equal in the hour of struggle."

"But I am not at home!" The sharp, harsh words, though spoken in an undertone in the adjoining boudoir, were heard by Augustine, and her heart beat violently.

"The lady is in there," replied the maid.

"You are an idiot! Show her in," replied the duchesse, whose voice was sweeter, and had assumed the dulcet tones of politeness. She evidently now meant to be heard.

Augustine shyly entered the room. At the end of the dainty boudoir she saw the duchesse lounging luxuriously on an ottoman covered with brown velvet and placed in the centre of a sort of apse outlined by soft folds of white muslin over a yellow lining. Ornaments of gilt bronze, arranged with exquisite taste, enhanced this sort of dais, under which the duchesse reclined like a Greek statue. The dark hue of the velvet gave relief to every fascinating charm. A subdued light, friendly to her beauty, fell like a reflection rather than a direct illumination. A few rare flowers raised their perfumed heads from costly Sèvres vases. At the moment when this picture was presented to Augustine's astonished eyes, she was approaching so noiselessly that she caught a glance from those of the enchantress. This look seemed to say to someone whom Augustine did not at first perceive, "Stay; you will see a pretty woman, and make her visit seem less of a bore."

On seeing Augustine, the duchesse rose and made her sit down by her.

"And to what do I owe the pleasure of this visit, madame?" she said with a most gracious smile.

"Why all the falseness?" thought Augustine, replying only with a bow.

Her silence was compulsory. The young woman saw before her a superfluous witness of the scene. This personage was, of all the Colonels in the army, the youngest, the most fashionable, and the finest man. His face, full of life and youth, but already expressive, was further enhanced by a small moustache twirled up into points, and as black as jet, by a full imperial, by whiskers carefully combed, and a forest of black hair in some disorder. He was whisking a riding whip with an air of ease and freedom which suited his self-satisfied expression and the elegance of his dress; the ribbons attached to his button-hole were carelessly tied, and he seemed to pride himself much more on his smart appearance than on his courage. Augustine looked at the Duchesse de Carigliano, and indicated the Colonel by a sidelong glance. All its mute appeal was understood.

"Good-bye, then, Monsieur d'Aiglemont, we shall meet in the Bois de Boulogne."*

These words were spoken by the siren as though they were the result of an agreement made before Augustine's arrival, and she winged them with a threatening look that the officer deserved perhaps for the admiration he showed in gazing at the modest flower, which contrasted so well with the haughty duchesse. The young fop bowed in silence, turned on the heels of his boots, and gracefully quitted the boudoir. At this instant, Augustine, watching her rival, whose eyes seemed to follow the brilliant officer, detected in that glance a sentiment of which the transient expression is known to every woman. She perceived with the deepest anguish that her visit would be useless; this lady, full of artifice, was too greedy of homage not to have a ruthless heart.

"Madame," said Augustine in a broken voice, "the step I am about to take will seem to you very strange; but there is a madness of despair which ought to excuse anything. I understand only too well why Théodore prefers your house to any other, and why your mind has so much power over his. Alas! I have only to look into myself to find more than ample reasons. But I am devoted to my husband, madame. Two years of tears have not effaced his image from my heart, though I have lost his. In my folly I dared to dream of a contest with you; and I have come to you to ask you by what means I may triumph over yourself. Oh, madame," cried the young wife, ardently seizing the hand which her rival allowed her to hold, "I will never pray to God for my own happiness with so much fervor as I will beseech Him for yours, if you will help me to win back Sommervieux's regard—I will not say his love. I have no hope but in you. Ah! tell me how you could please him, and make him forget the first days——" At these words Augustine broke down, suffocated with sobs she could not suppress. Ashamed of her weakness, she hid her face in her handkerchief, which she bathed with tears.

"What a child you are, my dear little beauty!" said the duchesse, carried away by the novelty of such a scene, and touched, in spite of herself, at receiving such homage from the most perfect virtue perhaps in Paris. She took the young wife's handkerchief, and herself wiped the tears from her eyes, soothing her by a few monosyllables murmured with gracious compassion. After a moment's silence the duchesse, grasping poor Augustine's hands in both her own—hands that had a rare character of dignity and powerful beauty—said in a gentle and friendly voice: "My first warning is to advise you not to weep so bitterly; tears are disfiguring. We must learn to deal firmly with the sorrows that make us ill, for love does not linger long by a sick-bed. Melancholy, at first, no doubt, lends a certain attractive grace, but it ends by dragging the features and blighting the loveliest face. And besides, our tyrants are so vain as to insist that their slaves should be always cheerful."

"But, madame, it is not in my power not to feel. How is it possible, without suffering a thousand deaths, to see the face which once beamed with love and gladness turn chill, colorless, and indifferent? I cannot control my heart!"

"So much the worse, sweet child. But I fancy I know all your story. In the first place, if your husband is unfaithful to you, understand clearly that I am not his accomplice. If I was anxious to have him in my drawing-room, it was, I own, out of vanity; he was famous, and he went nowhere. I like you too much already to tell you all the mad things he has done for my sake. I will only reveal one, because it may perhaps help us to bring him back to you, and to punish him for the audacity of his behavior to me. He will end by compromising me. I know the world too well, my dear, to abandon myself to the discretion of a too superior man. You should know that one may allow them to court one, but marry them—that is a mistake! We women ought to admire men of genius, and delight in them as a spectacle, but as to living with them? Never.—No, no. It is like wanting to find pleasure in inspecting the machinery of the opera instead of sitting in a box to enjoy its brilliant illusions. But this misfortune has fallen on you, my poor child, has it not? Well, then, you must try to arm yourself against tyranny."

"Ah, madame, before coming in here, only seeing you as I came in, I already detected some arts of which I had no suspicion."

"Well, come and see me sometimes, and it will not be

long before you have mastered the knowledge of these trifles, important, too, in their way. Outward things are, to fools, half of life; and in that matter more than one clever man is a fool, in spite of all his talent. But I dare wager you never could refuse your Théodore anything!"

"How refuse anything, madame, if one loves a man?"

"Poor innocent, I could adore you for your simplicity. You should know that the more we love the less we should allow a man, above all, a husband, to see the whole extent of our passion. The one who loves most is tyrannized over, and, which is worse, is sooner or later neglected. The one who wishes to rule should——"

"What, madame, must I then dissimulate, calculate, become false, form an artificial character, and live in it? How is it possible to live in such a way? Can you——" she hesitated; the duchesse smiled.

"My dear child," the great lady went on in a serious tone, "conjugal happiness has in all times been a speculation, a business demanding particular attention. If you persist in talking passion while I am talking marriage, we shall soon cease to understand each other. Listen to me," she went on, assuming a confidential tone. "I have been in the way of seeing some of the superior men of our day. Those who have married have for the most part chosen quite insignificant wives. Well, those wives governed them, as the Emperor governs us; and if they were not loved, they were at least respected. I like secrets—especially those which concern women—well enough to have amused myself by seeking the clue to the riddle. Well, my sweet child, those worthy women had the gift of analyzing their husbands' nature; instead of taking fright, like you, at their superiority, they very acutely noted the qualities they lacked, and either by possessing those qualities, or by feigning to possess them, they found means of making such a handsome display of them in their husbands' eyes that in the end they impressed them. Also, I must tell you, all these souls which appear so lofty have just a speck of madness in them, which we ought to know how to take advantage of. By firmly resolving to have the upper hand and never deviating from that aim, by bringing all our actions to bear on it, all our ideas, our cajolery, we subjugate these eminently capricious natures, which, by the very mutability of their thoughts, lend us the means of influencing them."

"Good heavens!" cried the young wife in dismay. "And this is life. It is a warfare— —"

"In which we must always threaten," said the duchesse, laughing. "Our power is wholly factitious. And we must never allow a man to despise us; it is impossible to recover from such a descent but by odious manoeuvring. Come," she added, "I will give you a means of bringing your husband to his senses."

She rose with a smile to guide the young and guileless apprentice to conjugal arts through the labyrinth of her palace. They came to a back-staircase, which led up to the reception rooms. As Madame de Carigliano pressed the secret springlock of the door she stopped, looking at Augustine with an inimitable gleam of shrewdness and grace. "The Duc de Carigliano adores me," said she. "Well, he dare not enter by this door without my leave. And he is a man in the habit of commanding thousands of soldiers. He knows how to face a battery, but before me,—he is afraid!"

Augustine sighed. They entered a sumptuous gallery, where the painter's wife was led by the duchesse up to the portrait painted by Théodore of Mademoiselle Guillaume. On seeing it, Augustine uttered a cry.

"I knew it was no longer in my house," she said, "but—here!— —"

"My dear child, I asked for it merely to see what pitch of idiocy a man of genius may attain to. Sooner or later

I should have returned it to you, for I never expected the pleasure of seeing the original here face to face with the copy. While we finish our conversation I will have it carried down to your carriage. And if, armed with such a talisman, you are not your husband's mistress for a hundred years, you are not a woman, and you deserve your fate."

Augustine kissed the duchesse's hand, and the lady clasped her to her heart, with all the more tenderness because she would forget her by the morrow. This scene might perhaps have destroyed for ever the candor and purity of a less virtuous woman than Augustine, for the astute politics of the higher social spheres were no more consonant to Augustine than the narrow reasoning of Joseph Lebas, or Madame Guillaume's vapid morality. Strange are the results of the false positions into which we may be brought by the slightest mistake in the conduct of life! Augustine was like an Alpine cowherd surprised by an avalanche; if he hesitates, if he listens to the shouts of his comrades, he is almost certainly lost. In such a crisis the heart steels itself or breaks.

Madame de Sommervieux returned home a prey to such agitation as it is difficult to describe. Her conversation with the Duchesse de Carigliano had roused in her mind a crowd of contradictory thoughts. Like the sheep in the fable, full of courage in the wolf's absence, she preached to herself, and laid down admirable plans of conduct; she devised a thousand coquettish stratagems; she even talked to her husband, finding, away from him, all the springs of true eloquence which never desert a woman; then, as she pictured to herself Théodore's clear and steadfast gaze, she began to quake. When she asked whether monsieur were at home her voice shook. On learning that he would not be in to dinner, she felt an unaccountable thrill of joy. Like a criminal who has appealed against sentence of death, a respite, however short, seemed to her a lifetime. She placed the portrait in

her room, and waited for her husband in all the agonies
of hope. That this venture must decide her future life,
she felt too keenly not to shiver at every sound, even
the low ticking of the clock, which seemed to aggravate
her terrors by doling them out to her. She tried to cheat
time by various devices. The idea struck her of dressing
in a way which would make her exactly like the portrait. Then, knowing her husband's restless temper, she
had her room lighted up with unusual brightness, feeling sure that when he came in curiosity would bring
him there at once. Midnight had struck when, at the
call of the groom, the street gate was opened, and the
artist's carriage rumbled in over the stones of the silent
courtyard.

"What is the meaning of this illumination?" asked
Théodore in glad tones, as he came into her room.

Augustine skillfully seized the auspicious moment;
she threw herself into her husband's arms, and pointed
to the portrait. The artist stood rigid as a rock, and his
eyes turned alternately on Augustine, on the accusing
dress. The frightened wife, half-dead, as she watched
her husband's changeful brow — that terrible brow —
saw the expressive furrows gathering like clouds; then
she felt her blood curdling in her veins when, with a
glaring look, and in a deep hollow voice, he began to
question her:

"Where did you find that picture?"

"The Duchesse de Carigliano returned it to me."

"You asked her for it?"

"I did not know that she had it."

The gentleness, or rather the exquisite sweetness of
this angel's voice, might have touched a cannibal, but
not an artist in the clutches of wounded vanity.

"It is worthy of her!" exclaimed the painter in a voice
of thunder. "I will be avenged!" he cried, striding up
and down the room. "She shall die of shame; I will paint
her! Yes, I will paint her as Messalina stealing out at

night from the palace of Claudius."

"Théodore!" said a faint voice.

"I will kill her!"

"My dear——"

"She is in love with that little cavalry colonel, because he rides well——"

"Théodore!"

"Let me be!" said the painter in a tone almost like a roar.

It would be odious to describe the whole scene. In the end the frenzy of passion prompted the artist to acts and words which any woman not so young as Augustine would have ascribed to madness.

At eight o'clock next morning Madame Guillaume, surprising her daughter, found her pale, with red eyes, her hair in disorder, holding a handkerchief soaked with tears, while she gazed at the floor strewn with the torn fragments of a dress and the broken fragments of a large gilt picture-frame. Augustine, almost senseless with grief, pointed to the wreck with a gesture of deep despair.

"I don't know that the loss is very great!" cried the old mistress of the Cat and Racket. "It was like you, no doubt; but I am told that there is a man on the boulevard who paints lovely portraits for fifty crowns."

"Oh, mother!"

"Poor child, you are quite right," replied Madame Guillaume, who misinterpreted the expression of her daughter's glance at her. "True, my child, no one ever can love you as fondly as a mother. My darling, I guess it all; but confide your sorrows to me, and I will comfort you. Did I not tell you long ago that the man was mad! Your maid has told me pretty stories. Why, he must be a perfect monster!"

Augustine laid a finger on her white lips, as if to implore a moment's silence. During this dreadful night misery had led her to that patient resignation which in mothers and loving wives transcends in its effects all human energy, and perhaps reveals in the heart of women the existence of certain chords which God has withheld from men.

An inscription engraved on a broken column in the cemetery at Montmartre states that Madame de Sommervieux died at the age of twenty-seven. In the simple words of this epitaph one of the timid creature's friends can read the last scene of a tragedy. Every year, on the second of November, the solemn day of the dead, he never passes this youthful monument without wondering whether it does not need a stronger woman than Augustine to endure the violent embrace of genius?

"The humble and modest flowers that bloom in the valley," he reflects, "perish perhaps when they are transplanted too near the skies, to the region where storms gather and the sun is scorching."

Maffliers, October 1829

Addendum to *At the Sign of the Cat and Racket*
The following personages appear in other stories of
The Human Comedy.

Aiglemont, General, Marquis Victor d'
  The Firm of Nucingen
  A Woman of Thirty

Birotteau, César
  César Birotteau
  The Rabouilleuse

Camusot
  Lost Illusions (A Distinguished Provincial at Paris)
  The Rabouilleuse
  Cousin Pons
  The Muse of the Department
  César Birotteau

Cardot, Jean-Jerome-Severin
  A Start in Life
  Lost Illusions
  A Distinguished Provincial at Paris
  The Rabouilleuse
  César Birotteau

Carigliano, Maréchal, Duc de
  Old Goriot
  Sarrasine

Carigliano, Duchesse de
  Lost Illusions (A Distinguished Provincial at Paris)
  The Peasants
  The Deputy for Arcis

Guillaume
  César Birotteau

Lebas, Joseph
César Birotteau
Cousin Bette

Lebas, Madame Joseph (Virginie)
César Birotteau
Cousin Bette

Lourdois
César Birotteau

Rabourdin, Xavier
The Bureaucrats
César Birotteau
The Petty Bourgeoisie

Roguin, Madame
César Birotteau
Pierrette
A Second Home
A Daughter of Eve

Sommervieux, Théodore de
The Bureaucrats
Modeste Mignon

Sommervieux, Madame Théodore de (Augustine)
César Birotteau

The Ball at Sceaux

(*Le Bal de Sceaux*)
Translated by Clara Bell

To Henri de Balzac, from his brother Honoré.

Invariable dans sa religion aristocratique, Monsieur DE FONTAINE
en avait aveuglément suivi les maximes.

LE BAL DE SCEAUX.

Plate II: *The Comte de Fontaine*
Illustration by Jean Louis Ernest Meissonier

The Comte de Fontaine, head of one of the oldest families in Poitou, had served the Bourbon cause* with intelligence and bravery during the war in La Vendée against the Republic. After having escaped all the dangers which threatened the royalist leaders during this stormy period of modern history, he was wont to say in jest, "I am one of the men who gave themselves to be killed on the steps of the throne." And the pleasantry had some truth in it, as spoken by a man left for dead at the bloody battle of Les Quatre Chemins. Though ruined by confiscation, the staunch Vendéen* steadily refused the lucrative posts offered to him by the Emperor Napoleon. Immovable in his aristocratic faith, he had blindly obeyed its precepts when he thought it fitting to choose a companion for life. In spite of the blandishments of a rich but revolutionary parvenu, who valued the alliance at a high figure, he married Mademoiselle de Kergarouët, without a fortune, but belonging to one of the oldest families in Brittany.

When the second revolution* burst on Monsieur de Fontaine he was encumbered with a large family. Though it was no part of the noble gentleman's views to solicit favors, he yielded to his wife's wish, left his country estate, of which the income barely sufficed to maintain his children, and came to Paris. Saddened by seeing the greediness of his former comrades in the rush for places and dignities under the new Constitution,* he was about to return to his property when he received a ministerial despatch, in which a well-known magnate

71

announced to him his nomination as *maréchal de camp*, or brigadier-general, under a rule which allowed the officers of the Catholic armies to count the twenty submerged years of Louis XVIII's reign as years of service. Some days later he further received, without any solicitation, *ex officio*, the crosses of the Legion of Honor and of Saint-Louis.*

Shaken in his determination by these successive favors, due, as he supposed, to the monarch's remembrance, he was no longer satisfied with taking his family, as he had piously done every Sunday, to cry "Vive le Roi" in the hall of the Tuileries when the royal family passed through on their way to chapel; he craved the favor of a private audience. The audience, at once granted, was in no sense private. The royal drawing-room was full of old adherents, whose powdered heads, seen from above, suggested a carpet of snow. There the comte met some old friends, who received him somewhat coldly; but the princes he thought *adorable*, an enthusiastic expression which escaped him when the most gracious of his masters, to whom the comte had supposed himself to be known only by name, came to shake hands with him, and spoke of him as the most thorough Vendéen of them all. Notwithstanding this ovation, none of these august persons thought of inquiring as to the sum of his losses, or of the money he had poured so generously into the chests of the Catholic regiments. He discovered, a little late, that he had made war at his own cost. Towards the end of the evening he thought he might venture on a witty allusion to the state of his affairs, similar, as it was, to that of many other gentlemen. His Majesty laughed heartily enough; any speech that bore the hall-mark of wit was certain to please him; but he nevertheless replied with one of those royal pleasantries whose sweetness is more formidable than the anger of a rebuke. One of the king's most intimate advisers took an opportunity of going up to the fortune-seeking Vendéen, and made him understand by a keen and polite hint that the time had not yet come for settling accounts with the sovereign; that there were bills of much longer standing than his on the books, and there, no doubt, they would remain, as part of the history of the Revolution. The comte prudently withdrew from the venerable group, which formed a respectful semi-circle before the august family; then, having extricated his sword, not without some difficulty, from among the lean legs which had got mixed up with it, he crossed the courtyard of the Tuileries and got into the hackney cab he had left on the quay. With the restive spirit, which is peculiar to the nobility of the old school, in whom still survives the memory of the League and the day of the Barricades (in 1588),* he bewailed himself in his cab, loudly enough to compromise him, over the change that had come over the Court. "Formerly," he said to himself, "every one could speak freely to the king of his own little affairs; the nobles could ask him a favor, or for money, when it suited them, and nowadays one cannot recover the money advanced for his service without raising a scandal! By Heaven! the cross of Saint-Louis and the rank of brigadier-general will not make good the three hundred thousand livres I have spent, out and out, on the royal cause. I must speak to the king, face to face, in his own room."

This scene cooled Monsieur de Fontaine's ardor all the more effectually because his requests for an interview were never answered. And, indeed, he saw the upstarts of the Empire obtaining some of the offices reserved, under the old monarchy, for the highest families.

"All is lost!" he exclaimed one morning. "The king has certainly never been other than a revolutionary. But for Monsieur, who never derogates, and is some comfort to his faithful adherents, I do not know what hands the crown of France might not fall into if things are to go on like this. Their cursed constitutional system is the worst possible government, and can never suit France. Louis XVIII and Monsieur Beugnot spoiled everything at Saint Ouen."*

The comte, in despair, was preparing to retire to his estate, abandoning, with dignity, all claims to repayment. At this moment the events of the 20th March (1815) gave warning of a fresh storm, threatening to overwhelm the legitimate monarch and his defenders. Monsieur de Fontaine, like one of those generous souls who do not dismiss a servant in a torrent of rain; borrowed on his lands to follow the routed monarchy, without knowing whether this complicity in emigration would prove more propitious to him than his past devotion. But when he perceived that the companions of the king's exile were in higher favor than the brave men who had protested, sword in hand, against the establishment of the republic, he may perhaps have hoped to derive greater profit from this journey into a foreign land than from active and dangerous service in the heart of his own country. Nor was his courtier-like calculation one of these rash speculations which promise splendid results on paper, and are ruinous in effect. He was—to quote the wittiest and most successful of our diplomates—one of the faithful five hundred who shared the exile of the Court at Ghent, and one of the fifty thousand who returned with it.* During the short banishment of royalty, Monsieur de Fontaine was so happy as to be employed by Louis XVIII, and found more than one opportunity of giving him proofs of great political honesty and sincere attachment. One evening, when the king had nothing better to do, he recalled Monsieur de Fontaine's witticism at the Tuileries. The old Vendéen did not let such a happy chance slip; he told his history with so much vivacity that a king, who never forgot anything, might remember it at a convenient season. The royal amateur of literature also observed the elegant style given to some notes which the discreet gentleman had been invited to recast. This little success stamped Monsieur de Fontaine on the king's memory as one of the loyal servants of the Crown.

At the second restoration the comte was one of those special envoys who were sent throughout the departments charged with absolute jurisdiction over the leaders of revolt; but he used his terrible powers with moderation. As soon as the temporary commission was ended, the High Provost found a seat in the Privy Council, became a deputy, spoke little, listened much, and changed his opinions very considerably. Certain circumstances, unknown to historians, brought him into such intimate relations with the sovereign, that one day, as he came in, the shrewd monarch addressed him thus: "My friend Fontaine, I shall take care never to appoint you to be director-general, or minister. Neither you nor I, as *employés*, could keep our place on account of our opinions. Representative government has this advantage; it saves Us the trouble We used to have, of dismissing Our Secretaries of State. Our Council is a perfect inn-parlor, whither public opinion sometimes sends strange travelers; however, We can always find a place for Our faithful adherents."

This ironical speech was introductory to a rescript giving Monsieur de Fontaine an appointment as administrator in the office of Crown lands. As a consequence of the intelligent attention with which he listened to his royal friend's sarcasms, his name always rose to His Majesty's lips when a commission was to be appointed of which the members were to receive a handsome salary. He had the good sense to hold his tongue about the favor with which he was honored, and knew how to entertain the monarch in those familiar chats in which Louis XVIII delighted as much as in a well-written note, by his brilliant manner of repeating political anecdotes, and the political or parliamentary tittle-tattle—if the expression may pass—which at that time was rife. It is well known that he was immensely amused by every detail of his *Gouvernementabilité*—a word adopted by his facetious Majesty.

Thanks to the Comte de Fontaine's good sense, wit, and tact, every member of his numerous family, however young, ended, as he jestingly told his sovereign, in attaching himself like a silkworm to the leaves of the Pay-List. Thus, by the king's intervention, his eldest son found a high and fixed position as a lawyer. The second, before the restoration a mere captain, was appointed to the command of a legion on the return from Ghent; then, thanks to the confusion of 1815, when the regulations were evaded, he passed into the bodyguard, returned to a line regiment, and found himself after the affair of the Trocadéro* a lieutenant-general with a commission in the Guards. The youngest, appointed *sous-préfet*,* ere long became a legal official and director of a municipal board of the city of Paris, where he was safe from changes in Legislature. These bounties, bestowed without parade, and as secret as the favor enjoyed by the comte, fell unperceived. Though the father and his three sons each had sinecures enough to enjoy an income in salaries almost equal to that of a chief of department, their political good fortune excited no envy. In those early days of the constitutional system, few persons had very precise ideas of the peaceful domain of the civil service, where astute favorites managed to find an equivalent for the demolished abbeys. Monsieur le Comte de Fontaine, who till lately boasted that he had not read the Charter, and displayed such indignation at the greed of courtiers, had, before long, proved to his august master that he understood, as well as the king himself, the spirit and resources of the representative system. At the same time, notwithstanding the established careers open to his three sons, and the pecuniary advantages derived from four official appointments, Monsieur de Fontaine was the head of too large a family to be able to re-establish his fortune easily and rapidly.

His three sons were rich in prospects, in favor, and in talent; but he had three daughters, and was afraid of wearying the monarch's benevolence. It occurred to him to mention only one by one, these virgins eager to light their torches. The king had too much good taste to leave his work incomplete. The marriage of the eldest with a Receiver-General, Planat de Baudry, was arranged by one of those royal speeches which cost nothing and are worth millions. One evening, when the sovereign was out of spirits, he smiled on hearing of the existence of another Demoiselle de Fontaine, for whom he found a husband in the person of a young magistrate, of inferior birth, no doubt, but wealthy, and whom he created Baron. When, the year after, the Vendéen spoke of Mademoiselle Émilie de Fontaine, the king replied in his thin sharp tones, "*Amicus Plato sed magis amica Natio.*"* Then, a few days later, he treated his "friend Fontaine" to a quatrain, harmless enough, which he styled an epigram, in which he made fun of these three daughters so skillfully introduced, under the form of a trinity. Nay, if report is to be believed, the monarch had found the point of the jest in the Unity of the three Divine Persons.

"If your Majesty would only condescend to turn the epigram into an epithalamium?" said the comte, trying to turn the sally to good account.

"Though I see the rhyme of it, I fail to see the reason," retorted the king, who did not relish any pleasantry, however mild, on the subject of his poetry.

From that day his intercourse with Monsieur de Fontaine showed less amenity. Kings enjoy contradicting more than people think. Like most youngest children, Émilie de Fontaine was a Benjamin spoilt by almost everybody. The king's coolness, therefore, caused the comte all the more regret, because no marriage was ever so difficult to arrange as that of this darling daughter. To understand all the obstacles we must make our way into the fine residence where the official was housed at the expense of the nation. Émilie had spent her childhood on the family estate, enjoying the abundance which suffices for the joys of early youth; her lightest wishes had been law to her sisters, her brothers, her mother, and even her father. All her relations doted on her. Having come to years of discretion just when her family was loaded with the favors of fortune, the enchantment of life continued. The luxury of Paris seemed to her just as natural as a wealth of flowers or fruit, or as the rural plenty which had been the joy of her first years. Just as in her childhood she had never been thwarted in the satisfaction of her playful desires, so now, at fourteen, she was still obeyed when she rushed into the whirl of fashion.

Thus, accustomed by degrees to the enjoyment of money, elegance of dress, of gilded drawing-rooms and fine carriages, became as necessary to her as the compliments of flattery, sincere or false, and the festivities and vanities of court life. Like most spoiled children, she tyrannized over those who loved her, and kept her blandishments for those who were indifferent. Her faults grew with her growth, and her parents were to gather the bitter fruits of this disastrous education. At the age of nineteen Émilie de Fontaine had not yet been pleased to make a choice from among the many young men whom her father's politics brought to his entertainments. Though so young, she asserted in society all the freedom of mind that a married woman can enjoy. Her beauty was so remarkable that, for her, to appear in a room was to be its queen; but, like sovereigns, she had no friends, though she was everywhere the object of attentions to which a finer nature than hers might perhaps have succumbed. Not a man, not even an old man, had it in him to contradict the opinions of a young girl whose lightest look could rekindle love in the coldest heart.

She had been educated with a care which her sisters had not enjoyed; painted pretty well, spoke Italian and English, and played the piano brilliantly; her voice, trained by the best masters, had a ring in it which made her singing irresistibly charming. Clever, and intimate with every branch of literature, she might have made folks believe that, as Mascarille says,* people of quality come into the world knowing everything. She could argue fluently on Italian or Flemish painting, on the Middle Ages or the Renaissance; pronounced at haphazard on books new or old, and could expose the defects of a work with a cruelly graceful wit. The simplest thing she said was accepted by an admiring crowd as a *fetfah* of the Sultan by the Turks.* She thus dazzled shallow persons; as to deeper minds, her natural tact enabled her to discern them, and for them she put forth so much fascination that, under cover of her charms, she escaped their scrutiny. This enchanting veneer covered a careless heart; the opinion—common to many young girls—that no one else dwelt in a sphere so lofty as to be able to understand the merits of her soul; and a pride based no less on her birth than on her beauty. In the absence of the overwhelming sentiment which, sooner or later, works havoc in a woman's heart, she spent her young ardor in an immoderate love of distinctions, and expressed the deepest contempt for persons of inferior birth. Supremely impertinent to all newly-created nobility, she made every effort to get her parents recognized as equals by the most illustrious families of the Saint-Germain quarter.*

These sentiments had not escaped the observing eye of Monsieur de Fontaine, who more than once, when his two elder girls were married, had smarted under Émilie's sarcasm. Logical readers will be surprised to see the old Royalist bestowing his eldest daughter on a Receiver-General, possessed, indeed, of some old hereditary estates, but whose name was not preceded by the little word to which the throne owed so many partisans,* and his second to a magistrate too lately baronified to obscure the fact that his father had sold firewood. This noteworthy change in the ideas of a noble on the verge of his sixtieth year—an age when men rarely renounce their convictions—was due not merely to his unfortunate residence in the modern Babylon, where, sooner or later, country folks all get their corners rubbed down; the Comte de Fontaine's new political conscience was also a result of the king's advice and friendship. The philosophical prince had taken pleasure in converting the Vendéen to the ideas required by the advance of the nineteenth century, and the new aspect of the Monarchy. Louis XVIII aimed at fusing parties as Napoleon had fused things and men. The legitimate king, who was not less clever perhaps than his rival, acted in a contrary direction. The last head of the House of Bourbon was just as eager to satisfy the third estate and the creations of the Empire, by curbing the clergy, as the first of the Napoleons had been to attract the grand old nobility, or to endow the Church. The Privy Councillor, being in the secret of these royal projects, had insensibly become one of the most prudent and influential leaders of that moderate party which most desired a fusion of opinion in the interests of the nation. He preached the expensive doctrines of constitutional government, and lent all his weight to encourage the political see-saw which enabled his master to rule France in the midst of storms. Perhaps Monsieur de Fontaine hoped that one of the sudden gusts of legislation, whose unexpected efforts then startled the oldest politicians, might carry him up to the rank of peer. One of his most rigid principles was to recognize no nobility in France but that of the peerage—the only families that might enjoy any privileges.

"A nobility bereft of privileges," he would say, "is a tool without a handle."

As far from Lafayette's party as he was from La Bourdonnaye's,* he ardently engaged in the task of general reconciliation, which was to result in a new era and splendid fortunes for France. He strove to convince the families who frequented his drawing-room, or those whom he visited, how few favorable openings would henceforth be offered by a civil or military career. He urged mothers to give their boys a start in independent and industrial professions, explaining that military posts and high Government appointments must at last pertain, in a quite constitutional order, to the younger sons of members of the peerage. According to him, the people had conquered a sufficiently large share in practical government by its elective assembly, its appointments to law-offices, and those of the exchequer, which, said he, would always, as heretofore, be the natural right of the distinguished men of the third estate.

These new notions of the head of the Fontaines, and the prudent matches for his eldest girls to which they had led, met with strong resistance in the bosom of his family. The Comtesse de Fontaine remained faithful to the ancient beliefs which no woman could disown, who, through her mother, belonged to the Rohans.* Although she had for a while opposed the happiness and fortune awaiting her two eldest girls, she yielded to those private considerations which husband and wife confide to each other when their heads are resting on the same pillow. Monsieur de Fontaine calmly pointed out to his wife, by exact arithmetic that their residence in Paris, the necessity for entertaining, the magnificence of the house which made up to them now for the privations so bravely shared in La Vendée, and the expenses of their sons, swallowed up the chief part of their income from salaries. They must therefore seize, as a boon from heaven, the opportunities which offered for settling their

girls with such wealth. Would they not some day enjoy sixty—eighty—a hundred thousand francs a year?
Such advantageous matches were not to be met with every day for girls without a portion. Again, it was time
that they should begin to think of economizing, to add
to the estate of Fontaine, and re-establish the old territo-
rial fortune of the family. The comtesse yielded to such
cogent arguments, as every mother would have done in
her place, though perhaps with a better grace; but she
declared that Émilie, at any rate, should marry in such
a way as to satisfy the pride she had unfortunately contributed to foster in the girl's young soul.

Thus events, which ought to have brought joy into the
family, had introduced a small leaven of discord. The
Receiver-General and the young lawyer were the objects of a ceremonious formality which the comtesse and
Émilie contrived to create. This etiquette soon found
even ampler opportunity for the display of domestic
tyranny; for Lieutenant-General de Fontaine married
Mademoiselle Mongenod, the daughter of a rich banker; the Président very sensibly found a wife in a young
lady whose father, twice or thrice a millionaire, had
traded in salt; and the third brother, faithful to his plebeian doctrines, married Mademoiselle Grossetête, the
only daughter of the Receiver-General at Bourges. The
three sisters-in-law and the two brothers-in-law found
the high sphere of political bigwigs, and the drawing-
rooms of the Faubourg Saint-Germain, so full of charm
and of personal advantages, that they united in forming
a little court round the overbearing Émilie. This treaty
between interest and pride was not, however, so firmly
cemented but that the young despot was, not infrequently, the cause of revolts in her little realm. Scenes,
which the highest circles would not have disowned,
kept up a sarcastic temper among all the members of
this powerful family; and this, without seriously diminishing the regard they professed in public, degenerated

sometimes in private into sentiments far from charitable. Thus the Lieutenant-General's wife, having become a baronne, thought herself quite as noble as a Kergarouët, and imagined that her good hundred thousand francs a year gave her the right to be as impertinent as her sister-in-law Émilie, whom she would sometimes wish to see happily married, as she announced that the daughter of some peer of France had married Monsieur So-and-So with no title to his name. The Vicomtesse de Fontaine amused herself by eclipsing Émilie in the taste and magnificence that were conspicuous in her dress, her furniture, and her carriages. The satirical spirit in which her brothers and sisters sometimes received the claims avowed by Mademoiselle de Fontaine roused her to wrath that a perfect hailstorm of sharp sayings could hardly mitigate. So when the head of the family felt a slight chill in the king's tacit and precarious friendship, he trembled all the more because, as a result of her sisters' defiant mockery, his favorite daughter had never looked so high.

In the midst of these circumstances, and at a moment when this petty domestic warfare had become serious, the monarch, whose favor Monsieur de Fontaine still hoped to regain, was attacked by the malady of which he was to die.* The great political chief, who knew so well how to steer his bark in the midst of tempests, soon succumbed. Uncertain then of favors to come, the Comte de Fontaine made every effort to collect the élite of marrying men about his youngest daughter. Those who may have tried to solve the difficult problem of settling a haughty and capricious girl, will understand the trouble taken by the unlucky father. Such an affair, carried out to the liking of his beloved child, would worthily crown the career the comte had followed for these ten years at Paris. From the way in which his family claimed salaries under every department, it might be compared with the House of Austria, which, by intermarriage, threatens to pervade Europe.* The old Vendéen was not to be discouraged in bringing forward suitors, so much had he his daughter's happiness at heart, but nothing could be more absurd than the way in which the impertinent young thing pronounced her verdicts and judged the merits of her adorers. It might have been supposed that, like a princess in the *Arabian Nights*, Émilie was rich enough and beautiful enough to choose from among all the princes in the world. Her objections were each more preposterous than the last: one had too thick knees and was bow-legged, another was short-sighted, this one's name was Durand,* that one limped, and almost all were too fat. Livelier, more attractive, and gayer than ever after dismissing two or three suitors, she rushed into the festivities of the winter season, and to balls, where her keen eyes criticised the celebrities of the day, delighted in encouraging proposals which she invariably rejected.

Nature had bestowed on her all the advantages needed for playing the part of Célimène.* Tall and slight, Émilie de Fontaine could assume a dignified or a frolicsome mien at her will. Her neck was rather long, allowing her to affect beautiful attitudes of scorn and impertinence. She had cultivated a large variety of those turns of the head and feminine gestures, which emphasize so cruelly or so happily a hint of a smile. Fine black hair, thick and strongly-arched eyebrows, lent her countenance an expression of pride, to which her coquettish instincts and her mirror had taught her to add terror by a stare, or gentleness by the softness of her gaze, by the set of the gracious curve of her lips, by the coldness or the sweetness of her smile. When Émilie meant to conquer a heart, her pure voice did not lack melody; but she could also give it a sort of curt clearness when she was minded to paralyze a partner's indiscreet tongue. Her colorless face and alabaster brow were like the limpid surface of a lake, which by turns is rippled by the impulse of a breeze and recovers its glad serenity when the air is still. More than one young man, a victim to her scorn, accused her of acting a part; but she justified herself by inspiring her detractors with the desire to please her, and then subjecting them to all her most contemptuous caprice. Among the young girls of fashion, not one knew better than she how to assume an air of reserve when a man of talent was introduced to her, or how to display the insulting politeness which treats an equal as an inferior, and to pour out her impertinence on all who tried to hold their heads on a level with hers. Wherever she went she seemed to be accepting homage rather than compliments, and even in a princess her airs and manner would have transformed the chair on which she sat into an imperial throne.

Monsieur de Fontaine discovered too late how utterly the education of the daughter he loved had been ruined by the tender devotion of the whole family. The admiration which the world is at first ready to bestow on a young girl, but for which, sooner or later, it takes its revenge, had added to Émilie's pride, and increased her self-confidence. Universal subservience had developed in her the selfishness natural to spoilt children, who, like kings, make a plaything of everything that comes to hand. As yet the graces of youth and the charms of talent hid these faults from every eye; faults all the more odious in a woman, since she can only please by self-sacrifice and unselfishness; but nothing escapes the eye of a good father, and Monsieur de Fontaine often tried to explain to his daughter the more important pages of the mysterious book of life. Vain effort! He had to lament his daughter's capricious indocility and ironical shrewdness too often to persevere in a task so difficult as that of correcting an ill-disposed nature. He contented himself with giving her from time to time some gentle and kind advice; but he had the sorrow of seeing his tenderest words slide from his daughter's heart as if it were of marble. A father's eyes are slow to be unsealed, and it needed more than one experience before the old Royalist perceived that his daughter's rare caresses were bestowed on him with an air of condescension. She was like young children, who seem to say to their mother, "Make haste to kiss me, that I may go to play." In short, Émilie vouchsafed to be fond of her parents. But often, by those sudden whims, which seem inexplicable in young girls, she kept aloof and scarcely ever appeared; she complained of having to share her father's and mother's heart with too many people; she was jealous of every one, even of her brothers and sisters. Then, after creating a desert about her, the strange girl accused all nature of her unreal solitude and her wilful griefs. Strong in the experience of her twenty years, she blamed fate, because, not knowing that the mainspring of happiness is in ourselves, she demanded it of the circumstances of life. She would have fled to the ends of the earth to escape a marriage such as those of her two sisters, and nevertheless her heart was full of horrible jealousy at seeing them married, rich, and happy. In short, she sometimes led her mother—who was as much a victim to her vagaries as Monsieur de Fontaine—to suspect that she had a touch of madness.

But such aberrations are quite inexplicable; nothing is commoner than this unconfessed pride developed in the heart of young girls belonging to families high in the social scale, and gifted by nature with great beauty. They are almost all convinced that their mothers, now forty or fifty years of age, can neither sympathize with their young souls, nor conceive of their imaginings. They fancy that most mothers, jealous of their girls, want to dress them in their own way with the premeditated purpose of eclipsing them or robbing them of admiration. Hence, often, secret tears and dumb revolt against supposed tyranny. In the midst of these woes, which become very real though built on an imaginary basis, they have also a mania for composing a scheme of life, while casting for themselves a brilliant horoscope; their magic consists in taking their dreams for reality; secretly, in their long meditations, they resolve to give their heart and hand to none but the man possessing this or the other qualification; and they paint in fancy a model to which, whether or no, the future lover must correspond. After some little experience of life, and the serious reflections that come with years, by dint of seeing the world and its prosaic round, by dint of observing unhappy examples, the brilliant hues of their ideal are extinguished. Then, one fine day, in the course of events, they are quite astonished to find themselves happy without the nuptial poetry of their day-dreams. It was on the strength of that poetry that Mademoiselle Émilie de Fontaine, in her slender wisdom, had drawn up a programme to which a suitor must conform to be excepted. Hence her disdain and sarcasm.

"Though young and of an ancient family, he must be a peer of France,"* said she to herself. "I could not bear not to see my coat-of-arms on the panels of my carriage among the folds of azure mantling, not to drive like the princes down the broad walk of the Champs-Élysées on the days of Longchamps in Holy Week.* Besides, my father says that it will someday be the highest dignity in France. He must be a soldier—but I reserve the right of making him retire; and he must bear an Order, that the sentries may present arms to us."

And these rare qualifications would count for nothing if this creature of fancy had not the most amiable temper, a fine figure, intelligence, and, above all, if he were not slender. To be lean, a personal grace which is but fugitive, especially under a representative government, was an indispensable condition. Mademoiselle de Fontaine had an ideal standard which was to be the model. A young man who at the first glance did not fulfil the requisite conditions did not even get a second look.

"Good Heavens! see how fat he is!" was with her the utmost expression of contempt.

To hear her, people of respectable corpulence were incapable of sentiment, bad husbands, and unfit for civilized society. Though it is esteemed a beauty in the East, to be fat seemed to her a misfortune for a woman; but in a man it was a crime. These paradoxical views were amusing, thanks to a certain liveliness of rhetoric. The comte felt nevertheless that by-and-by his daughter's affections, of which the absurdity would be evident to some women who were not less clear-sighted than merciless, would inevitably become a subject of constant ridicule. He feared lest her eccentric notions should deviate into bad style. He trembled to think that the pitiless world might already be laughing at a young woman who remained so long on the stage without arriving at any conclusion of the drama she was playing. More than one actor in it, disgusted by a refusal, seemed to be waiting for the slightest turn of ill-luck to take his revenge. The indifferent, the lookers-on were beginning to weary of it; admiration is always exhausting to human beings. The old Vendéen knew better than any one that if there is an art in choosing the right moment for coming forward on the boards of the world, on those of the Court, in a drawing-room or on the stage, it is still more difficult to quit them in the nick of time. So during the first winter after the accession of Charles X, he redoubled his efforts, seconded by his three sons and his sons-in-law, to assemble in the rooms of his official residence the best matches which Paris and the various deputations from departments could offer. The splendor of his entertainments, the luxury of his dining-room, and his dinners, fragrant with truffles, rivaled the famous banquets by which the ministers of that time secured the vote of their parliamentary recruits.

The Honorable Deputy was consequently pointed at

as a most influential corrupter of the legislative honesty of the illustrious Chamber that was dying as it would seem of indigestion. A whimsical result! his efforts to get his daughter married secured him a splendid popularity. He perhaps found some covert advantage in selling his truffles twice over. This accusation, started by certain mocking Liberals, who made up by their flow of words for their small following in the Chamber, was not a success. The Poitevin gentleman* had always been so noble and so honorable, that he was not once the object of those epigrams which the malicious journalism of the day hurled at the three hundred votes of the centre, at the Ministers, the cooks, the Directors-General, the princely Amphitryons, and the official supporters of the Villèle Ministry.*

At the close of this campaign, during which Monsieur de Fontaine had on several occasions brought out all his forces, he believed that this time the procession of suitors would not be a mere dissolving view in his daughter's eyes; that it was time she should make up her mind. He felt a certain inward satisfaction at having well fulfilled his duty as a father. And having left no stone unturned, he hoped that, among so many hearts laid at Émilie's feet, there might be one to which her caprice might give a preference. Incapable of repeating such an effort, and tired, too, of his daughter's conduct, one morning, towards the end of Lent, when the business at the Chamber did not demand his vote, he determined to ask what her views were. While his valet was artistically decorating his bald yellow head with the delta of powder which, with the hanging "*ailes de pigeon*,"* completed his venerable style of hairdressing, Émilie's father, not without some secret misgivings, told his old servant to go and desire the haughty damsel to appear in the presence of the head of the family.

"Joseph," he added, when his hair was dressed, "take away that towel, draw back the curtains, put those chairs square, shake the rug, and lay it quite straight. Dust everything.—Now, air the room a little by opening the window."

The comte multiplied his orders, putting Joseph out of breath, and the old servant, understanding his master's intentions, aired and tidied the room, of course the least cared for of any in the house, and succeeded in giving a look of harmony to the files of bills, the letter-boxes, the books and furniture of this sanctum, where the interests of the royal demesnes were debated over. When Joseph had reduced this chaos to some sort of order, and brought to the front such things as might be most pleasing to the eye, as if it were a shop front, or such as by their color might give the effect of a kind of official poetry, he stood for a minute in the midst of the labyrinth of papers piled in some places even on the floor, admired his handiwork, jerked his head, and went.

The anxious sinecure-holder did not share his retainer's favorable opinion. Before seating himself in his deep chair, whose rounded back screened him from draughts, he looked round him doubtfully, examined his dressing-gown with a hostile expression, shook off a few grains of snuff, carefully wiped his nose, arranged the tongs and shovel, made the fire, pulled up the heels of his slippers, pulled out his little queue of hair which had lodged horizontally between the collar of his waistcoat and that of his dressing-gown restoring it to its perpendicular position; then he swept up the ashes of the hearth, which bore witness to a persistent catarrh. Finally, the old man did not settle himself till he had once more looked all over the room, hoping that nothing could give occasion to the saucy and impertinent remarks with which his daughter was apt to answer his good advice. On this occasion he was anxious not to compromise his dignity as a father. He daintily took a pinch of snuff, cleared his throat two or three times, as if he were about to demand a count out of the House;

then he heard his daughter's light step, and she came in humming an air from *Il Barbiere*.*

"Good-morning, papa. What do you want with me so early?" Having sung these words, as though they were the refrain of the melody, she kissed the comte, not with the familiar tenderness which makes a daughter's love so sweet a thing, but with the light carelessness of a mistress confident of pleasing, whatever she may do.

"My dear child," said Monsieur de Fontaine, gravely, "I sent for you to talk to you very seriously about your future prospects. You are at this moment under the necessity of making such a choice of a husband as may secure your durable happiness——"

"My good father," replied Émilie, assuming her most coaxing tone of voice to interrupt him, "it strikes me that the armistice on which we agreed as to my suitors is not yet expired."

"Émilie, we must to-day forbear from jesting on so important a matter. For some time past the efforts of those who most truly love you, my dear child, have been concentrated on the endeavor to settle you suitably; and you would be guilty of ingratitude in meeting with levity those proofs of kindness which I am not alone in lavishing on you."

As she heard these words, after flashing a mischievously inquisitive look at the furniture of her father's study, the young girl brought forward the armchair which looked as if it had been least used by petitioners, set it at the side of the fireplace so as to sit facing her father, and settled herself in so solemn an attitude that it was impossible not to read in it a mocking intention, crossing her arms over the dainty trimmings of a pelerine *à la neige*,* and ruthlessly crushing its endless frills of white tulle. After a laughing side glance at her old father's troubled face, she broke silence.

"I never heard you say, my dear father, that the Government issued its instructions in its dressing-gown. However," and she smiled, "that does not matter; the mob are probably not particular. Now, what are your proposals for legislation, and your official introductions?"

"I shall not always be able to make them, headstrong girl!—Listen, Émilie. It is my intention no longer to compromise my reputation, which is part of my children's fortune, by recruiting the regiment of dancers which, spring after spring, you put to rout. You have already been the cause of many dangerous misunderstandings with certain families. I hope to make you perceive more truly the difficulties of your position and of ours. You are two-and-twenty, my dear child, and you ought to have been married nearly three years since. Your brothers and your two sisters are richly and happily provided for. But, my dear, the expenses occasioned by these marriages, and the style of housekeeping you require of your mother, have made such inroads on our income that I can hardly promise you a hundred thousand francs as a marriage portion. From this day forth I shall think only of providing for your mother, who must not be sacrificed to her children. Émilie, if I were to be taken from my family Madame de Fontaine could not be left at anybody's mercy, and ought to enjoy the affluence which I have given her too late as the reward of her devotion in my misfortunes. You see, my child, that the amount of your fortune bears no relation to your notions of grandeur. Even that would be such a sacrifice as I have not hitherto made for either of my children; but they have generously agreed not to expect in the future any compensation for the advantage thus given to a too favored child."

"In their position!" said Émilie, with an ironical toss of her head.

"My dear, do not so depreciate those who love you. Only the poor are generous as a rule; the rich have always excellent reasons for not handing over twenty thousand francs to a relation. Come, my child, do not pout, let us talk rationally.—Among the young marrying men have you noticed Monsieur de Manerville?"

"Oh, he minces his words—he says Zules instead of Jules; he is always looking at his feet, because he thinks them small, and he gazes at himself in the glass! Besides, he is fair. I don't like fair men."

"Well, then, Monsieur de Beaudenord?"

"He is not noble! he is ill made and stout. He is dark, it is true.—If the two gentlemen could agree to combine their fortunes, and the first would give his name and his figure to the second, who should keep his dark hair, then—perhaps——"

"What can you say against Monsieur de Rastignac?"

"Madame de Nucingen has made a banker of him," she said with meaning.

"And our cousin, the Vicomte de Portenduère?"

"A mere boy, who dances badly; besides, he has no fortune. And, after all, papa, none of these people have titles. I want, at least, to be a comtesse like my mother."

"Have you seen no one, then, this winter——"

"No, papa."

"What then do you want?"

"The son of a peer of France.

"My dear girl, you are mad!" said Monsieur de Fontaine, rising.

But he suddenly lifted his eyes to heaven, and seemed to find a fresh fount of resignation in some religious thought; then, with a look of fatherly pity at his daughter, who herself was moved, he took her hand, pressed it, and said with deep feeling: "God is my witness, poor mistaken child, I have conscientiously discharged my duty to you as a father—conscientiously, do I say? Most lovingly, my Émilie. Yes, God knows! This winter I have brought before you more than one good man, whose character, whose habits, and whose temper were known to me, and all seemed worthy of you. My child, my task is done. From this day forth you are the arbiter of your fate, and I consider myself both happy and unhappy at finding myself relieved of the heaviest of paternal functions. I know not whether you will for any long time, now, hear a voice which, to you, has never been stern; but remember that conjugal happiness does not rest so much on brilliant qualities and ample fortune as on reciprocal esteem. This happiness is, in its nature, modest, and devoid of show. So now, my dear, my consent is given beforehand, whoever the son-in-law may be whom you introduce to me; but if you should be unhappy, remember you will have no right to accuse your father. I shall not refuse to take proper steps and help you, only your choice must be serious and final. I will never twice compromise the respect due to my white hairs."

The affection thus expressed by her father, the solemn tones of his urgent address, deeply touched Mademoiselle de Fontaine; but she concealed her emotion, seated herself on her father's knees—for he had dropped all tremulous into his chair again—caressed him fondly, and coaxed him so engagingly that the old man's brow cleared. As soon as Émilie thought that her father had got over his painful agitation, she said in a gentle voice: "I have to thank you for your graceful attention, my dear father. You have had your room set in order to receive your beloved daughter. You did not perhaps know that you would find her so foolish and so headstrong. But, papa, is it so difficult to get married to a peer of France? You declared that they were manufactured by dozens. At least, you will not refuse to advise me."

"No, my poor child, no;—and more than once I may have occasion to cry, 'Beware!' Remember that the making of peers is so recent a force in our government machinery that they have no great fortunes. Those who are rich look to becoming richer. The wealthiest member of our peerage has not half the income of the least rich lord in the English Upper Chamber. Thus all the French peers are on the lookout for great heiresses for their sons, wherever they may meet with them. The necessity in which they find themselves of marrying for money will certainly exist for at least two centuries.

"Pending such a fortunate accident as you long for—and this fastidiousness may cost you the best years of your life—your attractions might work a miracle, for men often marry for love in these days. When experience lurks behind so sweet a face as yours it may achieve wonders. In the first place, have you not the gift of recognizing virtue in the greater or smaller dimensions of a man's body? This is no small matter! To so wise a young person as you are, I need not enlarge on all the difficulties of the enterprise. I am sure that you would never attribute good sense to a stranger because he had a handsome face, or all the virtues because he had a fine figure. And I am quite of your mind in thinking that the sons of peers ought to have an air peculiar to themselves, and perfectly distinctive manners. Though nowadays no external sign stamps a man of rank, those young men will have, perhaps, to you the indefinable something that will reveal it. Then, again, you have your heart well in hand, like a good horseman who is sure his steed cannot bolt. Luck be with you, my dear!"

"You are making game of me, papa. Well, I assure you that I would rather die in Mademoiselle de Condé's convent than not be the wife of a peer of France."

She slipped out of her father's arms, and proud of being her own mistress, went off singing the air of *Cara non dubitare*, in the "Matrimonio Segreto."*

As it happened, the family were that day keeping the anniversary of a family fête. At dessert Madame Planat, the Receiver-General's wife, spoke with some enthusiasm of a young American owning an immense fortune, who had fallen passionately in love with her sister, and made through her the most splendid proposals.

"A banker, I rather think," observed Émilie carelessly. "I do not like money dealers."

"But, Émilie," replied the Baron de Villaine, the husband of the comte's second daughter, "you do not like lawyers either; so that if you refuse men of wealth who have not titles, I do not quite see in what class you are to choose a husband."

"Especially, Émilie, with your standard of slimness," added the Lieutenant-General.

"I know what I want," replied the young lady.

"My sister wants a fine name, a fine young man, fine prospects, and a hundred thousand francs a year," said the Baronne de Fontaine. "Monsieur de Marsay, for instance."

"I know, my dear," retorted Émilie, "that I do not mean to make such a foolish marriage as some I have seen. Moreover, to put an end to these matrimonial discussions, I hereby declare that I shall look on anyone who talks to me of marriage as a foe to my peace of mind."

An uncle of Émilie's, a vice-admiral, whose fortune had just been increased by twenty thousand francs a year in consequence of the Act of Indemnity, and a man of seventy, feeling himself privileged to say hard things to his grand-niece, on whom he doted, in order to mollify the bitter tone of the discussion now exclaimed:

"Do not tease my poor little Émilie; don't you see she is waiting till the Duc de Bordeaux comes of age!"*

The old man's pleasantry was received with general laughter.

"Take care I don't marry you, old fool!" replied the young girl, whose last words were happily drowned in the noise.

"My dear children," said Madame de Fontaine, to soften this saucy retort, "Émilie, like you, will take no advice but her mother's."

"Bless me! I shall take no advice but my own in a matter which concerns no one but myself," said Mademoiselle de Fontaine very distinctly.

At this all eyes were turned to the head of the family. Every one seemed anxious as to what he would do to assert his dignity. The venerable gentleman enjoyed much consideration, not only in the world; happier than many fathers, he was also appreciated by his family, all its members having a just esteem for the solid qualities by which he had been able to make their fortunes. Hence he was treated with the deep respect which is shown by English families, and some aristocratic houses on the continent, to the living representatives of an ancient pedigree. Deep silence had fallen; and the guests looked alternately from the spoilt girl's proud and sulky pout to the severe faces of Monsieur and Madame de Fontaine.

"I have made my daughter Émilie mistress of her own fate," was the reply spoken by the comte in a deep voice.

Relations and guests gazed at Mademoiselle de Fontaine with mingled curiosity and pity. The words seemed to declare that fatherly affection was weary of the contest with a character that the whole family knew to be incorrigible. The sons-in-law muttered, and the brothers glanced at their wives with mocking smiles. From that moment every one ceased to take any interest in the haughty girl's prospects of marriage. Her old uncle was the only person who, as an old sailor, ventured to stand on her tack, and take her broadsides, without ever troubling himself to return her fire.

When the fine weather was settled, and after the budget was voted, the whole family—a perfect example of the parliamentary families on the northern side of the Channel who have a footing in every government department, and ten votes in the House of Commons— flew away like a brood of young birds to the charming neighborhoods of Aulnay, Antony, and Châtenay.* The wealthy Receiver-General had lately purchased in this part of the world a country-house for his wife, who remained in Paris only during the session. Though the fair Émilie despised the commonalty, her feeling was not carried so far as to scorn the advantages of a fortune acquired in a profession; so she accompanied her sister to the sumptuous villa, less out of affection for the members of her family who were visiting there, than because fashion has ordained that every woman who has any self-respect must leave Paris in the summer. The green seclusion of Sceaux* answered to perfection the requirements of good style and of the duties of an official position.

As it is extremely doubtful that the fame of the "Bal de Sceaux" should ever have extended beyond the borders of the Department of the Seine, it will be necessary to give some account of this weekly festivity, which at that time was important enough to threaten to become an institution. The environs of the little town of Sceaux enjoy a reputation due to the scenery, which is considered enchanting. Perhaps it is quite ordinary, and owes its fame only to the stupidity of the Paris townsfolk, who, emerging from the stony abyss in which they are buried, would find something to admire in the flats of La Beauce. However, as the poetic shades of Aulnay, the hillsides of Antony, and the valley of the Bièvre* are peopled with artists who have traveled far, by foreigners who are very hard to please, and by a great many pretty women not devoid of taste, it is to be supposed that the Parisians are right. But Sceaux possesses another attraction not less powerful to the Parisian. In the midst of a garden whence there are delightful views, stands a large rotunda open on all sides, with a light, spreading roof supported on elegant pillars. This rural baldachino shelters a dancing-floor. The most stuck-up landowners of the neighborhood rarely fail to make an excursion thither once or twice during the season, arriving at this rustic palace of Terpsichore either in dashing parties on horseback, or in the light and elegant carriages which powder the philosophical pedestrian with dust. The hope of meeting some women of fashion, and of being seen by them—and the hope, less often disappointed, of seeing young peasant girls, as wily as judges—crowds the ballroom at Sceaux with numerous swarms of lawyers' clerks, of the disciples of Æsculapius, and other youths whose complexions are kept pale and moist by the damp atmosphere of Paris back-shops. And a good many bourgeois marriages have had their beginning to the sound of the band occupying the centre of this circular ballroom. If that roof could speak, what love-stories could it not tell!

This interesting medley gave the Sceaux balls at that time a spice of more amusement than those of two or three places of the same kind near Paris; and it had incontestable advantages in its rotunda, and the beauty of its situation and its gardens. Émilie was the first to express a wish to play at being *common folk* at this gleeful suburban entertainment, and promised herself immense pleasure in mingling with the crowd. Everybody wondered at her desire to wander through such a mob; but is there not a keen pleasure to grand people in an *incognito*? Mademoiselle de Fontaine amused herself with imagining all these town-bred figures; she fancied herself leaving the memory of a bewitching glance and smile stamped on more than one shopkeeper's heart, laughed beforehand at the damsels' airs, and sharpened her pencils for the scenes she proposed to sketch in her satirical album. Sunday could not come soon enough to satisfy her impatience.

The party from the Villa Planat set out on foot, so

as not to betray the rank of the personages who were about to honor the ball with their presence. They dined early. And the month of May humored this aristocratic escapade by one of its finest evenings. Mademoiselle de Fontaine was quite surprised to find in the rotunda some quadrilles made up of persons who seemed to belong to the upper classes. Here and there, indeed, were some young men who look as though they must have saved for a month to shine for a day; and she perceived several couples whose too hearty glee suggested nothing conjugal; still, she could only glean instead of gathering a harvest. She was amused to see that pleasure in a cotton dress was so very like pleasure robed in satin, and that the girls of the middle class danced quite as well as ladies—nay, sometimes better. Most of the women were simply and suitably dressed. Those who in this assembly represented the ruling power, that is to say, the country-folk, kept apart with wonderful politeness. In fact, Mademoiselle Émilie had to study the various elements that composed the mixture before she could find any subject for pleasantry. But she had not time to give herself up to malicious criticism, or opportunity for hearing many of the startling speeches which caricaturists so gladly pick up. The haughty young lady suddenly found a flower in this wide field—the metaphor is reasonable—whose splendor and coloring worked on her imagination with all the fascination of novelty. It often happens that we look at a dress, a hanging, a blank sheet of paper, with so little heed that we do not at first detect a stain or a bright spot which afterwards strikes the eye as though it had come there at the very instant when we see it; and by a sort of moral phenomenon somewhat resembling this, Mademoiselle de Fontaine discovered in a young man the external perfection of which she had so long dreamed.

Seated on one of the clumsy chairs which marked the boundary line of the circular floor, she had placed herself at the end of the row formed by the family party, so as to be able to stand up or push forward as her fancy moved her, treating the living pictures and groups in the hall as if she were in a picture gallery; impertinently turning her eye-glass on persons not two yards away, and making her remarks as though she were criticising or praising a study of a head, a painting of *genre*. Her eyes, after wandering over the vast moving picture, were suddenly caught by this figure, which seemed to have been placed on purpose in one corner of the canvas, and in the best light, like a person out of all proportion with the rest.

The stranger, alone and absorbed in thought, leaned lightly against one of the columns that supported the roof; his arms were folded, and he leaned slightly on one side as though he had placed himself there to have his portrait taken by a painter. His attitude, though full of elegance and dignity, was devoid of affectation. Nothing suggested that he had half turned his head, and bent it a little to the right like Alexander, or Lord Byron, and some other great men, for the sole purpose of attracting attention. His fixed gaze followed a girl who was dancing, and betrayed some strong feeling. His slender, easy frame recalled the noble proportions of the Apollo. Fine black hair curled naturally over a high forehead. At a glance Mademoiselle de Fontaine observed that his linen was fine, his gloves fresh, and evidently bought of a good maker, and his feet were small and well shod in boots of Irish kid. He had none of the vulgar trinkets displayed by the dandies of the National Guard or the Lovelaces of the counting-house.* A black ribbon, to which an eye-glass was attached, hung over a waistcoat of the most fashionable cut. Never had the fastidious Émilie seen a man's eyes shaded by such long, curled lashes. Melancholy and passion were expressed in this face, and the complexion was of a manly olive hue. His mouth seemed ready to smile, unbending the corners of eloquent lips; but this, far from hinting at gaiety, revealed on the contrary a sort of pathetic grace. There was too much promise in that head, too much distinction in his whole person, to allow of one's saying, "What a handsome man!" or "What a fine man!" One wanted to know him. The most clear-sighted observer, on seeing this stranger, could not have helped taking him for a clever man attracted to this rural festivity by some powerful motive.

All these observations cost Émilie only a minute's attention, during which the privileged gentleman under her severe scrutiny became the object of her secret admiration. She did not say to herself, "He must be a peer of France!" but "Oh, if only he is noble, and he surely must be— —" Without finishing her thought, she suddenly rose, and followed by her brother the General, she made her way towards the column, affecting to watch the merry quadrille; but by a stratagem of the eye, familiar to women, she lost not a gesture of the young man as she went towards him. The stranger politely moved to make way for the newcomers, and went to lean against another pillar. Émilie, as much nettled by his politeness as she might have been by an impertinence, began talking to her brother in a louder voice than good taste enjoined; she turned and tossed her head, gesticulated eagerly, and laughed for no particular reason, less to amuse her brother than to attract the attention of the imperturbable stranger. None of her little arts succeeded. Mademoiselle de Fontaine then followed the direction in which his eyes were fixed, and discovered the cause of his indifference.

In the midst of the quadrille, close in front of them, a pale girl was dancing; her face was like one of the divinities which Girodet has introduced into his immense composition of French Warriors received by Ossian.* Émilie fancied that she recognized her as a distinguished *milady* who for some months had been living on a neighboring estate. Her partner was a lad of about fifteen, with red hands, and dressed in nankeen trousers, a blue coat, and white shoes, which showed that the damsel's love of dancing made her easy to please in the matter of partners. Her movements did not betray her apparent delicacy, but a faint flush already tinged her white cheeks, and her complexion was gaining color. Mademoiselle de Fontaine went nearer, to be able to examine the young lady at the moment when she returned to her place, while the side couples in their turn danced the figure. But the stranger went up to the pretty dancer, and leaning over, said in a gentle but commanding tone:

"Clara, my child, do not dance any more."

Clara made a little pouting face, bent her head, and finally smiled. When the dance was over, the young man wrapped her in a cashmere shawl with a lover's care, and seated her in a place sheltered from the wind. Very soon Mademoiselle de Fontaine, seeing them rise and walk round the place as if preparing to leave, found means to follow them under pretence of admiring the views from the garden. Her brother lent himself with malicious good-humor to the divagations of her rather eccentric wanderings. Émilie then saw the attractive couple get into an elegant tilbury, by which stood a mounted groom in livery. At the moment when, from his high seat, the young man was drawing the reins even, she caught a glance from his eye such as a man casts aimlessly at the crowd; and then she enjoyed the feeble satisfaction of seeing him turn his head to look at her. The young lady did the same. Was it from jealousy?

"I imagine you have now seen enough of the garden," said her brother. "We may go back to the dancing."

"I am ready," said she. "Do you think the girl can be a relation of Lady Dudley's?"

"Lady Dudley may have some male relation staying

with her," said the Baron de Fontaine; "but a young girl!—No!"

Next day Mademoiselle de Fontaine expressed a wish to take a ride. Then she gradually accustomed her old uncle and her brothers to escorting her in very early rides, excellent, she declared for her health. She had a particular fancy for the environs of the hamlet where Lady Dudley was living. Notwithstanding her cavalry manœuvres, she did not meet the stranger so soon as the eager search she pursued might have allowed her to hope. She went several times to the "Bal de Sceaux" without seeing the young Englishman who had dropped from the skies to pervade and beautify her dreams. Though nothing spurs on a young girl's infant passion so effectually as an obstacle, there was a time when Mademoiselle de Fontaine was on the point of giving up her strange and secret search, almost despairing of the success of an enterprise whose singularity may give some idea of the boldness of her temper. In point of fact, she might have wandered long about the village of Châtenay without meeting her Unknown. The fair Clara—since that was the name Émilie had overheard—was not English, and the stranger who escorted her did not dwell among the flowery and fragrant bowers of Châtenay.

One evening Émilie, out riding with her uncle, who, during the fine weather, had gained a fairly long truce from the gout, met Lady Dudley. The distinguished foreigner had with her in her open carriage Monsieur Vandenesse. Émilie recognized the handsome couple, and her suppositions were at once dissipated like a dream. Annoyed, as any woman must be whose expectations are frustrated, she touched up her horse so suddenly that her uncle had the greatest difficulty in following her, she had set off at such a pace.

"I am too old, it would seem, to understand these youthful spirits," said the old sailor to himself as he put his horse to a canter; "or perhaps young people are not what they used to be. But what ails my niece? Now she is walking at a foot-pace like a gendarme on patrol in the Paris streets. One might fancy she wanted to out-flank that worthy man, who looks to me like an author dreaming over his poetry, for he has, I think, a notebook in his hand. My word, I am a great simpleton! Is not that the very young man we are in search of!"

At this idea the old admiral moderated his horse's pace so as to follow his niece without making any noise. He had played too many pranks in the years 1771 and soon after, a time of our history when gallantry was held in honor, not to guess at once that by the merest chance Émilie had met the Unknown of the Sceaux gardens. In spite of the film which age had drawn over his gray eyes, the Comte de Kergarouët could recognize the signs of extreme agitation in his niece, under the unmoved expression she tried to give to her features. The girl's piercing eyes were fixed in a sort of dull amazement on the stranger, who quietly walked on in front of her.

"Ay, that's it," thought the sailor. "She is following him as a pirate follows a merchantman. Then, when she has lost sight of him, she will be in despair at not knowing who it is she is in love with, and whether he is a marquis or a shopkeeper. Really these young heads need an old fogy like me always by their side . . ."

He unexpectedly spurred his horse in such a way as to make his niece's bolt, and rode so hastily between her and the young man on foot that he obliged him to fall back on to the grassy bank which rose from the roadside. Then, abruptly drawing up, the comte exclaimed:

"Couldn't you get out of the way?"

"I beg your pardon, monsieur. But I did not know that it lay with me to apologize to you because you almost rode me down."

"There, enough of that, my good fellow!" replied the sailor harshly, in a sneering tone that was nothing less than insulting. At the same time the comte raised his hunting-crop as if to strike his horse, and touched the young fellow's shoulder, saying, "A liberal citizen is a reasoner; every reasoner should be prudent."

The young man went up the bankside as he heard the sarcasm; then he crossed his arms, and said in an excited tone of voice, "I cannot suppose, monsieur, as I look at your white hairs, that you still amuse yourself by provoking duels——"

"White hairs!" cried the sailor, interrupting him. "You lie in your throat. They are only gray."

A quarrel thus begun had in a few seconds become so fierce that the younger man forgot the moderation he had tried to preserve. Just as the Comte de Kergarouët saw his niece coming back to them with every sign of the greatest uneasiness, he told his antagonist his name, bidding him keep silence before the young lady entrusted to his care. The stranger could not help smiling as he gave a visiting card to the old man, desiring him to observe that he was living at a country-house at Chevreuse; and, after pointing this out to him, he hurried away.

"You very nearly damaged that poor young counter-jumper, my dear," said the comte, advancing hastily to meet Émilie. "Do you not know how to hold your horse in?—And there you leave me to compromise my dignity in order to screen your folly; whereas if you had but stopped, one of your looks, or one of your pretty speeches—one of those you can make so prettily when you are not pert—would have set everything right, even if you had broken his arm."

"But, my dear uncle, it was your horse, not mine, that caused the accident. I really think you can no longer ride; you are not so good a horseman as you were last year.—But instead of talking nonsense——"

"Nonsense, by Gad! Is it nothing to be so impertinent to your uncle?"

"Ought we not to go on and inquire if the young man is hurt? He is limping, uncle, only look!"

"No, he is running; I rated him soundly."

"Oh, yes, uncle; I know you there!"

"Stop," said the comte, pulling Émilie's horse by the bridle, "I do not see the necessity of making advances to some shopkeeper who is only too lucky to have been thrown down by a charming young lady, or the commander of *La Belle-Poule*."*

"Why do you think he is anything so common, my dear uncle? He seems to me to have very fine manners."

"Every one has manners nowadays, my dear."

"No, uncle, not every one has the air and style which come of the habit of frequenting drawing-rooms, and I am ready to lay a bet with you that the young man is of noble birth."

"You had not long to study him."

"No, but it is not the first time I have seen him."

"Nor is it the first time you have looked for him," replied the admiral with a laugh.

Émilie colored. Her uncle amused himself for some time with her embarrassment; then he said: "Émilie, you know that I love you as my own child, precisely because you are the only member of the family who has the legitimate pride of high birth. Devil take it, child, who could have believed that sound principles would become so rare? Well, I will be your confidant. My dear child, I see that his young gentleman is not indifferent to you. Hush! All the family would laugh at us if we sailed under the wrong flag. You know what that means. We two will keep our secret, and I promise to bring him straight into the drawing-room."

"When, uncle?"

"To-morrow."

"But, my dear uncle, I am not committed to anything?"

"Nothing whatever, and you may bombard him, set fire to him, and leave him to founder like an old hulk if you choose. He won't be the first, I fancy?"

"You *are* kind, uncle!"

As soon as the comte got home he put on his glasses, quietly took the card out of his pocket, and read, "Maximilien Longueville, Rue du Sentier."*

"Make yourself happy, my dear niece," he said to Émilie, "you may hook him with any easy conscience; he belongs to one of our historical families, and if he is not a peer of France, he infallibly will be."

"How do you know so much?"

"That is my secret."

"Then do you know his name?"

The old man bowed his gray head, which was not unlike a gnarled oak-stump, with a few leaves fluttering about it, withered by autumnal frosts; and his niece immediately began to try the ever-new power of her coquettish arts. Long familiar with the secret of cajoling the old man, she lavished on him the most childlike caresses, the tenderest names; she even went so far as to kiss him to induce him to divulge so important a secret. The old man, who spent his life in playing off these scenes on his niece, often paying for them with a present of jewelry, or by giving her his box at the Opera, this time amused himself with her entreaties, and, above all, her caresses. But as he spun out this pleasure too long, Émilie grew angry, passed from coaxing to sarcasm and sulks; then, urged by curiosity, she recovered herself. The diplomatic admiral extracted a solemn promise from his niece that she would for the future be gentler, less noisy, and less wilful, that she would spend less, and, above all, tell him everything. The treaty being concluded, and signed by a kiss impressed on Émilie's white brow, he led her into a corner of the room, drew her on to his knee, held the card under the thumbs so as to hide it, and then uncovered the letters one by one, spelling the name of Longueville; but he firmly refused to show her anything more.

This incident added to the intensity of Mademoiselle de Fontaine's secret sentiment, and during chief part of the night she evolved the most brilliant pictures from the dreams with which she had fed her hopes. At last, thanks to chance, to which she had so often appealed, Émilie could now see something very unlike a chimera at the fountain-head of the imaginary wealth with which she gilded her married life. Ignorant, as all young girls are, of the perils of love and marriage, she was passionately captivated by the externals of marriage and love. Is not this as much as to say that her feeling had birth like all the feelings of extreme youth—sweet but cruel mistakes, which exert a fatal influence on the lives of young girls so inexperienced as to trust their own judgment to take care of their future happiness?

Next morning, before Émilie was awake, her uncle had hastened to Chevreuse.* On recognizing, in the courtyard of an elegant little villa, the young man he had so determinedly insulted the day before, he went up to him with the pressing politeness of men of the old court.

"Why, my dear monsieur, who could have guessed that I should have a brush, at the age of seventy-three, with the son, or the grandson, of one of my best friends. I am a vice-admiral, monsieur; is not that as much as to say that I think no more of fighting a duel than of smoking a cigar? Why, in my time, no two young men could be intimate till they had seen the color of their blood! But 'sdeath, monsieur, last evening, sailor-like, I had taken a drop too much grog on board, and I ran you down. Shake hands; I would rather take a hundred rebuffs from a Longueville than cause his family the smallest regret."

However coldly the young man tried to behave to the Comte de Kergarouët, he could not resist the frank cordiality of his manner, and presently gave him his hand.

"You were going out riding," said the comte. "Do not let me detain you. But, unless you have other plans, I beg you will come to dinner to-day at the Villa Planat. My nephew, the Comte de Fontaine, is a man it is essential that you should know. Ah, ha! And I propose to make up to you for my clumsiness by introducing you to five of the prettiest women in Paris. So, so, young man, your brow is clearing! I am fond of young people, and I like to see them happy. Their happiness reminds me of the good times of my youth, when adventures were not lacking, any more than duels. We were gay dogs then! Nowadays you think and worry over everything, as though there had never been a fifteenth and a sixteenth century."

"But, monsieur, are we not in the right? The sixteenth century only gave religious liberty to Europe, and the nineteenth will give it political lib——"

"Oh, we will not talk politics. I am a perfect old woman—an *ultra* you see. But I do not hinder young men from being revolutionary, so long as they leave the king at liberty to disperse their assemblies."

When they had gone a little way, and the comte and his companion were in the heart of the woods, the old sailor pointed out a slender young birch sapling, pulled up his horse, took out one of his pistols, and the bullet was lodged in the heart of the tree, fifteen paces away.

"You see, my dear fellow, that I am not afraid of a duel," he said with comical gravity, as he looked at Monsieur Longueville.

"Nor am I," replied the young man, promptly cocking his pistol; he aimed at the hole made by the comte's bullet, and sent his own close to it.

"That is what I call a well-educated man," cried the

admiral with enthusiasm.

During this ride with the youth, whom he already regarded as his nephew, he found endless opportunities of catechizing him on all the trifles of which a perfect knowledge constituted, according to his private code, an accomplished gentleman.

"Have you any debts?" he at last asked of his companion, after many other inquiries.

"No, monsieur."

"What, you pay for all you have?"

"Punctually; otherwise we should lose our credit, and every sort of respect."

"But at least you have more than one mistress? Ah, you blush, comrade! Well, manners have changed. All these notions of lawful order, Kantism, and liberty have spoilt the young men. You have no Guimard now, no Duthé,* no creditors—and you know nothing of heraldry; why, my dear young friend, you are not fully fledged. The man who does not sow his wild oats in the spring sows them in the winter. If I have but eighty thousand francs a year at the age of seventy, it is because I ran through the capital at thirty. Oh! with my wife—in decency and honor. However, your imperfections will not interfere with my introducing you at the Pavillon Planat. Remember, you have promised to come, and I shall expect you."

"What an odd little old man!" said Longueville to himself. "He is so jolly and hale; but though he wishes to seem a good fellow, I will not trust him too far."

Next day, at about four o'clock, when the house party were dispersed in the drawing-rooms and billiard-room, a servant announced to the inhabitants of the Villa Planat, "Monsieur *de* Longueville." On hearing the name of the old admiral's protégé, every one, down to the player who was about to miss his stroke, rushed in, as much to study Mademoiselle de Fontaine's countenance as to judge of this phoenix of men, who had earned honorable mention to the detriment of so many rivals. A simple but elegant style of dress, an air of perfect ease, polite manners, a pleasant voice with a ring in it which found a response in the hearer's heart-strings, won the good-will of the family for Monsieur Longueville. He did not seem unaccustomed to the luxury of the Receiver-General's ostentatious mansion. Though his conversation was that of a man of the world, it was easy to discern that he had had a brilliant education, and that his knowledge was as thorough as it was extensive. He knew so well the right thing to say in a discussion on naval architecture, trivial, it is true, started by the old admiral, that one of the ladies remarked that he must have passed through the *École Polytechnique.**

"And I think, madame," he replied, "that I may regard it as an honor to have got in."

In spite of urgent pressing, he refused politely but firmly to be kept to dinner, and put an end to the persistency of the ladies by saying that he was the Hippocrates of his young sister, whose delicate health required great care.

"Monsieur is perhaps a medical man?" asked one of Émilie's sisters-in-law with ironical meaning.

"Monsieur has left the *École Polytechnique,*" Mademoiselle de Fontaine kindly put in; her face had flushed with richer color, as she learned that the young lady of the ball was Monsieur Longueville's sister.

"But, my dear, he may be a doctor and yet have been to the École Polytechnique—is it not so, monsieur?"

"There is nothing to prevent it, madame," replied the young man.

Every eye was on Émilie, who was gazing with uneasy curiosity at the fascinating stranger. She breathed more freely when he added, not without a smile, "I have not the honor of belonging to the medical profession; and I even gave up going into the Engineers in order to preserve my independence."

"And you did well," said the comte. "But how can you regard it as an honor to be a doctor?" added the Breton nobleman. "Ah, my young friend, such a man as you—"

"Monsieur le Comte, I respect every profession that has a useful purpose."

"Well, in that we agree. You respect those professions, I imagine, as a young man respects a dowager."

Monsieur Longueville made his visit neither too long nor too short. He left at the moment when he saw that he had pleased everybody, and that each one's curiosity about him had been roused.

"He is a cunning rascal!" said the comte, coming into the drawing-room after seeing him to the door.

Mademoiselle de Fontaine, who had been in the secret of this call, had dressed with some care to attract the young man's eye; but she had the little disappointment of finding that he did not bestow on her so much attention as she thought she deserved. The family were a good deal surprised at the silence into which she had retired. Émilie generally displayed all her arts for the benefit of newcomers, her witty prattle, and the inexhaustible eloquence of her eyes and attitudes. Whether it was that the young man's pleasing voice and attractive manners had charmed her, that she was seriously in love, and that this feeling had worked a change in her, her demeanor had lost all its affectations. Being simple and natural, she must, no doubt, have seemed more beautiful. Some of her sisters, and an old lady, a friend of the family, saw in this behavior a refinement of art. They supposed that Émilie, judging the man worthy of her, intended to delay revealing her merits, so as to dazzle him suddenly when she found that she pleased him. Every member of the family was curious to know what this capricious creature thought of the stranger; but when, during dinner, every one chose to endow Monsieur Longueville with some fresh quality which no one else had discovered, Mademoiselle de Fontaine sat for some time in silence. A sarcastic remark of her uncle's suddenly roused her from her apathy; she said, somewhat epigrammatically, that such heavenly perfection must cover some great defect, and that she would take good care how she judged so gifted a man at first sight.

"Those who please everybody, please nobody," she added; "and the worst of all faults is to have none."

Like all girls who are in love, Émilie cherished the hope of being able to hide her feelings at the bottom of her heart by putting the Argus-eyes that watched on the wrong tack; but by the end of a fortnight there was not a member of the large family party who was not in this little domestic secret. When Monsieur Longueville called for the third time, Émilie believed it was chiefly for her sake. This discovery gave her such intoxicating pleasure that she was startled as she reflected on it. There was something in it very painful to her pride. Accustomed as she was to be the centre of her world, she was obliged to recognize a force that attracted her outside herself; she tried to resist, but she could not chase from her heart the fascinating image of the young man.

Then came some anxiety. Two of Monsieur Longueville's qualities, very adverse to general curiosity, and especially to Mademoiselle de Fontaine's, were unexpected modesty and discretion. He never spoke of himself, of his pursuits, or of his family. The hints Émilie threw out in conversation, and the traps she laid to extract from the young fellow some facts concerning himself, he could evade with the adroitness of a diplomatist concealing a secret. If she talked of painting, he responded as a connoisseur; if she sat down to play, he showed without conceit that he was a very good pianist; one evening he delighted all the party by joining his delightful voice to Émilie's in one of Cimarosa's charming duets. But when they tried to find out whether he were a professional singer, he baffled them so pleasantly that he did not afford these women, practised as they were in the art of reading feelings, the least chance of discovering to what social sphere he belonged. However boldly the old uncle cast the boarding-hooks over the vessel, Longueville slipped away cleverly, so as to preserve the charm of mystery; and it was easy to him to remain the "handsome Stranger" at the Villa, because curiosity never overstepped the bounds of good breeding.

Émilie, distracted by this reserve, hoped to get more out of the sister than the brother, in the form of confidences. Aided by her uncle, who was as skilful in such manœuvres as in handling a ship, she endeavored to bring upon the scene the hitherto unseen figure of Mademoiselle Clara Longueville. The family party at the Villa Planat soon expressed the greatest desire to make the acquaintance of so amiable a young lady, and to give her some amusement. An informal dance was proposed and accepted. The ladies did not despair of making a young girl of sixteen talk.

Notwithstanding the little clouds piled up by suspicion and created by curiosity, a light of joy shone in Émilie's soul, for she found life delicious when thus intimately connected with another than herself. She began to understand the relations of life. Whether it is that happiness makes us better, or that she was too fully occupied to torment other people, she became less caustic, more gentle, and indulgent. This change in her temper enchanted and amazed her family. Perhaps, at last, her selfishness was being transformed to love. It was a deep delight to her to look for the arrival of her bashful and unconfessed adorer. Though they had not uttered a word of passion, she knew that she was loved, and with what art did she not lead the stranger to unlock the stores of his information, which proved to be varied! She perceived that she, too, was being studied, and that made her endeavor to remedy the defects her education had encouraged. Was not this her first homage to love, and a bitter reproach to herself? She desired to please, and she was enchanting; she loved, and she was idolized. Her family, knowing that her pride would sufficiently protect her, gave her enough freedom to enjoy the little childish delights which give to first love its charm and its violence. More than once the young man and Mademoiselle de Fontaine walked, *tête-à-tête*, in the avenues of the garden, where nature was dressed like a woman going to a ball. More than once they had those conversations, aimless and meaningless, in which the emptiest phrases are those which cover the deepest feelings. They often admired together the setting sun and its gorgeous coloring. They gathered daisies to pull the petals off, and sang the most impassioned duets, using the notes set down by Pergolesi or Rossini as faithful interpreters to express their secrets.

The day of the dance came. Clara Longueville and her brother, whom the servants persisted in honoring with the noble *de*, were the principle guests. For the first time in her life Mademoiselle de Fontaine felt pleasure in a young girl's triumph. She lavished on Clara in all sincerity the gracious petting and little attentions which women generally give each other only to excite the jealousy of men. Émilie, had, indeed, an object in view; she wanted to discover some secrets. But, being a girl, Mademoiselle Longueville showed even more mother-wit than her brother, for she did not even look as if she were hiding a secret, and kept the conversation to subjects unconnected with personal interests, while, at the same time, she gave it so much charm that Mademoiselle de Fontaine was almost envious, and called her "the Siren." Though Émilie had intended to make Clara talk, it was Clara, in fact, who questioned Émilie; she had meant to judge her, and she was judged by her; she was constantly provoked to find that she had betrayed her own character in some reply which Clara had extracted from her, while her modest and candid manner prohibited any suspicion of perfidy. There was a moment when Mademoiselle de Fontaine seemed sorry for an ill-judged sally against the commonalty to which Clara had led her.

"Mademoiselle," said the sweet child, "I have heard so much of you from Maximilien that I had the keenest desire to know you, out of affection for him; but is not a wish to know you a wish to love you?"

"My dear Clara, I feared I might have displeased you by speaking thus of people who are not of noble birth."

"Oh, be quite easy. That sort of discussion is pointless in these days. As for me, it does not affect me. I am beside the question."

Ambitious as the answer might seem, it filled Mademoiselle de Fontaine with the deepest joy; for, like all infatuated people, she explained it, as oracles are explained, in the sense that harmonized with her wishes; she began dancing again in higher spirits than ever, as she watched Longueville, whose figure and grace almost surpassed those of her imaginary ideal. She felt added satisfaction in believing him to be well born, her black eyes sparkled, and she danced with all the pleasure that comes of dancing in the presence of the being we love. The couple had never understood each other as well as at this moment; more than once they felt their finger tips thrill and tremble as they were married in the figures of the dance.

The early autumn had come to the handsome pair, in the midst of country festivities and pleasures; they had abandoned themselves softly to the tide of the sweetest sentiment in life, strengthening it by a thousand little which any one can imagine; for love is in some respects always the same. They studied each other through it all, as much as lovers can.

"Well, well; a flirtation never turned so quickly into a love match," said the old uncle, who kept an eye on the two young people as a naturalist watches an insect in the microscope.

The speech alarmed Monsieur and Madame Fontaine. The old Vendéen had ceased to be so indifferent to his daughter's prospects as he had promised to be. He went to Paris to seek information, and found none. Uneasy at this mystery, and not yet knowing what might be the outcome of the inquiry which he had begged a Paris friend to institute with reference to the family of Longueville, he thought it his duty to warn his daughter to behave prudently. The fatherly admonition was received with mock submission spiced with irony.

"At least, my dear Émilie, if you love him, do not own it to him."

"My dear father, I certainly do love him; but I will await your permission before I tell him so."

"But remember, Émilie, you know nothing of his family or his pursuits."

"I may be ignorant, but I am content to be. But, father, you wished to see me married; you left me at liberty to make my choice; my choice is irrevocably made—what more is needful?"

"It is needful to ascertain, my dear, whether the man of your choice is the son of a peer of France," the venerable gentleman retorted sarcastically.

Émilie was silent for a moment. She presently raised her head, looked at her father, and said somewhat anxiously, "Are not the Longuevilles— —?"

"They became extinct in the person of the old Duc de Rostein-Limbourg, who perished on the scaffold in 1793. He was the last representative of the last and younger branch."

"But, papa, there are some very good families descended from bastards. The history of France swarms with princes bearing the bar sinister on their shields."

"Your ideas are much changed," said the old man, with a smile.

The following day was the last that the Fontaine family were to spend at the Pavillon Planat. Émilie, greatly disturbed by her father's warning, awaited with extreme impatience the hour at which young Longueville was in the habit of coming, to wring some explanation from him. She went out after dinner, and walked alone across the shrubbery towards an arbor fit for lovers, where she knew that the eager youth would seek her; and as she hastened thither she considered of the best way to discover so important a matter without compromising herself—a rather difficult thing! Hitherto no direct avowal had sanctioned the feelings which bound her to this stranger. Like Maximilien, she had secretly enjoyed the sweetness of first love; but both were equally proud, and each feared to confess that love.

Maximilien Longueville, to whom Clara had communicated her not unfounded suspicions as to Émilie's character, was by turns carried away by the violence of a young man's passion, and held back by a wish to know and test the woman to whom he would be entrusting his happiness. His love had not hindered him from perceiving in Émilie the prejudices which marred her young nature; but before attempting to counteract them, he wished to be sure that she loved him, for he would no sooner risk the fate of his love than of his life. He had, therefore, persistently kept a silence to which his looks, his behavior, and his smallest actions gave the lie.

On her side, the self-respect natural to a young girl, augmented in Mademoiselle de Fontaine by the monstrous vanity founded on her birth and beauty, kept her from meeting the declaration half-way, which her growing passion sometimes urged her to invite. Thus the lovers had instinctively understood the situation without explaining to each other their secret motives. There are times in life when such vagueness pleases youthful minds. Just because each had postponed speaking too long, they seemed to be playing a cruel game of suspense. He was trying to discover whether he was beloved, by the effort any confession would cost his haughty mistress; she every minute hoped that he would break a too respectful silence.

Émilie, seated on a rustic bench, was reflecting on all that had happened in these three months full of enchantment. Her father's suspicions were the last that could appeal to her; she even disposed of them at once by two or three of those reflections natural to an inexperienced girl, which, to her, seemed conclusive. Above all, she was convinced that it was impossible that she should deceive herself. All the summer through she had not been able to detect in Maximilien a single gesture, or a single word, which could indicate a vulgar origin or vulgar occupations; nay more, his manner of discussing things revealed a man devoted to the highest interests of the nation. "Besides," she reflected, "an office clerk, a banker, or a merchant, would not be at leisure to spend a whole season in paying his addresses to me in the midst of woods and fields; wasting his time as freely as a nobleman who has life before him free of all care."

She had given herself up to meditations far more interesting to her than these preliminary thoughts, when a slight rustling in the leaves announced to her than Maximilien had been watching her for a minute, not probably without admiration.

"Do you know that it is very wrong to take a young girl thus unawares?" she asked him, smiling.

"Especially when they are busy with their secrets," replied Maximilien archly.

"Why should I not have my secrets? You certainly have yours."

"Then you really were thinking of your secrets?" he went on, laughing.

"No, I was thinking of yours. My own, I know."

"But perhaps my secrets are yours, and yours mine," cried the young man, softly seizing Mademoiselle de Fontaine's hand and drawing it through his arm.

After walking a few steps they found themselves under a clump of trees which the hues of the sinking sun wrapped in a haze of red and brown. This touch of natural magic lent a certain solemnity to the moment. The young man's free and eager action, and, above all, the throbbing of his surging heart, whose hurried beating spoke to Émilie's arm, stirred her to an emotion that was all the more disturbing because it was produced by the simplest and most innocent circumstances. The restraint under which the young girls of the upper class live gives incredible force to any explosion of feeling, and to meet an impassioned lover is one of the greatest dangers they can encounter. Never had Émilie and Maximilien allowed their eyes to say so much that they dared never speak. Carried a way by this intoxication, they easily forgot the petty stipulations of pride, and the cold hesitancies of suspicion. At first, indeed, they could only express themselves by a pressure of hands which interpreted their happy thoughts.

After slowly pacing a few steps in long silence, Mademoiselle de Fontaine spoke. "Monsieur, I have a question to ask you," she said trembling, and in an agitated voice. "But, remember, I beg, that it is in a manner compulsory on me, from the rather singular position I am in with regard to my family."

A pause, terrible to Émilie, followed these sentences, which she had almost stammered out. During the minute while it lasted, the girl, haughty as she was, dared not meet the flashing eye of the man she loved, for she was secretly conscious of the meanness of the next words she added: "Are you of noble birth?"

As soon as the words were spoken she wished herself at the bottom of a lake.

"Mademoiselle," Longueville gravely replied, and his face assumed a sort of stern dignity, "I promise to answer you truly as soon as you shall have answered in all sincerity a question I will put to you!"—He released her arm, and the girl suddenly felt alone in the world, as he said: "What is your object in questioning me as to my birth?"

She stood motionless, cold, and speechless.

"Mademoiselle," Maximilien went on, "let us go no further if we do not understand each other. I love you," he said, in a voice of deep emotion. "Well, then," he added, as he heard the joyful exclamation she could not suppress, "why ask me if I am of noble birth?"

"Could he speak so if he were not?" cried a voice within her, which Émilie believed came from the depths of her heart. She gracefully raised her head, seemed to find new life in the young man's gaze, and held out her hand as if to renew the alliance.

"You thought I cared very much for dignities?" said she with keen archness.

"I have no titles to offer my wife," he replied, in a half-sportive, half-serious tone. "But if I choose one of high rank, and among women whom a wealthy home has accustomed to the luxury and pleasures of a fine fortune, I know what such a choice requires of me. Love gives everything," he added lightly, "but only to lovers. Once married, they need something more than the vault of heaven and the carpet of a meadow."

"He is rich," she reflected. "As to titles, perhaps he only wants to try me. He has been told that I am mad about titles, and bent on marrying none but a peer's son. My priggish sisters have played me that trick."— "I assure you, monsieur," she said aloud, "that I have had very extravagant ideas about life and the world; but now," she added pointedly, looking at him in a perfectly distracting way, "I know where true riches are to be found for a wife."

"I must believe that you are speaking from the depths of your heart," he said, with gentle gravity. "But this winter, my dear Émilie, in less than two months perhaps, I may be proud of what I shall have to offer you if you care for the pleasures of wealth. This is the only secret I shall keep locked here," and he laid his hand on his heart, "for on its success my happiness depends. I dare not say ours."

"Yes, yes, ours!"

Exchanging such sweet nothings, they slowly made their way back to rejoin the company. Mademoiselle de Fontaine had never found her lover more amiable or wittier: his light figure, his engaging manners, seemed to her more charming than ever, since the conversation which had made her to some extent the possessor of a heart worthy to be the envy of every woman. They sang an Italian duet with so much expression that the audience applauded enthusiastically. Their *adieux* were in a conventional tone, which concealed their happiness. In short, this day had been to Émilie like a chain binding her more closely than ever to the Stranger's fate. The strength and dignity he had displayed in the scene when they had confessed their feelings had perhaps impressed Mademoiselle de Fontaine with the respect without which there is no true love.

When she was left alone in the drawing-room with her father, the old man went up to her affectionately, held her hands, and asked her whether she had gained any light at to Monsieur Longueville's family and fortune.

"Yes, my dear father," she replied, "and I am happier than I could have hoped. In short, Monsieur de Longueville is the only man I could ever marry."

"Very well, Émilie," said the comte, "then I know what remains for me to do."

"Do you know of any impediment?" she asked, in sincere alarm.

"My dear child, the young man is totally unknown to me; but unless he is not a man of honor, so long as you love him, he is as dear to me as a son."

"Not a man of honor!" exclaimed Émilie. "As to that, I am quite easy. My uncle, who introduced him to us, will answer for him. Say, my dear uncle, has he been a filibuster, an outlaw, a pirate?"

"I knew I should find myself in this fix!" cried the old sailor, waking up. He looked round the room, but his niece had vanished "like Saint-Elmo's fires," to use his favorite expression.

"Well, uncle," Monsieur de Fontaine went on, "how could you hide from us all you knew about this young man? You must have seen how anxious we have been. Is Monsieur de Longueville a man of family?"

"I don't know him from Adam or Eve," said the Comte de Kergarouët. "Trusting to that crazy child's tact, I got him here by a method of my own. I know that the boy shoots with a pistol to admiration, hunts well, plays wonderfully at billiards, at chess, and at backgammon; he handles the foils, and rides a horse like the late Chevalier de Saint-Georges.* He has a thorough knowledge of all our vintages. He is as good an arithmetician as Barême, draws, dances, and sings well. The devil's in it! what more do you want? If that is not a perfect gentleman, find me a *bourgeois* who knows all this, or any man who lives more nobly than he does. Does he do anything, I ask you? Does he compromise his dignity by hanging about an office, bowing down before the upstarts you call Directors-General? He walks upright. He is a man.—However, I have just found in my waistcoat pocket the card he gave me when he fancied I wanted to cut his throat, poor innocent. Young men are very simple-minded nowadays! Here it is."

"Rue du Sentier, No. 5," said Monsieur de Fontaine,

trying to recall among all the information he had received, something which might concern the stranger. "What the devil can it mean? Messrs. Palma, Werbrust & Co., wholesale dealers in muslins, calicoes, and printed cotton goods, live there. —Stay, I have it: Longueville the deputy has an interest in their house. Well, but so far as I know, Longueville has but one son of two-and-thirty, who is not at all like our man, and to whom he gave fifty thousand francs a year that he might marry a minister's daughter; he wants to be made a peer like the rest of 'em. —I never heard him mention this Maximilien. Has he a daughter? What is this girl Clara? Besides, it is open to any adventurer to call himself Longueville. But is not the house of Palma, Werbrust & Co. half ruined by some speculation in Mexico or the Indies? I will clear all this up."

"You speak a soliloquy as if you were on the stage, and seem to account me a cipher," said the old admiral suddenly. "Don't you know that if he is a gentleman, I have more than one bag in my hold that will stop any leak in his fortune?"

"As to that, if he is a son of Longueville's, he will want nothing; but," said Monsieur de Fontaine, shaking his head from side to side, "his father has not even washed off the stains of his origin. Before the Revolution he was an attorney, and the *de* he has since assumed no more belongs to him than half of his fortune."

"Pooh! pooh! happy those whose fathers were hanged!" cried the admiral gaily.

Three or four days after this memorable day, on one of those fine mornings in the month of November, which show the boulevards cleaned by the sharp cold of an early frost, Mademoiselle de Fontaine, wrapped in a new style of fur cape, of which she wished to set the fashion, went out with two of her sisters-in-law, on whom she had been wont to discharge her most cutting remarks. The three women were tempted to the drive, less by their desire to try a very elegant carriage, and wear gowns which were to set the fashion for the winter, than by their wish to see a cape which a friend had observed in a handsome lace and linen shop at the corner of the Rue de la Paix.* As soon as they were in the shop the Baronne de Fontaine pulled Émilie by the sleeve, and pointed out to her Maximilien Longueville seated behind the desk, and engaged in paying out the change for a gold piece to one of the workwomen with whom he seemed to be in consultation. The "handsome stranger" held in his hand a parcel of patterns, which left no doubt as to his honorable profession.

Émilie felt an icy shudder, though no one perceived it. Thanks to the good breeding of the best society, she completely concealed the rage in her heart, and answered her sister-in-law with the words, "I knew it," with a fullness of intonation and inimitable decision which the most famous actress of the time might have envied her. She went straight up to the desk. Longueville looked up, put the patterns in his pocket with distracting coolness, bowed to Mademoiselle de Fontaine, and came forward, looking at her keenly.

"Mademoiselle," he said to the shopgirl, who followed him, looking very much disturbed, "I will send to settle that account; my house deals in that way. But here," he whispered into her ear, as he gave her a thousand-franc note, "take this—it is between ourselves.—You will forgive me, I trust, mademoiselle," he added, turning to Émilie. "You will kindly excuse the tyranny of business matters."

"Indeed, monsieur, it seems to me that it is no concern of mine," replied Mademoiselle de Fontaine, looking at him with a bold expression of sarcastic indifference which might have made any one believe that she now saw him for the first time.

"Do you really mean it?" asked Maximilien in a

broken voice.

Émilie turned her back upon him with amazing insolence. These words, spoken in an undertone, had escaped the ears of her two sisters-in-law. When, after buying the cape, the three ladies got into the carriage again, Émilie, seated with her back to the horses, could not resist one last comprehensive glance into the depths of the odious shop, where she saw Maximilien standing with his arms folded, in the attitude of a man superior to the disaster that has so suddenly fallen on him. Their eyes met and flashed implacable looks. Each hoped to inflict a cruel wound on the heart of a lover. In one instant they were as far apart as if one had been in China and the other in Greenland.

Does not the breath of vanity wither everything? Mademoiselle de Fontaine, a prey to the most violent struggle that can torture the heart of a young girl, reaped the richest harvest of anguish that prejudice and narrow-mindedness ever sowed in a human soul. Her face, but just now fresh and velvety, was streaked with yellow lines and red patches; the paleness of her cheeks seemed every now and then to turn green. Hoping to hide her despair from her sisters, she would laugh as she pointed out some ridiculous dress or passer-by; but her laughter was spasmodic. She was more deeply hurt by their unspoken compassion than by any satirical comments for which she might have revenged herself. She exhausted her wit in trying to engage them in a conversation, in which she tried to expend her fury in senseless paradoxes, heaping on all men engaged in trade the bitterest insults and witticisms in the worst taste.

On getting home, she had an attack of fever, which at first assumed a somewhat serious character. By the end of a month the care of her parents and of the physician restored her to her family.

Every one hoped that this lesson would be severe

enough to subdue Émilie's nature; but she insensibly fell into her old habits and threw herself again into the world of fashion. She declared that there was no disgrace in making a mistake. If she, like her father, had a vote in the Chamber, she would move for an edict, she said, by which all merchants, and especially dealers in calico, should be branded on the forehead, like Berri sheep, down to the third generation. She wished that none but nobles should have the right to wear the antique French costume, which was so becoming to the courtiers of Louis XV. To hear her, it was a misfortune for France, perhaps, that there was no outward and visible difference between a merchant and a peer of France. And a hundred more such pleasantries, easy to imagine, were rapidly poured out when any accident brought up the subject.

But those who loved Émilie could see through all her banter a tinge of melancholy. It was clear that Maximilien Longueville still reigned over that inexorable heart. Sometimes she would be as gentle as she had been during the brief summer that had seen the birth of her love; sometimes, again, she was unendurable. Every one made excuses for her inequality of temper, which had its source in sufferings at once secret and known to all. The Comte de Kergarouët had some influence over her, thanks to his increased prodigality, a kind of consolation which rarely fails of its effect on a Parisian girl.

The first ball at which Mademoiselle de Fontaine appeared was at the Neapolitan ambassador's. As she took her place in the first quadrille she saw, a few yards away from her, Maximilien Longueville, who nodded slightly to her partner.

"Is that young man a friend of yours?" she asked, with a scornful air.

"Only my brother," he replied.

Émilie could not help starting. "Ah!" he continued, "and he is the noblest soul living— —"

"Do you know my name?" asked Émilie, eagerly interrupting him.

"No, mademoiselle. It is a crime, I confess, not to remember a name which is on every lip—I ought to say in every heart. But I have a valid excuse. I have but just arrived from Germany. My ambassador, who is in Paris on leave, sent me here this evening to take care of his amiable wife, whom you may see yonder in that corner."

"A perfect tragic mask!" said Émilie, after looking at the ambassadress.

"And yet that is her ballroom face!" said the young man, laughing. "I shall have to dance with her! So I thought I might have some compensation." Mademoiselle de Fontaine curtseyed. "I was very much surprised," the voluble young secretary went on, "to find my brother here. On arriving from Vienna I heard that the poor boy was ill in bed; and I counted on seeing him before coming to this ball; but good policy will always allow us to indulge family affection. The *Padrona della casa** would not give me time to call on my poor Maximilien."

"Then, monsieur, your brother is not, like you, in diplomatic employment."

"No," said the attaché, with a sigh, "the poor fellow sacrificed himself for me. He and my sister Clara have renounced their share of my father's fortune to make an eldest son of me. My father dreams of a peerage, like all who vote for the ministry. Indeed, it is promised him," he added in an undertone. "After saving up a little capital my brother joined a banking firm, and I hear he has just effected a speculation in Brazil which may make him a millionaire. You see me in the highest spirits at having been able, by my diplomatic connections, to contribute to his success. I am impatiently expecting a dispatch from the Brazilian Legation, which will help to lift the cloud from his brow. What do you think of him?"

"Well, your brother's face does not look to me like that of a man busied with money matters."

The young attaché shot a scrutinizing glance at the apparently calm face of his partner.

"What!" he exclaimed, with a smile, "can young ladies read the thoughts of love behind the silent brow?"

"Your brother is in love, then?" she asked, betrayed into a movement of curiosity.

"Yes; my sister Clara, to whom he is as devoted as a mother, wrote to me that he had fallen in love this summer with a very pretty girl; but I have had no further news of the affair. Would you believe that the poor boy used to get up at five in the morning, and went off to settle his business that he might be back by four o'clock in the country where the lady was? In fact, he ruined a very nice thoroughbred that I had just given him. Forgive my chatter, mademoiselle; I have but just come home from Germany. For a year I have heard no decent French, I have been weaned from French faces, and satiated with Germans, to such a degree that, I believe, in my patriotic mania, I could talk to the chimeras on a French candlestick. And if I talk with a lack of reserve unbecoming in a diplomatist, the fault is yours, mademoiselle. Was it not you who pointed out my brother? When he is the theme I become inexhaustible. I should like to proclaim to all the world how good and generous he is. He gave up no less than a hundred thousand francs a year, the income from the Longueville property."

If Mademoiselle de Fontaine had the benefit of these important revelations, it was partly due to the skill with which she continued to question her confiding partner from the moment when she found that he was the brother of her scorned lover.

"And could you, without being grieved, see your brother selling muslin and calico?" asked Émilie, at the end of the third figure of the quadrille.

"How do you know that?" asked the attaché. "Thank God, though I pour out a flood of words, I have already acquired the art of not telling more than I intend, like all the other diplomatic apprentices I know."

"You told me, I assure you."

Monsieur de Longueville looked at Mademoiselle de Fontaine with a surprise that was full of perspicacity. A suspicion flashed upon him. He glanced inquiringly from his brother to his partner, guessed everything, clasped his hands, fixed his eyes on the ceiling, and began to laugh, saying, "I am an idiot! You are the handsomest person here; my brother keeps stealing glances at you; he is dancing in spite of his illness, and you pretend not to see him. Make him happy," he added, as he led her back to her old uncle. "I shall not be jealous, but I shall always shiver a little at calling you my sister— —"

The lovers, however, were to prove as inexorable to each other as they were to themselves. At about two in the morning, refreshments were served in an immense corridor, where, to leave persons of the same coterie free to meet each other, the tables were arranged as in a restaurant. By one of those accidents which always happen to lovers, Mademoiselle de Fontaine found herself at a table next to that at which the more important guests were seated. Maximilien was of the group. Émilie, who lent an attentive ear to her neighbors' conversation, overheard one of those dialogues into which a young woman so easily falls with a young man who has the grace and style of Maximilien Longueville. The lady talking to the young banker was a Neapolitan duchess, whose eyes shot lightning flashes, and whose skin had the sheen of satin. The intimate terms on which Longueville affected to be with her stung Mademoiselle de Fontaine all the more because she had just given her lover back twenty times as much tenderness as she had ever felt for him before.

"Yes, monsieur, in my country true love can make every kind of sacrifice," the duchess was saying, in a simper.

"You have more passion than Frenchwomen," said Maximilien, whose burning gaze fell on Émilie. "They are all vanity."

"Monsieur," Émilie eagerly interposed, "is it not very wrong to calumniate your own country? Devotion is to be found in every nation."

"Do you imagine, mademoiselle," retorted the Italian, with a sardonic smile, "that a Parisian would be capable of following her lover all over the world?"

"Oh, madame, let us understand each other. She would follow him to a desert and live in a tent but not to sit in a shop."

A disdainful gesture completed her meaning. Thus, under the influence of her disastrous education, Émilie for the second time killed her budding happiness, and destroyed its prospects of life. Maximilien's apparent indifference, and a woman's smile, had wrung from her one of those sarcasms whose treacherous zest always let her astray.

"Mademoiselle," said Longueville, in a low voice, under cover of the noise made by the ladies as they rose from the table, "no one will ever more ardently desire your happiness than I; permit me to assure you of this, as I am taking leave of you. I am starting for Italy in a few days."

"With a duchess, no doubt?"

"No, but perhaps with a mortal blow."

"Is not that pure fancy?" asked Émilie, with an anxious glance.

"No," he replied. "There are wounds which never heal."

"You are not to go," said the girl, imperiously, and she smiled.

"I shall go," replied Maximilien, gravely.

"You will find me married on your return, I warn you," she said coquettishly.

"I hope so."

"Impertinent wretch!" she exclaimed. "How cruel a revenge!"

A fortnight later Maximilien set out with his sister Clara for the warm and poetic scenes of beautiful Italy, leaving Mademoiselle de Fontaine a prey to the most vehement regret. The young Secretary to the Embassy took up his brother's quarrel, and contrived to take signal vengeance on Émilie's disdain by making known the occasion of the lovers' separation. He repaid his fair partner with interest all the sarcasm with which she had formerly attacked Maximilien, and often made more than one Excellency smile by describing the fair foe of the counting-house, the amazon who preached a crusade against bankers, the young girl whose love had evaporated before a bale of muslin. The Comte de Fontaine was obliged to use his influence to procure an appointment to Russia for Auguste Longueville in order to protect his daughter from the ridicule heaped upon her by this dangerous young persecutor.

Not long after, the Ministry being compelled to raise a levy of peers to support the aristocratic party, trembling in the Upper Chamber under the lash of an illustrious writer,* gave Monsieur Guiraudin de Longueville a peerage, with the title of Vicomte. Monsieur de Fontaine also obtained a peerage, the reward due as much to his fidelity in evil days as to his name, which claimed a place in the hereditary Chamber.

About this time Émilie, now of age, made, no doubt, some serious reflections on life, for her tone and manners changed perceptibly. Instead of amusing herself by saying spiteful things to her uncle, she lavished on him the most affectionate attentions; she brought him his stick with a persevering devotion that made the cynical smile, she gave him her arm, rode in his carriage, and accompanied him in all his drives; she even persuaded him that she liked the smell of tobacco, and read him his favorite paper *La Quotidienne** in the midst of clouds of smoke, which the malicious old sailor intentionally blew over her; she learned piquet to be a match for the old comte; and this fantastic damsel even listened without impatience to his periodical narratives of the battles of the *Belle-Poule*, the manœuvres of the *Ville de Paris*, Monsieur de Suffren's first expedition, or the battle of Aboukir.*

Though the old sailor had often said that he knew his longitude and latitude too well to allow himself to be captured by a young corvette, one fine morning Paris drawing-rooms heard the news of the marriage of Mademoiselle de Fontaine to the Comte de Kergarouët. The young comtesse gave splendid entertainments to drown thought; but she, no doubt, found a void at the bottom of the whirlpool; luxury was ineffectual to disguise the emptiness and grief of her sorrowing soul; for the most part, in spite of the flashes of assumed gaiety, her beautiful face expressed unspoken melancholy. Émilie appeared, however, full of attentions and consideration for her old husband, who, on retiring to his rooms at night, to the sounds of a lively band, would often say, "I do not know myself. Was I to wait till the age of seventy-two to embark as pilot on board the *Belle Émilie* after twenty years of matrimonial galleys?"

The conduct of the young comtesse was marked by such strictness that the most clear-sighted criticism had no fault to find with her. Lookers on chose to think that the vice-admiral had reserved the right of disposing of his fortune to keep his wife more tightly in hand; but this was a notion as insulting to the uncle as to the niece. Their conduct was indeed so delicately judicious that the men who were most interested in guessing the secrets of the couple could never decide whether the old comte regarded her as a wife or as a daughter. He was often heard to say that he had rescued his niece as a castaway after shipwreck; and that, for his part, he had never taken a mean advantage of hospitality when he had saved an enemy from the fury of the storm. Though the comtesse aspired to reign in Paris and tried to keep pace with Mesdames the Duchesses de Maufrigneuse and du Chaulieu, the Marquises d'Espard and d'Aiglemont, the Comtesses Féraud, de Montcornet, and de Restaud, Madame de Camps, and Mademoiselle des Touches, she did not yield to the addresses of the young Vicomte de Portenduère, who made her his idol.

Two years after her marriage, in one of the old drawing-rooms in the Faubourg Saint-Germain, where she was admired for her character, worthy of the old school, Émilie heard the Vicomte de Longueville announced. In the corner of the room where she was sitting, playing piquet with the Bishop of Persepolis, her agitation was not observed; she turned her head and saw her former lover come in, in all the freshness of youth. His father's death, and then that of his brother, killed by the severe climate of Saint-Petersburg, had placed on Maximilien's head the hereditary plumes of the French peer's hat. His fortune matched his learning and his merits; only the day before his youthful and fervid eloquence had dazzled the Assembly. At this moment he stood before the comtesse, free, and graced with all the advantages she had formerly required of her ideal. Every mother with a daughter to marry made amiable advances to a man gifted with the virtues which they attributed to him, as they admired his attractive person; but Émilie knew, better than any one, that the Vicomte de Longueville had the steadfast nature in which a wise woman sees a guarantee of happiness. She looked at the admiral who, to use his favorite expression, seemed likely to hold his course for a long time yet, and cursed the follies of her youth.

At this moment Monsieur de Persepolis said with Episcopal grace: "Fair lady, you have thrown away the king of hearts—I have won. But do not regret your money. I keep it for my little seminaries."

Paris, December 1829

Addendum to *The Ball at Sceaux*
The following personages appear in other stories of
The Human Comedy.

Beaudenord, Godefroid de
Lost Illusions (A Distinguished Provincial at Paris)
The Firm of Nucingen

Dudley, Lady Arabella
The Lily of the Valley
The Magic Skin
The Secrets of the Princesse de Cadignan
A Daughter of Eve
Letters of Two Brides

Fontaine, Comte de
The Chouans
Modeste Mignon
César Birotteau
The Bureaucrats

Kergarouët, Comte de
The Purse
Ursule Mirouët

Louis XVIII, Louis-Stanislas-Xavier
The Chouans
The Brotherhood of Consolation
A Shadowy Affair
Scenes from a Courtesan's Life
The Lily of the Valley
Colonel Chabert
The Bureaucrats

Manerville, Paul Francois-Joseph, Comte de
The Thirteen
Lost Illusions (A Distinguished Provincial at Paris)
The Marriage Contract

Marsay, Henri de
The Thirteen
The Unconscious Humorists
Another Study of Woman
The Lily of the Valley
Old Goriot
Jealousies of a Country Town
Ursule Mirouët
The Marriage Contract
Lost Illusions (A Distinguished Provincial at Paris)
Letters of Two Brides
Modest Mignon
The Secrets of the Princesse de Cadignan
A Shadowy Affair
A Daughter of Eve

Palma (banker)
The Firm of Nucingen
César Birotteau
Gobseck
Lost Illusions (A Distinguished Provincial at Paris)

Portenduère, Vicomte Savinien de
Scenes from a Courtesan's Life
Ursule Mirouët
Béatrix

Rastignac, Eugene de
  Old Goriot
  Lost Illusions (A Distinguished Provincial at Paris)
  Scenes from a Courtesan's Life
  The Interdiction
  A Study of Woman
  Another Study of Woman
  The Magic Skin
  The Secrets of the Princesse de Cadignan
  A Daughter of Eve
  A Shadowy Affair
  The Firm of Nucingen
  Cousin Bette
  The Deputy for Arcis
  The Unconscious Humorists

Vandenesse, Marquise Charles de (Émilie de Fontaine)
  César Birotteau
  Ursule Mirouët
  A Daughter of Eve

Letters of Two Brides
(*Mémoires de deux Jeunes Mariées*)
Translated by R.S. Scott

To George Sand*

Your name, dear George, while casting a reflected radiance on my book, can gain no new glory from this page. And yet it is neither self-interest nor diffidence which has led me to place it there, but only the wish that it should bear witness to the solid friendship between us, which has survived our wanderings and separations, and triumphed over the busy malice of the world. This feeling is hardly likely now to change. The goodly company of friendly names, which will remain attached to my works, forms an element of pleasure in the midst of the vexation caused by their increasing number. Each fresh book, in fact, gives rise to fresh annoyance, were it only in the reproaches aimed at my too prolific pen, as though it could rival in fertility the world from which I draw my models! Would it not be a fine thing, George, if the future antiquarian of dead literatures were to find in this company none but great names and generous hearts, friends bound by pure and holy ties, the illustrious figures of the century? May I not justly pride myself on this assured possession, rather than on a popularity necessarily unstable? For him who knows you well, it is happiness to be able to sign himself, as I do here,

Your friend,
De Balzac
Paris, June 1840

« Si vous aviez à me reprendre en quoi que ce soit, je deviendrais
votre obligée. » Il a tressailli , le sang a coloré son teint olivâtre.

MÉMOIRES DE DEUX JEUNES MARIÉS.

Plate III: *Armande-Louise-Marie de Chaulieu*
and Don Felipe Hénarez, the Baron de Macumer
Illustration by Tony Johannot

I

LOUISE DE CHAULIEU TO RENÉE DE MAUCOMBE

Paris, September

Sweetheart, I too am free of school! And I am the first too, unless you have written to Blois, at our sweet tryst of letter-writing.

Raise those great black eyes of yours, fixed on my opening sentence, and keep this excitement for the letter which shall tell you of my first love. By the way, why always "first?" Is there, I wonder, a second love?

Don't go running on like this, you will say, but tell me rather how you made your escape from the convent where you were to take your vows. Well, dear, I don't know about the Carmelites, but the miracle of my own deliverance was, I can assure you, most humdrum. The cries of an alarmed conscience triumphed over the dictates of a stern policy—there's the whole mystery. The sombre melancholy which seized me after you left hastened the happy climax, my aunt did not want to see me die of a decline, and my mother, whose one unfailing cure for my malady was a novitiate, gave way before her.

So I am in Paris, thanks to you, my love! Dear Renée, could you have seen me the day I found myself parted from you, well might you have gloried in the deep impression you had made on so youthful a bosom. We

143

had lived so constantly together, sharing our dreams and letting our fancy roam together, that I verily believe our souls had become welded together, like those two Hungarian girls, whose death we heard about from Monsieur Beauvisage*—poor misnamed being! Never surely was man better cut out by nature for the post of convent physician!

Tell me, did you not droop and sicken with your darling? In my gloomy depression, I could do nothing but count over the ties which bind us. But it seemed as though distance had loosened them; I wearied of life, like a turtle-dove widowed of her mate. Death smiled sweetly on me, and I was proceeding quietly to die. To be at Blois, at the Carmelites, consumed by dread of having to take my vows there, a Mademoiselle de la Vallière,* but without her prelude, and without my Renée! How could I not be sick—sick unto death?

How different it used to be! That monotonous existence, where every hour brings its duty, its prayer, its task, with such desperate regularity that you can tell what a Carmelite sister is doing in any place, at any hour of the night or day; that deadly dull routine, which crushes out all interest in one's surroundings, had become for us two a world of life and movement. Imagination had thrown open her fairy realms, and in these our spirits ranged at will, each in turn serving as magic steed to the other, the more alert quickening the drowsy; the world from which our bodies were shut out became the playground of our fancy, which reveled there in frolicsome adventure. The very *Lives of the Saints* helped us to understand what was so carefully left unsaid! But the day when I was reft of your sweet company, I became a true Carmelite, such as they appeared to us, a modern Danaïde, who, instead of trying to fill a bottomless barrel, draws every day, from Heaven knows what deep, an empty pitcher, thinking to find it full.

My aunt knew nothing of this inner life. How could she, who has made a paradise for herself within the two acres of her convent, understand my revolt against life? A religious life, if embraced by girls of our age, demands either an extreme simplicity of soul, such as we, sweetheart, do not possess, or else an ardor for self-sacrifice like that which makes my aunt so noble a character. But she sacrificed herself for a brother to whom she was devoted; to do the same for an unknown person or an idea is surely more than can be asked of mortals.

For the last fortnight I have been gulping down so many reckless words, burying so many reflections in my bosom, and accumulating such a store of things to tell, fit for your ear alone, that I should certainly have been suffocated but for the resource of letter-writing as a sorry substitute for our beloved talks. How hungry one's heart gets! I am beginning my journal this morning, and I picture to myself that yours is already started, and that, in a few days, I shall be at home in your beautiful Gémenos valley,* which I know only through your descriptions, just as you will live that Paris life, revealed to you hitherto only in our dreams.

Well, then, sweet child, know that on a certain morning—a red-letter day in my life—there arrived from Paris a lady companion and Philippe, the last remaining of my grandmother's valets, charged to carry me off. When my aunt summoned me to her room and told me the news, I could not speak for joy, and only gazed at her stupidly.

"My child," she said, in her guttural voice, "I can see that you leave me without regret, but this farewell is not the last; we shall meet again. God has placed on your forehead the sign of the elect. You have the pride which leads to heaven or to hell, but your nature is too noble to choose the downward path. I know you better than you know yourself; with you, passion, I can see, will be very different from what it is with most women."

She drew me gently to her and kissed my forehead. The kiss made my flesh creep, for it burned with that consuming fire which eats away her life, which has turned to black the azure of her eyes, and softened the lines about them, has furrowed the warm ivory of her temples, and cast a sallow tinge over the beautiful face.

Before replying, I kissed her hands.

"Dear aunt," I said, "I shall never forget your kindness; and if it has not made your nunnery all that it ought to be for my health of body and soul, you may be sure nothing short of a broken heart will bring me back again—and that you would not wish for me. You will not see me here again till my royal lover has deserted me, and I warn you that if I catch him, death alone shall tear him from me. I fear no Montespan."

She smiled and said:

"Go, madcap, and take your idle fancies with you. There is certainly more of the bold Montespan in you than of the gentle la Vallière."

I threw my arms round her. The poor lady could not refrain from escorting me to the carriage. There her tender gaze was divided between me and the armorial bearings.

At Beaugency* night overtook me, still sunk in a stupor of the mind produced by these strange parting words. What can be awaiting me in this world for which I have so hungered?

To begin with, I found no one to receive me; my heart had been schooled in vain. My mother was at the Bois de Boulogne,* my father at the Council; my brother, the Duc de Rhétoré, never comes in, I am told, till it is time to dress for dinner. Miss Griffith (she is not unlike a griffin) and Philippe took me to my rooms.

The suite is the one which belonged to my beloved grandmother, the Princesse de Vaurémont, to whom I owe some sort of a fortune which no one has ever told me about. As you read this, you will understand the sadness which came over me as I entered a place sacred to so many memories, and found the rooms just as she had left them! I was to sleep in the bed where she died.

Sitting down on the edge of the sofa, I burst into tears, forgetting I was not alone, and remembering only how often I had stood there by her knees, the better to hear her words. There I had gazed upon her face, buried in its brown laces, and worn as much by age as by the pangs of approaching death. The room seemed to me still warm with the heat which she kept up there. How comes it that Armande-Louise-Marie de Chaulieu must be like some peasant girl, who sleeps in her mother's bed the very morrow of her death? For to me it was as though the princesse, who died in 1817, had passed away but yesterday.

I saw many things in the room which ought to have been removed. Their presence showed the carelessness with which people, busy with the affairs of state, may treat their own, and also the little thought which had been given since her death to this grand old lady, who will always remain one of the striking figures of the eighteenth century. Philippe seemed to divine something of the cause of my tears. He told me that the furniture of the princesse had been left to me in her will and that my father had allowed all the larger suites to remain dismantled, as the Revolution had left them. On hearing this I rose, and Philippe opened the door of the small drawing-room which leads into the reception-rooms.

In these I found all the well-remembered wreckage; the panels above the doors, which had contained valuable pictures, bare of all but empty frames; broken marbles, mirrors carried off. In old days I was afraid to go up the state staircase and cross these vast, deserted rooms; so I used to get to the princesse's rooms by a small staircase which runs under the arch of the larger one and leads to the secret door of her dressing-room.

My suite, consisting of a drawing-room, bedroom, and the pretty morning-room in scarlet and gold, of which I have told you, lies in the wing on the side of the Invalides.* The house is only separated from the boulevard by a wall, covered with creepers, and by a splendid avenue of trees, which mingle their foliage with that of the young elms on the sidewalk of the boulevard. But for the blue-and-gold dome of the Invalides and its gray stone mass, you might be in a wood.

The style of decoration in these rooms, together with their situation, indicates that they were the old show suite of the duchesses, while the ducs must have had theirs in the wing opposite. The two suites are decorously separated by the two main blocks, as well as by the central one, which contained those vast, gloomy, resounding halls shown me by Philippe, all despoiled of their splendor, as in the days of my childhood.

Philippe grew quite confidential when he saw the surprise depicted on my countenance. For you must know that in this home of diplomacy the very servants have a reserved and mysterious air. He went on to tell me that it was expected a law would soon be passed restoring to the fugitives of the Revolution the value of their property, and that my father is waiting to do up his house till this restitution is made, the king's architect having estimated the damage at three hundred thousand livres.

This piece of news flung me back despairing on my drawing-room sofa. Could it be that my father, instead of spending this money in arranging a marriage for me, would have left me to die in the convent? This was the first thought to greet me on the threshold of my home.

Ah! Renée, what would I have given then to rest my head upon your shoulder, or to transport myself to the days when my grandmother made the life of these rooms? You two in all the world have been alone in loving me—you away at Maucombe, and she who survives only in my heart, the dear old lady, whose still youthful eyes used to open from sleep at my call. How well we understood each other!

These memories suddenly changed my mood. What at first had seemed profanation, now breathed of holy association. It was sweet to inhale the faint odor of the powder she loved still lingering in the room; sweet to sleep beneath the shelter of those yellow damask curtains with their white pattern, which must have retained something of the spirit emanating from her eyes and breath. I told Philippe to rub up the old furniture and make the rooms look as if they were lived in; I explained to him myself how I wanted everything arranged, and where to put each piece of furniture. In this way I entered into possession, and showed how an air of youth might be given to the dear old things.

The bedroom is white in color, a little dulled with time, just as the gilding of the fanciful arabesques shows here and there a patch of red; but this effect harmonizes well with the faded colors of the Savonnerie tapestry, which was presented to my grandmother by Louis XV along with his portrait. The timepiece was a gift from the Maréchal de Saxe, and the china ornaments on the mantelpiece came from the Maréchal de Richelieu.* My grandmother's portrait, painted at the age of twenty-five, hangs in an oval frame opposite that of the king. The prince, her husband, is conspicuous by his absence. I like this frank negligence, untinged by hypocrisy—a characteristic touch which sums up her charming personality. Once when my grandmother was seriously ill, her confessor was urgent that the prince, who was waiting in the drawing-room, should be admitted.

"He can come in with the doctor and his drugs," was the reply.

The bed has a canopy and well-stuffed back, and the

149

curtains are looped up with fine wide bands. The furniture is of gilded wood, upholstered in the same yellow damask with white flowers which drapes the windows, and which is lined there with a white silk that looks as though it were watered. The panels over the doors have been painted, by what artist I can't say, but they represent one a sunrise, the other a moonlight scene.

The fireplace is a very interesting feature in the room. It is easy to see that life in the last century centered largely round the hearth, where great events were enacted. The copper gilt grate is a marvel of workmanship, and the mantelpiece is most delicately finished; the fire-irons are beautifully chased; the bellows are a perfect gem. The tapestry of the screen comes from the Gobelins and is exquisitely mounted; charming fantastic figures run all over the frame, on the feet, the supporting bar, and the wings; the whole thing is wrought like a fan.

Dearly should I like to know who was the giver of this dainty work of art, which was such a favorite with her. How often have I seen the old lady, her feet upon the bar, reclining in the easy-chair, with her dress half raised in front, toying with the snuff-box, which lay upon the ledge between her box of pastilles and her silk mitts. What a coquette she was! to the day of her death she took as much pains with her appearance as though the beautiful portrait had been painted only yesterday, and she were waiting to receive the throng of exquisites from the Court! How the armchair recalls to me the inimitable sweep of her skirts as she sank back in it!

These women of a past generation have carried off with them secrets which are very typical of their age. The princesse had a certain turn of the head, a way of dropping her glance and her remarks, a choice of words, which I look for in vain, even in my mother. There was subtlety in it all, and there was good-nature; the points were made without any affectation. Her talk was at once lengthy and concise; she told a good story, and could put her meaning in three words. Above all, she was extremely free-thinking, and this has undoubtedly had its effect on my way of looking at things.

From seven years old till I was ten, I never left her side; it pleased her to attract me as much as it pleased me to go. This preference was the cause of more than one passage at arms between her and my mother, and nothing intensifies feeling like the icy breath of persecution. How charming was her greeting, "Here you are, little rogue!" when curiosity had taught me how to glide with stealthy snake-like movements to her room. She felt that I loved her, and this childish affection was welcome as a ray of sunshine in the winter of her life.

I don't know what went on in her rooms at night, but she had many visitors; and when I came on tiptoe in the morning to see if she were awake, I would find the drawing-room furniture disarranged, the card-tables set out, and patches of snuff scattered about.

This drawing-room is furnished in the same style as the bedroom. The chairs and tables are oddly shaped, with claw feet and hollow mouldings. Rich garlands of flowers, beautifully designed and carved, wind over the mirrors and hang down in festoons. On the consoles are fine china vases. The ground colors are scarlet and white. My grandmother was a high-spirited, striking brunette, as might be inferred from her choice of colors. I have found in the drawing-room a writing-table I remember well; the figures on it used to fascinate me; it is plaited in graven silver, and was a present from one of the Genoese Lomellini. Each side of the table represents the occupations of a different season; there are hundreds of figures in each picture, and all in relief.

I remained alone for two hours, while old memories rose before me, one after another, on this spot, hallowed by the death of a woman most remarkable even among the witty and beautiful Court ladies of Louis XV's day.

You know how abruptly I was parted from her, at a

151

day's notice, in 1816.

"Go and bid good-bye to your grandmother," said my mother.

The princesse received me as usual, without any display of feeling, and expressed no surprise at my departure.

"You are going to the convent, dear," she said, "and will see your aunt there, who is an excellent woman. I shall take care, though, that they don't make a victim of you; you shall be independent, and able to marry whom you please."

Six months later she died. Her will had been given into the keeping of the Prince de Talleyrand, the most devoted of all her old friends. He contrived, while paying a visit to Mademoiselle de Chargebœuf, to intimate to me, through her, that my grandmother forbade me to take the vows. I hope, sooner or later, to meet the prince, and then I shall doubtless learn more from him.

Thus, sweetheart, if I have found no one in flesh and blood to meet me, I have comforted myself with the shade of the dear princesse, and have prepared myself for carrying out one of our pledges, which was, as you know, to keep each other informed of the smallest details in our homes and occupations. It makes such a difference to know where and how the life of one we love is passed. Send me a faithful picture of the veriest trifles around you, omitting nothing, not even the sunset lights among the tall trees.

October 19th

It was three in the afternoon when I arrived. About half-past five, Rose came and told me that my mother had returned, so I went downstairs to pay my respects to her.

My mother lives in a suite on the ground floor, exactly corresponding to mine, and in the same block. I am just over her head, and the same secret staircase serves for both. My father's rooms are in the block opposite, but are larger by the whole of the space occupied by the grand staircase on our side of the building. These ancestral mansions are so spacious, that my father and mother continue to occupy the ground-floor rooms, in spite of the social duties which have once more devolved on them with the return of the Bourbons,* and are even able to receive in them.

I found my mother, dressed for the evening, in her drawing-room, where nothing is changed. I came slowly down the stairs, speculating with every step how I should be met by this mother who had shown herself so little of a mother to me, and from whom, during eight years, I had heard nothing beyond the two letters of which you know. Judging it unworthy to simulate an affection I could not possibly feel, I put on the air of a pious imbecile, and entered the room with many inward qualms, which however soon disappeared. My mother's tack was equal to the occasion. She made no pretence of emotion; she neither held me at arm's-length nor hugged me to her bosom like a beloved daughter, but greeted me as though we had parted the evening before. Her manner was that of the kindliest and most sincere friend, as she addressed me like a grown person, first kissing me on the forehead.

"My dear little one," she said, "if you were to die at the convent, it is much better to live with your family. You frustrate your father's plans and mine; but the age of blind obedience to parents is past. Monsieur de Chaulieu's intention, and in this I am quite at one with him, is to lose no opportunity of making your life pleasant and of letting you see the world. At your age I should have thought as you do, therefore I am not vexed with you; it is impossible you should understand what we expected from you. You will not find any absurd severity in me; and if you have ever thought me heartless, you will soon find out your mistake. Still, though I wish you to feel perfectly free, I think that, to begin with, you would do well to follow the counsels of a mother, who wishes to be a sister to you."

I was quite charmed by the duchesse, who talked in a gentle voice, straightening my convent tippet as she spoke. At the age of thirty-eight she is still exquisitely beautiful. She has dark-blue eyes, with silken lashes, a smooth forehead, and a complexion so pink and white that you might think she paints. Her bust and shoulders are marvelous, and her waist is as slender as yours. Her hand is milk-white and extraordinarily beautiful; the nails catch the light in their perfect polish, the thumb is like ivory, the little finger stands just a little apart from the rest, and the foot matches the hand; it is the Spanish foot of Mademoiselle de Vandenesse. If she is like this at forty, at sixty she will still be a beautiful woman.

I replied, sweetheart, like a good little girl. I was as nice to her as she to me, nay, nicer. Her beauty completely vanquished me; it seemed only natural that such a woman should be absorbed in her regal part. I told her this as simply as though I had been talking to you. I daresay it was a surprise to her to hear words of affection from her daughter's mouth, and the unfeigned homage of my admiration evidently touched her deeply. Her manner changed and became even more engaging; she dropped all formality as she said:

"I am much pleased with you, and I hope we shall remain good friends."

The words struck me as charmingly naive, but I did not let this appear, for I saw at once that the prudent course was to allow her to believe herself much deeper and cleverer than her daughter. So I only stared vacantly and she was delighted. I kissed her hands repeatedly, telling her how happy it made me to be so treated and to feel at my ease with her. I even confided to her my previous tremors. She smiled, put her arm round my neck, and drawing me towards her, kissed me on the forehead most affectionately.

"Dear child," she said, "we have people coming to dinner to-day. Perhaps you will agree with me that it is better for you not to make your first appearance in society till you have been in the dressmaker's hands; so, after you have seen your father and brother, you can go upstairs again."

I assented most heartily. My mother's exquisite dress was the first revelation to me of the world which our dreams had pictured; but I did not feel the slightest desire to rival her.

My father now entered, and the duchesse presented me to him.

He became all at once most affectionate, and played the father's part so well, that I could not but believe his heart to be in it. Taking my two hands in his, and kissing them, with more of the lover than the father in his manner, he said:

"So this is my rebel daughter!"

And he drew me towards him, with his arm passed tenderly round my waist, while he kissed me on the cheeks and forehead.

"The pleasure with which we shall watch your success in society will atone for the disappointment we felt at your change of vocation," he said. Then, turning to my mother, "Do you know that she is going to turn out very pretty, and you will be proud of her some day?— Here is your brother, Rhétoré.—Alphonse," he said to a fine young man who came in, "here is your convent-bred sister, who threatens to send her nun's frock to the deuce."

My brother came up in a leisurely way and took my hand, which he pressed.

"Come, come, you may kiss her," said my father.

And he kissed me on both cheeks.

"I am delighted to see you," he said, "and I take your side against my father."

I thanked him, but could not help thinking he might have come to Blois when he was at Orléans visiting our marquis brother in his quarters.

Fearing the arrival of strangers, I now withdrew. I tidied up my rooms, and laid out on the scarlet velvet of my lovely table all the materials necessary for writing to you, meditating all the while on my new situation.

This, my fair sweetheart, is a true and veracious account of the return of a girl of eighteen, after an absence of nine years, to the bosom of one of the noblest families in the kingdom. I was tired by the journey as well as by all the emotions I had been through, so I went to bed in convent fashion, at eight o'clock after supper. They have preserved even a little Saxe service which the dear princesse used when she had a fancy for taking her meals alone.

II
THE SAME TO THE SAME

November 25th

Next day I found my rooms done out and dusted, and even flowers put in the vases, by old Philippe. I began to feel at home. Only it didn't occur to anybody that a Carmelite schoolgirl has an early appetite, and Rose had no end of trouble in getting breakfast for me.

"Mademoiselle goes to bed at dinner-time," she said to me, "and gets up when the duc is just returning home."

I began to write. About one o'clock my father knocked at the door of the small drawing-room and asked if he might come in. I opened the door; he came in, and found me writing to you.

"My dear," he began, "you will have to get yourself clothes, and to make these rooms comfortable. In this purse you will find twelve thousand francs, which is the yearly income I purpose allowing you for your expenses. You will make arrangements with your mother as to some governess whom you may like, in case Miss Griffith doesn't please you, for Madame de Chaulieu will not have time to go out with you in the mornings. A carriage and man-servant shall be at your disposal."

"Let me keep Philippe," I said.

"So be it," he replied. "But don't be uneasy; you have money enough of your own to be no burden either to your mother or me."

"May I ask how much I have?"

"Certainly, my child," he said. "Your grandmother left you five hundred thousand francs; this was the amount of her savings, for she would not alienate a foot of land from the family. This sum has been placed in Government stock, and, with the accumulated interest, now brings in about forty thousand francs a year. With this I had purposed making an independence for your second brother, and it is here that you have upset my plans. Later, however, it is possible that you may fall in with them. It shall rest with yourself, for I have confidence in your good sense far more than I had expected.

"I do not need to tell you how a daughter of the Chaulieus ought to behave. The pride so plainly written in your features is my best guarantee. Safeguards, such as common folk surround their daughters with, would be an insult in our family. A slander reflecting on your name might cost the life of the man bold enough to utter it, or the life of one of your brothers, if by chance the right should not prevail. No more on this subject. Good-bye, little one."

He kissed me on the forehead and went out. I cannot understand the relinquishment of this plan after nine years' persistence in it. My father's frankness is what I like. There is no ambiguity about his words. My money ought to belong to his marquis son. Who, then, has had bowels of mercy? My mother? My father? Or could it be my brother?

I remained sitting on my grandmother's sofa, staring at the purse which my father had left on the mantelpiece, at once pleased and vexed that I could not withdraw my mind from the money. It is true, further speculation was useless. My doubts had been cleared up and there was something fine in the way my pride was spared.

Philippe has spent the morning rushing about among the various shops and workpeople who are to undertake the task of my metamorphosis. A famous dressmaker, by name Victorine, has come, as well as a woman for underclothing, and a shoemaker. I am as impatient as a child to know what I shall be like when I emerge from the sack which constituted the conventual uniform; but all these tradespeople take a long time; the corsetmaker requires a whole week if my figure is not to be spoilt. You see, I have a figure, dear; this becomes serious. Janssen, the operatic shoemaker, solemnly assures me that I have my mother's foot. The whole morning has gone in these weighty occupations. Even a glovemaker has come to take the measure of my hand. The underclothing woman has got my orders.

At the meal which I call dinner, and the others lunch, my mother told me that we were going together to the milliner's to see some hats, so that my taste should be formed, and I might be in a position to order my own.

This burst of independence dazzles me. I am like a blind man who has just recovered his sight. Now I begin to understand the vast interval which separates a Carmelite sister from a girl in society. Of ourselves we could never have conceived it.

During this lunch my father seemed absent-minded, and we left him to his thoughts; he is deep in the king's confidence. I was entirely forgotten; but, from what I have seen, I have no doubt he will remember me when he has need of me. He is a very attractive man in spite of his fifty years. His figure is youthful; he is well made, fair, and extremely graceful in his movements. He has a diplomatic face, at once dumb and expressive; his nose is long and slender, and he has brown eyes.

What a handsome pair! Strange thoughts assail me as it becomes plain to me that these two, so perfectly matched in birth, wealth, and mental superiority, live entirely apart, and have nothing in common but their name. The show of unity is only for the world.

The cream of the Court and diplomatic circles were here last night. Very soon I am going to a ball given by the Duchesse de Maufrigneuse, and I shall be presented to the society I am so eager to know. A dancing-master is coming every morning to give me lessons, for I must be able to dance in a month, or I can't go to the ball.

Before dinner, my mother came to talk about the governess with me. I have decided to keep Miss Griffith, who was recommended by the English ambassador. Miss Griffith is the daughter of a clergyman; her mother was of good family, and she is perfectly well bred. She is thirty-six, and will teach me English. The good soul is quite handsome enough to have ambitions; she is Scotch—poor and proud—and will act as my chaperon. She is to sleep in Rose's room. Rose will be under her orders. I saw at a glance that my governess would be governed by me. In the six days we have been together, she has made very sure that I am the only person likely to take an interest in her; while, for my part, I have ascertained that, for all her statuesque features, she will prove accommodating. She seems to me a kindly soul, but cautious. I have not been able to extract a word of what passed between her and my mother.

Another trifling piece of news! My father has this morning refused the appointment as Minister of State which was offered him. This accounts for his preoccupied manner last night. He says he would prefer an embassy to the worries of public debate. Spain in especial attracts him.

This news was told me at lunch, the one moment of the day when my father, mother, and brother see each other in an easy way. The servants then only come when they are rung for. The rest of the day my brother, as well as my father, spends out of the house. My mother has her toilet to make; between two and four she is never visible; at four o'clock she goes out for an hour's drive; when she is not dining out, she receives from six to seven, and the evening is given to entertainments of various kinds—theatres, balls, concerts, at homes. In short, her life is so full, that I don't believe she ever has a quarter of an hour to herself. She must spend a considerable time dressing in the morning; for at lunch, which takes place between eleven and twelve, she is exquisite. The meaning of the things that are said about her is dawning on me. She begins the day with a bath barely warmed, and a cup of cold coffee with cream; then she dresses. She is never, except on some great emergency, called before nine o'clock. In summer there are morning rides, and at two o'clock she receives a young man whom I have never yet contrived to see.

Behold our family life! We meet at lunch and dinner, though often I am alone with my mother at this latter meal, and I foresee that still oftener I shall take it in my own rooms (following the example of my grandmother) with only Miss Griffith for company, for my mother frequently dines out. I have ceased to wonder at the indifference my family have shown to me. In Paris, my dear, it is a miracle of virtue to love the people who live with you, for you see little enough of them; as for the absent—they do not exist!

Knowing as this may sound, I have not yet set foot in the streets, and am deplorably ignorant. I must wait till I am less of the country cousin and have brought my dress and deportment into keeping with the society I am about to enter, the whirl of which amazes me even here, where only distant murmurs reach my ear. So far I have not gone beyond the garden; but the Italian Opera opens in a few days, and my mother has a box there. I am crazy with delight at the thought of hearing Italian music and seeing French acting.

Already I begin to drop convent habits for those of society. I spend the evening writing to you till the moment for going to bed arrives. This has been postponed to ten o'clock, the hour at which my mother goes out, if she is not at the theatre. There are twelve theatres in Paris.

I am grossly ignorant and I read a lot, but quite indiscriminately, one book leading to another. I find the names of fresh books on the cover of the one I am reading; but as I have no one to direct me, I light on some which are fearfully dull. What modern literature I have read all turns upon love, the subject which used to bulk so largely in our thoughts, because it seemed that our fate was determined by man and for man. But how inferior are these authors to two little girls, known as Sweetheart and Darling—otherwise Renée and Louise. Ah! my love, what wretched plots, what ridiculous situations, and what poverty of sentiment! Two books, however, have given me wonderful pleasure—*Corinne* and *Adolphe*.* Apropos of this, I asked my father one day whether it would be possible for me to see Madame de Staël. My father, mother, and Alphonse all burst out laughing, and Alphonse said:

"Where in the world has she sprung from?"

To which my father replied:

"What fools we are! She springs from the Carmelites."

"My child, Madame de Staël is dead," said my mother gently.

When I finished *Adolphe*, I asked Miss Griffith how a woman could be betrayed.

"Why, of course, when she loves," was her reply.

Renée, tell me, do you think we could be betrayed by a man?

Miss Griffith has at last discerned that I am not an utter ignoramus, that I have somewhere a hidden vein of knowledge, the knowledge we learned from each other in our random arguments. She sees that it is only superficial facts of which I am ignorant. The poor thing has opened her heart to me. Her curt reply to my question, when I compare it with all the sorrows I can imagine, makes me feel quite creepy. Once more she urged me not to be dazzled by the glitter of society, to be always on my guard, especially against what most attracted me. This is the sum-total of her wisdom, and I can get nothing more out of her. Her lectures, therefore, become a trifle monotonous, and she might be compared in this respect to the bird which has only one cry.

III

THE SAME TO THE SAME

December

My Darling,—Here I am ready to make my bow to the world. By way of preparation I have been trying to commit all the follies I could think of before sobering down for my entry. This morning, I have seen myself, after many rehearsals, well and duly equipped—stays, shoes, curls, dress, ornaments,—all in order. Following the example of duelists before a meeting, I tried my arms in the privacy of my chamber. I wanted to see how I would look, and had no difficulty in discovering a certain air of victory and triumph, bound to carry all before it. I mustered all my forces, in accordance with that splendid maxim of antiquity, "Know thyself!" and boundless was my delight in thus making my own acquaintance. Griffith was the sole spectator of this doll's play, in which I was at once doll and child. You think you know me? You are hugely mistaken.

Here is a portrait, then, Renée, of your sister, formerly disguised as a Carmelite, now brought to life again as a frivolous society girl. She is one of the greatest beauties in France—Provence, of course, excepted. I don't see that I can give a more accurate summary of this interesting topic.

True, I have my weak points; but were I a man, I should adore them. They arise from what is most promising in me. When you have spent a fortnight admiring the exquisite curves of your mother's arms, and that mother the Duchesse de Chaulieu, it is impossible, my dear, not to deplore your own angular elbows. Yet there is consolation in observing the fineness of the wrist, and a certain grace of line in those hollows, which will yet fill out and show plump, round, and well modeled, under the satiny skin. The somewhat crude outline of the arms is seen again in the shoulders. Strictly speaking, indeed, I have no shoulders, but only two bony blades, standing out in harsh relief. My figure also lacks pliancy; there is a stiffness about the side lines.

Poof! There's the worst out. But then the contours are bold and delicate, the bright, pure flame of health bites into the vigorous lines, a flood of life and of blue blood pulses under the transparent skin, and the fairest daughter of Eve would seem a negress beside me! I have the foot of a gazelle! My joints are finely turned, my features of a Greek correctness. It is true, madame, that the flesh tints do not melt into each other; but, at least, they stand out clear and bright. In short, I am a very pretty green fruit, with all the charm of unripeness. I see a great likeness to the face in my aunt's old missal, which rises out of a violet lily.

There is no silly weakness in the blue of my insolent eyes; the white is pure mother-of-pearl, prettily marked with tiny veins, and the thick, long lashes fall like a silken fringe. My forehead sparkles, and the hair grows deliciously; it ripples into waves of pale gold, growing browner towards the centre, whence escape little rebel locks, which alone would tell that my fairness is not of the insipid and hysterical type. I am a tropical blonde, with plenty of blood in my veins, a blonde more apt to strike than to turn the cheek. What do you think the hairdresser proposed? He wanted, if you please, to smooth my hair into two bands, and place over my forehead a pearl, kept in place by a gold chain! He said it would recall the Middle Ages.

I told him I was not aged enough to have reached the middle, or to need an ornament to freshen me up!

The nose is slender, and the well-cut nostrils are separated by a sweet little pink partition—an imperious, mocking nose, with a tip too sensitive ever to grow fat or red. Sweetheart, if this won't find a husband for a dowerless maiden, I'm a donkey. The ears are daintily curled, a pearl hanging from either lobe would show yellow. The neck is long, and has an undulating motion full of dignity. In the shade the white ripens to a golden tinge. Perhaps the mouth is a little large. But how expressive! what a color on the lips! how prettily the teeth laugh!

Then, dear, there is a harmony running through all. What a gait! what a voice! We have not forgotten how our grandmother's skirts fell into place without a touch. In a word, I am lovely and charming. When the mood comes, I can laugh one of our good old laughs, and no one will think the less of me; the dimples, impressed by Comedy's light fingers on my fair cheeks, will command respect. Or I can let my eyes fall and my heart freeze under my snowy brows. I can pose as a Madonna with melancholy, swan-like neck, and the painters' virgins will be nowhere; my place in heaven would be far above them. A man would be forced to chant when he spoke to me.

So, you see, my panoply is complete, and I can run the whole gamut of coquetry from deepest bass to shrillest treble. It is a huge advantage not to be all of one piece. Now, my mother is neither playful nor virginal. Her only attitude is an imposing one; when she ceases to be majestic, she is ferocious. It is difficult for her to heal the wounds she makes, whereas I can wound and heal together. We are absolutely unlike, and therefore there could not possibly be rivalry between us, unless indeed we quarreled over the greater or less perfection of our extremities, which are similar. I take after my father, who is shrewd and subtle. I have the manner of my grandmother and her charming voice, which becomes falsetto when forced, but is a sweet-toned chest voice at the ordinary pitch of a quiet talk.

I feel as if I had left the convent to-day for the first time. For society I do not yet exist; I am unknown to it. What a ravishing moment! I still belong only to myself, like a flower just blown, unseen yet of mortal eye.

In spite of this, my sweet, as I paced the drawing-room during my self-inspection, and saw the poor cast-off school-clothes, a queer feeling came over me. Regret for the past, anxiety about the future, fear of society, a long farewell to the pale daisies which we used to pick and strip of their petals in light-hearted innocence, there was something of all that; but strange, fantastic visions also rose, which I crushed back into the inner depths, whence they had sprung, and whither I dared not follow them.

My Renée, I have a regular trousseau! It is all beautifully laid away and perfumed in the cedar-wood drawers with lacquered front of my charming dressing-table. There are ribbons, shoes, gloves, all in lavish abundance. My father has kindly presented me with the pretty gewgaws a girl loves—a dressing-case, toilet service, scent-box, fan, sunshade, prayer-book, gold chain, cashmere shawl. He has also promised to give me riding lessons. And I can dance! To-morrow, yes, to-morrow evening, I come out!

My dress is white muslin, and on my head I wear a garland of white roses in Greek style. I shall put on my Madonna face; I mean to play the simpleton, and have all the women on my side. My mother is miles away from any idea of what I write to you. She believes me quite destitute of mind, and would be dumfounded if she read my letter. My brother honors me with a profound contempt, and is uniformly and politely indifferent.

He is a handsome young fellow, but melancholy, and given to moods. I have divined his secret, though neither the duc nor duchesse has an inkling of it. In spite of his youth and his title, he is jealous of his father. He has no position in the State, no post at Court, he never has to say, "I am going to the Chamber." I alone in the house have sixteen hours for meditation. My father is absorbed in public business and his own amusements; my mother, too, is never at leisure; no member of the household practises self-examination, they are constantly in company, and have hardly time to live.

I should immensely like to know what is the potent charm wielded by society to keep people prisoner from nine every evening till two or three in the morning, and force them to be so lavish alike of strength and money. When I longed for it, I had no idea of the separations it brought about, or its overmastering spell. But, then, I forget, it is Paris which does it all.

It is possible, it seems, for members of one family to live side by side and know absolutely nothing of each other. A half-fledged nun arrives, and in a couple of weeks has grasped domestic details, of which the master diplomatist at the head of the house is quite ignorant. Or perhaps he *does* see, and shuts his eyes deliberately, as part of the father's role. There is a mystery here which I must plumb.

IV

THE SAME TO THE SAME

December 15th

Yesterday, at two o'clock, I went to drive in the Champs-Élysées and the Bois de Boulogne. It was one of those autumn days which we used to find so beautiful on the banks of the Loire. So I have seen Paris at last! The Place Louis XV* is certainly very fine, but the beauty is that of man's handiwork.

I was dressed to perfection, pensive, with set face (though inwardly much tempted to laugh), under a lovely hat, my arms crossed. Would you believe it? Not a single smile was thrown at me, not one poor youth was struck motionless as I passed, not a soul turned to look again; and yet the carriage proceeded with a deliberation worthy of my pose.

No, I am wrong, there was one—a duc, and a charming man—who suddenly reined in as we went by. The individual who thus saved appearances for me was my father, and he proclaimed himself highly gratified by what he saw. I met my mother also, who sent me a butterfly kiss from the tips of her fingers. The worthy Griffith, who fears no man, cast her glances hither and thither without discrimination. In my judgment, a young woman should always know exactly what her eye is resting on.

I was mad with rage. One man actually inspected my carriage without noticing me. This flattering homage probably came from a carriage-maker. I have been quite out in the reckoning of my forces. Plainly, beauty, that rare gift which comes from heaven, is commoner in Paris than I thought. I saw hats doffed with deference to simpering fools; a purple face called forth murmurs of, "It is she!" My mother received an immense amount of admiration. There is an answer to this problem, and I mean to find it.

The men, my dear, seemed to me generally very ugly. The very few exceptions are bad copies of us. Heaven knows what evil genius has inspired their costume; it is amazingly inelegant compared with those of former generations. It has no distinction, no beauty of color or romance; it appeals neither to the senses, nor the mind, nor the eye, and it must be very uncomfortable. It is meagre and stunted. The hat, above all, struck me; it is a sort of truncated column, and does not adapt itself in the least to the shape of the head; but I am told it is easier to bring about a revolution than to invent a graceful hat. Courage in Paris recoils before the thought of appearing in a round felt; and for lack of one day's daring, men stick all their lives to this ridiculous headpiece. And yet Frenchmen are said to be fickle!

The men are hideous anyway, whatever they put on their heads. I have seen nothing but worn, hard faces, with no calm nor peace in the expression; the harsh lines and furrows speak of foiled ambition and smarting vanity. A fine forehead is rarely seen.

"And these are the product of Paris!" I said to Miss Griffith.

"Most cultivated and pleasant men," she replied.

I was silent. The heart of a spinster of thirty-six is a well of tolerance.

In the evening I went to the ball, where I kept close to my mother's side. She gave me her arm with a devotion which did not miss its reward. All the honors were for her; I was made the pretext for charming compliments. She was clever enough to find me fools for my partners, who one and all expatiated on the heat and the beauty of the ball, till you might suppose I was freezing and blind. Not one failed to enlarge on the strange, unheard-of, extraordinary, odd, remarkable fact—that he saw me for the first time.

My dress, which dazzled me as I paraded alone in my white-and-gold drawing-room, was barely noticeable amidst the gorgeous finery of most of the married women. Each had her band of faithful followers, and they all watched each other askance. A few were radiant in triumphant beauty, and amongst these was my mother. A girl at a ball is a mere dancing-machine—a thing of no consequence whatever.

The men, with rare exceptions, did not impress me more favorably here than at the Champs-Élysées. They have a used-up look; their features are meaningless, or rather they have all the same meaning. The proud, stalwart bearing which we find in the portraits of our ancestors—men who joined moral to physical vigor—has disappeared. Yet in this gathering there was one man of remarkable ability, who stood out from the rest by the beauty of his face. But even he did not rouse in me the feeling which I should have expected. I do not know his works, and he is a man of no family. Whatever the genius and the merits of a plebeian or a commoner, he could never stir my blood. Besides, this man was obviously so much more taken up with himself than with anybody else, that I could not but think these great brain-workers must look on us as things rather than persons. When men of intellectual power love, they ought to give up writing, otherwise their love is not the real thing. The lady of their heart does not come first in all their thoughts. I seemed to read all this in the bearing of the man I speak of. I am told he is a professor, orator, and author, whose ambition makes him the slave of every bigwig.

My mind was made up on the spot. It was unworthy of me, I determined, to quarrel with society for not being impressed by my merits, and I gave myself up to the simple pleasure of dancing, which I thoroughly enjoyed. I heard a great deal of inept gossip about people of whom I know nothing; but perhaps it is my ignorance on many subjects which prevents me from appreciating it, as I saw that most men and women took a lively pleasure in certain remarks, whether falling from their own lips or those of others. Society bristles with enigmas which look hard to solve. It is a perfect maze of intrigue. Yet I am fairly quick of sight and hearing, and as to my wits, Mademoiselle de Maucombe does not need to be told!

I returned home tired with a pleasant sort of tiredness, and in all innocence began describing my sensations to my mother, who was with me. She checked me with the warning that I must never say such things to any one but her.

"My dear child," she added, "it needs as much tact to know when to be silent as when to speak."

This advice brought home to me the nature of the sensations which ought to be concealed from every one, not excepting perhaps even a mother. At a glance I measured the vast field of feminine duplicity. I can assure you, sweetheart, that we, in our unabashed simplicity, would pass for two very wide-awake little scandal-mongers. What lessons may be conveyed in a finger on the lips, in a word, a look! All in a moment I was seized with excessive shyness. What! may I never again speak of the natural pleasure I feel in the exercise of dancing? "How then," I said to myself, "about the deeper feelings?"

I went to bed sorrowful, and I still suffer from the shock produced by this first collision of my frank, joyous nature with the harsh laws of society. Already the highway hedges are flecked with my white wool! Farewell, beloved.

V

RENÉE DE MAUCOMBE TO LOUISE DE CHAULIEU

October

How deeply your letter moved me; above all, when I compare our widely different destinies! How brilliant is the world you are entering, how peaceful the retreat where I shall end my modest career!

In the Castle of Maucombe, which is so well known to you by description that I shall say no more of it, I found my room almost exactly as I left it; only now I can enjoy the splendid view it gives of the Gémenos valley, which my childish eyes used to see without comprehending. A fortnight after my arrival, my father and mother took me, along with my two brothers, to dine with one of our neighbors, Monsieur de l'Estorade, an old gentleman of good family, who has made himself rich, after the provincial fashion, by scraping and paring.

Monsieur de l'Estorade was unable to save his only son from the clutches of Bonaparte; after successfully eluding the conscription, he was forced to send him to the army in 1813, to join the Emperor's bodyguard. After Leipsic no more was heard of him.* Monsieur de Montriveau, whom the father interviewed in 1814, declared that he had seen him taken by the Russians. Madame de l'Estorade died of grief whilst a vain search was being made in Russia. The baron, a very pious old man, practised that fine theological virtue which we used to cultivate at Blois—Hope! Hope made him see his son in dreams. He hoarded his income for him, and guarded carefully the portion of inheritance which fell to him from the family of the late Madame de l'Estorade, no one venturing to ridicule the old man.

At last it dawned upon me that the unexpected return of this son was the cause of my own. Who could have imagined, whilst fancy was leading us a giddy dance, that my destined husband was slowly traveling on foot through Russia, Poland, and Germany? His bad luck only forsook him at Berlin, where the French Minister helped his return to his native country. Monsieur de l'Estorade, the father, who is a small landed proprietor in Provence, with an income of about ten thousand livres, has not sufficient European fame to interest the

171

world in the wandering Knight de l'Estorade, whose name smacks of his adventures.

The accumulated income of twelve thousand livres from the property of Madame de l'Estorade, with the addition of the father's savings, provides the poor guard of honor with something like two hundred and fifty thousand livres, not counting house and lands—quite a considerable fortune in Provence. His worthy father had bought, on the very eve of the chevalier's return, a fine but badly-managed estate, where he designs to plant ten thousand mulberry-trees, raised in his nursery with a special view to this acquisition. The baron, having found his long-lost son, has now but one thought, to marry him, and marry him to a girl of good family.

My father and mother entered into their neighbor's idea with an eye to my interests so soon as they discovered that Renée de Maucombe would be acceptable without a dowry, and that the money the said Renée ought to inherit from her parents would be duly acknowledged as hers in the contract. In a similar way, my younger brother, Jean de Maucombe, as soon as he came of age, signed a document stating that he had received from his parents an advance upon the estate equal in amount to one-third of whole. This is the device by which the nobles of Provence elude the infamous Civil Code of Monsieur de Bonaparte, a code which will drive as many girls of good family into convents as it will find husbands for.* The French nobility, from the little I have been able to gather, seem to be divided on these matters.

The dinner, darling, was a first meeting between your sweetheart and the exile. The Comte de Maucombe's servants donned their old laced liveries and hats, the coachman his great top-boots; we sat five in the antiquated carriage, and arrived in state about two o'clock—the dinner was for three—at the grange, which is the dwelling of the Baron de l'Estorade.

My father-in-law to be has, you see, no castle, only a simple country house, standing beneath one of our hills, at the entrance of that noble valley, the pride of which is undoubtedly the Castle of Maucombe. The building is quite unpretentious: four pebble walls covered with a yellowish wash, and roofed with hollow tiles of a good red, constitute the grange. The rafters bend under the weight of this brick-kiln. The windows, inserted casually, without any attempt at symmetry, have enormous shutters, painted yellow. The garden in which it stands is a Provençal garden, enclosed by low walls, built of big round pebbles set in layers, alternately sloping or upright, according to the artistic taste of the mason, which finds here its only outlet. The mud in which they are set is falling away in places.

Thanks to an iron railing at the entrance facing the road, this simple farm has a certain air of being a country-seat. The railing, long sought with tears, is so emaciated that it recalled Sister Angélique to me. A flight of stone steps leads to the door, which is protected by a pent-house roof, such as no peasant on the Loire would tolerate for his coquettish white stone house, with its blue roof, glittering in the sun. The garden and surrounding walks are horribly dusty, and the trees seem burnt up. It is easy to see that for years the baron's life has been a mere rising up and going to bed again, day after day, without a thought beyond that of piling up coppers. He eats the same food as his two servants, a Provençal lad and the old woman who used to wait on his wife. The rooms are scantily furnished.

Nevertheless, the house of l'Estorade had done its best; the cupboards had been ransacked, and its last man beaten up for the dinner, which was served to us on old silver dishes, blackened and battered. The exile, my darling pet, is like the railing, emaciated! He is pale and silent, and bears traces of suffering. At thirty-seven he might be fifty. The once beautiful ebon locks of youth are streaked with white like a lark's wing. His fine blue eyes are cavernous; he is a little deaf, which suggests the Knight of the Sorrowful Countenance.*

Spite of all this, I have graciously consented to become Madame de l'Estorade and to receive a dowry of two hundred and fifty thousand livres, but only on the express condition of being allowed to work my will upon the grange and make a park there. I have demanded from my father, in set terms, a grant of water, which can be brought thither from Maucombe. In a month I shall be Madame de l'Estorade; for, dear, I have made a good impression. After the snows of Siberia a man is ready enough to see merit in those black eyes, which according to you, used to ripen fruit with a look. Louis de l'Estorade seems well content to marry the Renée de Maucombe—such is your friend's splendid title.

Whilst you are preparing to reap the joys of that many-sided existence which awaits a young lady of the Chaulieu family, and to queen it in Paris, your poor little sweetheart, Renée, that child of the desert, has fallen from the empyrean, whither together we had soared, into the vulgar realities of a life as homely as a daisy's. I have vowed to myself to comfort this young man, who has never known youth, but passed straight from his mother's arms to the embrace of war, and from the joys of his country home to the frosts and forced labor of Siberia.

Humble country pleasures will enliven the monotony of my future. It shall be my ambition to enlarge the oasis round my house, and to give it the lordly shade of fine trees. My turf, though Provençal, shall be always green. I shall carry my park up the hillside and plant on the highest point some pretty kiosque, whence, perhaps, my eyes may catch the shimmer of the Mediterranean. Orange and lemon trees, and all choicest things that grow, shall embellish my retreat; and there will I be a mother among my children. The poetry of Nature, which nothing can destroy, shall hedge us round; and standing loyally at the post of duty, we need fear no danger. My religious feelings are shared by my father-in-law and by the chevalier.

Ah! darling, my life unrolls itself before my eyes like one of the great highways of France, level and easy, shaded with evergreen trees. This century will not see another Bonaparte; and my children, if I have any, will not be rent from me. They will be mine to train and make men of—the joy of my life. If you also are true to your destiny, you who ought to find your mate amongst the great ones of the earth, the children of your Renée will not lack a zealous protectress.

Farewell, then, for me at least, to the romances and thrilling adventures in which we used ourselves to play the part of heroine. The whole story of my life lies before me now; its great crises will be the teething and nutrition of the young Masters de l'Estorade, and the mischief they do to my shrubs and me. To embroider their caps, to be loved and admired by a sickly man at the mouth of the Gémenos valley—there are my pleasures. Perhaps some day the country dame may go and spend a winter in Marseilles; but danger does not haunt the purlieus of a narrow provincial stage. There will be nothing to fear, not even an admiration such as could only make a woman proud. We shall take a great deal of interest in the silkworms for whose benefit our mulberry-leaves will be sold! We shall know the strange vicissitudes of life in Provence, and the storms that may attack even a peaceful household. Quarrels will be impossible, for Monsieur de l'Estorade has formally announced that he will leave the reins in his wife's hands; and as I shall do nothing to remind him of this wise resolve, it is likely he may persevere in it.

You, my dear Louise, will supply the romance of my life. So you must narrate to me in full all your adventures, describe your balls and parties, tell me what you wear, what flowers crown your lovely golden locks, and what are the words and manners of the men you meet. Your other self will be always there—listening, dancing, feeling her finger-tips pressed—with you. If only I could have some fun in Paris now and then, while you played the house-mother at La Crampade! such is the name of our grange. Poor Monsieur de l'Estorade, who fancies he is marrying one woman! Will he find out there are two?

I am writing nonsense now, and as henceforth I can only be foolish by proxy, I had better stop. One kiss, then, on each cheek—my lips are still virginal, he has only dared to take my hand. Oh! our deference and propriety are quite disquieting, I assure you. There, I am off again. Good-bye, dear.

P. S.—I have just opened your third letter. My dear, I have about one thousand livres to dispose of; spend them for me on pretty things, such as we can't find here, nor even at Marseilles. While speeding on your own business, give a thought to the recluse of La Crampade. Remember that on neither side have the heads of the family any people of taste in Paris to make their purchases. I shall reply to your letter later.

VI
DON FÉLIPE HÉNAREZ TO DON FERNAND

Paris, September

The address of this letter, my brother, will show you that the head of your house is out of reach of danger. If the massacre of our ancestors in the Court of Lions* made Spaniards and Christians of us against our will, it left us a legacy of Arab cunning; and it may be that I owe my safety to the blood of the Abencerrages* still flowing in my veins.

Fear made Ferdinand's acting so good, that Valdez

actually believed in his protestations.* But for me the poor Admiral would have been done for. Nothing, it seems, will teach the Liberals what a king is. This particular Bourbon has been long known to me; and the more His Majesty assured me of his protection, the stronger grew my suspicions. A true Spaniard has no need to repeat a promise. A flow of words is a sure sign of duplicity.

Valdez took ship on an English vessel. For myself, no sooner did I see the cause of my beloved Spain wrecked in Andalusia, than I wrote to the steward of my Sardinian estate to make arrangements for my escape. Some hardy coral fishers were despatched to wait for me at a point on the coast; and when Ferdinand urged the French to secure my person, I was already in my Barony of Macumer, amidst brigands who defy all law and all avengers.

The last Hispano-Moorish family of Granada has found once more the shelter of an African desert, and even a Saracen horse, in an estate which comes to it from Saracens. How the eyes of these brigands—who but yesterday had dreaded my authority—sparkled with savage joy and pride when they found they were protecting against the King of Spain's vendetta the Duc de Soria, their master and a Hénarez—the first who had come to visit them since the time when the island belonged to the Moors. More than a score of rifles were ready to point at Ferdinand of Bourbon, son of a race which was still unknown when the Abencerrages arrived as conquerors on the banks of the Loire.

My idea had been to live on the income of these huge estates, which, unfortunately, we have so greatly neglected; but my stay there convinced me that this was impossible, and that Queverdo's reports were only too correct. The poor man had twenty-two lives at my disposal, and not a single *réal*; prairies of twenty thousand acres, and not a house; virgin forests, and not a stick of furniture! A million *piastres* and a resident master for half a century would be necessary to make these magnificent lands pay. I must see to this.

The conquered have time during their flight to ponder their own case and that of their vanquished party. At the spectacle of my noble country, a corpse for monks to prey on, my eyes filled with tears; I read in it the presage of Spain's gloomy future.

At Marseilles I heard of Riego's end*. Painfully did it come home to me that my life also would henceforth be a martyrdom, but a martyrdom protracted and unnoticed. Is existence worthy the name, when a man can no longer die for his country or live for a woman? To love, to conquer, this twofold form of the same thought, is the law graven on our sabres, emblazoned on the vaulted roofs of our palaces, ceaselessly whispered by the water, which rises and falls in our marble fountains. But in vain does it nerve my heart; the sabre is broken, the palace in ashes, the living spring sucked up by the barren sand.

Here, then, is my last will and testament.

Don Fernand, you will understand now why I put a check upon your ardor and ordered you to remain faithful to the *rey netto*.* As your brother and friend, I implore you to obey me; as your master, I command. You will go to the king and will ask from him the grant of my dignities and property, my office and titles. He will perhaps hesitate, and may treat you to some regal scowls; but you must tell him that you are loved by Marie Hérédia, and that Marie can marry none but a Duc de Soria. This will make the king radiant. It is the immense fortune of the Hérédia family which alone has stood between him and the accomplishment of my ruin. Your proposal will seem to him, therefore, to deprive me of a last resource, and he will gladly hand over to you my spoils.

You will then marry Marie. The secret of the mutual

love against which you fought was no secret to me, and I have prepared the old comte to see you take my place. Marie and I were merely doing what was expected of us in our position and carrying out the wishes of our fathers; everything else is in your favor. You are beautiful as a child of love, and are possessed of Marie's heart. I am an ill-favored Spanish grandee, for whom she feels an aversion to which she will not confess. Some slight reluctance there may be on the part of the noble Spanish girl on account of my misfortunes, but this you will soon overcome.

Duc de Soria, your predecessor would neither cost you a regret nor rob you of a *maravedi*. My mother's diamonds, which will suffice to make me independent, I will keep, because the gap caused by them in the family estate can be filled by Marie's jewels. You can send them, therefore, by my nurse, old Urraca, the only one of my servants whom I wish to retain. No one can prepare my chocolate as she does.

During our brief revolution, my life of unremitting toil was reduced to the barest necessaries, and these my salary was sufficient to provide. You will therefore find the income of the last two years in the hands of your steward. This sum is mine; but a Duc de Soria cannot marry without a large expenditure of money, therefore we will divide it. You will not refuse this wedding-present from your brigand brother. Besides, I mean to have it so.

The Barony of Macumer, not being Spanish territory, remains to me. Thus I have still a country and a name, should I wish to take up a position in the world again.

Thank Heaven, this finishes our business, and the house of Soria is saved!

At the very moment when I drop into simple Baron de Macumer, the French cannon announce the arrival of the Duc d'Angoulême.* You will understand why I break off. . .

179

October

When I arrived here I had not ten doubloons in my pocket. He would indeed be a poor sort of leader who, in the midst of calamities he has not been able to avert, has found means to feather his own nest. For the vanquished Moor there remains a horse and the desert; for the Christian foiled of his hopes, the cloister and a few gold pieces.

But my present resignation is mere weariness. I am not yet so near the monastery as to have abandoned all thoughts of life. Ozalga had given me several letters of introduction to meet all emergencies, amongst these one to a bookseller, who takes with our fellow-countrymen the place which Galignani* holds with the English in Paris. This man has found eight pupils for me at three francs a lesson. I go to my pupils every alternate day, so that I have four lessons a day and earn twelve francs, which is more than I require. When Urraca comes I shall make some Spanish exile happy by passing on to him my connection.

I lodge in the Rue Hillerin-Bertin* with a poor widow, who takes boarders. My room faces south and looks out on a little garden. It is perfectly quiet; I have green trees to look upon, and spend the sum of one piastre a day. I am amazed at the amount of calm, pure pleasure which I enjoy in this life, after the fashion of Dionysius at Corinth.* From sunrise until ten o'clock I smoke and take my chocolate, sitting at my window and contemplating two Spanish plants, a broom which rises out of a clump of jessamine—gold on a white ground, colors which must send a thrill through any scion of the Moors. At ten o'clock I start for my lessons, which last till four, when I return for dinner. Afterwards I read and smoke till I go to bed.

I can put up for a long time with a life like this, compounded of work and meditation, of solitude and society. Be happy, therefore, Fernand; my abdication has brought no afterthoughts; I have no regrets like Charles V, no longing to try the game again like Napoleon.* Five days and nights have passed since I wrote my will; to my mind they might have been five centuries. Honor, titles, wealth, are for me as though they had never existed.

Now that the conventional barrier of respect which hedged me round has fallen, I can open my heart to you, dear boy. Though cased in the armor of gravity, this heart is full of tenderness and devotion, which have found no object, and which no woman has divined, not even she who, from her cradle, has been my destined bride. In this lies the secret of my political enthusiasm. Spain has taken the place of a mistress and received the homage of my heart. And now Spain, too, is gone! Beggared of all, I can gaze upon the ruin of what once was me and speculate over the mysteries of my being.

Why did life animate this carcass, and when will it depart? Why has that race, pre-eminent in chivalry, breathed all its primitive virtues—its tropical love, its fiery poetry—into this its last offshoot, if the seed was never to burst its rugged shell, if no stem was to spring forth, no radiant flower scatter aloft its Eastern perfumes? Of what crime have I been guilty before my birth that I can inspire no love? Did fate from my very infancy decree that I should be stranded, a useless hulk, on some barren shore! I find in my soul the image of the deserts where my fathers ranged, illumined by a scorching sun which shrivels up all life. Proud remnant of a fallen race, vain force, love run to waste, an old man in the prime of youth, here better than elsewhere shall I await the last grace of death. Alas! under this murky sky no spark will kindle these ashes again to flame. Thus my last words may be those of Christ, God, Thou hast forsaken me! Cry of agony and terror, to the core of which no mortal has ventured yet to penetrate!

You can realize now, Fernand, what a joy it is to me to

181

live afresh in you and Marie. I shall watch you henceforth with the pride of a creator satisfied in his work.
Love each other well and go on loving if you would not
give me pain; any discord between you would hurt me
more than it would yourselves.

Our mother had a presentiment that events would
one day serve her wishes. It may be that the longing of a
mother constitutes a pact between herself and God. Was
she not, moreover, one of those mysterious beings who
can hold converse with Heaven and bring back thence
a vision of the future? How often have I not read in the
lines of her forehead that she was coveting for Fernand
the honors and the wealth of Félipe! When I said so to
her, she would reply with tears, laying bare the wounds
of a heart, which of right was the undivided property
of both her sons, but which an irresistible passion gave
to you alone.

Her spirit, therefore, will hover joyfully above your
heads as you bow them at the altar. My mother, have
you not a caress for your Félipe now that he has yielded to your favorite even the girl whom you regretfully
thrust into his arms? What I have done is pleasing to
our womankind, to the dead, and to the king; it is the
will of God. Make no difficulty then, Fernand; obey,
and be silent.

P. S. Tell Urraca to be sure and call me nothing but
Monsieur Hénarez. Don't say a word about me to Marie.
You must be the one living soul to know the secrets of
the last Christianized Moor, in whose veins runs the
blood of a great family, which took its rise in the desert
and is now about to die out in the person of a solitary
exile. Farewell.

VII
LOUISE DE CHAULIEU TO RENÉE DE MAUCOMBE

What! To be married so soon. But this is unheard of. At the end of a month you become engaged to a man who is a stranger to you, and about whom you know nothing. The man may be deaf—there are so many kinds of deafness!—he may be sickly, tiresome, insufferable!

Don't you see, Renée, what they want with you? You are needful for carrying on the glorious stock of the l'Estorades, that is all. You will be buried in the provinces. Are these the promises we made each other? Were I you, I would sooner set off to the Hyères islands in a caique, on the chance of being captured by an Algerian corsair and sold to the Grand Turk. Then I should be a Sultana some day, and wouldn't I make a stir in the harem while I was young—yes, and afterwards too!

You are leaving one convent to enter another. I know you; you are a coward, and you will submit to the yoke of family life with a lamblike docility. But I am here to direct you; you must come to Paris. There we shall drive the men wild and hold a court like queens. Your husband, sweetheart, in three years from now may become a member of the Chamber. I know all about members now, and I will explain it to you. You will work that machine very well; you can live in Paris, and become there what my mother calls a woman of fashion. Oh! you needn't suppose I will leave you in your grange!

Monday

For a whole fortnight now, my dear, I have been living the life of society; one evening at the Italiens, another at the Grand Opera,* and always a ball afterwards. Ah! society is a witching world. The music of the Opera enchants me; and whilst my soul is plunged in divine pleasure, I am the centre of admiration and the focus of all the opera-glasses. But a single glance will make the boldest youth drop his eyes.

I have seen some charming young men there; all the same, I don't care for any of them; not one has roused in me the emotion which I feel when I listen to Garcia in his splendid duet with Pellegrini in *Otello*. Heavens! how jealous Rossini must have been to express jealousy so well! What a cry in "*Il mio cor si divide!*"* I'm speaking Greek to you, for you never heard Garcia, but then you know how jealous I am!

What a wretched dramatist Shakespeare is! Othello is in love with glory; he wins battles, he gives orders, he struts about and is all over the place while Desdemona sits at home; and Desdemona, who sees herself neglected for the silly fuss of public life, is quite meek all the time. Such a sheep deserves to be slaughtered. Let the man whom I deign to love beware how he thinks of anything but loving me!

For my part, I like those long trials of the old-fashioned chivalry. That lout of a young lord, who took offence because his sovereign-lady sent him down among the lions to fetch her glove, was, in my opinion, very impertinent, and a fool too. Doubtless the lady had in reserve for him some exquisite flower of love, which he lost, as he well deserved—the puppy!

But here am I running on as though I had not a great piece of news to tell you. My father is certainly going to represent our master the King at Madrid. I say *our* master, for I shall make part of the embassy. My mother wishes to remain here, and my father will take me so as to have some woman with him.

My dear, this seems to you, no doubt, very simple, but there are horrors behind it, all the same: in a fortnight I have probed the secrets of the house. My mother would accompany my father to Madrid if he would take Monsieur de Canalis as a secretary to the embassy. But the king appoints the secretaries; the duc dare neither annoy the king, who hates to be opposed, nor vex my mother; and the wily diplomat believes he has cut the knot by leaving the duchesse here. Monsieur de Canalis, who is the great poet of the day, is the young man who cultivates my mother's society, and who no doubt studies diplomacy with her from three o'clock to five. Diplomacy must be a fine subject, for he is as regular as a gambler on the Stock Exchange.

The Duc de Rhétoré, our elder brother, solemn, cold, and whimsical, would be extinguished by his father at Madrid, therefore he remains in Paris. Miss Griffith has found out also that Alphonse is in love with a ballet-girl at the Opera. How is it possible to fall in love with legs and pirouettes? We have noticed that my brother comes to the theatre only when Tullia dances there; he applauds the steps of this creature, and then goes out. Two ballet-girls in a family are, I fancy, more destructive than the plague. My second brother is with his regiment, and I have not yet seen him. Thus it comes about that I have to act as the Antigone of His Majesty's ambassador. Perhaps I may get married in Spain, and perhaps my father's idea is a marriage there without dowry, after the pattern of yours with this broken-down guard of honor. My father asked if I would go with him, and offered me the use of his Spanish master.

"Spain, the country for castles in the air!" I cried. "Perhaps you hope that it may mean marriages for me!"

For sole reply he honored me with a meaning look. For some days he has amused himself with teasing me at lunch; he watches me, and I dissemble. In this way I have played with him cruelly as father and ambassador *in petto*. Hadn't he taken me for a fool? He asked me what I thought of this and that young man, and of some girls whom I had met in several houses. I replied with quite inane remarks on the color of their hair, their faces, and the difference in their figures. My father seemed disappointed at my crassness, and inwardly blamed himself for having asked me.

"Still, father," I added, "don't suppose I am saying what I really think: mother made me afraid the other day that I had spoken more frankly than I ought of my impressions."

"With your family you can speak quite freely," my mother replied.

"Very well, then," I went on. "The young men I have met so far strike me as too self-centered to excite interest in others; they are much more taken up with themselves than with their company. They can't be accused of lack of candor at any rate. They put on a certain expression to talk to us, and drop it again in a moment, apparently satisfied that we don't use our eyes. The man as he converses is the lover; silent, he is the husband. The girls, again, are so artificial that it is impossible to know what they really are, except from the way they dance; their figures and movements alone are not a sham. But what has alarmed me most in this fashionable society is its brutality. The little incidents which take place when supper is announced give one some idea—to compare small things with great—of what a popular rising might be. Courtesy is only a thin veneer on the general selfishness. I imagined society very different. Women count for little in it; that may perhaps be a survival of Bonapartist ideas."

"Armande is coming on extraordinarily," said my mother.

"Mother, did you think I should never get beyond asking to see Madame de Staël?"

My father smiled, and rose from the table.

Saturday

My dear, I have left one thing out. Here is the tidbit I have reserved for you. The love which we pictured must be extremely well hidden; I have seen not a trace of it.

True, I have caught in drawing-rooms now and again a quick exchange of glances, but how colorless it all is! Love, as we imagined it, a world of wonders, of glorious dreams, of charming realities, of sorrows that waken sympathy, and smiles that make sunshine, does not exist. The bewitching words, the constant interchange of happiness, the misery of absence, the flood of joy at the presence of the beloved one—where are they? What soil produces these radiant flowers of the soul? Which is wrong? We or the world?

I have already seen hundreds of men, young and middle-aged; not one has stirred the least feeling in me. No proof of admiration and devotion on their part, not even a sword drawn in my behalf, would have moved me. Love, dear, is the product of such rare conditions that it is quite possible to live a lifetime without coming across the being on whom nature has bestowed the power of making one's happiness. The thought is enough to make one shudder; for if this being is found too late, what then?

For some days I have begun to tremble when I think of the destiny of women, and to understand why so many wear a sad face beneath the flush brought by the unnatural excitement of social dissipation. Marriage is a mere matter of chance. Look at yours. A storm of wild thoughts has passed over my mind. To be loved every day the same, yet with a difference, to be loved as much after ten years of happiness as on the first day!—such a love demands years. The lover must be allowed to languish, curiosity must be piqued and satisfied, feeling roused and responded to.

Is there, then, a law for the inner fruits of the heart, as there is for the visible fruits of nature? Can joy be made lasting? In what proportion should love mingle tears with pleasures? The cold policy of the funereal, monotonous, persistent routine of the convent seemed to me at these moments the only real life; while the wealth, the splendor, the tears, the delights, the triumph, the joy, the satisfaction, of a love equal, shared, and sanctioned, appeared a mere idle vision.

I see no room in this city for the gentle ways of love, for precious walks in shady alleys, the full moon sparkling on the water, while the suppliant pleads in vain. Rich, young, and beautiful, I have only to love, and love would become my sole occupation, my life; yet in the three months during which I have come and gone, eager and curious, nothing has appealed to me in the bright, covetous, keen eyes around me. No voice has thrilled me, no glance has made the world seem brighter.

Music alone has filled my soul, music alone has at all taken the place of our friendship. Sometimes, at night, I will linger for an hour by my window, gazing into the garden, summoning the future, with all it brings, out of the mystery which shrouds it. There are days too when, having started for a drive, I get out and walk in the Champs-Élysées, and picture to myself that the man who is to waken my slumbering soul is at hand, that he will follow and look at me. Then I meet only mountebanks, vendors of gingerbread, jugglers, passers-by hurrying to their business, or lovers who try to escape notice. These I am tempted to stop, asking them, "You who are happy, tell me what is love."

But the impulse is repressed, and I return to my carriage, swearing to die an old maid. Love is undoubtedly an incarnation, and how many conditions are needful before it can take place! We are not certain of never quarreling with ourselves, how much less so when there are two? This is a problem which God alone can solve.

I begin to think that I shall return to the convent. If I remain in society, I shall do things which will look like follies, for I cannot possibly reconcile myself to what I see. I am perpetually wounded either in my sense of delicacy, my inner principles, or my secret thoughts.

Ah! my mother is the happiest of women, adored as

she is by Canalis, her great little man. My love, do you know I am seized sometimes with a horrible craving to know what goes on between my mother and that young man? Griffith tells me she has gone through all these moods; she has longed to fly at women, whose happiness was written in their face; she has blackened their character, torn them to pieces. According to her, virtue consists in burying all these savage instincts in one's innermost heart. But what then of the heart? It becomes the sink of all that is worst in us.

It is very humiliating that no adorer has yet turned up for me. I am a marriageable girl, but I have brothers, a family, relations, who are sensitive on the point of honor. Ah! if that is what keeps men back, they are poltroons.

The part of Chimène in the *Cid* and that of the Cid* delight me. What a marvelous play! Well, good-bye.

VIII

THE SAME TO THE SAME

January

Our master is a poor refugee, forced to keep in hiding on account of the part he played in the revolution which the Duc d'Angoulême has just quelled—a triumph to which we owe some splendid fêtes. Though a Liberal, and doubtless a man of the people, he has awakened my interest: I fancy that he must have been condemned to death. I make him talk for the purpose of getting at his secret; but he is of a truly Castilian taciturnity, proud as though he were Gonsalvo di Cordova,* and nevertheless angelic in his patience and gentleness. His pride is not irritable like Miss Griffith's, it belongs to his inner nature; he forces us to civility because his own manners are so perfect, and holds us at a distance by the respect he shows us. My father declares that there is a great deal of the nobleman in Señor Hénarez, whom, among ourselves, he calls in fun Don Hénarez.

A few days ago I took the liberty of addressing him thus. He raised his eyes, which are generally bent on the ground, and flashed a look from them that quite abashed me; my dear, he certainly has the most beautiful eyes imaginable. I asked him if I had offended him in any way, and he said to me in his grand, rolling Spanish:

"I am here only to teach you Spanish."

I blushed and felt quite snubbed. I was on the point of making some pert answer, when I remembered what our dear mother in God used to say to us, and I replied instead:

"It would be a kindness to tell me if you have anything to complain of."

A tremor passed through him, the blood rose in his olive cheeks; he replied in a voice of some emotion:

"Religion must have taught you, better than I can, to respect the unhappy. Had I been a *don* in Spain, and lost everything in the triumph of Ferdinand VII, your witticism would be unkind; but if I am only a poor teacher of languages, is it not a heartless satire? Neither is worthy of a young lady of rank."

I took his hand, saying:

"In the name of religion also, I beg you to pardon me."

He bowed, opened my Quixote, and sat down.

This little incident disturbed me more than the harvest of compliments, gazing and pretty speeches on my most successful evening. During the lesson I watched him attentively, which I could do the more safely, as he never looks at me.

As the result of my observations, I made out that the tutor, whom we took to be forty, is a young man, some years under thirty. My governess, to whom I had handed him over, remarked on the beauty of his black hair and of his pearly teeth. As to his eyes, they are velvet and fire; but he is plain and insignificant. Though the Spaniards have been described as not a cleanly people, this man is most carefully got up, and his hands are whiter than his face. He stoops a little, and has an extremely large, oddly-shaped head. His ugliness, which, however, has a dash of piquancy, is aggravated by smallpox marks, which seam his face. His forehead is very prominent, and the shaggy eyebrows meet, giving a repellent air of harshness. There is a frowning, plaintive look on his face, reminding one of a sickly child, which owes its life to superhuman care, as Sister Marthé did. As my father observed, his features are a shrunken reproduction of those of Cardinal Ximenes. The natural dignity of our tutor's manners seems to disconcert the dear duc, who doesn't like him, and is never at ease with him; he can't bear to come in contact with superiority of any kind.

As soon as my father knows enough Spanish, we start for Madrid. When Hénarez returned, two days after the reproof he had given me, I remarked by way of showing my gratitude:

"I have no doubt that you left Spain in consequence of political events. If my father is sent there, as seems to be expected, we shall be in a position to help you, and might be able to obtain your pardon, in case you are under sentence."

"It is impossible for any one to help me," he replied.

"But," I said, "is that because you refuse to accept any help, or because the thing itself is impossible?"

"Both," he said, with a bow, and in a tone which forbade continuing the subject.

My father's blood chafed in my veins. I was offended by this haughty demeanor, and promptly dropped Señor Hénarez.

All the same, my dear, there is something fine in this rejection of any aid. "He would not accept even our friendship," I reflected, whilst conjugating a verb.

Suddenly I stopped short and told him what was in my mind, but in Spanish. Hénarez replied very politely that equality of sentiment was necessary between friends, which did not exist in this case, and therefore it was useless to consider the question.

"Do you mean equality in the amount of feeling on either side, or equality in rank?" I persisted, determined to shake him out of this provoking gravity.

He raised once more those awe-inspiring eyes, and mine fell before them. Dear, this man is a hopeless enigma. He seemed to ask whether my words meant love; and the mixture of joy, pride, and agonized doubt in his glance went to my heart. It was plain that advances, which would be taken for what they were worth in France, might land me in difficulties with a Spaniard, and I drew back into my shell, feeling not a little foolish.

The lesson over, he bowed, and his eyes were eloquent of the humble prayer: "Don't trifle with a poor wretch."

This sudden contrast to his usual grave and dignified manner made a great impression on me. It seems horrible to think and to say, but I can't help believing that there are treasures of affection in that man.

IX

MADAME DE L'ESTORADE TO MADEMOISELLE DE CHAULIEU

December

All is over, my dear child, and it is Madame de l'Estorade who writes to you. But between us there is no change; it is only a girl the less.

Don't be troubled; I did not give my consent recklessly or without much thought. My life is henceforth mapped out for me, and the freedom from all uncertainty as to the road for me to follow suits my mind and disposition. A great moral power has stepped in, and once for all swept what we call chance out of my life. We have the property to develop, our home to beautify and adorn; for me there is also a household to direct and sweeten and a husband to reconcile to life. In all probability I shall have a family to look after, children to educate.

What would you have? Everyday life cannot be cast in heroic mould. No doubt there seems, at any rate at first sight, no room left in this scheme of life for that longing after the infinite which expands the mind and soul. But what is there to prevent me from launching on that boundless sea our familiar craft? Nor must you suppose that the humble duties to which I dedicate my life give no scope for passion. To restore faith in happiness to an unfortunate, who has been the sport of adverse circumstances, is a noble work, and one which alone may suffice to relieve the monotony of my existence. I can see no opening left for suffering, and I see a great deal of good to be done. I need not hide from you that the love I have for Louis de l'Estorade is not of the kind which makes the heart throb at the sound of a step, and thrills us at the lightest tones of a voice, or the caress of a burning glance; but, on the other hand, there is nothing in him which offends me.

What am I to do, you will ask, with that instinct for all which is great and noble, with those mental energies, which have made the link between us, and which we still possess? I admit that this thought has troubled me. But are these faculties less ours because we keep them concealed, using them only in secret for the welfare of the family, as instruments to produce the happiness of those confided to our care, to whom we are bound to give ourselves without reserve? The time during which a woman can look for admiration is short, it will soon be past; and if my life has not been a great one, it will at least have been calm, tranquil, free from shocks.

Nature has favored our sex in giving us a choice

between love and motherhood. I have made mine. My children shall be my gods, and this spot of earth my Eldorado.

I can say no more to-day. Thank you much for all the things you have sent me. Give a glance at my needs on the enclosed list. I am determined to live in an atmosphere of refinement and luxury, and to take from provincial life only what makes its charm. In solitude a woman can never be vulgarized—she remains herself. I count greatly on your kindness for keeping me up to the fashion. My father-in-law is so delighted that he can refuse me nothing, and turns his house upside down. We are getting workpeople from Paris and renovating everything.

X

MADEMOISELLE DE CHAULIEU TO MADAME DE L'ESTORADE

January

Oh! Renée, you have made me miserable for days! So that bewitching body, those beautiful proud features, that natural grace of manner, that soul full of priceless gifts, those eyes, where the soul can slake its thirst as at a fountain of love, that heart, with its exquisite delicacy, that breadth of mind, those rare powers—fruit of nature and of our interchange of thought—treasures whence should issue a unique satisfaction for passion and desire, hours of poetry to outweigh years, joys to make a man serve a lifetime for one gracious gesture,—all this is to be buried in the tedium of a tame, commonplace marriage, to vanish in the emptiness of an existence which you will come to loath! I hate your children before they are born. They will be monsters!

So you know all that lies before you; you have nothing left to hope, or fear, or suffer? And supposing the glorious morning rises which will bring you face to face with the man destined to rouse you from the sleep into which you are plunging! . . . Ah! a cold shiver goes through me at the thought!

Well, at least you have a friend. You, it is understood, are to be the guardian angel of your valley. You will grow familiar with its beauties, will live with it in all its aspects, till the grandeur of nature, the slow growth of vegetation, compared with the lightning rapidity of thought, become like a part of yourself; and as your eye rests on the laughing flowers, you will question your own heart. When you walk between your husband, silent and contented, in front, and your children screaming and romping behind, I can tell you beforehand what you will write to me. Your misty valley, your hills, bare or clothed with magnificent trees, your meadow, the wonder of Provence, with its fresh water dispersed in little runlets, the different effects of the atmosphere, this whole world of infinity which laps you round, and which God has made so various, will recall to you the infinite sameness of your soul's life. But at least I shall be there, my Renée, and in me you will find a heart which no social pettiness shall ever corrupt, a heart all your own.

Monday

My dear, my Spaniard is quite adorably melancholy; there is something calm, severe, manly, and mysterious about him which interests me profoundly. His unvarying solemnity and the silence which envelops him act like an irritant on the mind. His mute dignity is worthy of a fallen king. Griffith and I spend our time over him as though he were a riddle.

How odd it is! A language-master captures my fancy as no other man has done. Yet by this time I have passed in review all the young men of family, the attachés to embassies, and the ambassadors, generals, and inferior officers, the peers of France, their sons and nephews, the court, and the town.

The coldness of the man provokes me. The sandy waste which he tries to place, and does place, between us is covered by his deep-rooted pride; he wraps himself in mystery. The hanging back is on his side, the boldness on mine. This odd situation affords me the more amusement because the whole thing is mere trifling. What is a man, a Spaniard, and a teacher of languages to me? I make no account of any man whatever, were he a king. We are worth far more, I am sure, than the greatest of them. What a slave I would have made of Napoleon! If he had loved me, shouldn't he have felt the whip!

Yesterday I aimed a shaft at Monsieur Hénarez which must have touched him to the quick. He made no reply; the lesson was over, and he bowed with a glance at me, in which I read that he would never return. This suits me capitally; there would be something ominous in starting an imitation *Nouvelle Héloïse*.* I have just been reading Rousseau's, and it has left me with a strong distaste for love. Passion which can argue and moralize seems to me detestable.

Clarissa also is much too pleased with herself and her long, little letter; but Richardson's work is an admirable picture, my father tells me, of English women.* Rousseau's seems to me a sort of philosophical sermon, cast in the form of letters.

Love, as I conceive it, is a purely subjective poem. In all that books tell us about it, there is nothing which is not at once false and true. And so, my pretty one, as you will henceforth be an authority only on conjugal love, it seems to me my duty—in the interest, of course, of our common life—to remain unmarried, and have a grand passion, so that we may enlarge our experience.

Tell me every detail of what happens to you, especially in the first few days, with that strange animal called a husband. I promise to do the same for you if ever I am loved. Farewell, poor martyred darling.

XI

MADAME DE L'ESTORADE TO MADEMOISELLE DE CHAULIEU

La Crampade

You and your Spaniard make me shudder, my darling. I write this line to beg of you to dismiss him. All that you say of him corresponds with the character of those dangerous adventurers who, having nothing to lose, will take any risk. This man cannot be your husband, and must not be your lover. I will write to you more fully about the inner history of my married life when my heart is free from the anxiety your last letter has roused in it.

XII

MADEMOISELLE DE CHAULIEU TO MADAME DE L'ESTORADE

February

At nine o'clock this morning, sweetheart, my father was announced in my rooms. I was up and dressed. I found him solemnly seated beside the fire in the drawing-room, looking more thoughtful than usual. He pointed to the armchair opposite to him. Divining his meaning, I sank into it with a gravity, which so well aped his, that he could not refrain from smiling, though the smile was dashed with melancholy.

"You are quite a match for your grandmother in quick-wittedness," he said.

"Come, father, don't play the courtier here," I replied; "you want something from me."

He rose, visibly agitated, and talked to me for half an hour. This conversation, dear, really ought to be preserved. As soon as he had gone, I sat down to my table and tried to recall his words. This is the first time that I have seen my father revealing his inner thoughts.

He began by flattering me, and he did not do it badly. I was bound to be grateful to him for having understood and appreciated me.

"Armande," he said, "I was quite mistaken in you, and you have agreeably surprised me. When you arrived from the convent, I took you for an average young girl, ignorant and not particularly intelligent, easily to be bought off with gewgaws and ornaments, and with little turn for reflection."

"You are complimentary to young girls, father."

"Oh! there is no such thing as youth nowadays," he said, with the air of a diplomat. "Your mind is amazingly open. You take everything at its proper worth; your clear-sightedness is extraordinary, there is no hoodwinking you. You pass for being blind, and all the time you have laid your hand on causes, while other people are still puzzling over effects. In short, you are a minister in petticoats, the only person here capable of understanding me. It follows, then, that if I have any sacrifice to ask from you, it is only to yourself I can turn for help in persuading you.

"I am therefore going to explain to you, quite frankly, my former plans, to which I still adhere. In order to recommend them to you, I must show that they are connected with feelings of a very high order, and I shall thus be obliged to enter into political questions of the greatest importance to the kingdom, which might be wearisome to any one less intelligent than you are. When you have heard me, I hope you will take time for consideration, six months if necessary. You are entirely your own mistress; and if you decline to make the sacrifice I ask, I shall bow to your decision and trouble you no further."

This preface, my sweetheart, made me really serious, and I said:

"Speak, father."

Here, then, is the deliverance of the statesman:

"My child, France is in a very critical position, which is understood only by the king and a few superior minds. But the king is a head without arms; the great nobles, who are in the secret of the danger, have no authority over the men whose co-operation is needful in order to bring about a happy result. These men, cast up by popular election, refuse to lend themselves as instruments. Even the able men among them carry on the work of pulling down society, instead of helping us to strengthen the edifice.

"In a word, there are only two parties—the party of Marius and the party of Sulla.* I am for Sulla against Marius. This, roughly speaking, is our position. To go more into details: the Revolution is still active; it is embedded in the law and written on the soil; it fills people's minds. The danger is all the greater because the greater number of the king's counselors, seeing it destitute of armed forces and of money, believe it completely vanquished. The king is an able man, and not easily blinded; but from day to day he is won over by his brother's partisans, who want to hurry things on. He has not two years to live, and thinks more of a peaceful deathbed than of anything else.

"Shall I tell you, my child, which is the most destructive of all the consequences entailed by the Revolution? You would never guess. In Louis XVI the Revolution has decapitated every head of a family. The family has ceased to exist; we have only individuals. In their desire to become a nation, Frenchmen have abandoned the idea of empire; in proclaiming the equal rights of all children to their father's inheritance, they have killed the family spirit and created the State treasury. But all this has paved the way for weakened authority, for the blind force of the masses, for the decay of art and the supremacy of individual interests, and has left the road open to the foreign invader.

"We stand between two policies—either to found the State on the basis of the family, or to rest it on individual interest—in other words, between democracy and aristocracy, between free discussion and obedience, between Catholicism and religious indifference. I am among the few who are resolved to oppose what is called the people, and that in the people's true interest. It is not now a question of feudal rights, as fools are told, nor of rank; it is a question of the State and of the existence of France. The country which does not rest on the foundation of paternal authority cannot be stable. That is the foot of the ladder of responsibility and subordination, which has for its summit the king.

"The king stands for us all. To die for the king is to die for oneself, for one's family, which, like the kingdom, cannot die. All animals have certain instincts; the instinct of man is for family life. A country is strong which consists of wealthy families, every member of whom is interested in defending a common treasure; it is weak when composed of scattered individuals, to whom it matters little whether they obey seven or one, a Russian or a Corsican, so long as each keeps his own plot of land, blind, in their wretched egotism, to the fact that the day is coming when this too will be torn from them.

"Terrible calamities are in store for us, in case our party fails. Nothing will be left but penal or fiscal laws—your money or your life. The most generous nation on the earth will have ceased to obey the call of noble instincts. Wounds past curing will have been fostered and aggravated, an all pervading jealousy being the first. Then the upper classes will be submerged; equality of desire will be taken for equality of strength; true distinction, even when proved and recognized, will be threatened by the advancing tide of middle-class prejudice. It was possible to choose one man out of a thousand, but, amongst three millions, discrimination becomes impossible, when all are moved by the same ambitions and attired in the same livery of mediocrity. No foresight will warn this victorious horde of that other terrible horde, soon to be arrayed against them in the peasant proprietors; in other words, twenty million acres of land, alive, stirring, arguing, deaf to reason, insatiable of appetite, obstructing progress, masters in their brute force— —"

"But," said I, interrupting my father, "what can I do to help the State. I feel no vocation for playing Joan of Arc in the interests of the family, or for finding a martyr's block in the convent."

"You are a little hussy," cried my father. "If I speak sensibly to you, you are full of jokes; when I jest, you talk like an ambassadress."

"Love lives on contrasts," was my reply.

And he laughed till the tears stood in his eyes.

"You will reflect on what I have told you; you will do justice to the large and confiding spirit in which I have broached the matter, and possibly events may assist my plans. I know that, so far as you are concerned, they are injurious and unfair, and this is the reason why I appeal for your sanction of them less to your heart and your imagination than to your reason. I have found more judgment and commonsense in you than in any one I know— —"

"You flatter yourself," I said, with a smile, "for I am every inch your child!"

"In short," he went on, "one must be logical. You can't have the end without the means, and it is our duty to set an example to others. From all this I deduce that you ought not to have money of your own till your younger brother is provided for, and I want to employ the whole of your inheritance in purchasing an estate for him to go with the title."

"But," I said, "you won't interfere with my living in my own fashion and enjoying life if I leave you my fortune?"

"Provided," he replied, "that your view of life does not conflict with the family honor, reputation, and, I may add, glory."

"Come, come," I cried, "what has become of my excellent judgment?"

"There is not in all France," he said with bitterness, "a man who would take for wife a daughter of one of our noblest families without a dowry and bestow one on her. If such a husband could be found, it would be among the class of rich *parvenus*; on this point I belong to the eleventh century."

"And I also," I said. "But why despair? Are there no aged peers?"

"You are an apt scholar, Louise!" he exclaimed.

Then he left me, smiling and kissing my hand.

I received your letter this very morning, and it led me to contemplate that abyss into which you say that I may fall. A voice within seemed to utter the same warning. So I took my precautions. Hénarez, my dear, dares to look at me, and his eyes are disquieting. They inspire me with what I can only call an unreasoning dread. Such a man ought no more to be looked at than a frog; he is ugly and fascinating.

For two days I have been hesitating whether to tell my father point-blank that I want no more Spanish lessons and have Hénarez sent about his business. But in spite of all my brave resolutions, I feel that the horrible sensation which comes over me when I see that man has become necessary to me. I say to myself, "Once more, and then I will speak."

His voice, my dear, is sweetly thrilling; his speaking is just like la Fodor's singing. His manners are simple, entirely free from affectation. And what teeth!

Just now, as he was leaving, he seemed to divine the interest I take in him, and made a gesture—oh! most respectfully—as though to take my hand and kiss it; then checked himself, apparently terrified at his own boldness and the chasm he had been on the point of bridging. There was the merest suggestion of all this, but I understood it and smiled, for nothing is more pathetic than to see the frank impulse of an inferior checking itself abashed. The love of a plebeian for a girl of noble birth implies such courage!

My smile emboldened him. The poor fellow looked blindly about for his hat; he seemed determined not to find it, and I handed it to him with perfect gravity. His eyes were wet with unshed tears. It was a mere passing moment, yet a world of facts and ideas were contained in it. We understood each other so well that, on a sudden, I held out my hand for him to kiss.

Possibly this was equivalent to telling him that love might bridge the interval between us. Well, I cannot tell what moved me to do it. Griffith had her back turned as I proudly extended my little white paw. I felt the fire of his lips, tempered by two big tears. Oh! my love, I lay in my armchair, nerveless, dreamy. I was happy, and I cannot explain to you how or why. What I felt only a poet could express. My condescension, which fills me with shame now, seemed to me then something to be proud of; he had fascinated me, that is my one excuse.

Friday

This man is really very handsome. He talks admirably, and has remarkable intellectual power. My dear, he is a very Bossuet in force and persuasiveness when he explains the mechanism, not only of the Spanish tongue, but also of human thought and of all language. His mother tongue seems to be French. When I expressed surprise at this, he replied that he came to France when quite a boy, following the King of Spain to Valençay.*

What has passed within this enigmatic being? He is no longer the same man. He came, dressed quite simply, but just as any gentleman would for a morning walk. He put forth all his eloquence, and flashed wit, like rays from a beacon, all through the lesson. Like a man roused from lethargy, he revealed to me a new world of thoughts. He told me the story of some poor devil of a valet who gave up his life for a single glance from a queen of Spain.

"What could he do but die?" I exclaimed.

This delighted him, and he looked at me in a way which was truly alarming.

In the evening I went to a ball at the Duchesse de Lenoncourt's. The Prince de Talleyrand happened to be there; and I got Monsieur de Vandenesse, a charming young man, to ask him whether, among the guests at his country-place in 1809, he remembered any one of the name of Hénarez. Vandenesse reported the prince's reply, word for word, as follows:

"Hénarez is the Moorish name of the Soria family, who are, they say, descendants of the Abencerrages, converted to Christianity. The old duc and his two sons were with the king. The eldest, the present Duc de Soria, has just had all his property, titles, and dignities confiscated by King Ferdinand, who in this way avenges a long-standing feud. The duc made a huge mistake in consenting to form a constitutional ministry with Valdez. Happily, he escaped from Cadiz before the arrival of the Duc d'Angoulême, who, with the best will in the world, could not have saved him from the king's wrath."

This information gave me much food for reflection. I cannot describe to you the suspense in which I passed the time till my next lesson, which took place this morning.

During the first quarter of an hour I examined him closely, debating inwardly whether he were duke or commoner, without being able to come to any conclusion. He seemed to read my fancies as they arose and to take pleasure in thwarting them. At last I could endure it no longer. Putting down my book suddenly, I broke off the translation I was making of it aloud, and said to him in Spanish:

"You are deceiving us. You are no poor middle-class Liberal. You are the Duc de Soria!"

"Mademoiselle," he replied, with a gesture of sorrow, "unhappily, I am not the Duc de Soria."

I felt all the despair with which he uttered the word "unhappily." Ah! my dear, never should I have conceived it possible to throw so much meaning and passion into a single word. His eyes had dropped, and he dared no longer look at me.

"Monsieur de Talleyrand," I said, "in whose house you spent your years of exile, declares that any one bearing the name of Hénarez must either be the late Duc de Soria or a lacquey."

He looked at me with eyes like two black burning coals, at once blazing and ashamed. The man might have been in the torture-chamber. All he said was:

"My father was in truth the servant of the King of Spain."

Griffith could make nothing of this sort of lesson. An awkward silence followed each question and answer.

"In one word," I said, "are you a nobleman or not?"

"You know that in Spain even beggars are noble."

This reticence provoked me. Since the last lesson I had given play to my imagination in a little practical joke. I had drawn an ideal portrait of the man whom I should wish for my lover in a letter which I designed giving to him to translate. So far, I had only put Spanish into French, not French into Spanish; I pointed this out to him, and begged Griffith to bring me the last letter I had received from a friend of mine.

"I shall find out," I thought, from the effect my sketch has on him, "what sort of blood runs in his veins."

I took the paper from Griffith's hands, saying:

"Let me see if I have copied it rightly."

For it was all in my writing. I handed him the paper, or, if you will, the snare, and I watched him while he read as follows:

He who is to win my heart, my dear, must be harsh and unbending with men, but gentle with women. His eagle eye must have power to quell with a single glance the least approach to ridicule. He will have a pitying smile for those who would jeer at sacred things, above all, at that poetry of the heart, without which life would be but a dreary commonplace. I have the greatest scorn for those who would rob us of the living fountain of religious beliefs, so rich in solace. His faith, therefore, should have the simplicity of a child, though united to the firm conviction of an intelligent man, who has examined the foundations of his creed. His fresh and original way of looking at things must be entirely free from affectation or desire to show off. His words will be few and fit, and his mind so richly stored, that he cannot possibly become a bore to himself any more than to others.

All his thoughts must have a high and chivalrous character, without alloy of self-seeking; while his actions should be marked by a total absence of interested or sordid motives. Any weak points he may have will arise from the very elevation of his views above those of the common herd, for in every respect I would have him superior to his age. Ever mindful of the delicate attentions due to the weak, he will be gentle to all women, but not prone lightly to fall in love with any; for love will seem to him too serious to turn into a game.

Thus it might happen that he would spend his life in ignorance of true love, while all the time possessing those qualities most fitted to inspire it. But if ever he find the ideal woman who has haunted his waking dreams, if he meet with a nature capable of understanding his own, one who could fill his soul and pour sunlight over his life, could shine as a star through the mists of this chill and gloomy world, lend fresh charm to existence, and draw music from the hitherto silent chords of his being—needless to say, he would recognize and welcome his good fortune.

And she, too, would be happy. Never, by word or look, would he wound the tender heart which abandoned itself to him, with the blind trust of a child reposing in its mother's arms. For were the vision shattered, it would be the wreck of her inner life. To the mighty waters of love she would confide her all!

The man I picture must belong, in expression, in attitude, in gait, in his way of performing alike the smallest and the greatest actions, to that race of the truly great who are always simple and natural. He need not be good-looking, but his hands must be beautiful. His upper lip will curl with a careless, ironic smile for the general public, whilst he reserves for those he loves the heavenly, radiant glance in which he puts his soul.

"Will mademoiselle allow me," he said in Spanish, in a voice full of agitation, "to keep this writing in memory of her? This is the last lesson I shall have the honor of giving her, and that which I have just received in these words may serve me for an abiding rule of life. I left Spain, a fugitive and penniless, but I have to-day received from my family a sum sufficient for my needs. You will allow me to send some poor Spaniard in my place."

In other words, he seemed to me to say, "This little game must stop." He rose with an air of marvelous dignity, and left me quite upset by such unheard-of delicacy in a man of his class. He went downstairs and asked to speak with my father.

At dinner my father said to me with a smile:

"Louise, you have been learning Spanish from an ex-minister and a man condemned to death."

"The Duc de Soria," I said.

"Duc!" replied my father. "No, he is not that any longer; he takes the title now of Baron de Macumer from a property which still remains to him in Sardinia. He is something of an original, I think."

"Don't brand with that word, which with you always implies some mockery and scorn, a man who is your equal, and who, I believe, has a noble nature."

"Baronne de Macumer?" exclaimed my father, with a laughing glance at me.

Pride kept my eyes fixed on the table.

"But," said my mother, "Hénarez must have met the

Mes yeux ont été magiquement attirés par deux yeux de feu
qui brillaient comme deux escarboucles dans un coin du parterre.

MÉMOIRES DE DEUX JEUNES MARIÉS.

Plate IV: *Armande-Louise-Marie de Chaulieu*
Illustration by Tony Johannot

Spanish ambassador on the steps?"

"Yes," replied my father, "the ambassador asked me if I was conspiring against the king, his master; but he greeted the ex-grandee of Spain with much deference, and placed his services at his disposal."

All this, dear, Madame de l'Estorade, happened a fortnight ago, and it is a fortnight now since I have seen the man who loves me, for that he loves me there is not a doubt. What is he about? If only I were a fly, or a mouse, or a sparrow! I want to see him alone, myself unseen, at his house. Only think, a man exists, to whom I can say, "Go and die for me!" And he is so made that he would go, at least I think so. Anyhow, there is in Paris a man who occupies my thoughts, and whose glance pours sunshine into my soul. Is not such a man an enemy, whom I ought to trample under foot? What? There is a man who has become necessary to me—a man without whom I don't know how to live! You married, and I—in love! Four little months, and those two doves, whose wings erst bore them so high, have fluttered down upon the flat stretches of real life!

Sunday

Yesterday, at the Italian Opera, I could feel some one was looking at me; my eyes were drawn, as by a magnet, to two wells of fire, gleaming like carbuncles in a dim corner of the orchestra. Hénarez never moved his eyes from me. The wretch had discovered the one spot from which he could see me—and there he was. I don't know what he may be as a politician, but for love he has a genius: "Behold, my fair Renée, where our business now stands," as the great Corneille has said.

XIII

MADAME DE L'ESTORADE TO MADEMOISELLE DE CHAULIEU

La Crampade, February

My dear Louise,—I was bound to wait some time before writing to you; but now I know, or rather I have learned, many things which, for the sake of your future happiness, I must tell you. The difference between a girl and a married woman is so vast, that the girl can no more comprehend it than the married woman can go back to girlhood again.

I chose to marry Louis de l'Estorade rather than return to the convent; that at least is plain. So soon as I realized that the convent was the only alternative to marrying Louis, I had, as girls say, to "submit," and my submission once made, the next thing was to examine the situation and try to make the best of it.

The serious nature of what I was undertaking filled me at first with terror. Marriage is a matter concerning the whole of life, whilst love aims only at pleasure. On the other hand, marriage will remain when pleasures have vanished, and it is the source of interests far more precious than those of the man and woman entering on the alliance. Might it not therefore be that the only requisite for a happy marriage was friendship—a friendship which, for the sake of these advantages, would shut its eyes to many of the imperfections of humanity? Now there was no obstacle to the existence of friendship between myself and Louis de l'Estorade. Having renounced all idea of finding in marriage those transports of love on which our minds used so often, and with such perilous rapture, to dwell, I found a gentle calm settling over me. "If debarred from love, why not seek for happiness?" I said to myself. "Moreover, I am loved, and the love offered me I shall accept. My married life will be no slavery, but rather a perpetual reign. What is there to say against such a situation for a woman who wishes to remain absolute mistress of herself?"

The important point of separating marriage from marital rights was settled in a conversation between Louis and me, in the course of which he gave proof of an excellent temper and a tender heart. Darling, my desire was to prolong that fair season of hope which, never culminating in satisfaction, leaves to the soul its virginity. To grant nothing to duty or the law, to be guided entirely by one's own will, retaining perfect independence—what could be more attractive, more honorable?

A contract of this kind, directly opposed to the legal contract, and even to the sacrament itself, could be concluded only between Louis and me. This difficulty, the first which has arisen, is the only one which has delayed the completion of our marriage. Although, at first, I may have made up my mind to accept anything rather than return to the convent, it is only in human nature, having got an inch, to ask for an ell, and you and I, sweet love, are of those who would have it all.

I watched Louis out of the corner of my eye, and put it to myself, "Has suffering had a softening or a hardening effect on him?" By dint of close study, I arrived at the conclusion that his love amounted to a passion. Once transformed into an idol, whose slightest frown would turn him white and trembling, I realized that I might venture anything. I drew him aside in the most natural manner on solitary walks, during which I discreetly sounded his feelings. I made him talk, and got him to expound to me his ideas and plans for our future. My questions betrayed so many preconceived notions, and went so straight for the weak points in this terrible dual existence, that Louis has since confessed to me the alarm it caused him to find in me so little of the ignorant maiden.

Then I listened to what he had to say in reply. He got mixed up in his arguments, as people do when handicapped by fear; and before long it became clear that chance had given me for adversary one who was the less fitted for the contest because he was conscious of what you magniloquently call my "greatness of soul." Broken by sufferings and misfortune, he looked on himself as a sort of wreck, and three fears in especial haunted him.

First, we are aged respectively thirty-seven and seventeen; and he could not contemplate without quaking the twenty years that divide us. In the next place, he shares our views on the subject of my beauty, and it is cruel for him to see how the hardships of his life have robbed him of youth. Finally, he felt the superiority of my womanhood over his manhood. The consciousness of these three obvious drawbacks made him distrustful of himself; he doubted his power to make me happy, and guessed that he had been chosen as the lesser of two evils.

One evening he tentatively suggested that I only married him to escape the convent.

"I cannot deny it," was my grave reply.

My dear, it touched me to the heart to see the two great tears which stood in his eyes. Never before had I experienced the shock of emotion which a man can impart to us.

"Louis," I went on, as kindly as I could, "it rests entirely with you whether this marriage of convenience becomes one to which I can give my whole heart. The favor I am about to ask from you will demand unselfishness on your part, far nobler than the servitude to which a man's love, when sincere, is supposed to reduce him. The question is, Can you rise to the height of friendship such as I understand it?

"Life gives us but one friend, and I wish to be yours. Friendship is the bond between a pair of kindred souls, united in their strength, and yet independent. Let us be friends and comrades to bear jointly the burden of life.

Leave me absolutely free. I would put no hindrance in the way of your inspiring me with a love similar to your own; but I am determined to be yours only of my own free gift. Create in me the wish to give up my freedom, and at once I lay it at your feet.

"Infuse with passion, then, if you will, this friendship, and let the voice of love disturb its calm. On my part I will do what I can to bring my feelings into accord with yours. One thing, above all, I would beg of you. Spare me the annoyances to which the strangeness of our mutual position might give rise to our relations with others. I am neither whimsical nor prudish, and should be sorry to get that reputation; but I feel sure that I can trust to your honor when I ask you to keep up the outward appearance of wedded life."

Never, dear, have I seen a man so happy as my proposal made Louis. The blaze of joy which kindled in his eyes dried up the tears.

"Do not fancy," I concluded, "that I ask this from any wish to be eccentric. It is the great desire I have for your respect which prompts my request. If you owe the crown of your love merely to the legal and religious ceremony, what gratitude could you feel to me later for a gift in which my goodwill counted for nothing? If during the time that I remained indifferent to you (yielding only a passive obedience, such as my mother has just been urging on me) a child were born to us, do you suppose that I could feel towards it as I would towards one born of our common love? A passionate love may not be necessary in marriage, but, at least, you will admit that there should be no repugnance. Our position will not be without its dangers; in a country life, such as ours will be, ought we not to bear in mind the evanescent nature of passion? Is it not simple prudence to make provision beforehand against the calamities incident to change of feeling?"

He was greatly astonished to find me at once so

reasonable and so apt at reasoning; but he made me a solemn promise, after which I took his hand and pressed it affectionately.

We were married at the end of the week. Secure of my freedom, I was able to throw myself gaily into the petty details which always accompany a ceremony of the kind, and to be my natural self. Perhaps I may have been taken for an old bird, as they say at Blois. A young girl, delighted with the novel and hopeful situation she had contrived to make for herself, and may have passed for a strong-minded female.

Dear, the difficulties which would beset my life had appeared to me clearly as in a vision, and I was sincerely anxious to make the happiness of the man I married. Now, in the solitude of a life like ours, marriage soon becomes intolerable unless the woman is the presiding spirit. A woman in such a case needs the charm of a mistress, combined with the solid qualities of a wife. To introduce an element of uncertainty into pleasure is to prolong illusion, and render lasting those selfish satisfactions which all creatures hold, and should shroud a woman in expectancy, crown her sovereign, and invest her with an exhaustless power, a redundancy of life, that makes everything blossom around her. The more she is mistress of herself, the more certainly will the love and happiness she creates be fit to weather the storms of life.

But, above all, I have insisted on the greatest secrecy in regard to our domestic arrangements. A husband who submits to his wife's yoke is justly held an object of ridicule. A woman's influence ought to be entirely concealed. The charm of all we do lies in its unobtrusiveness. If I have made it my task to raise a drooping courage and restore their natural brightness to gifts which I have dimly descried, it must all seem to spring from Louis himself.

Such is the mission to which I dedicate myself, a

mission surely not ignoble, and which might well satisfy a woman's ambition. Why, I could glory in this secret which shall fill my life with interest, in this task towards which my every energy shall be bent, while it remains concealed from all but God and you.

I am very nearly happy now, but should I be so without a friendly heart in which to pour the confession? For how make a confidant of him? My happiness would wound him, and has to be concealed. He is sensitive as a woman, like all men who have suffered much.

For three months we remained as we were before marriage. As you may imagine, during this time I made a close study of many small personal matters, which have more to do with love than is generally supposed. In spite of my coldness, Louis grew bolder, and his nature expanded. I saw on his face a new expression, a look of youth. The greater refinement which I introduced into the house was reflected in his person. Insensibly I became accustomed to his presence, and made another self of him. By dint of constant watching I discovered how his mind and countenance harmonize. "The animal that we call a husband," to quote your words, disappeared, and one balmy evening I discovered in his stead a lover, whose words thrilled me and on whose arm I leant with pleasure beyond words. In short, to be open with you, as I would be with God, before whom concealment is impossible, the perfect loyalty with which he had kept his oath may have piqued me, and I felt a fluttering of curiosity in my heart. Bitterly ashamed, I struggled with myself. Alas! when pride is the only motive for resistance, excuses for capitulation are soon found.

We celebrated our union in secret, and secret it must remain between us. When you are married you will approve this reserve. Enough that nothing was lacking either of satisfaction for the most fastidious sentiment, or of that unexpectedness which brings, in a sense, its own sanction. Every witchery of imagination, of passion, of reluctance overcome, of the ideal passing into reality, played its part.

Yet, in spite of all this enchantment, I once more stood out for my complete independence. I can't tell you all my reasons for this. To you alone shall I confide even as much as this. I believe that women, whether passionately loved or not, lose much in their relation with their husbands by not concealing their feelings about marriage and the way they look at it.

My one joy, and it is supreme, springs from the certainty of having brought new life to my husband before I have borne him any children. Louis has regained his youth, strength, and spirits. He is not the same man. With magic touch I have effaced the very memory of his sufferings. It is a complete metamorphosis. Louis is really very attractive now. Feeling sure of my affection, he throws off his reserve and displays unsuspected gifts.

To be the unceasing spring of happiness for a man who knows it and adds gratitude to love, ah! dear one, this is a conviction which fortifies the soul, even more than the most passionate love can do. The force thus developed—at once impetuous and enduring, simple and diversified—brings forth ultimately the family, that noble product of womanhood, which I realize now in all its animating beauty.

The old father has ceased to be a miser. He gives blindly whatever I wish for. The servants are content; it seems as though the bliss of Louis had let a flood of sunshine into the household, where love has made me queen. Even the old man would not be a blot upon my pretty home, and has brought himself into line with all my improvements; to please me he has adopted the dress, and with the dress, the manners of the day.

We have English horses, a coupé, a barouche, and a tilbury. The livery of our servants is simple but in good taste. Of course we are looked on as spendthrifts. I apply all my intellect (I am speaking quite seriously) to managing my household with economy, and obtaining for it the maximum of pleasure with the minimum of cost.

I have already convinced Louis of the necessity of getting roads made, in order that he may earn the reputation of a man interested in the welfare of his district. I insist too on his studying a great deal. Before long I hope to see him a member of the Council General of the Department,* through the influence of my family and his mother's. I have told him plainly that I am ambitious, and that I was very well pleased his father should continue to look after the estate and practise economies, because I wished him to devote himself exclusively to politics. If we had children, I should like to see them all prosperous and with good State appointments. Under penalty, therefore, of forfeiting my esteem and affection, he must get himself chosen deputy for the department at the coming elections; my family would support his candidature, and we should then have the delight of spending all our winters in Paris. Ah! my love, by the ardor with which he embraced my plans, I can gauge the depth of his affection.

To conclude here is a letter he wrote me yesterday from Marseilles, where he had gone to spend a few hours:

MY SWEET RENÉE, — When you gave me permission to love you, I began to believe in happiness; now, I see it unfolding endlessly before me. The past is merely a dim memory, a shadowy background, without which my present bliss would show less radiant. When I am with you, love so transports me that I am powerless to express the depth of my affection; I can but worship and admire. Only at a distance does the power of speech return. You are supremely beautiful, Renée, and your beauty is of the statuesque and regal type, on which time leaves but little impression. No doubt the love of husband and wife depends less on outward beauty than on graces of character, which are yours also in perfection; still, let me say that

217

the certainty of having your unchanging beauty, on which to feast my eyes, gives me a joy that grows with every glance. There is a grace and dignity in the lines of your face, expressive of the noble soul within, and breathing of purity beneath the vivid coloring. The brilliance of your dark eyes, the bold sweep of your forehead, declare a spirit of no common elevation, sound and trustworthy in every relation, and well braced to meet the storms of life, should such arise. The keynote of your character is its freedom from all pettiness. You do not need to be told all this; but I write it because I would have you know that I appreciate the treasure I possess. Your favors to me, however slight, will always make my happiness in the far-distant future as now; for I am sensible how much dignity there is in our promise to respect each other's liberty. Our own impulse shall with us alone dictate the expression of feeling. We shall be free even in our fetters. I shall have the more pride in wooing you again now that I know the reward you place on victory. You cannot speak, breathe, act, or think, without adding to the admiration I feel for your charm both of body and mind. There is in you a rare combination of the ideal, the practical, and the bewitching which satisfies alike judgment, a husband's pride, desire, and hope, and which extends the boundaries of love beyond those of life itself. Oh! my loved one, may the genius of love remain faithful to me, and the future be full of those delights by means of which you have glorified all that surrounds me! I long for the day which shall make you a mother, that I may see you content with the fullness of your life, may hear you, in the sweet voice I love and with the thoughts, bless the love which has refreshed my soul and given new vigor to my powers, the love which is my pride, and whence I have drawn, as from a magic fountain, fresh life. Yes, I shall be all that you would have me. I shall take a leading part in the public life of the district, and on you shall fall the rays of a glory which will owe its existence to the desire of pleasing you.

So much for my pupil, dear! Do you suppose he could have written like this before? A year hence his style will have still further improved. Louis is now in his first transport; what I look forward to is the uniform and continuous sensation of content which ought to be the fruit of a happy marriage, when a man and woman, in perfect trust and mutual knowledge, have solved the problem of giving variety to the infinite. This is the task set before every true wife; the answer begins to dawn on me, and I shall not rest till I have made it mine.

You see that he fancies himself—vanity of men!—the chosen of my heart, just as though there were no legal bonds. Nevertheless, I have not yet got beyond that external attraction which gives us strength to put up with a good deal. Yet Louis is lovable; his temper is wonderfully even, and he performs, as a matter of course, acts on which most men would plume themselves. In short, if I do not love him, I shall find no difficulty in being good to him.

So here are my black hair and my black eyes—whose lashes act, according to you, like Venetian blinds—my commanding air, and my whole person, raised to the rank of sovereign power! Ten years hence, dear, why should we not both be laughing and gay in your Paris, whence I shall carry you off now and again to my beautiful oasis in Provence?

Oh! Louise, don't spoil the splendid future which awaits us both! Don't do the mad things with which you threaten me. My husband is a young man, prematurely old; why don't you marry some young-hearted graybeard in the Chamber of Peers?* There lies your vocation.

XIV

THE DUC DE SORIA TO THE BARON DE MACUMER

Madrid

MY DEAR BROTHER,—You did not make me Duc de Soria in order that my actions should belie the name. How could I tolerate my happiness if I knew you to be a wanderer, deprived of the comforts which wealth everywhere commands? Neither Marie nor I will consent to marry till we hear that you have accepted the money which Urraca will hand over to you. These two millions are the fruit of your own savings and Marie's.

We have both prayed, kneeling before the same altar—and with what earnestness, God knows!—for your happiness. My dear brother, it cannot be that these prayers will remain unanswered. Heaven will send you the love which you seek, to be the consolation of your exile. Marie read your letter with tears, and is full of admiration for you. As for me, I consent, not for my own sake, but for that of the family. The king justified your expectations. Oh! that I might avenge you by letting him see himself, dwarfed before the scorn with which you flung him his toy, as you might toss a tiger its food.

The only thing I have taken for myself, dear brother, is my happiness. I have taken Marie. For this I shall always be beholden to you, as the creature to the Creator. There will be in my life and in Marie's one day not less glorious than our wedding day—it will be the day when we hear that your heart has found its mate, that a woman loves you as you ought to be, and would be, loved. Do not forget that if you live for us, we also live for you.

You can write to us with perfect confidence under cover to the Nuncio, sending your letters *via* Rome. The French ambassador at Rome will, no doubt, undertake to forward them to Monsignore Bemboni, at the State Secretary's office, whom our legate will have advised. No other way would be safe. Farewell, dear exile, dear despoiled one. Be proud at least of the happiness which you have brought to us, if you cannot be happy in it. God will doubtless hear our prayers, which are full of your name.

FERNANDO

XV

LOUISE DE CHAULIEU TO MADAME DE L'ESTORADE

March

Ah! my love, marriage is making a philosopher of you! Your darling face must, indeed, have been jaundiced when you wrote me those terrible views of human life and the duty of women. Do you fancy you will convert me to matrimony by your programme of subterranean labors?

Alas! is this then the outcome for you of our too-instructed dreams! We left Blois all innocent, armed with the pointed shafts of meditation, and, lo! the weapons of that purely ideal experience have turned against your own breast! If I did not know you for the purest and most angelic of created beings, I declare I should say that your calculations smack of vice. What, my dear, in the interest of your country home, you submit your pleasures to a periodic thinning, as you do your timber. Oh! rather let me perish in all the violence of the heart's storms than live in the arid atmosphere of your cautious arithmetic!

As girls, we were both unusually enlightened, because of the large amount of study we gave to our chosen subjects; but, my child, philosophy without love, or disguised under a sham love, is the most hideous of conjugal hypocrisies. I should imagine that even the biggest of fools might detect now and again the owl of wisdom squatting in your bower of roses—a ghastly phantom sufficient to put to flight the most promising of passions. You make your own fate, instead of waiting, a plaything in its hands.

We are each developing in strange ways. A large dose of philosophy to a grain of love is your recipe; a large dose of love to a grain of philosophy is mine. Why, Rousseau's Julie, whom I thought so learned, is a mere beginner to you. Woman's virtue, quotha! How you have weighed up life! Alas! I make fun of you, and, after all, perhaps you are right.

In one day you have made a holocaust of your youth and become a miser before your time. Your Louis will be happy, I daresay. If he loves you, of which I make no doubt, he will never find out, that, for the sake of your family, you are acting as a courtesan does for money; and certainly men seem to find happiness with them, judging by the fortunes they squander thus. A keen-sighted husband might no doubt remain in love with you, but what sort of gratitude could he feel in the long run for a woman who had made of duplicity a sort of moral armor, as indispensable as her stays?

Love, dear, is in my eyes the first principle of all the virtues, conformed to the divine likeness. Like all other first principles, it is not a matter of arithmetic; it is the Infinite in us. I cannot but think you have been trying to justify in your own eyes the frightful position of a girl, married to a man for whom she feels nothing more than esteem. You prate of duty, and make it your rule and measure; but surely to take necessity as the spring of action is the moral theory of atheism? To follow the impulse of love and feeling is the secret law of every woman's heart. You are acting a man's part, and your Louis will have to play the woman!

Oh! my dear, your letter has plunged me into an endless train of thought. I see now that the convent can never take the place of mother to a girl. I beg of you, my grand angel with the black eyes, so pure and proud, so serious and so pretty, do not turn away from these cries, which the first reading of your letter has torn from me! I have taken comfort in the thought that, while I was lamenting, love was doubtless busy knocking down the scaffolding of reason.

It may be that I shall do worse than you without any reasoning or calculations. Passion is an element in life bound to have a logic not less pitiless than yours.

Monday

Yesterday night I placed myself at the window as I was going to bed, to look at the sky, which was wonderfully clear. The stars were like silver nails, holding up a veil of blue. In the silence of the night I could hear some one breathing, and by the half-light of the stars I saw my Spaniard, perched like a squirrel on the branches of one of the trees lining the boulevard, and doubtless lost in admiration of my windows.

The first effect of this discovery was to make me withdraw into the room, my feet and hands quite limp and nerveless; but, beneath the fear, I was conscious of a delicious undercurrent of joy. I was overpowered but happy. Not one of those clever Frenchmen, who aspire to marry me, has had the brilliant idea of spending the night in an elm-tree at the risk of being carried off by the watch. My Spaniard has, no doubt, been there for some time. Ah! he won't give me any more lessons, he wants to receive them—well, he shall have one. If only he knew what I said to myself about his superficial ugliness! Others can philosophize besides you, Renée! It was horrid, I argued, to fall in love with a handsome man. Is it not practically avowing that the senses count for three parts out of four in a passion which ought to be super-sensual?

Having got over my first alarm, I craned my neck behind the window in order to see him again—and well was I rewarded! By means of a hollow cane he blew me in through the window a letter, cunningly rolled round a leaden pellet.

Good Heavens! will he suppose I left the window open on purpose?

But what was to be done? To shut it suddenly would be to make oneself an accomplice.

I did better. I returned to my window as though I had seen nothing and heard nothing of the letter, then I said aloud:

"Come and look at the stars, Griffith."

Griffith was sleeping as only old maids can. But the Moor, hearing me, slid down, and vanished with ghostly rapidity.

He must have been dying of fright, and so was I, for I did not hear him go away; apparently he remained at the foot of the elm. After a good quarter of an hour, during which I lost myself in contemplation of the heavens, and battled with the waves of curiosity, I closed my widow and sat down on the bed to unfold the delicate bit of paper, with the tender touch of a worker amongst the ancient manuscripts at Naples. It felt red hot to my fingers. "What a horrible power this man has over me!" I said to myself.

All at once I held out the paper to the candle—I would burn it without reading a word. Then a thought stayed me, "What can he have to say that he writes so secretly?" Well, dear, I *did* burn it, reflecting that, though any other girl in the world would have devoured the letter, it was not fitting that I—Armande-Louise-Marie de Chaulieu—should read it.

The next day, at the Italian Opera, he was at his post. But I feel sure that, ex-prime minister of a constitutional government though he is, he could not discover the slightest agitation of mind in any movement of mine. I might have seen nothing and received nothing the evening before. This was most satisfactory to me, but he looked very sad. Poor man! in Spain it is so natural for love to come in at the window!

During the interval, it seems, he came and walked in the passages. This I learned from the chief secretary of the Spanish embassy, who also told the story of a noble action of his.

As Duc de Soria he was to marry one of the richest heiresses in Spain, the young Princess Marie Hérédia, whose wealth would have mitigated the bitterness of exile. But it seems that Marie, disappointing the wishes of the fathers, who had betrothed them in their earliest childhood, loved the younger son of the house of Soria, to whom my Félipe, gave her up. Allowing himself to be despoiled by the King of Spain.

"He would perform this piece of heroism quite simply," I said to the young man.

"You know him then?" was his ingenuous reply.

My mother smiled.

"What will become of him, for he is condemned to death?" I asked.

"Though dead to Spain, he can live in Sardinia."

"Ah! then Spain is the country of tombs as well as castles?" I said, trying to carry it off as a joke.

"There is everything in Spain, even Spaniards of the old school," my mother replied.

"The Baron de Macumer obtained a passport, not without difficulty, from the King of Sardinia," the young diplomatist went on. "He has now become a Sardinian subject, and he possesses a magnificent estate in the island with full feudal rights. He has a palace at Sassari. If Ferdinand VII were to die, Macumer would probably go in for diplomacy, and the Court of Turin would make him ambassador. Though young, he is—"

"Ah! he is young?"

"Certainly, mademoiselle . . . though young, he is one of the most distinguished men in Spain."

I scanned the house meanwhile through my opera-glass, and seemed to lend an inattentive ear to the secretary; but, between ourselves, I was wretched at having burnt his letter. In what terms would a man like that express his love? For he does love me. To be loved, adored in secret; to know that in this house, where all the great men of Paris were collected, there was one entirely devoted to me, unknown to everybody! Ah! Renée, now I understand the life of Paris, its balls, and its gaieties. It all flashed on me in the true light. When we love, we must have society, were it only to sacrifice it to our love. I felt a different creature—and such a happy one! My vanity, pride, self-love,—all were flattered. Heaven knows what glances I cast upon the audience!

"Little rogue!" the duchesse whispered in my ear with a smile.

Yes, Renée, my wily mother had deciphered the hidden joy in my bearing, and I could only haul down my flag before such feminine strategy. Those two words taught me more of worldly wisdom than I have been able to pick up in a year—for we are in March now. Alas! no more Italian Opera in another month. How will life be possible without that heavenly music, when one's heart is full of love?

When I got home, my dear, with determination worthy of a Chaulieu, I opened my window to watch a shower of rain. Oh! if men knew the magic spell that a heroic action throws over us, they would indeed rise to greatness! a poltroon would turn hero! What I had learned about my Spaniard drove me into a very fever. I felt certain that he was there, ready to aim another letter at me.

I was right, and this time I burnt nothing. Here, then, is the first love-letter I have received, madame logician: each to her kind:—

Louise, it is not for your peerless beauty I love you, nor for your gifted mind, your noble feeling, the wondrous charm of all you say and do, nor yet for your pride, your queenly scorn of baser mortals—a pride blent in you with charity, for what angel could be more tender?—Louise, I love you because, for the sake of a poor exile, you have unbent this lofty majesty, because by a gesture, a glance, you have brought consolation to a man so far beneath you that the utmost he could hope for was your pity, the pity of a generous heart. You are the one woman whose eyes have shone with a tenderer light when bent on me.

And because you let fall this glance—a mere grain of dust, yet a grace surpassing any bestowed on me when I stood at the summit of a subject's ambition—I long to tell you, Louise, how dear you are to me, and that my love is for yourself alone, without a thought beyond, a love that far more than fulfils the conditions laid down by you for an ideal passion.

Know, then, idol of my highest heaven, that there is in the world an offshoot of the Saracen race, whose life is in your hands, who will receive your orders as a slave, and deem it an honor to execute them. I have given myself to you absolutely and for the mere joy of giving, for a single glance of your eye, for a touch of the hand which one day you offered to your Spanish master. I am but your servitor, Louise; I claim no more.

No, I dare not think that I could ever be loved; but perchance my devotion may win for me toleration. Since that morning when you smiled upon me with generous girlish impulse, divining the misery of my lonely and rejected heart, you reign there alone. You are the absolute ruler of my life, the queen of my thoughts, the god of my heart; I find you in the sunshine of my home, the fragrance of my flowers, the balm of the air I breathe, the pulsing of my blood, the light that visits me in sleep.

One thought alone troubled this happiness—your ignorance. All unknown to you was this boundless devotion, the trusty arm, the blind slave, the silent tool, the wealth—for henceforth all I possess is mine only as a trust—which lay at your disposal; unknown to you, the heart waiting to receive your confidence, and yearning to replace all that your life (I know it well) has lacked—the liberal ancestress, so ready to meet your needs, a father to whom you could look for protection in every difficulty, a friend, a brother. The secret of your isolation is no secret to me! If I am bold, it is because I long that you should know how much is yours.

Take all, Louise, and is so doing bestow on me the one life possible for me in this world—the life of devotion. In placing the yoke on my neck, you run no risk; I ask nothing but the joy of knowing myself yours. Needless even to say you will never love me; it cannot be otherwise. I must love you from afar, without hope, without reward beyond my own love.

In my anxiety to know whether you will accept me as your servant, I have racked my brain to find some way in

227

which you may communicate with me without any danger of compromising yourself. Injury to your self-respect there can be none in sanctioning a devotion which has been yours for many days without your knowledge. Let this, then, be the token. At the Opera this evening, if you carry in your hand a bouquet consisting of one red and one white camellia—emblem of a man's blood at the service of the purity he worships—that will be my answer. I ask no more; thenceforth, at any moment, ten years hence or to-morrow, whatever you demand shall be done, so far as it is possible for man to do it, by your happy servant,

FÉLIPE HÉNAREZ

P. S.—You must admit, dear, that great lords know how to love! See the spring of the African lion! What restrained fire! What loyalty! What sincerity! How high a soul in low estate! I felt quite small and dazed as I said to myself, "What shall I do?"

It is the mark of a great man that he puts to flight all ordinary calculations. He is at once sublime and touching, childlike and of the race of giants. In a single letter Hénarez has outstripped volumes from Lovelace or Saint-Preux.* Here is true love, no beating about the bush. Love may be or it may not, but where it is, it ought to reveal itself in its immensity.

Here am I, shorn of all my little arts! To refuse or accept! That is the alternative boldly presented me, without the ghost of an opening for a middle course. No fencing allowed! This is no longer Paris; we are in the heart of Spain or the far East. It is the voice of Abencerrage, and it is the scimitar, the horse, and the head of Abencerrage which he offers, prostrate before a Catholic Eve! Shall I accept this last descendant of the Moors? Read again and again his Hispano-Saracenic letter, Renée dear, and you will see how love makes a clean sweep of all the Judaic bargains of your philosophy.

Renée, your letter lies heavy on my heart; you have

vulgarized life for me. What need have I for finessing? Am I not mistress for all time of this lion whose roar dies out in plaintive and adoring sighs? Ah! how he must have raged in his lair of the Rue Hillerin-Bertin! I know where he lives, I have his card: *F., Baron de Macumer.*

He has made it impossible for me to reply. All I can do is to fling two camellias in his face. What fiendish arts does love possess—pure, honest, simple-minded love! Here is the most tremendous crisis of a woman's heart resolved into an easy, simple action. Oh, Asia! I have read the Nights, here is their very essence: two flowers, and the question is settled. We clear the fourteen volumes of Harlowe with a bouquet. I writhe before this letter, like a thread in the fire. To take, or not to take, my two camellias. Yes or No, kill or give life! At last a voice cries to me, "Test him!" And I will test him.

XVI

THE SAME TO THE SAME

March

I am dressed in white—white camellias in my hair, and another in my hand. My mother has red camellias; so it would not be impossible to take one from her—if I wished! I have a strange longing to put off the decision to the last moment, and make him pay for his red camellia by a little suspense.

What a vision of beauty! Griffith begged me to stop for a little and be admired. The solemn crisis of the evening and the drama of my secret reply have given me a color; on each cheek I sport a red camellia laid upon a white!

1 a.m.

Everybody admired me, but only one adored. He hung his head as I entered with a white camellia, but turned pale as the flower when, later, I took a red one from my mother's hand. To arrive with the two flowers might possibly have been accidental; but this deliberate action was a reply. My confession, therefore, is fuller than it need have been.

The opera was *Romeo and Juliet*. As you don't know the duet of the two lovers, you can't understand the bliss of two neophytes in love, as they listen to this divine outpouring of the heart.

On returning home I went to bed, but only to count the steps which resounded on the sidewalk. My heart and head, darling, are all on fire now. What is he doing? What is he thinking of? Has he a thought, a single thought, that is not of me? Is he, in very truth, the devoted slave he painted himself? How to be sure? Or, again, has it ever entered his head that, if I accept him, I lay myself open to the shadow of a reproach or am in any sense rewarding or thanking him? I am harrowed by the hair-splitting casuistry of the heroines in *Cyrus* and *Astræa*,* by all the subtle arguments of the court of love.

Has he any idea that, in affairs of love, a woman's most trifling actions are but the issue of long brooding and inner conflicts, of victories won only to be lost! What are his thoughts at this moment? How can I give him my orders to write every evening the particulars of the day just gone? He is my slave whom I ought to keep busy. I shall deluge him with work!

Sunday Morning

Only towards morning did I sleep a little. It is midday now. I have just got Griffith to write the following letter:

TO THE BARON DE MACUMER:
Mademoiselle de Chaulieu begs me, Monsieur le Baron, to ask you to return to her the copy of a letter written to her by

a friend, which is in her own handwriting, and which you carried away.—Believe me, etc.,

GRIFFITH

My dear, Griffith has gone out; she has gone to the Rue Hillerin-Bertin; she had handed in this little love-letter for my slave, who returned to me in an envelope my sweet portrait, stained with tears. He has obeyed. Oh! my sweet, it must have been dear to him! Another man would have refused to send it in a letter full of flattery; but the Saracen has fulfilled his promises. He has obeyed. It moves me to tears.

XVII

THE SAME TO THE SAME

April 2nd

Yesterday the weather was splendid. I dressed myself like a girl who wants to look her best in her sweetheart's eyes. My father, yielding to my entreaties, has given me the prettiest turnout in Paris—two dapple-gray horses and a barouche, which is a masterpiece of elegance. I was making a first trial of this, and peeped out like a flower from under my sunshade lined with white silk.

As I drove up the avenue of the Champs-Élysées, I saw my Abencerrage approaching on an extraordinarily beautiful horse. Almost every man nowadays is a finished jockey, and they all stopped to admire and inspect it. He bowed to me, and on receiving a friendly sign of encouragement, slackened his horse's pace so that I was able to say to him:

"You are not vexed with me for asking for my letter; it was no use to you." Then in a lower voice, "You have already transcended the ideal. . . . Your horse makes you an object of general interest," I went on aloud.

"My steward in Sardinia sent it to me. He is very proud of it; for this horse, which is of Arab blood, was born in my stables."

231

This morning, my dear, Hénarez was on an English sorrel, also very fine, but not such as to attract attention. My light, mocking words had done their work. He bowed to me and I replied with a slight inclination of the head.

The Duc d'Angoulême has bought Macumer's horse. My slave understood that he was deserting the role of simplicity by attracting the notice of the crowd. A man ought to be remarked for what he is, not for his horse, or anything else belonging to him. To have too beautiful a horse seems to me a piece of bad taste, just as much as wearing a huge diamond pin. I was delighted at being able to find fault with him. Perhaps there may have been a touch of vanity in what he did, very excusable in a poor exile, and I like to see this childishness.

Oh! my dear old preacher, do my love affairs amuse you as much as your dismal philosophy gives me the creeps? Dear Philip the Second in petticoats, are you comfortable in my barouche? Do you see those velvet eyes, humble, yet so eloquent, and glorying in their servitude, which flash on me as some one goes by? He is a hero, Renée, and he wears my livery, and always a red camellia in his buttonhole, while I have always a white one in my hand.

How clear everything becomes in the light of love! How well I know my Paris now! It is all transfused with meaning. And love here is lovelier, grander, more bewitching than elsewhere.

I am convinced now that I could never flirt with a fool or make any impression on him. It is only men of real distinction who can enter into our feelings and feel our influence. Oh! my poor friend, forgive me. I forgot our l'Estorade. But didn't you tell me you were going to make a genius of him? I know what that means. You will dry nurse him till some day he is able to understand you.

Good-bye. I am a little off my head, and must stop.

XVIII
MADAME DE L'ESTORADE TO LOUISE DE CHAULIEU

April

My angel—or ought I not rather to say my imp of evil?—you have, without meaning it, grieved me sorely. I would say wounded were we not one soul. And yet it is possible to wound oneself.

How plain it is that you have never realized the force of the word *indissoluble* as applied to the contract binding man and woman! I have no wish to controvert what has been laid down by philosophers or legislators—they are quite capable of doing this for themselves—but, dear one, in making marriage irrevocable and imposing on it a relentless formula, which admits of no exceptions, they have rendered each union a thing as distinct as one individual is from another. Each has its own inner laws which differ from those of others. The laws regulating married life in the country, for instance, cannot be the same as those regulating a household in town, where frequent distractions give variety to life. Or conversely, married life in Paris, where existence is one perpetual whirl, must demand different treatment from the more peaceful home in the provinces.

But if place alters the conditions of marriage, much more does character. The wife of a man born to be a leader need only resign herself to his guidance; whereas the wife of a fool, conscious of superior power, is bound to take the reins in her own hand if she would avert calamity.

You speak of vice; and it is possible that, after all, reason and reflection produce a result not dissimilar from what we call by that name. For what does a woman mean by it but perversion of feeling through calculation? Passion is vicious when it reasons, admirable only when it springs from the heart and spends itself in sublime impulses that set at naught all selfish considerations. Sooner or later, dear one, you too will say, "Yes! dissimulation is the necessary armor of a woman, if by dissimulation be meant courage to bear in silence, prudence to foresee the future."

Every married woman learns to her cost the existence of certain social laws, which, in many respects, conflict with the laws of nature. Marrying at our age, it would be possible to have a dozen children. What is this but another name for a dozen crimes, a dozen misfortunes? It would be handing over to poverty and despair twelve innocent darlings; whereas two children would mean the happiness of both, a double blessing, two lives capable of developing in harmony with the customs and laws of our time. The natural law and the code are in hostility, and we are the battle ground. Would you give the name of vice to the prudence of the wife who guards her family from destruction through its own acts? One calculation or a thousand, what matter, if the decision no longer rests with the heart?

And of this terrible calculation you will be guilty some day, my noble Baronne de Macumer, when you are the proud and happy wife of the man who adores you; or rather, being a man of sense, he will spare you by making it himself. (You see, dear dreamer, that I have studied the code in its bearings on conjugal relations.) And when at last that day comes, you will understand that we are answerable only to God and to ourselves for the means we employ to keep happiness alight in the heart of our homes. Far better is the calculation which succeeds in this than the reckless passion which introduces trouble, heart-burnings, and dissension.

I have reflected painfully on the duties of a wife and mother of a family. Yes, sweet one, it is only by a sublime hypocrisy that we can attain the noblest ideal of a perfect woman. You tax me with insincerity because I dole out to Louis, from day to day, the measure of his intimacy with me; but is it not too close an intimacy which provokes rupture? My aim is to give him, in the very interest of his happiness, many occupations, which will all serve as distractions to his love; and this is not the reasoning of passion. If affection be inexhaustible, it is not so with love: the task, therefore, of a woman—truly no light one—is to spread it out thriftily over a lifetime.

At the risk of exciting your disgust, I must tell you that I persist in the principles I have adopted, and hold myself both heroic and generous in so doing. Virtue, my pet, is an abstract idea, varying in its manifestations with the surroundings. Virtue in Provence, in Constantinople, in London, and in Paris bears very different fruit, but is none the less virtue. Each human life is a substance compacted of widely dissimilar elements, though, viewed from a certain height, the general effect is the same.

If I wished to make Louis unhappy and to bring about a separation, all I need do is to leave the helm in his hands. I have not had your good fortune in meeting with a man of the highest distinction, but I may perhaps have the satisfaction of helping him on the road to it. Five years hence let us meet in Paris and see! I believe we shall succeed in mystifying you. You will tell me then that I was quite mistaken, and that Monsieur de l'Estorade is a man of great natural gifts.

As for this brave love, of which I know only what you tell me, these tremors and night watches by starlight on the balcony, this idolatrous worship, this deification of woman—I knew it was not for me. You can enlarge the borders of your brilliant life as you please; mine is hemmed in to the boundaries of La Crampade.

And you reproach me for the jealous care which alone can nurse this modest and fragile shoot into a wealth of lasting and mysterious happiness! I believed myself to have found out how to adapt the charm of a mistress to the position of a wife, and you have almost made me blush for my device. Who shall say which of us is right, which is wrong? Perhaps we are both right and both wrong. Perhaps this is the heavy price which society exacts for our furbelows, our titles, and our children.

I too have my red camellias, but they bloom on my lips in smiles for my double charge—the father and the son—whose slave and mistress I am. But, my dear, your last letters made me feel what I have lost! You have taught me all a woman sacrifices in marrying. One single glance did I take at those beautiful wild plateaus where you range at your sweet will, and I will not tell you the tears that fell as I read. But regret is not remorse, though it may be first cousin to it.

You say, "Marriage has made you a philosopher!" Alas! bitterly did I feel how far this was from the truth, as I wept to think of you swept away on love's torrent. But my father has made me read one of the profoundest thinkers of these parts, the man on whom the mantle of Boussuet has fallen, one of those hard-headed theorists whose words force conviction. While you were reading *Corinne*, I conned Bonald;* and here is the whole secret of my philosophy. He revealed to me the Family in its strength and holiness. According to Bonald, your father was right in his homily.

Farewell, my dear fancy, my friend, my wild other self.

XIX
LOUISE DE CHAULIEU TO MADAME DE L'ESTORADE

Well, my Renée, you are a love of a woman, and I quite agree now that we can only be virtuous by cheating. Will that satisfy you? Moreover, the man who loves us is our property; we can make a fool or a genius of him as we please; only, between ourselves, the former happens more commonly. You will make yours a genius, and you won't tell the secret—there are two heroic actions, if you will!

Ah! if there were no future life, how nicely you would be sold, for this is martyrdom into which you are plunging of your own accord. You want to make him ambitious and to keep him in love! Child that you are, surely the last alone is sufficient.

Tell me, to what point is calculation a virtue, or virtue calculation? You won't say? Well, we won't quarrel over that, since we have Bonald to refer to. We are, and intend to remain, virtuous; nevertheless at this moment I believe that you, with all your pretty little knavery, are a better woman than I am.

Yes, I am shockingly deceitful. I love Félipe, and I conceal it from him with an odious hypocrisy. I long to see him leap from his tree to the top of the wall, and from the wall to my balcony—and if he did, how I should wither him with my scorn! You see, I am frank enough with you.

What restrains me? Where is the mysterious power which prevents me from telling Félipe, dear fellow, how supremely happy he has made me by the outpouring of his love—so pure, so absolute, so boundless, so unobtrusive, and so overflowing?

Madame de Mirbel* is painting my portrait, and I intend to give it to him, my dear. What surprises me more and more every day is the animation which love puts into life. How full of interest is every hour, every action, every trifle! and what amazing confusion between the past, the future, and the present! One lives in three tenses at once. Is it still so after the heights of happiness are reached? Oh! tell me, I implore you, what is happiness? Does it soothe, or does it excite? I am horribly restless; I seem to have lost all my bearings; a force in my heart drags me to him, spite of reason and spite of propriety. There is this gain, that I am better able to enter into your feelings.

Félipe's happiness consists in feeling himself mine;

the aloofness of his love, his strict obedience, irritate me, just as his attitude of profound respect provoked me when he was only my Spanish master. I am tempted to cry out to him as he passes, "Fool, if you love me so much as a picture, what will it be when you know the real me?"

Oh! Renée, you burn my letters, don't you? I will burn yours. If other eyes than ours were to read these thoughts which pass from heart to heart, I should send Félipe to put them out, and perhaps to kill the owners, by way of additional security.

Monday

Oh! Renée, how is it possible to fathom the heart of man? My father ought to introduce me to Monsieur Bonald, since he is so learned; I would ask him. I envy the privilege of God, who can read the undercurrents of the heart.

Does he still worship? That is the whole question.

If ever, in gesture, glance, or tone, I were to detect the slightest falling off in the respect he used to show me in the days when he was my instructor in Spanish, I feel that I should have strength to put the whole thing from me. "Why these fine words, these grand resolutions?" you will say. Dear, I will tell you.

My fascinating father, who treats me with the devotion of an Italian *cavaliere servente** for his lady, had my portrait painted, as I told you, by Madame de Mirbel. I contrived to get a copy made, good enough to do for the duc, and sent the original to Félipe. I despatched it yesterday, and these lines with it:

Don Félipe, your single-hearted devotion is met by a blind confidence. Time will show whether this is not to treat a man as more than human.

It was a big reward. It looked like a promise and—dreadful to say—a challenge; but—which will seem to you still more dreadful—I quite intended that it should suggest both these things, without going so far as to actually to commit me. If in his reply there is "Dear Louise!" or even "Louise," he is done for!

Tuesday

No, he is not done for. The constitutional minister is perfect as a lover. Here is his letter:—

Every moment passed away from your sight has been filled by me with ideal pictures of you, my eyes closed to the outside world and fixed in meditation on your image, which used to obey the summons too slowly in that dim palace of dreams, glorified by your presence. Henceforth my gaze will rest upon this wondrous ivory—this talisman, might I not say?—since your blue eyes sparkle with life as I look, and paint passes into flesh and blood. If I have delayed writing, it is because I could not tear myself away from your presence, which wrung from me all that I was bound to keep most secret.

Yes, closeted with you all last night and to-day, I have, for the first time in my life, given myself up to full, complete, and boundless happiness. Could you but see yourself where I have placed you, between the Virgin and God, you might have some idea of the agony in which the night has passed. But I would not offend you by speaking of it; for one glance from your eyes, robbed of the tender sweetness which is my life, would be full of torture for me, and I implore your clemency therefore in advance. Queen of my life and of my soul, oh! that you could grant me but one-thousandth part of the love I bear you!

This was the burden of my prayer; doubt worked havoc in my soul as I oscillated between belief and despair, between life and death, darkness and light. A criminal whose verdict hangs in the balance is not more racked with suspense than I, as I own to my temerity. The smile imaged on your lips, to which my eyes turned ever and again, and alone able to calm the storm roused by the dread of displeasing you. From my birth no one, not even my mother, has smiled on me. The beautiful young girl who was designed for me rejected my heart and gave hers to my brother. Again, in politics all my efforts have been defeated. In the eyes of my king I have read only thirst for vengeance; from childhood he has been my enemy, and the vote of the Cortes* which placed me in power was regarded by him as a personal insult.

Less than this might breed despondency in the stoutest heart. Besides, I have no illusion; I know the gracelessness of my person, and am well aware how difficult it is to do justice to the heart within so rugged a shell. To be loved had ceased to be more than a dream to me when I met you. Thus when I bound myself to your service I knew that devotion alone could excuse my passion.

But, as I look upon this portrait and listen to your smile that whispers of rapture, the rays of a hope which I had sternly banished pierced the gloom, like the light of dawn, again to be obscured by rising mists of doubt and fear of your displeasure, if the morning should break to day. No, it is impossible you should love me yet—I feel it; but in time, as you make proof of the strength, the constancy, and depth of my affection, you may yield me some foothold in your heart. If my daring offends you, tell me so without anger, and I will return to my former part. But if you consent to try and love me, be merciful and break it gently to one who has placed the happiness of his life in the single thought of serving you.

My dear, as I read these last words, he seemed to rise before me, pale as the night when the camellias told their story and he knew his offering was accepted. These words, in their humility, were clearly something quite different from the usual flowery rhetoric of lovers, and a wave of feeling broke over me; it was the breath of happiness.

The weather has been atrocious; impossible to go to the Bois without exciting all sorts of suspicions. Even my mother, who often goes out, regardless of rain, remains at home, and alone.

Wednesday evening

I have just seen *him* at the Opera, my dear; he is another man. He came to our box, introduced by the Sardinian ambassador.

Having read in my eyes that this audacity was taken in good part, he seemed awkwardly conscious of his limbs, and addressed the Marquise d'Espard as "mademoiselle." A light far brighter than the glare of the chandeliers flashed from his eyes. At last he went out with the air of a man who didn't know what he might do next.

"The Baron de Macumer is in love!" exclaimed Madame de Maufrigneuse.

"Strange, isn't it, for a fallen minister?" replied my mother.

I had sufficient presence of mind myself to regard with curiosity Mesdames de Maufrigneuse and d'Espard and my mother, as though they were talking a foreign language and I wanted to know what it was all about, but inwardly my soul sank in the waves of an intoxicating joy. There is only one word to express what I felt, and that is: rapture. Such love as Félipe's surely makes him worthy of mine. I am the very breath of his life, my hands hold the thread that guides his thoughts. To be quite frank, I have a mad longing to see him clear every obstacle and stand before me, asking boldly for my hand. Then I should know whether this storm of love would sink to placid calm at a glance from me.

Ah! my dear, I stopped here, and I am still all in a tremble. As I wrote, I heard a slight noise outside, and rose to see what it was. From my window I could see him coming along the ridge of the wall at the risk of his life. I went to the bedroom window and made him a sign, it was enough; he leaped from the wall—ten feet—and then ran along the road, as far as I could see him, in order to show me that he was not hurt. That he should think of my fear at the moment when he must have been stunned by his fall, moved me so much that I am still crying; I don't know why. Poor ungainly man! what was he coming for? what had he to say to me?

I dare not write my thoughts, and shall go to bed joyful, thinking of all that we would say if we were together. Farewell, fair silent one. I have not time to scold you for not writing, but it is more than a month since I have heard from you! Does this mean that you are at last happy? Have you lost the "complete independence" which you were so proud of, and which to-night has so nearly played me false?

XX
RENÉE DE L'ESTORADE TO LOUISE DE CHAULIEU

May

If love be the life of the world, why do austere philosophers count it for nothing in marriage? Why should Society take for its first law that the woman must be sacrificed to the family, introducing thus a note of discord into the very heart of marriage? And this discord was foreseen, since it was to meet the dangers arising from it that men were armed with new-found powers against us. But for these, we should have been able to bring their whole theory to nothing, whether by the force of love or of a secret, persistent aversion.

I see in marriage, as it at present exists, two opposing forces which it was the task of the lawgiver to reconcile. "When will they be reconciled?" I said to myself, as I read your letter. Oh! my dear, one such letter alone is enough to overthrow the whole fabric constructed by the sage of Aveyron,* under whose shelter I had so cheerfully ensconced myself! The laws were made by old men—any woman can see that—and they have been prudent enough to decree that conjugal love, apart from passion, is not degrading, and that a woman in yielding herself may dispense with the sanction of love, provided the man can legally call her his. In their exclusive concern for the family they have imitated Nature, whose one care is to propagate the species.

Formerly I was a person, now I am a chattel. Not a few tears have I gulped down, alone and far from every one. How gladly would I have exchanged them for a consoling smile! Why are our destinies so unequal? Your soul expands in the atmosphere of a lawful passion. For you, virtue will coincide with pleasure. If you encounter pain, it will be of your own free choice. Your duty, if you marry Félipe, will be one with the sweetest, freest indulgence of feeling. Our future is big with the answer to my question, and I look for it with restless eagerness.

You love and are adored. Oh! my dear, let this noble romance, the old subject of our dreams, take full possession of your soul. Womanly beauty, refined and spiritualized in you, was created by God, for His own purposes, to charm and to delight. Yes, my sweet, guard well the secret of your heart, and submit Félipe to those ingenious devices of ours for testing a lover's metal. Above all, make trial of your own love, for this is even more important. It is so easy to be misled by the deceptive glamour of novelty and passion, and by the vision of happiness.

Alone of the two friends, you remain in your maiden independence; and I beseech you, dearest, do not risk the irrevocable step of marriage without some guarantee. It happens sometimes, when two are talking together, apart from the world, their souls stripped of social disguise, that a gesture, a word, a look lights up, as by a flash, some dark abyss. You have courage and strength to tread boldly in paths where others would be lost.

You have no conception in what anxiety I watch you. Across all this space I see you; my heart beats with yours. Be sure, therefore, to write and tell me everything. Your letters create an inner life of passion within my homely, peaceful household, which reminds me of a level highroad on a gray day. The only event here, my sweet, is that I am playing cross-purposes with myself. But I don't want to tell you about it just now; it must wait for another day. With dogged obstinacy, I pass from despair to hope, now yielding, now holding back. It may be that I ask from life more than we have a right to claim. In youth we are so ready to believe that the ideal and the real will harmonize!

I have been pondering alone, seated beneath a rock in my park, and the fruit of my pondering is that love in marriage is a happy accident on which it is impossible to base a universal law. My Aveyron philosopher is right in looking on the family as the only possible unit in society, and in placing woman in subjection to the family, as she has been in all ages. The solution of this great—for us almost awful—question lies in our first child. For this reason, I would gladly be a mother, were it only to supply food for the consuming energy of my soul.

Louis's temper remains as perfect as ever; his love is of the active, my tenderness of the passive, type. He is happy, plucking the flowers which bloom for him, without troubling about the labor of the earth which has produced them. Blessed self-absorption! At whatever cost to myself, I fall in with his illusions, as a mother, in my idea of her, should be ready to spend herself to satisfy a fancy of her child. The intensity of his joy blinds him, and even throws its reflection upon me. The smile or look of satisfaction which the knowledge of his content brings to my face is enough to satisfy him. And so, "my child" is the pet name which I give him when we are alone.

And I wait for the fruit of all these sacrifices which remain a secret between God, myself, and you. On motherhood I have staked enormously; my credit account is now too large, I fear I shall never receive full payment. To it I look for employment of my energy, expansion of my heart, and the compensation of a world of joys. Pray Heaven I be not deceived! It is a question of all my future and, horrible thought, of my virtue.

XXI

LOUISE DE CHAULIEU TO RENÉE DE L'ESTORADE

June

Dear wedded sweetheart, — Your letter has arrived at the very moment to hearten me for a bold step which I have been meditating night and day. I feel within me a strange craving for the unknown, or, if you will, the forbidden, which makes me uneasy and reveals a conflict in progress in my soul between the laws of society and of nature. I cannot tell whether nature in me is the stronger of the two, but I surprise myself in the act of meditating between the hostile powers.

In plain words, what I wanted was to speak with Félipe, alone, at night, under the lime-trees at the bottom of our garden. There is no denying that this desire beseems the girl who has earned the epithet of an "up-to-date young lady," bestowed on me by the duchesse in jest, and which my father has approved.

Yet to me there seems a method in this madness. I should recompense Félipe for the long nights he has passed under my window, at the same time that I should test him, by seeing what he thinks of my escapade and how he comports himself at a critical moment. Let him cast a halo round my folly—behold in him my husband; let him show one iota less of the tremulous respect with which he bows to me in the Champs-Élysées—farewell, Don Félipe.

As for society, I run less risk in meeting my lover thus than when I smile to him in the drawing-rooms of Madame de Maufrigneuse and the old Marquise de Beauséant, where spies now surround us on every side; and Heaven only knows how people stare at the girl, suspected of a weakness for a grotesque, like

245

Macumer.

I cannot tell you to what a state of agitation I am reduced by dreaming of this idea, and the time I have given to planning its execution. I wanted you badly. What happy hours we should have chattered away, lost in the mazes of uncertainty, enjoying in anticipation all the delights and horrors of a first meeting in the silence of night, under the noble lime-trees of the Chaulieu mansion, with the moonlight dancing through the leaves! As I sat alone, every nerve tingling, I cried, "Oh! Renée, where are you?" Then your letter came, like a match to gunpowder, and my last scruples went by the board.

Through the window I tossed to my bewildered adorer an exact tracing of the key of the little gate at the end of the garden, together with this note:

Your madness must really be put a stop to. If you broke your neck, you would ruin the reputation of the woman you profess to love. Are you worthy of a new proof of regard, and do you deserve that I should talk with you under the limes at the foot of the garden at the hour when the moon throws them into shadow?

Yesterday at one o'clock, when Griffith was going to bed, I said to her:

"Take your shawl, dear, and come out with me. I want to go to the bottom of the garden without anyone knowing."

Without a word, she followed me. Oh! my Renée, what an awful moment when, after a little pause full of delicious thrills of agony, I saw him gliding along like a shadow. When he had reached the garden safely, I said to Griffith:

"Don't be astonished, but the Baron de Macumer is here, and, indeed, it is on that account I brought you with me."

No reply from Griffith.

"What would you have with me?" said Félipe, in a tone of such agitation that it was easy to see he was driven beside himself by the noise, slight as it was, of our dresses in the silence of the night and of our steps upon the gravel.

"I want to say to you what I could not write," I replied.

Griffith withdrew a few steps. It was one of those mild nights, when the air is heavy with the scent of flowers. My head swam with the intoxicating delight of finding myself all but alone with him in the friendly shade of the lime-trees, beyond which lay the garden, shining all the more brightly because the white facade of the house reflected the moonlight. The contrast seemed, as it were, an emblem of our clandestine love leading up to the glaring publicity of a wedding. Neither of us could do more at first than drink in silently the ecstasy of a moment, as new and marvelous for him as for me. At last I found tongue to say, pointing to the elm-tree:

"Although I am not afraid of scandal, you shall not climb that tree again. We have long enough played schoolboy and schoolgirl, let us rise now to the height of our destiny. Had that fall killed you, I should have died disgraced . . ."

I looked at him. Every scrap of color had left his face.

"And if you had been found there, suspicion would have attached either to my mother or to me . . ."

"Forgive me," he murmured.

"If you walk along the boulevard, I shall hear your step; and when I want to see you, I will open my window. But I would not run such a risk unless some emergency arose. Why have you forced me by your rash act to commit another, and one which may lower me in your eyes?"

The tears which I saw in his eyes were to me the most

eloquent of answers.

"What I have done to-night," I went on with a smile, "must seem to you the height of madness . . ."

After we had walked up and down in silence more than once, he recovered composure enough to say:

"You must think me a fool; and, indeed, the delirium of my joy has robbed me of both nerve and wits. But of this at least be assured, whatever you do is sacred in my eyes from the very fact that it seemed right to you. I honor you as I honor only God besides. And then, Miss Griffith is here."

"She is here for the sake of the others, not for us," I put in hastily.

My dear, he understood me at once.

"I know very well," he said, with the humblest glance at me, "that whether she is there or not makes no difference. Unseen of men, we are still in the presence of God, and our own esteem is not less important to us than that of the world."

"Thank you, Félipe," I said, holding out my hand to him with a gesture which you ought to see. "A woman, and I am nothing, if not a woman, is on the road to loving the man who understands her. Oh! only on the road," I went on, with a finger on my lips. "Don't let your hopes carry you beyond what I say. My heart will belong only to the man who can read it and know its every turn. Our views, without being absolutely identical, must be the same in their breadth and elevation. I have no wish to exaggerate my own merits; doubtless what seem virtues in my eyes have their corresponding defects. All I can say is, I should be heartbroken without them."

"Having first accepted me as your servant, you now permit me to love you," he said, trembling and looking in my face at each word. "My first prayer has been more than answered."

"But," I hastened to reply, "your position seems

to me a better one than mine. I should not object to change places, and this change it lies with you to bring about."

"In my turn, I thank you," he replied. "I know the duties of a faithful lover. It is mine to prove that I am worthy of you; the trials shall be as long as you choose to make them. If I belie your hopes, you have only— God! that I should say it—to reject me."

"I know that you love me," I replied. "*So far,*" with a cruel emphasis on the words, "you stand first in my regard. Otherwise you would not be here."

Then we began to walk up and down as we talked, and I must say that so soon as my Spaniard had recovered himself he put forth the genuine eloquence of the heart. It was not passion it breathed, but a marvelous tenderness of feeling which he beautifully compared to the divine love. His thrilling voice, which lent an added charm to thoughts, in themselves so exquisite, reminded me of the nightingale's note. He spoke low, using only the middle tones of a fine instrument, and words flowed upon words with the rush of a torrent. It was the overflow of the heart.

"No more," I said, "or I shall not be able to tear myself away."

And with a gesture I dismissed him.

"You have committed yourself now, mademoiselle," said Griffith.

"In England that might be so, but not in France," I replied with nonchalance. "I intend to make a love match, and am feeling my way—that is all."

You see, dear, as love did not come to me, I had to do as Mahomet did with the mountain.

Friday

Once more I have seen my slave. He has become very timid, and puts on an air of pious devotion, which I like, for it seems to say that he feels my power and fascination in every fibre. But nothing in his look or manner can rouse in these society sibyls any suspicion of the boundless love which I see. Don't suppose though, dear, that I am carried away, mastered, tamed; on the contrary, the taming, mastering, and carrying away are on my side . . .

In short, I am quite capable of reason. Oh! to feel again the terror of that fascination in which I was held by the schoolmaster, the plebeian, the man I kept at a distance!

The fact is that love is of two kinds—one which commands, and one which obeys. The two are quite distinct, and the passion to which the one gives rise is not the passion of the other. To get her full of life, perhaps a woman ought to have experience of both. Can the two passions ever co-exist? Can the man in whom we inspire love inspire it in us? Will the day ever come when Félipe is my master? Shall I tremble then, as he does now? These are questions which make me shudder.

He is very blind! In his place I should have thought Mademoiselle de Chaulieu, meeting me under the limes, a cold, calculating coquette, with starched manners. No, that is not love, it is playing with fire. I am still fond of Félipe, but I am calm and at my ease with him now. No more obstacles! What a terrible thought! It is all ebb-tide within, and I fear to question my heart. His mistake was in concealing the ardor of his love; he ought to have forced my self-control.

In a word, I was naughty, and I have not got the reward such naughtiness brings. No, dear, however sweet the memory of that half-hour beneath the trees, it is nothing like the excitement of the old time with its: "Shall I go? Shall I not go? Shall I write to him? Shall I not write?"

Is it thus with all our pleasures? Is suspense always better than enjoyment? Hope than fruition? Is it the rich who in very truth are the poor? Have we not both perhaps exaggerated feeling by giving to imagination too free a rein? There are times when this thought freezes me. Shall I tell you why? Because I am meditating another visit to the bottom of the garden—without Griffith. How far could I go in this direction? Imagination knows no limit, but it is not so with pleasure. Tell me, dear be-furbeloved professor, how can one reconcile the two goals of a woman's existence?

XXII

LOUISE TO FÉLIPE

I am not pleased with you. If you did not cry over Racine's *Bérénice*,* and feel it to be the most terrible of tragedies, there is no kinship in our souls; we shall never get on together, and had better break off at once. Let us meet no more. Forget me; for if I do not have a satisfactory reply, I shall forget you. You will become Monsieur le Baron de Macumer for me, or rather you will cease to be at all.

Yesterday at Madame d'Espard's you had a self-satisfied air which disgusted me. No doubt, apparently, about your conquest! In sober earnest, your self-possession alarms me. Not a trace in you of the humble slave of your first letter. Far from betraying the absent-mindedness of a lover, you polished epigrams! This is not the attitude of a true believer, always prostrate before his divinity.

If you do not feel me to be the very breath of your life, a being nobler than other women, and to be judged by other standards, then I must be less than a woman in your sight. You have roused in me a spirit of mistrust, Félipe, and its angry mutterings have drowned the accents of tenderness. When I look back upon what has passed between us, I feel in truth that I have a right to be suspicious. For know, Prime Minister of all the Spains, that I have reflected much on the defenceless condition of our sex. My innocence has held a torch, and my fingers are not burnt. Let me repeat to you, then, what my youthful experience taught me.

In all other matters, duplicity, faithlessness, and broken pledges are brought to book and punished; but not so with love, which is at once the victim, the accuser, the counsel, judge, and executioner. The cruelest treachery, the most heartless crimes, are those which remain for ever concealed, with two hearts alone for witness. How indeed should the victim proclaim them without injury to herself? Love, therefore, has its own code, its own penal system, with which the world has no concern.

Now, for my part, I have resolved never to pardon a serious misdemeanor, and in love, pray, what is not serious? Yesterday you had all the air of a man successful in his suit. You would be wrong to doubt it; and yet, if this assurance robbed you of the charming simplicity which sprang from uncertainty, I should blame you severely. I would have you neither bashful nor self-complacent; I would not have you in terror of losing my affection—that would be an insult—but neither would I have you wear your love lightly as a thing of course. Never should your heart be freer than mine. If you know nothing of the torture that a single stab of doubt brings to the soul, tremble lest I give you a lesson!

In a single glance I confided my heart to you, and you read the meaning. The purest feelings that ever took root in a young girl's breast are yours. The thought and meditation of which I have told you served only to enrich the mind; but if ever the wounded heart turns to the brain for counsel, be sure the young girl would show some kinship with the demon of knowledge and of daring.

I swear to you, Félipe, if you love me, as I believe you do and if I have reason to suspect the least falling off in the fear, obedience, and respect which you have hitherto professed, if the pure flame of passion which first kindled the fire of my heart should seem to me any day to burn less vividly, you need fear no reproaches. I would not weary you with letters bearing any trace of weakness, pride, or anger, nor even with one of warning like this. But if I spoke no words, Félipe, my face would tell you that death was near. And yet I should not die till I had branded you with infamy, and sown eternal sorrow in your heart; you would see the girl you loved dishonored and lost in this world, and know her doomed to everlasting suffering in the next.

Do not therefore, I implore you, give me cause to envy the old, happy Louise, the object of your pure worship, whose heart expanded in the sunshine of happiness, since, in the words of Dante, she possessed: *Senza brama, sicura ricchezza!** I have searched the *Inferno* through to find the most terrible punishment, some torture of the mind to which I might link the vengeance of God.

Yesterday, as I watched you, doubt went through me like a sharp, cold dagger's point. Do you know what that means? I mistrusted you, and the pang was so terrible, I could not endure it longer. If my service be too hard, leave it, I would not keep you. Do I need any proof of your cleverness? Keep for me the flowers of your wit. Show to others no fine surface to call forth flattery, compliments, or praise. Come to me, laden with hatred or scorn, the butt of calumny, come to me with the news that women flout you and ignore you, and not one loves you; then, ah! then you will know the treasures of Louise's heart and love.

We are only rich when our wealth is buried so deep that all the world might trample it under foot, unknowing. If you were handsome, I don't suppose I should have looked at you twice, or discovered one of the thousand reasons out of which my love sprang. True, we know no more of these reasons than we know why it is the sun makes the flowers to bloom, and ripens the fruit. Yet I could tell you of one reason very dear to me.

The character, expression, and individuality that ennoble your face are a sealed book to all but me. Mine is the power which transforms you into the most lovable of men, and that is why I would keep your mental gifts also for myself. To others they should be as meaningless as your eyes, the charm of your mouth and features. Let it be mine alone to kindle the beacon of your intelligence, as I bring the lovelight into your eyes. I would have you the Spanish grandee of old days, cold, ungracious, haughty, a monument to be gazed at from afar, like the ruins of some barbaric power, which no one ventures to explore. Now, you have nothing better to do than to open up pleasant promenades for the public, and show yourself of a Parisian affability!

Is my ideal portrait, then, forgotten? Your excessive cheerfulness was redolent of your love. Had it not been for a restraining glance from me, you would have proclaimed to the most sharp-sighted, keen-witted, and unsparing of Paris salons, that your inspiration was drawn from Armande-Louise-Marie de Chaulieu.

I believe in your greatness too much to think for a moment that your love is ruled by policy; but if you did not show a childlike simplicity when with me, I could only pity you. Spite of this first fault, you are still deeply admired by

LOUISE DE CHAULIEU

XXIII
FÉLIPE TO LOUISE

When God beholds our faults, He sees also our repentance. Yes, my beloved mistress, you are right. I felt that I had displeased you, but knew not how. Now that you have explained the cause of your trouble, I find in it fresh motive to adore you. Like the God of Israel, you are a jealous deity, and I rejoice to see it. For what is holier and more precious than jealousy? My fair guardian angel, jealousy is an ever-wakeful sentinel; it is to love what pain is to the body, the faithful herald of evil. Be jealous of your servant, Louise, I beg of you; the harder you strike, the more contrite will he be and kiss the rod, in all submission, which proves that he is not indifferent to you.

But, alas! dear, if the pains it cost me to vanquish my timidity and master feelings you thought so feeble were invisible to you, will Heaven, think you, reward them? I assure you, it needed no slight effort to show myself to you as I was in the days before I loved. At Madrid I was considered a good talker, and I wanted you to see for yourself the few gifts I may possess. If this were vanity, it has been well punished.

Your last glance utterly unnerved me. Never had I so quailed, even when the army of France was at the gates of Cadiz and I read peril for my life in the dissembling words of my royal master. Vainly I tried to discover the cause of your displeasure, and the lack of sympathy between us which this fact disclosed was terrible to me. For in truth I have no wish but to act by your will, think your thoughts, see with your eyes, respond to your joy and suffering, as my body responds to heat and cold. The crime and the anguish lay for me in the breach of unison in that common life of feeling which you have made so fair.

"I have vexed her!" I exclaimed over and over again, like one distraught. My noble, my beautiful Louise, if anything could increase the fervor of my devotion or confirm my belief in your delicate moral intuitions, it would be the new light which your words have thrown upon my own feelings. Much in them, of which my mind was formerly but dimly conscious, you have now made clear. If this be designed as chastisement, what can be the sweetness of your rewards?

Louise, for me it was happiness enough to be accepted as your servant. You have given me the life of which I despaired. No longer do I draw a useless breath, I have something to spend myself for; my force has an outlet, if only in suffering for you. Once more I say, as I have said before, that you will never find me other than I was when first I offered myself as your lowly bondman. Yes, were you dishonored and lost, to use your own words, my heart would only cling the more closely to you for your self-sought misery. It would be my care to staunch your wounds, and my prayers should importune God with the story of your innocence and your wrongs.

Did I not tell you that the feelings of my heart for you are not a lover's only, that I will be to you father, mother, sister, brother—ay, a whole family—anything or nothing, as you may decree? And is it not your own wish which has confined within the compass of a lover's feeling so many varying forms of devotion? Pardon me, then, if at times the father and brother disappear behind the lover, since you know they are none the less there, though screened from view. Would that you could read the feelings of my heart when you appear before me, radiant in your beauty, the centre of admiring eyes, reclining calmly in your carriage in the Champs-Élysées, or seated in your box at the Opera! Then would you know how absolutely free from selfish taint is the pride with which I hear the praises of your loveliness and grace, praises which warm my heart even to the strangers who utter them! When by chance you have raised me to elysium by a friendly greeting, my pride is mingled with humility, and I depart as though God's blessing rested on me. Nor does the joy vanish without leaving a long track of light behind. It breaks on me through the clouds of my cigarette smoke. More than ever do I feel how every drop of this surging blood throbs for you.

Can you be ignorant how you are loved? After seeing you, I return to my study, and the glitter of its Saracenic ornaments sinks to nothing before the brightness of your portrait, when I open the spring that keeps it locked up from every eye and lose myself in endless musings or link my happiness to verse. From the heights of heaven I look down upon the course of a life such as my hopes dare to picture it! Have you never, in the silence of the night, or through the roar of the town, heard the whisper of a voice in your sweet, dainty ear? Does no one of the thousand prayers that I speed to you reach home?

By dint of silent contemplation of your pictured face, I have succeeded in deciphering the expression of every feature and tracing its connection with some grace of the spirit, and then I pen a sonnet to you in Spanish on the harmony of the twofold beauty in which nature has clothed you. These sonnets you will never see, for my poetry is too unworthy of its theme, I dare not send it to you. Not a moment passes without thoughts of you, for my whole being is bound up in you, and if you ceased to be its animating principle, every part would ache.

Now, Louise, can you realize the torture to me of knowing that I had displeased you, while entirely ignorant of the cause? The ideal double life which seemed so fair was cut short. My heart turned to ice within me as, hopeless of any other explanation, I concluded that you had ceased to love me. With heavy heart, and yet not wholly without comfort, I was falling back upon my old post as servant; then your letter came and turned all to joy. Oh! might I but listen for ever to such chiding!

Once a child, picking himself up from a tumble, turned to his mother with the words "Forgive me." Hiding his own hurt, he sought pardon for the pain he had caused her. Louise, I was that child, and such as I was then, I am now. Here is the key to my character, which your slave in all humility places in your hands.

But do not fear, there will be no more stumbling. Keep tight the chain which binds me to you, so that a touch may communicate your lightest wish to him who will ever remain your slave,

FÉLIPE

XXIV

LOUISE DE CHAULIEU TO RENÉE DE L'ESTORADE

October 1825

My dear friend,—How is it possible that you, who brought yourself in two months to marry a broken-down invalid in order to mother him, should know anything of that terrible shifting drama, enacted in the recesses of the heart, which we call love—a drama where death lies in a glance or a light reply?

I had reserved for Félipe one last supreme test which was to be decisive. I wanted to know whether his love was the love of a Royalist for his king, who can do no wrong. Why should the loyalty of a Catholic be less supreme?

He walked with me a whole night under the limes at the bottom of the garden, and not a shadow of suspicion crossed his soul. Next day he loved me better, but the feeling was as reverent, as humble, as regretful as ever; he had not presumed an iota. Oh! he is a very Spaniard, a very Abencerrage. He scaled my wall to come and kiss the hand which in the darkness I reached down to him from my balcony. He might have broken his neck; how many of our young men would do the like?

But all this is nothing; Christians suffer the horrible pangs of martyrdom in the hope of heaven. The day before yesterday I took aside the royal ambassador-to-be at the court of Spain, my much respected father, and said to him with a smile:

"Monsieur, some of your friends will have it that you are marrying your dear Armande to the nephew of an ambassador who has been very anxious for this connection, and has long begged for it. Also, that the marriage-contract arranges for his nephew to succeed on his death to his enormous fortune and his title, and bestows on the young couple in the meantime an income of a hundred thousand livres, on the bride a dowry of eight hundred thousand francs. Your daughter weeps, but bows to the unquestioned authority of her honored parent. Some people are unkind enough to say that, behind her tears, she conceals a worldly and ambitious soul.

"Now, we are going to the gentleman's box at the Opera to-night, and Monsieur le Baron de Macumer will visit us there."

"Macumer needs a touch of the spur then," said my father, smiling at me, as though I were a female ambassador.

"You mistake Clarissa Harlowe for Figaro!" I cried, with a glance of scorn and mockery. "When you see me with my right hand ungloved, you will give the lie to this impertinent gossip, and will mark your displeasure at it."

"I may make my mind easy about your future. You have no more got a girl's headpiece than Jeanne d'Arc had a woman's heart. You will be happy, you will love nobody, and will allow yourself to be loved."

This was too much. I burst into laughter.

"What is it, little flirt?" he said.

"I tremble for my country's interests . . ."

And seeing him look quite blank, I added:

"At Madrid!"

"You have no idea how this little nun has learned, in a year's time, to make fun of her father," he said to the duchesse.

"Armande makes light of everything," my mother replied, looking me in the face.

"What do you mean?" I asked.

"Why, you are not even afraid of rheumatism on these damp nights," she said, with another meaning glance at me.

"Oh!" I answered, "the mornings are so hot!"

The duchesse looked down.

"It's high time she were married," said my father,

"and it had better be before I go."

"If you wish it," I replied demurely.

Two hours later, my mother and I, the Duchesse de Maufrigneuse and Madame d'Espard, were all four blooming like roses in the front of the box. I had seated myself sideways, giving only a shoulder to the house, so that I could see everything, myself unseen, in that spacious box which fills one of the two angles at the back of the hall, between the columns.

Macumer came, stood up, and put his opera-glasses before his eyes so that he might be able to look at me comfortably.

In the first interval entered the young man whom I call "king of the profligates." The Comte Henri de Marsay, who has great beauty of an effeminate kind, entered the box with an epigram in his eyes, a smile upon his lips, and an air of satisfaction over his whole countenance. He first greeted my mother, Madame d'Espard, and the Duchesse de Maufrigneuse, the Comte d'Esgrignon, and Monsieur de Canalis; then turning to me, he said:

"I do not know whether I shall be the first to congratulate you on an event which will make you the object of envy to many."

"Ah! a marriage!" I cried. "Is it left for me, a girl fresh from the convent, to tell you that predicted marriages never come off."

Monsieur de Marsay bent down, whispering to Macumer, and I was convinced, from the movement of his lips, that what he said was this:

"Baron, you are perhaps in love with that little coquette, who has used you for her own ends; but as the question is one not of love, but of marriage, it is as well for you to know what is going on."

Macumer treated this officious scandal-monger to one of those glances of his which seem to me so eloquent of noble scorn, and replied to the effect that he was "not in love with any little coquette." His whole bearing so delighted me, that directly I caught sight of my father, the glove was off.

Félipe had not a shadow of fear or doubt. How well did he bear out my expectations! His faith is only in me, society cannot hurt him with its lies. Not a muscle of the Arab's face stirred, not a drop of the blue blood flushed his olive cheek.

The two young comtes went out, and I said, laughing, to Macumer:

"Monsieur de Marsay has been treating you to an epigram on me."

"He did more," he replied. "It was an epithalamium."

"You speak Greek to me," I said, rewarding him with a smile and a certain look which always embarrasses him.

My father meantime was talking to Madame de Maufrigneuse.

"I should think so!" he exclaimed. "The gossip which gets about is scandalous. No sooner has a girl come out than everyone is keen to marry her, and the ridiculous stories that are invented! I shall never force Armande to marry against her will. I am going to take a turn in the promenade, otherwise people will be saying that I allowed the rumor to spread in order to suggest the marriage to the ambassador; and Cæsar's daughter ought to be above suspicion, even more than his wife — if that were possible."

The Duchesse de Maufrigneuse and Madame d'Espard shot glances first at my mother, then at the baron, brimming over with sly intelligence and repressed curiosity. With their serpent's cunning they had at last got an inkling of something going on. Of all mysteries in life, love is the least mysterious! It exhales from women, I believe, like a perfume, and she who can conceal it is a very monster! Our eyes prattle even more than our tongues.

Having enjoyed the delightful sensation of finding

Félipe rise to the occasion, as I had wished, it was only in nature I should hunger for more. So I made the signal agreed on for telling him that he might come to my window by the dangerous road you know of. A few hours later I found him, upright as a statue, glued to the wall, his hand resting on the balcony of my window, studying the reflections of the light in my room.

"My dear Félipe," I said, "You have acquitted yourself well to-night; you behaved exactly as I should have done had I been told that you were on the point of marrying."

"I thought," he replied, "that you would hardly have told others before me."

"And what right have you to this privilege?"

"The right of one who is your devoted slave."

"In very truth?"

"I am, and shall ever remain so."

"But suppose this marriage was inevitable; suppose that I had agreed . . ."

Two flashing glances lit up the moonlight—one directed to me, the other to the precipice which the wall made for us. He seemed to calculate whether a fall together would mean death; but the thought merely passed like lightning over his face and sparkled in his eyes. A power, stronger than passion, checked the impulse.

"An Arab cannot take back his word," he said in a husky voice. "I am your slave to do with as you will; my life is not mine to destroy."

The hand on the balcony seemed as though its hold were relaxing. I placed mine on it as I said:

"Félipe, my beloved, from this moment I am your wife in thought and will. Go in the morning to ask my father for my hand. He wishes to retain my fortune; but if you promise to acknowledge receipt of it in the contract, his consent will no doubt be given. I am no longer Armande de Chaulieu. Leave me at once; no breath of scandal must touch Louise de Macumer."

He listened with blanched face and trembling limbs, then, like a flash, had cleared the ten feet to the ground in safety. It was a moment of agony, but he waved his hand to me and disappeared.

"I am loved then," I said to myself, "as never woman was before." And I fell asleep in the calm content of a child, my destiny for ever fixed.

About two o'clock next day my father summoned me to his private room, where I found the duchesse and Macumer. There was an interchange of civilities. I replied quite simply that if my father and Monsieur Hénarez were of one mind, I had no reason to oppose their wishes. Thereupon my mother invited the baron to dinner; and after dinner, we all four went for a drive in the Bois de Boulogne, where I had the pleasure of smiling ironically to Monsieur de Marsay as he passed on horseback and caught sight of Macumer sitting opposite to us beside my father.

My bewitching Félipe has had his cards reprinted as follows:

HÉNAREZ
Baron de Macumer, formerly Duc de Soria

Every morning he brings me with his own hands a splendid bouquet, hidden in which I never fail to find a letter, containing a Spanish sonnet in my honor, which he has composed during the night.

Not to make this letter inordinately large, I send you as specimens only the first and last of these sonnets, which I have translated for your benefit, word for word, and line for line:—

FIRST SONNET

Many a time I've stood, clad in thin silken vest,
Drawn sword in hand, with steady pulse,
Waiting the charge of a raging bull,
And the thrust of his horn, sharper-pointed than Phœbe's
    crescent.

I've scaled, on my lips the lilt of an Andalusian dance,
The steep redoubt under a rain of fire;
I've staked my life upon a hazard of the dice
Careless, as though it were a gold doubloon.

My hand would seek the ball out of the cannon's mouth,
But now meseems I grow more timid than a crouching hair,
Or a child spying some ghost in the curtain's folds.

For when your sweet eye rests on me,
Any icy sweat covers my brow, my knees give way,
I tremble, shrink, my courage gone.

SECOND SONNET

Last night I fain would sleep to dream of thee,
But jealous sleep fled my eyelids,
I sought the balcony and looked towards heaven,
Always my glance flies upward when I think of thee.

Strange sight! whose meaning love alone can tell,
The sky had lost its sapphire hue,
The stars, dulled diamonds in their golden mount,
Twinkled no more nor shed their warmth.

The moon, washed of her silver radiance lily-white,
Hung mourning over the gloomy plain, for thou hast robbed
The heavens of all that made them bright.

The snowy sparkle of the moon is on thy lovely brow,
Heaven's azure centres in thine eyes,
Thy lashes fall like starry rays.

What more gracious way of saying to a young girl that
she fills your life? Tell me what you think of this love,
which expends itself in lavishing the treasures alike of
the earth and of the soul. Only within the last ten days
have I grasped the meaning of that Spanish gallantry,
so famous in old days.

Ah me! dear, what is going on now at La Crampade? How often do I take a stroll there, inspecting the growth of our crops! Have you no news to give of our mulberry trees, our last winter's plantations? Does everything prosper as you wish? And while the buds are opening on our shrubs—I will not venture to speak of the bedding-out plants—have they also blossomed in the bosom of the wife? Does Louis continue his policy of madrigals? Do you enter into each other's thoughts? I wonder whether your little runlet of wedding peace is better than the raging torrent of my love! Has my sweet lady professor taken offence? I cannot believe it; and if it were so, I should send Félipe off at once, post-haste, to fling himself at her knees and bring back to me my pardon or her head. Sweet love, my life here is a splendid success, and I want to know how it fares with life in Provence. We have just increased our family by the addition of a Spaniard with the complexion of a Havana cigar, and your congratulations still tarry.

Seriously, my sweet Renée, I am anxious. I am afraid lest you should be eating your heart out in silence, for fear of casting a gloom over my sunshine. Write to me at once, naughty child! and tell me your life in its every minutest detail; tell me whether you still hold back, whether your "independence" still stands erect, or has fallen on its knees, or is sitting down comfortably, which would indeed be serious. Can you suppose that the incidents of your married life are without interest for me? I muse at times over all that you have said to me. Often when, at the Opera, I seem absorbed in watching the pirouetting dancers, I am saying to myself, "It is half-past nine, perhaps she is in bed. What is she about? Is she happy? Is she alone with her independence? or has her independence gone the way of other dead and castoff independences?"

A thousand loves.

XXV
RENÉE DE L'ESTORADE TO LOUISE DE CHAULIEU

Saucy girl! Why should I write? What could I say? Whilst your life is varied by social festivities, as well as by the anguish, the tempers, and the flowers of love—all of which you describe so graphically, that I might be watching some first-rate acting at the theatre—mine is as monotonous and regular as though it were passed in a convent.

We always go to bed at nine and get up with daybreak. Our meals are served with a maddening punctuality. Nothing ever happens. I have accustomed myself without much difficulty to this mapping out of the day, which perhaps is, after all, in the nature of things. Where would the life of the universe be but for that subjection to fixed laws which, according to the astronomers, so Louis tells me, rule the spheres! It is not order of which we weary.

Then I have laid upon myself certain rules of dress, and these occupy my time in the mornings. I hold it part of my duty as a wife to look as charming as possible. I feel a certain satisfaction in it, and it causes lively pleasure to the good old man and to Louis. After lunch, we walk. When the newspapers arrive, I disappear to look after my household affairs or to read—for I read a great deal—or to write to you. I come back to the others an hour before dinner; and after dinner we play cards, or receive visits, or pay them. Thus my days pass between a contented old man, who has done with passions, and the man who owes his happiness to me. Louis's happiness is so radiant that it has at last warmed my heart.

For women, happiness no doubt cannot consist in the mere satisfaction of desire. Sometimes, in the evening, when I am not required to take a hand in the game, and can sink back in my armchair, imagination bears me on its strong wings into the very heart of your life. Then, its riches, its changeful tints, its surging passions become my own, and I ask myself to what end such a stormy preface can lead. May I not swallow up the book itself? For you, my darling, the illusions of love are possible; for me, only the facts of homely life remain. Yes, your love seems to me a dream!

Therefore I find it hard to understand why you are determined to throw so much romance over it. Your ideal man must have more soul than fire, more nobility and self-command than passion. You persist in trying to clothe in living form the dream ideal of a girl on the threshold of life; you demand sacrifices for the pleasure of rewarding them; you submit your Félipe to tests in order to ascertain whether desire, hope, and curiosity are enduring in their nature. But, child, behind all your fantastic stage scenery rises the altar, where everlasting bonds are forged. The very morrow of your marriage the graceful structure raised by your subtle strategy may fall before that terrible reality which makes of a girl a woman, of a gallant a husband. Remember that there is not exemption for lovers. For them, as for ordinary folk like Louis and me, there lurks beneath the wedding rejoicings the great "Perhaps" of Rabelais.*

I do not blame you, though, of course, it was rash, for talking with Félipe in the garden, or for spending a night with him, you on your balcony, he on his wall; but you make a plaything of life, and I am afraid that life may some day turn the tables. I dare not give you the counsel which my own experience would suggest; but let me repeat once more from the seclusion of my valley that the viaticum of married life lies in these words—resignation and self-sacrifice. For, spite of all your tests, your coyness, and your vigilance, I can see that marriage will mean to you what it has been to me. The greater the passion, the steeper the precipice we have hewn for our fall—that is the only difference.

Oh! what I would give to see the Baron de Macumer

and talk with him for an hour or two! Your happiness lies so near my heart.

XXVI
LOUISE DE MACUMER TO RENÉE DE L'ESTORADE

March 1825

As Félipe has carried out, with a truly Saracenic generosity, the wishes of my father and mother in acknowledging the fortune he has not received from me, the duchesse has become even more friendly to me than before. She calls me little sly-boots, little woman of the world, and says I know how to use my tongue.

"But, dear mamma," I said to her the evening before the contract was signed, "you attribute to cunning and smartness on my part what is really the outcome of the truest, simplest, most unselfish, most devoted love that ever was! I assure you that I am not at all the 'woman of the world' you do me the honor of believing me to be."

"Come, come, Armande," she said, putting her arm on my neck and drawing me to her, in order to kiss my forehead, "you did not want to go back to the convent, you did not want to die an old maid, and, like a fine, noble-hearted Chaulieu, as you are, you recognized the necessity of building up your father's family. (The duc was listening. If you knew, Renée, what flattery lies for him in these words.) I have watched you during the whole winter, poking your little nose into all that goes on, forming very sensible opinions about men and the present state of society in France. And you have picked out the one Spaniard capable of giving you the splendid position of a woman who reigns supreme in her own house. My little girl, you treated him exactly as Tullia treats your brother."

"What lessons they give in my sister's convent!" exclaimed my father.

A glance at my father cut him short at once; then, turning to the duchesse, I said:

"Madame, I love my future husband, Félipe de Soria, with all the strength of my soul. Although this love sprang up without my knowledge, and though I fought it stoutly when it first made itself felt, I swear to you that I never gave way to it till I had recognized in the Baron de Macumer a character worthy of mine, a heart of which the delicacy, the generosity, the devotion, and the temper are suited to my own."

"But, my dear," she began, interrupting me, "he is as ugly as . . ."

"As anything you like," I retorted quickly, "but I love his ugliness."

"If you love him, Armande," said my father, "and have the strength to master your love, you must not risk your happiness. Now, happiness in marriage depends largely on the first days—"

"Days only?" interrupted my mother. Then, with a glance at my father, she continued, "You had better leave us, my dear, to have our talk together."

"You are to be married, dear child," the duchesse then began in a low voice, "in three days. It becomes my duty, therefore, without silly whimpering, which would be unfitting our rank in life, to give you the serious advice which every mother owes to her daughter. You are marrying a man whom you love, and there is no reason why I should pity you or myself. I have only known you for a year; and if this period has been long enough for me to learn to love you, it is hardly sufficient to justify floods of tears at the idea of losing you. Your mental gifts are even more remarkable than those of your person; you have gratified maternal pride, and have shown yourself a sweet and loving daughter. I, in my turn, can promise you that you will always find a staunch friend in your mother. You smile? Alas! it too often happens that a mother who has lived on excellent terms with her daughter, as long as the daughter is a mere girl, comes to cross purposes with her when they are both women together.

"It is your happiness which I want, so listen to my words. The love which you now feel is that of a young girl, and is natural to us all, for it is woman's destiny to cling to a man. Unhappily, pretty one, there is but one man in the world for a woman! And sometimes this man, whom fate has marked out for us, is not the one whom we, mistaking a passing fancy for love, choose as husband. Strange as what I say may appear to you, it is worth noting. If we cannot love the man we have chosen, the fault is not exclusively ours, it lies with both, or sometimes with circumstances over which we have no control. Yet there is no reason why the man chosen for us by our family, the man to whom our fancy has gone out, should not be the man whom we can love. The barriers which arise later between husband and wife are often due to lack of perseverance on both sides. The task of transforming a husband into a lover is not less delicate than that other task of making a husband of the lover, in which you have just proved yourself marvelously successful.

"I repeat it, your happiness is my object. Never allow yourself, then, to forget that the first three months of your married life may work your misery if you do not submit to the yoke with the same forbearance, tenderness, and intelligence that you have shown during the days of courtship. For, my little rogue, you know very well that you have indulged in all the innocent pleasures of a clandestine love affair. If the culmination of your love begins with disappointment, dislike, nay, even with pain, well, come and tell me about it. Don't hope for too much from marriage at first; it will perhaps give you more discomfort than joy. The happiness of your life requires at least as patient cherishing as the early shoots of love.

"To conclude, if by chance you should lose the lover, you will find in his place the father of your children. In this, my dear child, lies the whole secret of social life. Sacrifice everything to the man whose name you bear, the man whose honor and reputation cannot suffer in the least degree without involving you in frightful consequences. Such sacrifice is thus not only an absolute duty for women of our rank, it is also their wisest policy. This, indeed, is the distinctive mark of great moral principles, that they hold good and are expedient from whatever aspect they are viewed. But I need say no more to you on this point.

"I fancy you are of a jealous disposition, and, my dear, if you knew how jealous I am! But you must not be stupid over it. To publish your jealousy to the world is like playing at politics with your cards upon the table, and those who let their own game be seen learn nothing of their opponents'. Whatever happens, we must know how to suffer in silence."

She added that she intended having some plain talk about me with Macumer the evening before the wedding.

Raising my mother's beautiful arm, I kissed her hand and dropped on it a tear, which the tone of real feeling in her voice had brought to my eyes. In the advice she had given me, I read high principle worthy of herself and of me, true wisdom, and a tenderness of heart unspoilt by the narrow code of society. Above all, I saw that she understood my character. These few simple words summed up the lessons which life and experience had brought her, perhaps at a heavy price. She was moved, and said, as she looked at me:

"Dear little girl, you've got a nasty crossing before you. And most women, in their ignorance or their disenchantment, are as wise as the Earl of Westmoreland!"

We both laughed; but I must explain the joke. The evening before, a Russian princess had told us an anecdote of this gentleman. He had suffered frightfully from sea-sickness in crossing the Channel, and turned tail when he got near Italy, because he had heard some one speak of "crossing" the Alps. "Thank you; I've had quite enough crossings already," he said.

You will understand, Renée, that your gloomy philosophy and my mother's lecture were calculated to revive the fears which used to disturb us at Blois. The nearer marriage approached, the more did I need to summon all my strength, my resolution, and my affection to face this terrible passage from maidenhood to womanhood. All our conversations came back to my mind, I re-read your letters and discerned in them a vague undertone of sadness.

This anxiety had one advantage at least; it helped me to the regulation expression for a bride as commonly depicted. The consequence was that on the day of signing the contract everybody said I looked charming and quite the right thing. This morning, at the *Mairie*,* it was an informal business, and only the witnesses were present.

I am writing this tail to my letter while they are putting out my dress for dinner. We shall be married at midnight at the Church of Sainte-Valère,* after a very gay evening. I confess that my fears give me a martyr-like and modest air to which I have no right, but which will be admired—why, I cannot conceive. I am delighted to see that poor Félipe is every whit as timorous as I am; society grates on him, he is like a bat in a glass shop.

"Thank Heaven, the day won't last for ever!" he whispered to me in all innocence.

In his bashfulness and timidity he would have liked to have no one there.

The Sardinian ambassador, when he came to sign the contract, took me aside in order to present me with a pearl necklace, linked together by six splendid diamonds—a gift from my sister-in-law, the Duchesse de Soria. Along with the necklace was a sapphire brace-let, on the under side of which were engraved the words, "unknown, beloved." Two charming letters came with these presents, which, however, I could not accept with-out consulting Félipe.

"For," I said, "I should not like to see you wearing or-naments that came from any one but me."

He kissed my hand, quite moved, and replied:

"Wear them for the sake of the inscription, and also for the kind feeling, which is sincere."

Saturday Evening

Here, then, my poor Renée, are the last words of your girl friend. After the midnight Mass, we set off for an es-tate which Félipe, with kind thought for me, has bought in Nivernais, on the way to Provence. Already my name is Louise de Macumer, but I leave Paris in a few hours as Louise de Chaulieu. However I am called, there will never be for you but one Louise.

XXVII

THE SAME TO THE SAME

October 1825

I have not written to you, dear, since our marriage, near-ly eight months ago. And not a line from you! Madame, you are inexcusable.

To begin with, we set off in a post-chaise for the Castle of Chantepleurs, the property which Macumer has bought in Nivernais. It stands on the banks of the Loire, sixty leagues from Paris. Our servants, with the excep-tion of my maid, were there before us, and we arrived, after a very rapid journey, the next evening. I slept all the way from Paris to beyond Montargis.* My lord and master put his arm round me and pillowed my head on his shoulder, upon an arrangement of handkerchiefs.

273

This was the one liberty he took; and the almost motherly tenderness which got the better of his drowsiness, touched me strangely. I fell asleep then under the fire of his eyes, and awoke to find them still blazing; the passionate gaze remained unchanged, but what thoughts had come and gone meanwhile! Twice he had kissed me on the forehead.

At Briare* we had breakfast in the carriage. Then followed a talk like our old talks at Blois, while the same Loire we used to admire called forth our praises, and at half-past seven we entered the noble long avenue of lime-trees, acacias, sycamores, and larches which leads to Chantepleurs. At eight we dined; at ten we were in our bedroom, a charming Gothic room, made comfortable with every modern luxury. Félipe, who is thought so ugly, seemed to me quite beautiful in his graceful kindness and the exquisite delicacy of his affection. Of passion, not a trace. All through the journey he might have been an old friend of fifteen years' standing. Later, he has described to me, with all the vivid touches of his first letter, the furious storms that raged within and were not allowed to ruffle the outer surface.

"So far, I have found nothing very terrible in marriage," I said, as I walked to the window and looked out on the glorious moon which lit up a charming park, breathing of heavy scents.

He drew near, put his arm again round me, and said:

"Why fear it? Have I ever yet proved false to my promise in gesture or look? Why should I be false in the future?"

Yet never were words or glances more full of mastery; his voice thrilled every fibre of my heart and roused a sleeping force; his eyes were like the sun in power.

"Oh!" I exclaimed, "what a world of Moorish perfidy in this attitude of perpetual prostration!"

He understood, my dear.

So, my fair sweetheart, if I have let months slip by without writing, you can now divine the cause. I have to recall the girl's strange past in order to explain the woman to myself. Renée, I understand you now. Not to her dearest friend, not to her mother, not, perhaps, even to herself, can a happy bride speak of her happiness. This memory ought to remain absolutely her own, an added rapture—a thing beyond words, too sacred for disclosure!

Is it possible that the name of duty has been given to the delicious frenzy of the heart, to the overwhelming rush of passion? And for what purpose? What malevolent power conceived the idea of crushing a woman's sensitive delicacy and all the thousand wiles of her modesty under the fetters of constraint? What sense of duty can force from her these flowers of the heart, the roses of life, the passionate poetry of her nature, apart from love? To claim feeling as a right! Why, it blooms of itself under the sun of love, and shrivels to death under the cold blast of distaste and aversion! Let love guard his own rights!

Oh! my noble Renée! I understand you now. I bow to your greatness, amazed at the depth and clearness of your insight. Yes, the woman who has not used the marriage ceremony, as I have done, merely to legalize and publish the secret election of her heart, has nothing left but to fly to motherhood. When earth fails, the soul makes for heaven!

One hard truth emerges from all that you have said. Only men who are really great know how to love, and now I understand the reason of this. Man obeys two forces—one sensual, one spiritual. Weak or inferior men mistake the first for the last, whilst great souls know how to clothe the merely natural instinct in all the graces of the spirit. The very strength of this spiritual passion imposes severe self-restraint and inspires them with reverence for women. Clearly, feeling is sensitive

275

in proportion to the calibre of the mental powers generally, and this is why the man of genius alone has something of a woman's delicacy. He understands and divines woman, and the wings of passion on which he raises her are restrained by the timidity of the sensitive spirit. But when the mind, the heart, and the senses all have their share in the rapture which transports us—ah! then there is no falling to earth, rather it is to heaven we soar, alas! for only too brief a visit.

Such, dear soul, is the philosophy of the first three months of my married life. Félipe is angelic. Without figure of speech, he is another self, and I can think aloud with him. His greatness of soul passes my comprehension. Possession only attaches him more closely to me, and he discovers in his happiness new motives for loving me. For him, I am the nobler part of himself. I can foresee that years of wedded life, far from impairing his affection, will only make it more assured, develop fresh possibilities of enjoyment, and bind us in more perfect sympathy. What a delirium of joy!

It is part of my nature that pleasure has an exhilarating effect on me; it leaves sunshine behind, and becomes a part of my inner being. The interval which parts one ecstasy from another is like the short night which marks off our long summer days. The sun which flushed the mountain tops with warmth in setting finds them hardly cold when it rises. What happy chance has given me such a destiny? My mother had roused a host of fears in me; her forecast, which, though free from the alloy of vulgar pettiness, seemed to me redolent of jealousy, has been falsified by the event. Your fears and hers, my own—all have vanished in thin air!

We remained at Chantepleurs seven months and a half, for all the world like a couple of runaway lovers fleeing the parental warmth, while the roses of pleasure crowned our love and embellished our dual solitude. One morning, when I was even happier than usual, I began to muse over my lot, and suddenly Renée and her prosaic marriage flashed into my mind. It seemed to me that now I could grasp the inner meaning in your life. Oh! my sweet, why do we speak a different tongue? Your marriage of convenience and my love match are two worlds, as widely separated as the finite from infinity. You still walk the earth, whilst I range the heavens! Your sphere is human, mine divine! Love crowned me queen, you reign by reason and duty. So lofty are the regions where I soar, that a fall would shiver me to atoms.

But no more of this. I shrink from painting to you the rainbow brightness, the profusion, the exuberant joy of love's springtime, as we know it.

For ten days we have been in Paris, staying in a charming house in the Rue du Bac,* prepared for us by the architect to whom Félipe intrusted the decoration of Chantepleurs. I have been listening, in all the full content of an assured and sanctioned love, to that divine music of Rossini's, which used to soothe me when, as a restless girl, I hungered vaguely after experience. They say I am more beautiful, and I have a childish pleasure in hearing myself called "madame."

Friday Morning

Renée, my fair saint, the happiness of my own life pulls me for ever back to you. I feel that I can be more to you than ever before, you are so dear to me! I have studied your wedded life closely in the light of my own opening chapters; and you seem to me to come out of the scrutiny so great, so noble, so splendid in your goodness, that I here declare myself your inferior and humble admirer, as well as your friend. When I think what marriage has been to me, it seems to me that I should have died, had it turned out otherwise. And *you live!* Tell me what your heart feeds on! Never again shall I make fun of you. Mockery, my sweet, is the child of ignorance; we jest at what we know nothing of. "Recruits will laugh where the veteran soldier looks grave," was a remark made to me by the Comte de Chaulieu, that poor cavalry officer whose campaigning so far has consisted in marches from Paris to Fontainebleau and back again.

I surmise, too, my dear love, that you have not told me all. There are wounds which you have hidden. You suffer; I am convinced of it. In trying to make out at this distance and from the scraps you tell me the reasons of your conduct, I have weaved together all sorts of romantic theories about you. "She has made a mere experiment in marriage," I thought one evening, "and what is happiness for me had proved only suffering to her. Her sacrifice is barren of reward, and she would not make it greater than need be. The unctuous axioms of social morality are only used to cloak her disappointment." Ah! Renée, the best of happiness is that it needs no dogma and no fine words to pave the way; it speaks for itself, while theory has been piled upon theory to justify the system of women's vassalage and thralldom. If self-denial be so noble, so sublime, what, pray, of my joy, sheltered by the gold-and-white canopy of the church, and witnessed by the hand and seal of the most sour-faced of mayors? Is it a thing out of nature?

For the honor of the law, for her own sake, but most of all to make my happiness complete, I long to see my Renée content. Oh! tell me that you see a dawn of love for this Louis who adores you! Tell me that the solemn, symbolic torch of Hymen has not alone served to lighten your darkness, but that love, the glorious sun of our hearts, pours his rays on you. I come back always, you see, to this midday blaze, which will be my destruction, I fear.

Dear Renée, do you remember how, in your outbursts of girlish devotion, you would say to me, as we sat under the vine-covered arbor of the convent garden, "I love you so, Louise, that if God appeared to me in a vision, I would pray Him that all the sorrows of life might be mine, and all the joy yours. I burn to suffer for you"? Now, darling, the day has come when I take up your prayer, imploring Heaven to grant you a share in my happiness.

I must tell you my idea. I have a shrewd notion that you are hatching ambitious plans under the name of Louis de l'Estorade. Very good; get him elected deputy at the approaching election, for he will be very nearly forty then; and as the Chamber* does not meet till six months later, he will have just attained the age necessary to qualify for a seat. You will come to Paris—there, isn't that enough? My father, and the friends I shall have made by that time, will learn to know and admire you; and if your father-in-law will agree to found a family, we will get the title of Comte for Louis. That is something at least! And we shall be together.

XXVIII
RENÉE DE L'ESTORADE TO LOUISE DE MACUMER

December 1825

My thrice happy Louise, your letter made me dizzy. For a few moments I held it in my listless hands, while a tear or two sparkled on it in the setting sun. I was alone beneath the small barren rock where I have had a seat placed; far off, like a lance of steel, the Mediterranean shone. The seat is shaded by aromatic shrubs, and I have had a very large jessamine, some honeysuckle, and Spanish brooms transplanted there, so that some day the rock will be entirely covered with climbing plants. The wild vine has already taken root there. But winter draws near, and all this greenery is faded like a piece of old tapestry. In this spot I am never molested; it is understood that here I wish to be alone. It is named Louise's seat—a proof, is it not, that even in solitude I am not alone here?

If I tell you all these details, to you so paltry, and try to describe the vision of green with which my prophetic gaze clothes this bare rock—on which top some freak of nature has set up a magnificent parasol pine—it is because in all this I have found an emblem to which I cling.

It was while your blessed lot was filling me with joy and—must I confess it?—with bitter envy too, that I felt the first movement of my child within, and this mystery of physical life reacted upon the inner recesses of my soul. This indefinable sensation, which partakes of the nature at once of a warning, a delight, a pain, a promise, and a fulfilment; this joy, which is mine alone, unshared by mortal, this wonder of wonders, has whispered to me that one day this rock shall be a carpet of flowers, resounding to the merry laughter of children, that I shall at last be blessed among women, and from me shall spring forth fountains of life. Now I know what I have lived for! Thus the first certainty of bearing within me another life brought healing to my wounds. A joy that beggars description has crowned for me those long days of sacrifice, in which Louis had already found his.

Sacrifice! I said to myself, how far does it excel passion! What pleasure has roots so deep as one which is not personal but creative? Is not the spirit of Sacrifice a power mightier than any of its results? Is it not that mysterious, tireless divinity, who hides beneath innumerable spheres in an unexplored centre, through which all worlds in turn must pass? Sacrifice, solitary and secret, rich in pleasures only tasted in silence, which none can guess at, and no profane eye has ever seen; Sacrifice, jealous God and tyrant, God of strength and victory, exhaustless spring which, partaking of the very essence of all that exists, can by no expenditure be drained below its own level;—Sacrifice, there is the keynote of my life.

For you, Louise, love is but the reflex of Félipe's

passion; the life which I shed upon my little ones will come back to me in ever-growing fullness. The plenty of your golden harvest will pass; mine, though late, will be but the more enduring, for each hour will see it renewed. Love may be the fairest gem which Society has filched from Nature; but what is motherhood save Nature in her most gladsome mood? A smile has dried my tears. Love makes my Louis happy, but marriage has made me a mother, and who shall say I am not happy also?

With slow steps, then, I returned to my white grange, with the green shutters, to write you these thoughts.

So it is, darling, that the most marvelous, and yet the simplest, process of nature has been going on in me for five months; and yet—in your ear let me whisper it—so far it agitates neither my heart nor my understanding. I see all around me happy; the grandfather-to-be has become a child again, trespassing on the grandchild's place; the father wears a grave and anxious look; they are all most attentive to me, all talk of the joy of being a mother. Alas! I alone remain cold, and I dare not tell you how dead I am to all emotion, though I affect a little in order not to damp the general satisfaction. But with you I may be frank; and I confess that, at my present stage, motherhood is a mere affair of the imagination.

Louis was to the full as much surprised as I. Does not this show how little, unless by his impatient wishes, the father counts for in this matter? Chance, my dear, is the sovereign deity in child-bearing. My doctor, while maintaining that this chance works in harmony with nature, does not deny that children who are the fruit of passionate love are bound to be richly endowed both physically and mentally, and that often the happiness which shone like a radiant star over their birth seems to watch over them through life. It may be then, Louise, that motherhood reserves joys for you which I shall never know. It may be that the feeling of a mother for the child of a man whom she adores, as you adore Félipe, is different from that with which she regards the offspring of reason, duty, and desperation!

Thoughts such as these, which I bury in my inmost heart, add to the preoccupation only natural to a woman soon to be a mother. And yet, as the family cannot exist without children, I long to speed the moment from which the joys of family, where alone I am to find my life, shall date their beginning. At present I live a life all expectation and mystery, except for a sickening physical discomfort, which no doubt serves to prepare a woman for suffering of a different kind. I watch my symptoms; and in spite of the attentions and thoughtful care with which Louis's anxiety surrounds me, I am conscious of a vague uneasiness, mingled with the nausea, the distaste for food, and abnormal longings common to my condition. If I am to speak candidly, I must confess, at the risk of disgusting you with the whole business, to an incomprehensible craving for rotten fruit. My husband goes to Marseilles to fetch the finest oranges the world produces—from Malta, Portugal, Corsica—and these I don't touch. Then I hurry there myself, sometimes on foot, and in a little back street, running down to the harbor, close to the Town Hall, I find wretched, half-putrid oranges, two for a sou, which I devour eagerly. The bluish, greenish shades on the mouldy parts sparkle like diamonds in my eyes, they are flowers to me; I forget the putrid odor, and find them delicious, with a piquant flavor, and stimulating as wine. My dear, they are the first love of my life! Your passion for Félipe is nothing to this! Sometimes I can slip out secretly and fly to Marseilles, full of passionate longings, which grow more intense as I draw near the street. I tremble lest the woman should be sold out of rotten oranges; I pounce on them and devour them as I stand. It seems to me an ambrosial food, and yet I have seen Louis turn aside, unable to bear the smell. Then came to my mind the ghastly words of Obermann in his gloomy elegy, which I wish I had never read, "Roots slake their thirst in foulest streams."* Since I took to this diet, the sickness has ceased, and I feel much stronger. This depravity of taste must have a meaning, for it seems to be part of a natural process and to be common to most women, sometimes going to most extravagant lengths.

When my situation is more marked, I shall not go beyond the grounds, for I should not like to be seen under these circumstances. I have the greatest curiosity to know at what precise moment the sense of motherhood begins. It cannot possibly be in the midst of frightful suffering, the very thought of which makes me shudder.

Farewell, favorite of fortune! Farewell, my friend, in whom I live again, and through whom I am able to picture to myself this brave love, this jealousy all on fire at a look, these whisperings in the ear, these joys which create for women, as it were, a new atmosphere, a new daylight, fresh life! Ah! pet, I too understand love. Don't weary of telling me everything. Keep faithful to our bond. I promise, in my turn, to spare you nothing.

Nay—to conclude in all seriousness—I will not conceal from you that, on reading your letter a second time, I was seized with a dread which I could not shake off. This superb love seems like a challenge to Providence. Will not the sovereign master of this earth, Calamity, take umbrage if no place be left for him at your feast? What mighty edifice of fortune has he not overthrown? Oh! Louise, forget not, in all this happiness, your prayers to God. Do good, be kind and merciful; let your moderation, if it may be, avert disaster. Religion has meant much more to me since I left the convent and since my marriage; but your Paris news contains no mention of it. In your glorification of Félipe it seems to me you reverse the saying, and invoke God less than His saint.

But, after all, this panic is only excess of affection.

You go to church together, I do not doubt, and do good in secret. The close of this letter will seem to you very primitive, I expect, but think of the too eager friendship which prompts these fears—a friendship of the type of La Fontaine's, which takes alarms at dreams, at half-formed, misty ideas. You deserve to be happy, since, through it all, you still think of me, no less than I think of you, in my monotonous life, which, though it lacks color, is yet not empty, and, if uneventful, is not unfruitful. God bless you, then!

XXIX

MONSIEUR DE L'ESTORADE TO THE BARONNE DE MACUMER

December 1825

MADAME,—It is the desire of my wife that you should not learn first from the formal announcement of an event which has filled us with joy. Renée has just given birth to a fine boy, whose baptism we are postponing till your return to Chantepleurs. Renée and I both earnestly hope that you may then come as far as La Crampade, and will consent to act as godmother to our firstborn. In this hope, I have had him placed on the register under the name of Armand-Louis de l'Estorade.

Our dear Renée suffered much, but bore it with angelic patience. You, who know her, will easily understand that the assurance of bringing happiness to us all supported her through this trying apprenticeship to motherhood.

Without indulging in the more or less ludicrous exaggerations to which the novel sensation of being a father is apt to give rise, I may tell you that little Armand is a beautiful infant, and you will have no difficulty in believing it when I add that he has Renée's features and eyes. So far, at least, this gives proof of intelligence.

The physician and accoucheur assure us that Renée is now quite out of danger; and as she is proving an admirable nurse—Nature has endowed her so generously!—my father and I are able to give free rein to our joy. Madame, may I be allowed to express the hope that this joy, so vivid and intense, which has brought fresh life into our house, and has changed the face of existence for my dear wife, may ere long be yours?

Renée has had a suite of rooms prepared, and I only wish I could make them worthy of our guests. But the cordial friendliness of the reception which awaits you may perhaps atone for any lack of splendor.

I have heard from Renée, madame, of your kind thought in regard to us, and I take this opportunity of thanking you for it, the more gladly because nothing could now be more appropriate. The birth of a grandson has reconciled my father to sacrifices which bear hardly on an old man. He has just bought two estates, and La Crampade is now a property with an annual rental of thirty thousand francs. My father intends asking the king's permission to form an entailed estate of it; and if you are good enough to get for him the title of which you spoke in your last letter, you will have already done much for your godson.

For my part, I shall carry out your suggestions solely with the object of bringing you and Renée together during the sessions of the Chamber. I am working hard with the view of becoming what is called a specialist. But nothing could give me greater encouragement in my labors than the thought that you will take an interest in my little Armand. Come, then, we beg of you, and with your beauty and your grace, your playful fancy and your noble soul, enact the part of good fairy to my son and heir. You will thus, madame, add undying gratitude to the respectful regard of

Your very humble, obedient servant,

LOUIS DE L'ESTORADE

XXX

LOUISE DE MACUMER TO RENÉE DE L'ESTORADE

January 1826

Macumer has just wakened me, darling, with your husband's letter. First and foremost—Yes. We shall be going
to Chantepleurs about the end of April. To me it will be
a piling up of pleasure to travel, to see you, and to be
the godmother of your first child. I must, please, have
Macumer for godfather. To take part in a ceremony of
the Church with another as my partner would be hateful to me. Ah! if you could see the look he gave me as I
said this, you would know what store this sweetest of
lovers sets on his wife!

"I am the more bent on our visiting La Crampade together, Félipe," I went on, "because I might have a child
there. I too, you know, would be a mother! . . . And yet,
can you fancy me torn in two between you and the infant? To begin with, if I saw any creature—were it even
my own son—taking my place in your heart, I couldn't
answer for the consequences. Medea may have been
right after all. The Greeks had some good notions!"

And he laughed.

So, my sweetheart, you have the fruit without the
flowers; I the flowers without the fruit. The contrast
in our lives still holds good. Between the two of us we
have surely enough philosophy to find the moral of it
some day. Bah! only ten months married! Too soon, you
will admit, to give up hope.

We are leading a gay, yet far from empty life, as is
the way with happy people. The days are never long
enough for us. Society, seeing me in the trappings of a
married woman, pronounces the Baronne de Macumer
much prettier than Louise de Chaulieu: a happy love
is a most becoming cosmetic. When Félipe and I drive
along the Champs-Élysées in the bright sunshine of
a crisp January day, beneath the trees, frosted with

clusters of white stars, and face all Paris on the spot where last year we met with a gulf between us, the contrast calls up a thousand fancies. Suppose, after all, your last letter should be right in its forecast, and we are too presumptuous!

If I am ignorant of a mother's joys, you shall tell me about them; I will learn by sympathy. But my imagination can picture nothing to equal the rapture of love. You will laugh at my extravagance; but, I assure you, that a dozen times in as many months the longing has seized me to die at thirty, while life was still untarnished, amidst the roses of love, in the embrace of passion. To bid farewell to the feast at its brightest, before disappointment has come, having lived in this sunshine and celestial air, and well-nigh spent myself in love, not a leaf dropped from my crown, not an illusion perished in my heart, what a dream is there! Think what it would be to bear about a young heart in an aged body, to see only cold, dumb faces around me, where even strangers used to smile; to be a worthy matron! Can Hell have a worse torture?

On this very subject, in fact, Félipe and I have had our first quarrel. I contended that he ought to have sufficient moral strength to kill me in my sleep when I have reached thirty, so that I might pass from one dream to another. The wretch declined. I threatened to leave him alone in the world, and, poor child, he turned white as a sheet. My dear, this distinguished statesman is neither more nor less than a baby. It is incredible what youth and simplicity he contrived to hide away. Now that I allow myself to think aloud with him, as I do with you, and have no secrets from him, we are always giving each other surprises.

Dear Renée, Félipe and Louise, the pair of lovers, want to send a present to the young mother. We would like to get something that would give you pleasure, and we don't share the popular taste for surprises; so tell me quite frankly, please, what you would like. It ought to be something which would recall us to you in a pleasant way, something which you will use every day, and which won't wear out with use. The meal which with us is most cheerful and friendly is lunch, and therefore the idea occurred to me of a special luncheon service, ornamented with figures of babies. If you approve of this, let me know at once; for it will have to be ordered immediately if we are to bring it. Paris artists are gentlemen of far too much importance to be hurried. This will be my offering to Lucina.

Farewell, dear nursing mother. May all a mother's delights be yours! I await with impatience your first letter, which will tell me all about it, I hope. Some of the details in your husband's letter went to my heart. Poor Renée, a mother has a heavy price to pay. I will tell my godson how dearly he must love you.

No end of love, my sweet one.

XXXI
RENÉE DE L'ESTORADE TO LOUISE DE MACUMER

It is nearly five months now since baby was born, and not once, dear heart, have I found a single moment for writing to you. When you are a mother yourself, you will be more ready to excuse me, than you are now; for you have punished me a little bit in making your own letters so few and far between. Do write, my darling! Tell me of your pleasures; lay on the blue as brightly as you please. It will not hurt me, for I am happy now, happier than you can imagine.

I went in state to the parish church to hear the Mass for recovery from childbirth, as is the custom in the old families of Provence. I was supported on either side by the two grandfathers—Louis's father and my own. Never had I knelt before God with such a flood of gratitude in my heart. I have so much to tell you of, so many feelings to describe, that I don't know where to begin; but from amidst these confused memories, one rises distinctly, that of my prayer in the church.

When I found myself transformed into a joyful mother, on the very spot where, as a girl, I had trembled for my future, it seemed to my fancy that the Virgin on the altar bowed her head and pointed to the infant Christ, who smiled at me! My heart full of pure and heavenly love, I held out little Armand for the priest to bless and bathe, in anticipation of the regular baptism to come later. But you will see us together then, Armand and me.

My child—come see how readily the word comes, and indeed there is none sweeter to a mother's heart and mind or on her lips—well, then, dear child, during the last two months I used to drag myself wearily and heavily about the gardens, not realizing yet how precious was the burden, spite of all the discomforts it brought! I was haunted by forebodings so gloomy and ghastly, that they got the better even of curiosity; in vain did I picture the delights of motherhood. My heart made no response even to the thought of the little one, who announced himself by lively kicking. That is a sensation, dear, which may be welcome when it is familiar; but as a novelty, it is more strange than pleasing. I speak for myself at least; you know I would never affect anything I did not really feel, and I look on my child as a gift straight from Heaven. For one who saw in it rather the image of the man she loved, it might be different.

But enough of such sad thoughts, gone, I trust, for ever.

When the crisis came, I summoned all my powers of resistance, and braced myself so well for suffering, that I bore the horrible agony—so they tell me—quite marvelously. For about an hour I sank into a sort of stupor, of the nature of a dream. I seemed to myself then two beings—an outer covering racked and tortured by red-hot pincers, and a soul at peace. In this strange state the pain formed itself into a sort of halo hovering over me. A gigantic rose seemed to spring out of my head and grow ever larger and larger, till it enfolded me in its blood-red petals. The same color dyed the air around, and everything I saw was blood-red. At last the climax came, when soul and body seemed no longer able to hold together; the spasms of pain gripped me like death itself. I screamed aloud, and found fresh strength against this fresh torture. Suddenly this concert of hideous cries was overborne by a joyful sound—the shrill wail of the newborn infant. No words can describe that moment. It was as though the universe took part in my cries, when all at once the chorus of pain fell hushed before the child's feeble note.

They laid me back again in the large bed, and it felt like paradise to me, even in my extreme exhaustion. Three or four happy faces pointed through tears to the child. My dear, I exclaimed in terror:

"It's just like a little monkey! Are you really and truly certain it is a child?"

I fell back on my side, miserably disappointed at my first experience of motherly feeling.

"Don't worry, dear," said my mother, who had installed herself as nurse. "Why, you've got the finest baby in the world. You mustn't excite yourself; but give your whole mind now to turning yourself as much as possible into an animal, a milch cow, pasturing in the meadow."

I fell asleep then, fully resolved to let nature have her way.

Ah! my sweet, how heavenly it was to waken up from all the pain and haziness of the first days, when everything was still dim, uncomfortable, confused. A ray of light pierced the darkness; my heart and soul, my inner self—a self I had never known before—rent the envelope of gloomy suffering, as a flower bursts its sheath at the first warm kiss of the sun, at the moment when the little wretch fastened on my breast and sucked. Not even the sensation of the child's first cry was so exquisite as this. This is the dawn of motherhood, this is the *Fiat lux!*

Here is happiness, joy ineffable, though it comes not without pangs. Oh! my sweet jealous soul, how you will relish a delight which exists only for ourselves, the child, and God! For this tiny creature all knowledge is summed up in its mother's breast. This is the one bright spot in its world, towards which its puny strength goes forth. Its thoughts cluster round this spring of life, which it leaves only to sleep, and whither it returns on waking. Its lips have a sweetness beyond words, and their pressure is at once a pain and a delight, a delight which by every excess becomes pain, or a pain which culminates in delight. The sensation which rises from it, and which penetrates to the very core of my life, baffles all description. It seems a sort of centre whence a myriad joy-bearing rays gladden the heart and soul. To bear a child is nothing; to nourish it is birth renewed every hour.

Oh! Louise, there is no caress of lover with half the power of those little pink hands, as they stray about, seeking whereby to lay hold on life. And the infant glances, now turned upon the breast, now raised to meet our own! What dreams come to us as we watch the clinging nursling! All our powers, whether of mind or body, are at its service; for it we breathe and think, in it our longings are more than satisfied! The sweet sensation of warmth at the heart, which the sound of his first cry brought to me—like the first ray of sunshine on the earth—came again as I felt the milk flow into his mouth, again as his eyes met mine, and at this moment I have felt it once more as his first smile gave token of a mind working within—for he has laughed, my dear! A laugh, a glance, a bite, a cry—four miracles of gladness which go straight to the heart and strike chords that respond to no other touch. A child is tied to our heart-strings, as the spheres are linked to their creator; we cannot think of God except as a mother's heart writ large.

It is only in the act of nursing that a woman realizes her motherhood in visible and tangible fashion; it is a joy of every moment. The milk becomes flesh before our eyes; it blossoms into the tips of those delicate flower-like fingers; it expands in tender, transparent nails; it spins the silky tresses; it kicks in the little feet. Oh! those baby feet, how plainly they talk to us! In them the child finds its first language.

Yes, Louise, nursing is a miracle of transformation going on before one's bewildered eyes. Those cries, they go to your heart and not your ears; those smiling eyes and lips, those plunging feet, they speak in words which could not be plainer if God traced them before you in letters of fire! What else is there in the world to care about? The father? Why, you could kill him if he dreamed of waking the baby! Just as the child is the world to us, so do we stand alone in the world for the child. The sweet consciousness of a common life is ample recompense for all the trouble and suffering—for suffering there is. Heaven save you, Louise, from ever knowing the maddening agony of a wound which gapes afresh with every pressure of rosy lips, and is so hard to heal—the heaviest tax perhaps imposed on beauty. For know, Louise, and beware! it visits only a fair and delicate skin.

My little ape has in five months developed into the prettiest darling that ever mother bathed in tears of joy, washed, brushed, combed, and made smart; for God knows what unwearied care we lavish upon those tender blossoms! So my monkey has ceased to exist, and behold in his stead a *baby*, as my English nurse says, a regular pink-and-white baby. He cries very little too now, for he is conscious of the love bestowed on him; indeed, I hardly ever leave him, and I strive to wrap him round in the atmosphere of my love.

Dear, I have a feeling now for Louis which is not love, but which ought to be the crown of a woman's love where it exists. Nay, I am not sure whether this tender fondness, this unselfish gratitude, is not superior to love. From all that you have told me of it, dear pet, I gather that love has something terribly earthly about it, whilst a strain of holy piety purifies the affection a happy mother feels for the author of her far-reaching and enduring joys. A mother's happiness is like a beacon, lighting up the future, but reflected also on the past in the guise of fond memories.

The old l'Estorade and his son have moreover redoubled their devotion to me; I am like a new person to them. Every time they see me and speak to me, it is with a fresh holiday joy, which touches me deeply. The grandfather has, I verily believe, turned child again; he looks at me admiringly, and the first time I came down to lunch he was moved to tears to see me eating and suckling the child. The moisture in these dry old eyes, generally expressive only of avarice, was a wonderful comfort to me. I felt that the good soul entered into my joy.

As for Louis, he would shout aloud to the trees and stones of the highway that he has a son; and he spends whole hours watching your sleeping godson. He does not know, he says, when he will grow used to it. These extravagant expressions of delight show me how great must have been their fears beforehand. Louis has confided in me that he had believed himself condemned to be childless. Poor fellow! he has all at once developed very much, and he works even harder than he did. The father in him has quickened his ambition.

For myself, dear soul, I grow happier and happier every moment. Each hour creates a fresh tie between the mother and her infant. The very nature of my feelings proves to me that they are normal, permanent, and indestructible; whereas I shrewdly suspect love, for instance, of being intermittent. Certainly it is not the same at all moments, the flowers which it weaves into the web of life are not all of equal brightness; love, in short, can and must decline. But a mother's love has no ebb-tide to fear; rather it grows with the growth of the child's needs, and strengthens with its strength. Is it not at once a passion, a natural craving, a feeling, a duty, a necessity, a joy? Yes, darling, here is woman's true sphere. Here the passion for self-sacrifice can expend itself, and no jealousy intrudes.

Here, too, is perhaps the single point on which society and nature are at one. Society, in this matter, enforces the dictates of nature, strengthening the maternal instinct by adding to it family spirit and the desire of perpetuating a name, a race, an estate. How tenderly must not a woman cherish the child who has been the first to open up to her these joys, the first to call forth the energies of her nature and to instruct her in the grand art of motherhood! The right of the eldest, which in the earliest times formed a part of the natural order and was lost in the origins of society, ought never, in my opinion, to have been questioned. Ah! how much a mother learns from her child! The constant protection of a helpless being forces us to so strict an alliance with virtue, that a woman never shows to full advantage except as a mother. Then alone can her character expand in the fulfilment of all life's duties and the enjoyment of all its pleasures. A woman who is not a mother is maimed and incomplete. Hasten, then, my sweetest, to fulfil your mission. Your present happiness will then be multiplied by the wealth of my delights.

23rd

I had to tear myself from you because your godson was crying. I can hear his cry from the bottom of the garden. But I would not let this go without a word of farewell.

I have just been reading over what I have said, and am horrified to see how vulgar are the feelings expressed! What I feel, every mother, alas! since the beginning must have felt, I suppose, in the same way, and put into the same words. You will laugh at me, as we do at the naive father who dilates on the beauty and cleverness of his (of course) quite exceptional offspring. But the refrain of my letter, darling, is this, and I repeat it: I am as happy now as I used to be miserable. This grange—and is it not going to be an estate, a family property?—has become my land of promise. The desert is past and over. A thousand loves, darling pet. Write to me, for now I can read without a tear the tale of your happy love. Farewell.

XXXII

MADAME DE MACUMER TO MADAME DE L'ESTORADE

March 1826

Do you know, dear, that it is more than three months since I have written to you or heard from you? I am the more guilty of the two, for I did not reply to your last, but you don't stand on punctilio surely?

Macumer and I have taken your silence for consent as regards the baby-wreathed luncheon service, and the little cherubs are starting this morning for Marseilles. It took six months to carry out the design. And so when Félipe asked me to come and see the service before it was packed, I suddenly waked up to the fact that we had not interchanged a word since the letter of yours which gave me an insight into a mother's heart.

My sweet, it is this terrible Paris—there's my excuse. What, pray, is yours? Oh! what a whirlpool is society! Didn't I tell you once that in Paris one must be as the Parisians? Society there drives out all sentiment; it lays an embargo on your time; and unless you are very careful, soon eats away your heart altogether. What an amazing masterpiece is the character of Célimène in Molière's *Le Misanthrope!** She is the society woman, not only of Louis XIV's time, but of our own, and of all, time.

Where should I be but for my breastplate—the love I bear Félipe? This very morning I told him, as the outcome of these reflections, that he was my salvation. If my evenings are a continuous round of parties, balls, concerts, and theatres, at night my heart expands again, and is healed of the wounds received in the world by the delights of the passionate love which await my return.

I dine at home only when we have friends, so-called, with us, and spend the afternoon there only on my day, for I have a day now—Wednesday—for receiving. I have entered the lists with Mesdames d'Espard and de Maufrigneuse, and with the old Duchesse de Lenoncourt, and my house has the reputation of being a very lively one. I allowed myself to become the fashion, because I saw how much pleasure my success gave Félipe. My mornings are his; from four in the afternoon till two in the morning I belong to Paris. Macumer makes an admirable host, witty and dignified, perfect in courtesy, and with an air of real distinction. No woman could help loving such a husband even if she had chosen him without consulting her heart.

My father and mother have left for Madrid. Louis XVIII being out of the way, the duchesse had no difficulty in obtaining from our good-natured Charles X the appointment of her fascinating poet; so he is carried off in the capacity of attaché.

My brother, the Duc de Rhétoré, deigns to recognize me as a person of mark. As for my younger brother, The Comte de Chaulieu, this buckram warrior owes me everlasting gratitude. Before my father left, he spent my fortune in acquiring for the comte an estate of forty thousand francs a year, entailed on the title, and his marriage with Mademoiselle de Mortsauf, an heiress from Touraine, is definitely arranged. The king, in order to preserve the name and titles of the de Lenoncourt and de Givry families from extinction, is to confer these, together with the armorial bearings, by patent on my brother. Certainly it would never have done to allow these two fine names and their splendid motto, *Faciem semper monstramus*,* to perish. Mademoiselle de Mortsauf, who is granddaughter and sole heiress of the Duc de Lenoncourt-Givry, will, it is said, inherit altogether more than one hundred thousand livres a year. The only stipulation my father has made is that the de Chaulieu arms should appear in the centre of the de Lenoncourt escutcheon. Thus my brother will be Duc de Lenoncourt. The young de Mortsauf, to whom everything would otherwise go, is in the last stage of consumption; his death is looked for every day. The marriage will take place next winter when the family are out of mourning. I am told that I shall have a charming sister-in-law in Mademoiselle de Mortsauf.

So you see that my father's reasoning is justified. The outcome of it all has won me many compliments, and my marriage is explained to everybody's satisfaction. To complete our success, the Prince de Talleyrand, out of affection for my grandmother, is showing himself a warm friend to Macumer. Society, which began by criticising me, has now passed to cordial admiration.

In short, I now reign a queen where, barely two years ago, I was an insignificant item. Macumer finds himself the object of universal envy, as the husband of "the most charming woman in Paris." At least a score of women, as you know, are always in that proud position. Men murmur sweet things in my ear, or content themselves with greedy glances. This chorus of longing and admiration is so soothing to one's vanity, that I confess I begin to understand the unconscionable price women are ready to pay for such frail and precarious privileges. A triumph of this kind is like strong wine to vanity, self-love, and all the self-regarding feelings. To pose perpetually as a divinity is a draught so potent in its intoxicating effects, that I am no longer surprised to see women grow selfish, callous, and frivolous in the heart of this adoration. The fumes of society mount to the head. You lavish the wealth of your soul and spirit, the treasures of your time, the noblest efforts of your will, upon a crowd of people who repay you in smiles and jealousy. The false coin of their pretty speeches, compliments, and flattery is the only return they give for the solid gold of your courage and sacrifices, and all the thought that must go to keep up without flagging the standard of beauty, dress, sparkling talk, and general affability. You are perfectly aware how much it costs, and that the whole thing is a fraud, but you cannot keep out of the vortex.

Ah! my sweetheart, how one craves for a real friend! How precious to me are the love and devotion of Félipe, and how my heart goes out to you! Joyfully indeed are we preparing for our move to Chantepleurs, where we can rest from the comedy of the Rue de Bac and of the Paris drawing-rooms. Having just read your letter again, I feel that I cannot better describe this demoniac paradise than by saying that no woman of fashion in Paris can possibly be a good mother.

Good-bye, then, for a short time, dear one. We shall stay at Chantepleurs only a week at most, and shall be with you about May 10th. So we are actually to meet again after more than two years! What changes since then! Here we are, both matrons, both in our promised land—I of love, you of motherhood.

If I have not written, my sweetest, it is not because I have forgotten you. And what of the monkey godson? Is he still pretty and a credit to me? He must be more than nine months old now. I should dearly like to be present when he makes his first steps upon this earth; but

Macumer tells me that even precocious infants hardly walk at ten months.

We shall have some good gossips there, and "cut pinafores," as the Blois folk say. I shall see whether a child, as the saying goes, spoils the pattern.

P. S.—If you deign to reply from your maternal heights, address to Chantepleurs. I am just off.

XXXIII

MADAME DE L'ESTORADE TO MADAME DE MACUMER

My child,—If ever you become a mother, you will find out that it is impossible to write letters during the first two months of your nursing. Mary, my English nurse, and I are both quite knocked up. It is true I had not told you that I was determined to do everything myself. Before the event I had with my own fingers sewn the baby clothes and embroidered and edged with lace the little caps. I am a slave, my pet, a slave day and night.

To begin with, Master Armand-Louis takes his meals when it pleases him, and that is always; then he has often to be changed, washed, and dressed. His mother is so fond of watching him sleep, of singing songs to him, of walking him about in her arms on a fine day, that she has little time left to attend to herself. In short, what society has been to you, my child—our child—has been to me!

I cannot tell you how full and rich my life has become, and I long for your coming that you may see for yourself. The only thing is, I am afraid he will soon be teething, and that you will find a peevish, crying baby. So far he has not cried much, for I am always at hand. Babies only cry when their wants are not understood, and I am constantly on the lookout for his. Oh! my sweet, my heart has opened up so wide, while you allow yours to shrink and shrivel at the bidding of society! I look for your coming with all a hermit's longing. I want so much to know what you think of l'Estorade, just as you no doubt are curious for my opinion of Macumer.

Write to me from your last resting-place. The gentlemen want to go and meet our distinguished guests. Come, Queen of Paris, come to our humble grange, where love at least will greet you!

XXXIV

MADAME DE MACUMER TO THE VICOMTESSE DE L'ESTORADE

April 1826

The name on this address will tell you, dear, that my petition has been granted. Your father-in-law is now Comte de l'Estorade. I would not leave Paris till I had obtained the gratification of your wishes, and I am writing in the presence of the Keeper of the Seals,* who has come to tell me that the patent is signed.

Good-bye for a short time!

XXXV

THE SAME TO THE SAME

Marseilles, July

I am ashamed to think how my sudden flight will have taken you by surprise. But since I am above all honest, and since I love you not one bit the less, I shall tell you the truth in four words: I am horribly jealous!

Félipe's eyes were too often on you. You used to have little talks together at the foot of your rock, which were a torture to me; and I was fast becoming irritable and unlike myself. Your truly Spanish beauty could not fail to recall to him his native land, and along with it Marie Hérédia, and I can be jealous of the past too. Your magnificent black hair, your lovely dark eyes, your brow, where the peaceful joy of motherhood stands out radiant against the shadows which tell of past suffering, the freshness of your southern skin, far fairer than that of a blonde like me, the splendid lines of your figure, the breasts, on which my godson hangs, peeping through the lace like some luscious fruit,—all this stabbed me in the eyes and in the heart. In vain did I stick cornflowers in my curls, in vain set off with cherry-colored ribbons the tameness of my pale locks, everything looked washed out when Renée appeared—a Renée so unlike the one I expected to find in your oasis.

Then Félipe made too much of the child, whom I found myself beginning to hate. Yes, I confess it, that exuberance of life which fills your house, making it gay with shouts and laughter—I wanted it for myself. I read a regret in Macumer's eyes, and, unknown to him, I cried over it two whole nights. I was miserable in your house. You are too beautiful as a woman, too triumphant as a mother, for me to endure your company.

Ah! you complained of your lot. Hypocrite! What would you have? L'Estorade is most presentable; he talks well; he has fine eyes; and his black hair, dashed with white, is very becoming; his southern manners, too, have something attractive about them. As far as I can make out, he will, sooner or later, be elected deputy for the Bouches-du-Rhône;* in the Chamber he is sure to come to the front, for you can always count on me to promote your interests. The sufferings of his exile have given him that calm and dignified air which goes halfway, in my opinion, to make a politician. For the whole art of politics, dear, seems to me to consist in looking serious. At this rate, Macumer, as I told him, ought certainly to have a high position in the state.

And so, having completely satisfied myself of your happiness, I fly off contented to my dear Chantepleurs, where Félipe must really achieve his aspirations. I have made up my mind not to receive you there without a fine baby at my breast to match yours.

Oh! I know very well I deserve all the epithets you can hurl at me. I am a fool, a wretch, an idiot. Alas! that is just what jealousy means. I am not vexed with you, but I was miserable, and you will forgive me for escaping from my misery. Two days more, and I should have made an exhibition of myself; yes, there would have been an outbreak of vulgarity.

But in spite of the rage gnawing at my heart, I am glad to have come, glad to have seen you in the pride of your beautiful motherhood, my friend still, as I remain yours in all the absorption of my love. Why, even here at Marseilles, only a step from your door, I begin to feel proud of you and of the splendid mother that you will make.

How well you judged your vocation! You seem to me born for the part of mother rather than of lover, exactly as the reverse is true of me. There are women capable of neither, hard-favored or silly women. A good mother and a passionately loving wife have this in common, that they both need intelligence and discretion ever at hand, and an unfailing command of every womanly art and grace. Oh! I watched you well; need I add, sly puss, that I admired you too! Your children will be happy, but not spoilt, with your tenderness lapping them round and the clear light of your reason playing softly on them.

Tell Louis the truth about my going away, but find some decent excuse for your father-in-law, who seems to act as steward for the establishment; and be careful to do the same for your family—a true Provençal version of the Harlowe family. Félipe does not know why I left, and he will never know. If he asks, I shall contrive to find some colorable pretext, probably that you were jealous of me! Forgive me this little conventional fib.

Good-bye. I write in haste, as I want you to get this at lunch-time; and the postilion, who has undertaken to convey it to you, is here, refreshing himself while he waits.

Many kisses to my dear little godson. Be sure you come to Chantepleurs in October. I shall be alone there all the time that Macumer is away in Sardinia, where he is designing great improvements in his estate. At least that is his plan for the moment, and his pet vanity consists in having a plan. Then he feels that he has a will of his own, and this makes him very uneasy when he unfolds it to me. Good-bye!

XXXVI

THE VICOMTESSE DE L'ESTORADE
TO THE BARONNE DE MACUMER

Dear,—no words can express the astonishment of all our party when, at luncheon, we were told that you had both gone, and, above all, when the postilion who took you to Marseilles handed me your mad letter. Why, naughty child, it was of your happiness, and nothing else, that made the theme of those talks below the rock, on the "Louise" seat, and you had not the faintest justification for objecting to them. *Ingrata!* My sentence on you is that you return here at my first summons. In that horrid letter, scribbled on the inn paper, you did not tell me what would be your next stopping place; so I must address this to Chantepleurs.

Listen to me, dear sister of my heart. Know first, that my mind is set on your happiness. Your husband, dear Louise, commands respect, not only by his natural gravity and dignified expression, but also because he somehow impresses one with the splendid power revealed in his piquant plainness and in the fire of his velvet eyes; and you will understand that it was some little time before I could meet him on those easy terms which are almost necessary for intimate conversation. Further, this man has been Prime Minister, and he idolizes you; whence it follows that he must be a profound dissembler. To fish up secrets, therefore, from the rocky caverns of this diplomatic soul is a work demanding a skilful hand no less than a ready brain. Nevertheless, I succeeded at last, without rousing my victim's suspicions, in discovering many things of which you, my pet, have no conception.

You know that, between us two, my part is rather that of reason, yours of imagination: I personify sober duty, you reckless love. It has pleased fate to continue in our lives this contrast in character which was imperceptible to all except ourselves. I am a simple country vicomtesse, very ambitious, and making it her task to lead her family on the road to prosperity. On the other hand, Macumer, late Duc de Soria, has a name in the world, and you, a duchesse by right, reign in Paris, where reigning is no easy matter even for kings. You have a considerable fortune, which will be doubled if Macumer carries out his projects for developing his great estates in Sardinia, the resources of which are matter of common talk at Marseilles. Deny, if you can, that if either has the right to be jealous, it is not you. But, thank God, we have both hearts generous enough to place our friendship beyond reach of such vulgar pettiness.

I know you, dear; I know that, ere now, you are ashamed of having fled. But don't suppose that your flight will save you from a single word of discourse which I had prepared for your benefit to-day beneath the rock. Read carefully then, I beg of you, what I say, for it concerns you even more closely than Macumer, though he also enters largely into my sermon.

Firstly, my dear, you do not love him. Before two years are over, you will be sick of adoration. You will never look on Félipe as a husband; to you he will always be the lover whom you can play with, for that is how all women treat their lovers. You do not look up to him, or reverence, or worship him as a woman should the god of her idolatry. You see, I have made a study of love, my sweet, and more than once have I taken soundings in the depth of my own heart. Now, as the result of a careful diagnosis of your case, I can say with confidence, this is not love.

Yes, dear Queen of Paris, you cannot escape the destiny of all queens. The day will come when you long to be treated as a light-o'-love, to be mastered and swept off your feet by a strong man, one who will not prostrate himself in adoration before you, but will seize your arm roughly in a fit of jealousy. Macumer loves you too fondly ever to be able either to resist you or find fault with you. A single glance from you, a single coaxing word, would melt his sternest resolution. Sooner or later, you will learn to scorn this excessive devotion. He spoils you, alas! just as I used to spoil you at the convent, for you are a most bewitching woman, and there is no escaping your siren-like charms.

Worse than all, you are candid, and it often happens that our happiness depends on certain social hypocrisies to which you will never stoop. For instance, society will not tolerate a frank display of the wife's power over her husband. The convention is that a man must no more show himself the lover of his wife, however passionately he adores her, than a married woman may play the part of a mistress. This rule you both disregard.

In the first place, my child, from what you have yourself told me, it is clear that the one unpardonable sin in society is to be happy. If happiness exists, no one must know of it. But this is a small point. What seems to me important is that the perfect equality which reigns between lovers ought never to appear in the case of husband and wife, under pain of undermining the whole fabric of society and entailing terrible disasters. If it is painful to see a man whom nature has made a nonentity, how much worse is the spectacle of a man of parts brought to that position? Before very long you will have reduced Macumer to the mere shadow of a man. He will cease to have a will and character of his own, and become mere clay in your hands. You will have so completely moulded him to your likeness, that your household will consist of only one person instead of two, and that one necessarily imperfect. You will regret it bitterly; but when at last you deign to open your eyes, the evil will be past cure. Do what we will, women do not, and never will, possess the qualities which are characteristic of men, and these qualities are absolutely indispensable to family life. Already Macumer, blinded though he is, has a dim foreshadowing of this future; he feels himself less a man through his love. His visit to Sardinia is a proof to me that he hopes by this temporary separation to succeed in recovering his old self.

You never scruple to use the power which his love has placed in your hand. Your position of vantage may be read in a gesture, a look, a tone. Oh! darling, how truly are you the mad wanton your mother called you! You do not question, I fancy, that I am greatly Louis's superior. Well, I would ask you, have you ever heard me contradict him? Am I not always, in the presence of others, the wife who respects in him the authority of the family? Hypocrisy! you will say. Well, listen to me. It is true that if I want to give him any advice which I think may be of use to him, I wait for the quiet and seclusion of our bedroom to explain what I think and wish; but, I assure you, sweetheart, that even there I never arrogate to myself the place of mentor. If I did not remain in private the same submissive wife that I appear to others, he would lose confidence in himself. Dear, the good we do to others is spoilt unless we efface ourselves so completely that those we help have no sense of inferiority. There is a wonderful sweetness in these hidden sacrifices, and what a triumph for me in your unsuspecting praises of Louis! There can be no doubt also that the happiness, the comfort, the hope of the last two years have restored what misfortune, hardship, solitude, and despondency has robbed him of.

This, then, is the sum-total of my observations. At the present moment you love in Félipe, not your husband, but yourself. There is truth in your father's words; concealed by the spring-flowers of your passion lies all the great lady's selfishness. Ah! my child, how I must love you to speak such bitter truths!

Let me tell you, if you will promise never to breathe a word of this to the baron, the end of our talk. We had been singing your praises in every key, for he soon discovered that I loved you like a fondly-cherished sister, and having insensibly brought him to a confidential mood, I ventured to say:

"Louise has never yet had to struggle with life. She has been the spoilt child of fortune, and she might yet have to pay for this were you not there to act the part of father as well as lover."

"Ah! but is it possible? . . ." He broke off abruptly, like a man who sees himself on the edge of a precipice. But the exclamation was enough for me. No doubt, if you had stayed, he would have spoken more freely later.

My sweet, think of the day awaiting you when your husband's strength will be exhausted, when pleasure will have turned to satiety, and he sees himself, I will not say degraded, but shorn of his proper dignity before you. The stings of conscience will then waken a sort of remorse in him, all the more painful for you, because you will feel yourself responsible, and you will end by despising the man whom you have not accustomed yourself to respect. Remember, too, that scorn with a woman is only the earliest phase of hatred. You are too noble and generous, I know, ever to forget the sacrifices which Félipe has made for you; but what further sacrifices will be left for him to make when he has, so to speak, served up himself at the first banquet? Woe to the man, as to the woman, who has left no desire unsatisfied! All is over then. To our shame or our glory—the point is too nice for me to decide—it is of love alone that women are insatiable.

Oh! Louise, change yet, while there is still time. If you would only adopt the same course with Macumer that I have done with l'Estorade, you might rouse the sleeping lion in your husband, who is made of the stuff of heroes. One might almost say that you grudge him his greatness. Would you feel no pride in using your power for other ends than your own gratification, in awakening the genius of a gifted man, as I in raising to a higher level one of merely common parts?

Had you remained with us, I should still have written this letter, for in talking you might have cut me short or got the better of me with your sharp tongue. But I know that you will read this thoughtfully and weigh my warnings. Dear heart, you have everything in life to make you happy, do not spoil your chances; return to Paris, I entreat you, as soon as Macumer comes back. The engrossing claims of society, of which I complained, are necessary for both of you; otherwise you would spend your life in mutual self-absorption. A married woman ought not to be too lavish of herself. The mother of a family, who never gives her household an opportunity of missing her, runs the risk of palling on them. If I have several children, as I trust for my own sake I may, I assure you I shall make a point of reserving to myself certain hours which shall be held sacred; even to one's children one's presence should not be a matter of daily bread.

Farewell, my dear jealous soul! Do you know that many women would be highly flattered at having roused this passing pang in you? Alas! I can only mourn, for what is not mother in me is your dear friend. A thousand loves. Make what excuse you will for leaving; if you are not sure of Macumer, I *am* of Louis.

XXXVII
THE BARONNE DE MACUMER
TO THE VICOMTESSE DE L'ESTORADE

Genoa

My beloved beauty,—I was bitten with the fancy to see something of Italy, and I am delighted at having carried off Macumer, whose plans in regard to Sardinia are postponed.

This country is simply ravishing. The churches—above all, the chapels—have a seductive, bewitching air, which must make every female Protestant yearn after Catholicism. Macumer has been received with acclamation, and they are all delighted to have made an Italian of so distinguished a man. Félipe could have the Sardinian embassy at Paris if I cared about it, for I am made much of at court.

If you write, address your letters to Florence. I have not time now to go into any details, but I will tell you the story of our travels whenever you come to Paris. We only remain here a week, and then go on to Florence, taking Leghorn on the way. We shall stay a month in Tuscany and a month at Naples, so as to reach Rome in November. Thence we return home by Venice, where we shall spend the first fortnight of December, and arrive in Paris, *via* Milan and Turin, for January.

Our journey is a perfect honeymoon; the sight of new places gives fresh life to our passion. Macumer did not know Italy at all, and we have begun with that splendid Cornice road, which might be the work of fairy architects.

Good-bye, darling. Don't be angry if I don't write. It is impossible to get a minute to oneself in traveling; my whole time is taken up with seeing, admiring, and realizing my impressions. But not a word to you of these till memory has given them their proper atmosphere.

XXXVIII
THE VICOMTESSE DE L'ESTORADE
TO THE BARONNE DE MACUMER

September

MY DEAR LOUISE,—There is lying for you at Chantepleurs a full reply to the letter you wrote me from Marseilles. This honeymoon journey, so far from diminishing the fears I there expressed, makes me beg of you to get my letter sent on from Nivernais.

The Government, it is said, are resolved on dissolution. This is unlucky for the Crown, since the last session of this loyal Parliament would have been devoted to the passing of laws, essential to the consolidation of its power; and it is not less so for us, as Louis will not be forty till the end of 1827. Fortunately, however, my father has agreed to stand, and he will resign his seat when the right moment arrives.

Your godson has found out how to walk without his godmother's help. He is altogether delicious, and begins to make the prettiest little signs to me, which bring home to one that here is really a thinking being, not a mere animal or sucking machine. His smiles are full of meaning. I have been so successful in my profession of nurse that I shall wean Armand in December. A year at the breast is quite enough; children who are suckled longer are said to grow stupid, and I am all for popular sayings.

You must make a tremendous sensation in Italy, my fair one with the golden locks. A thousand loves.

XXXIX
THE BARONNE DE MACUMER
TO THE VICOMTESSE DE L'ESTORADE

Your atrocious letter has reached me here, the steward having forwarded it by my orders. Oh! Renée . . . but

I will spare you the outburst of my wounded feelings, and simply tell you the effect your letter produced.

We had just returned from a delightful reception given in our honor by the ambassador, where I appeared in all my glory, and Macumer was completely carried away in a frenzy of love which I could not describe. Then I read him your horrible answer to my letter, and I read it sobbing, at the risk of making a fright of myself. My dear Arab fell at my feet, declaring that you raved. Then he carried me off to the balcony of the palace where we are staying, from which we have a view over part of the city; there he spoke to me words worthy of the magnificent moonlight scene which lay stretched before us. We both speak Italian now, and his love, told in that voluptuous tongue, so admirably adapted to the expression of passion, sounded in my ears like the most exquisite poetry. He swore that, even were you right in your predictions, he would not exchange for a lifetime a single one of our blessed nights or charming mornings. At this reckoning he has already lived a thousand years. He is content to have me for his mistress, and would claim no other title than that of lover. So proud and pleased is he to see himself every day the chosen of my heart, that were Heaven to offer him the alternative between living as you would have us to for another thirty years with five children, and five years spent amid the dear roses of our love, he would not hesitate. He would take my love, such as it is, and death.

While he was whispering this in my ear, his arm round me, my head resting on his shoulder, the cries of a bat, surprised by an owl, disturbed us. This death-cry struck me with such terror that Félipe carried me half-fainting to my bed. But don't be alarmed! Though this augury of evil still resounds in my soul, I am quite myself this morning. As soon as I was up, I went to Félipe, and, kneeling before him, my eyes fixed on his, his hands clasped in mine, I said to him:—

"My love, I am a child, and Renée may be right after all. It may be only your love that I love in you; but at least I can assure you that this is the one feeling of my heart, and that I love you as it is given me to love. But if there be aught in me, in my lightest thought or deed, which jars on your wishes or conception of me, I implore you to tell me, to say what it is. It will be a joy to me to hear you and to take your eyes as the guiding-stars of my life. Renée has frightened me, for she is a true friend."

Macumer could not find voice to reply, tears choked him.

I can thank you now, Renée. But for your letter I should not have known the depths of love in my noble, kingly Macumer. Rome is the city of love; it is there that passion should celebrate its feast, with art and religion as confederates.

At Venice we shall find the Duc and Duchesse de Soria. If you write, address now to Paris, for we shall leave Rome in three days. The ambassador's was a farewell party.

P. S.—Dear, silly child, your letter only shows that you knew nothing of love, except theoretically. Learn then that love is a quickening force which may produce fruits so diverse that no theory can embrace or co-ordinate them. A word this for my little Professor with her armor of stays.

XL

THE COMTESSE DE L'ESTORADE
TO THE BARONNE DE MACUMER

January 1827

My father has been elected to the Chamber, my father-in-law is dead, and I am on the point of my second confinement; these are the chief events marking the end of the year for us. I mention them at once, lest the sight of the black seal should frighten you.

My dear, your letter from Rome made my flesh creep. You are nothing but a pair of children. Félipe is either a dissembling diplomat or else his love for you is the love a man might have for a courtesan, on whom he squanders his all, knowing all the time that she is false to him. Enough of this. You say I rave, so I had better hold my tongue. Only this would I say, from the comparison of our two very different destinies I draw this harsh moral—Love not if you would be loved.

My dear, when Louis was elected to the provincial Council, he received the cross of the Legion of Honor.* That is now nearly three years ago; and as my father—whom you will no doubt see in Paris during the course of the session—has asked the rank of Officer of the Legion for his son-in-law, I want to know if you will do me the kindness to take in hand the bigwig, whoever he may be, to whom this patronage belongs, and to keep an eye upon the little affair. But, whatever you do, don't get entangled in the concerns of my honored father. The Comte de Maucombe is fishing for the title of Marquis for himself; but keep your good services for me, please. When Louis is a deputy—next winter that is—we shall come to Paris, and then we will move heaven and earth to get some Government appointment for him, so that we may be able to save our income by living on his salary. My father sits between the centre and the right; a title will content him. Our family was distinguished even in the days of King René,* and Charles X will hardly say no to a Maucombe; but what I fear is that my father may take it into his head to ask some favor for my younger brother. Now, if the marquisate is dangled out of his reach, he will have no thoughts to spare from himself.

January 15th

Ah! Louise, I have been in hell. If I can bear to tell you of my anguish, it is because you are another self; even so, I don't know whether I shall ever be able to live again in thought those five ghastly days. The mere word "convulsions" makes my very heart sick. Five days! to me they were five centuries of torture. A mother who has not been through this martyrdom does not know what suffering is. So frenzied was I that I even envied you, who never had a child!

The evening before that terrible day the weather was close, almost hot, and I thought my little Armand was affected by it. Generally so sweet and caressing, he was peevish, cried for nothing, wanted to play, and then broke his toys. Perhaps this sort of fractiousness is the usual sign of approaching illness with children. While I was wondering about it, I noticed Armand's cheeks flush, but this I set down to teething, for he is cutting four large teeth at once. So I put him to bed beside me, and kept constantly waking through the night. He was a little feverish, but not enough to make me uneasy, my mind being still full of the teething. Towards morning he cried "Mamma!" and asked by signs for something to drink; but the cry was spasmodic, and there were convulsive twitchings in the limbs, which turned me to ice. I jumped out of bed to fetch him a drink. Imagine my horror when, on my handing him the cup, he remained motionless, only repeating "Mamma!" in that strange, unfamiliar voice, which was indeed by this time hardly a voice at all. I took his hand, but it did not respond to my pressure; it was quite stiff. I put the cup to his lips; the poor little fellow gulped down three or four mouthfuls in a convulsive manner that was terrible to see, and the water made a strange sound in his throat. He clung to me desperately, and I saw his eyes roll, as though some hidden force within were pulling at them, till only the whites were visible; his limbs were turning rigid. I screamed aloud, and Louis came.

"A doctor! quick! . . . he is dying," I cried.

Louis vanished, and my poor Armand again gasped, "Mamma! Mamma!" The next moment he lost all consciousness of his mother's existence. The pretty veins on his forehead swelled, and the convulsions began. For a whole hour before the doctors came, I held in my arms that merry baby, all lilies and roses, the blossom of my life, my pride, and my joy, lifeless as a piece of wood; and his eyes! I cannot think of them without horror. My pretty Armand was a mere mummy—black, shriveled, misshapen.

A doctor, two doctors, brought from Marseilles by Louis, hovered about like birds of ill omen; it made me shudder to look at them. One spoke of brain fever, the other saw nothing but an ordinary case of convulsions in infancy. Our own country doctor seemed to me to have the most sense, for he offered no opinion. "It's teething," said the second doctor.—"Fever," said the first. Finally it was agreed to put leeches on his neck and ice on his head. It seemed to me like death. To look on, to see a corpse, all purple or black, and not a cry, not a movement from this creature but now so full of life and sound—it was horrible!

At one moment I lost my head, and gave a sort of hysterical laugh, as I saw the pretty neck which I used to devour with kisses, with the leeches feeding on it, and his darling head in a cap of ice. My dear, we had to cut those lovely curls, of which we were so proud and with which you used to play, in order to make room for the ice. The convulsions returned every ten minutes with the regularity of labor pains, and then the poor baby writhed and twisted, now white, now violet. His supple limbs clattered like wood as they struck. And this unconscious flesh was the being who smiled and prattled, and used to say Mamma! At the thought, a storm of agony swept tumultuously over my soul, like the sea tossing in a hurricane. It seemed as though every tie which binds a child to its mother's heart was strained to rending. My mother, who might have given me help, advice, or comfort, was in Paris. Mothers, it is my belief, know more than doctors do about convulsions.

After four days and nights of suspense and fear, which almost killed me, the doctors were unanimous in advising the application of a horrid ointment, which would produce open sores. Sores on my Armand! who only five days before was playing about, and laughing, and trying to say "Godmother!" I would not have it done, preferring to trust in nature. Louis, who believes in doctors, scolded me. A man remains the same through everything. But there are moments when this terrible disease takes the likeness of death, and in one of these it seemed borne in upon me that this hateful remedy was the salvation of Armand. Louise, the skin was so dry, so rough and parched, that the ointment would not act. Then I broke into weeping, and my tears fell so long and so fast, that the bedside was wet through. And the doctors were at dinner!

Seeing myself alone with the child, I stripped him of all medical appliances, and seizing him like a mad woman, pressed him to my bosom, laying my forehead against his, and beseeching God to grant him the life which I was striving to pass into his veins from mine. For some minutes I held him thus, longing to die with him, so that neither life nor death might part us. Dear, I felt the limbs relaxing; the writhings ceased, the child stirred, and the ghastly, corpselike tints faded away! I screamed, just as I did when he was taken ill; the doctors hurried up, and I pointed to Armand.

"He is saved!" exclaimed the oldest of them.

What music in those words! The gates of heaven opened! And, in fact, two hours later Armand came back to life; but I was utterly crushed, and it was only the healing power of joy which saved me from a serious illness. My God! by what tortures do you bind a mother to her child! To fasten him to our heart, need the nails be driven into the very quick? Was I not mother enough before? I, who wept tears of joy over his broken syllables and tottering steps, who spent hours together planning how best to perform my duty, and fit myself for the sweet post of mother? Why these horrors, these ghastly scenes, for a mother who already idolized her child?

As I write, our little Armand is playing, shouting, laughing. What can be the cause of this terrible disease with children? Vainly do I try to puzzle it out, remembering that I am again with child. Is it teething? Is it some peculiar process in the brain? Is there something wrong with the nervous system of children who are subject to convulsions? All these thoughts disquiet me, in view alike of the present and the future. Our country doctor holds to the theory of nervous trouble produced by teething. I would give every tooth in my head to see little Armand's all through. The sight of one of those little white pearls peeping out of the swollen gum brings a cold sweat over me now. The heroism with which the little angel bore his sufferings proves to me that he will be his mother's son. A look from him goes to my very heart.

Medical science can give no satisfactory explanation as to the origin of this sort of tetanus, which passes off as rapidly as it comes on, and can apparently be neither guarded against nor cured. One thing alone, as I said before, is certain, that it is hell for a mother to see her child in convulsions. How passionately do I clasp him to my heart! I could walk for ever with him in my arms!

To have suffered all this only six weeks before my confinement made it much worse; I feared for the coming child. Farewell, my dear beloved. Don't wish for a child—there is the sum and substance of my letter!

XLI
THE BARONNE DE MACUMER
TO THE VICOMTESSE DE L'ESTORADE

Paris

Poor sweet,—Macumer and I forgave you all your naughtiness when we heard of your terrible trouble. I thrilled with pain as I read the details of the double agony, and there seem compensations now in being childless.

I am writing at once to tell you that Louis has been promoted. He can now wear the ribbon of an officer of the Legion. You are a lucky woman, Renée, and you will probably have a little girl, since that used to be your wish!

The marriage of my brother with Mademoiselle de Mortsauf was celebrated on our return. Our gracious king, who really is extraordinarily kind, has given my brother the reversion of the post of first gentleman of the chamber, which his father-in-law now fills, on the one condition that the scutcheon of the Mortsaufs should be placed side by side with that of the Lenoncourts.

"The office ought to go with the title," he said to the Duc de Lenoncourt-Givry.

My father is justified a hundred-fold. Without the help of my fortune nothing of all this could have taken place. My father and mother came from Madrid for the wedding, and return there, after the reception which I give to-morrow for the bride and bridegroom.

The carnival will be a very gay one. The Duc and Duchesse de Soria are in Paris, and their presence makes me a little uneasy. Marie Hérédia is certainly one of the most beautiful women in Europe, and I don't like the way Félipe looks at her. Therefore I am doubly lavish of sweetness and caresses. Every look and gesture speak the words which I am careful my lips should not utter, "*She* could not love like this!" Heaven knows how lovely and fascinating I am! Yesterday Madame de Maufrigneuse said to me:

"Dear child, who can compete with you?"

Then I keep Félipe so well amused, that his sister-in-law must seem as lively as a Spanish cow in comparison. I am the less sorry that a little Abencerrage is not on his way, because the duchesse will no doubt stay in Paris over her confinement, and she won't be a beauty any longer. If the baby is a boy, it will be called Félipe, in honor of the exile. An unkind chance has decreed that I shall, a second time, serve as godmother.

Good-bye, dear, I shall go to Chantepleurs early this year, for our Italian tour was shockingly expensive. I shall leave about the end of March, and retire to economize in Nivenais. Besides, I am tired of Paris. Félipe sighs, as I do, after the beautiful quiet of the park, our cool meadows, and our Loire, with its sparkling sands, peerless among rivers. Chantepleurs will seem delightful to me after the pomps and vanities of Italy; for, after all, splendor becomes wearisome, and a lover's glance has more beauty than a *capo d'opéra* or a *bel quadro!**

We shall expect you there. Don't be afraid that I shall be jealous again. You are free to take what soundings you please in Macumer's heart, and fish up all the interjections and doubts you can. I am supremely indifferent. Since that day at Rome Félipe's love for me has grown. He told me yesterday (he is looking over my shoulder now) that his sister-in-law, the Princess Hérédia, his destined bride of old, the dream of his youth, had no brains. Oh! my dear, I am worse than a ballet-dancer! If you knew what joy that slighting remark gave me! I have pointed out to Félipe that she does not speak French correctly. She says *esemple* for *exemple*, *sain* for *cinq*, *cheu* for *je*. She is beautiful of course, but quite without charm or the slightest scintilla of wit. When a compliment is paid her, she looks at you as though she didn't know what to do with such a strange thing. Félipe, being what he is, could not have lived two months with Marie after his marriage. Don Fernand, the Duc de Soria, suits her very well. He has generous instincts, but it's easy to see he has been a spoilt child. I am tempted to be naughty and make you laugh; but I won't draw the long bow. Ever so much love, darling.

XLII
RENÉE TO LOUISE

My little girl is two months old. She is called Jeanne-Athénaïs, and has for godmother and godfather my mother, and an old grand-uncle of Louis's.

As soon as I possibly can, I shall start for my visit to Chantepleurs, since you are not afraid of a nursing mother. Your godson can say your name now; he calls it *Matoumer*, for he can't say *c* properly. You will be quite delighted with him. He has got all his teeth, and eats meat now like a big boy; he is all over the place, trotting about like a little mouse; but I watch him all the time with anxious eyes, and it makes me miserable that I cannot keep him by me when I am laid up. The time is more than usually long with me, as the doctors consider some special precautions necessary. Alas! my child, habit does not inure one to child-bearing. There are the same old discomforts and misgivings. However (don't show this to Félipe), this little girl takes after me, and she may yet cut out your Armand.

My father thought Félipe looking very thin, and my dear pet also not quite so blooming. Yet the Duc and Duchesse de Soria have gone; not a loophole for jealousy is left! Is there any trouble which you are hiding from me? Your letter is neither so long nor so full of loving thoughts as usual. Is this only a whim of my dear whimsical friend?

I am running on too long. My nurse is angry with me for writing, and Mademoiselle Athénaïs de l'Estorade wants her dinner. Farewell, then; write me some nice long letters.

XLIII

MADAME DE MACUMER TO THE COMTESSE DE L'ESTORADE

For the first time in my life, my dear Renée, I have been alone and crying. I was sitting under a willow, on a wooden bench by the side of the long Chantepleurs marsh. The view there is charming, but it needs some merry children to complete it, and I wait for you. I have been married nearly three years, and no child! The thought of your quiver full drove me to explore my heart.

And this is what I find there. "Oh! if I had to suffer a hundred-fold what Renée suffered when my god-son was born; if I had to see my child in convulsions, even so would to God that I might have a cherub of my own, like your Athénaïs!" I can see her from here in my mind's eye, and I know she is beautiful as the day, for you tell me nothing about her—that is just like my Renée! I believe you divine my trouble.

Each time my hopes are disappointed, I fall a prey for some days to the blackest melancholy. Then I compose sad elegies. When shall I embroider little caps and sew lace edgings to encircle a tiny head? When choose the cambric for the baby-clothes? Shall I never hear baby lips shout "Mamma," and have my dress pulled by a teasing despot whom my heart adores? Are there to be no wheelmarks of a little carriage on the gravel, no broken toys littered about the courtyard? Shall I never visit the toy-shops, as mothers do, to buy swords, and dolls, and baby-houses? And will it never be mine to watch the unfolding of a precious life—another Félipe, only more dear? I would have a son, if only to learn how a lover can be more to one in his second self.

My park and castle are cold and desolate to me. A

childless woman is a monstrosity of nature; we exist only to be mothers. Oh! my sage in woman's livery, how well you have conned the book of life! Everywhere, too, barrenness is a dismal thing. My life is a little too much like one of Gessner's or Florian's sheepfolds, which Rivarol longed to see invaded by a wolf.* I too have it in me to make sacrifices! There are forces in me, I feel, which Félipe has no use for; and if I am not to be a mother, I must be allowed to indulge myself in some romantic sorrow.

I have just made this remark to my belated Moor, and it brought tears to his eyes. He cannot stand any joking on his love, so I let him off easily, and only called him a paladin of folly.

At times I am seized with a desire to go on pilgrimage, to bear my longings to the shrine of some madonna or to a watering-place. Next winter I shall take medical advice. I am too much enraged with myself to write more. Good-bye.

XLIV

THE SAME TO THE SAME

Paris, 1829

A whole year passed, my dear, without a letter! What does this mean? I am a little hurt. Do you suppose that your Louis, who comes to see me almost every alternate day, makes up for you? It is not enough to know that you are well and that everything prospers with you; for I love you, Renée, and I want to know what you are feeling and thinking of, just as I say everything to you, at the risk of being scolded, or censured, or misunderstood. Your silence and seclusion in the country, at the time when you might be in Paris enjoying all the Parliamentary honors of the Comte de l'Estorade, cause me serious anxiety. You know that your husband's "gift of gab" and unsparing zeal have won for him quite a position here, and he will doubtless receive some very good post when the session is over. Pray, do you spend your life writing him letters of advice? Numa was not so far removed from his Egeria.*

Why did you not take this opportunity of seeing Paris? I might have enjoyed your company for four months. Louis told me yesterday that you were coming to fetch him, and would have your third confinement in Paris— you terrible mother Gigogne!* After bombarding Louis with queries, exclamations, and regrets, I at last defeated his strategy so far as to discover that his grand-uncle, the godfather of Athénaïs, is very ill. Now I believe that you, like a careful mother, would be quite equal to angling with the member's speeches and fame for a fat legacy from your husband's last remaining relative on the mother's side. Keep your mind easy, my Renée— we are all at work for Louis, Lenoncourts, Chaulieus, and the whole band of Madame de Macumer's followers. Martignac* will probably put him into the Audit Department. But if you won't tell me why you bury yourself in the country, I shall be cross.

Tell me, are you afraid that the political wisdom of the house of l'Estorade should seem to centre in you? Or is it the uncle's legacy? Perhaps you were afraid you would be less to your children in Paris? Ah! what I would give to know whether, after all, you were not simply too vain to show yourself in Paris for the first time in your present condition! Vain thing! Farewell.

XLV
RENÉE TO LOUISE

You complain of my silence; have you forgotten, then, those two little brown heads, at once my subjects and my tyrants? And as to staying at home, you have yourself hit upon several of my reasons. Apart from the condition of our dear uncle, I didn't want to drag with

Ces deux petits font alors de mon lit le théâtre de leurs jeux.

MÉMOIRES DE DEUX JEUNES MARIÉS.

Plate V: *The Comtesse Louis de l'Estorade and her Children*
Illustration by Tony Johannot

me to Paris a boy of four and a little girl who will soon be three, when I am again expecting my confinement. I had no intention of troubling you and upsetting your husband with such a party. I did not care to appear, looking my worst, in the brilliant circle over which you preside, and I detest life in hotels and lodgings.

When I come to spend the session in Paris, it will be in my own house. Louis's uncle, when he heard of the rank his grand-nephew had received, made me a present of two hundred thousand francs (the half of his savings) with which to buy a house in Paris, and I have charged Louis to find one in your neighborhood. My mother has given me thirty thousand francs for the furnishing, and I shall do my best not to disgrace the dear sister of my election—no pun intended.

I am grateful to you for having already done so much at Court for Louis. But though Monsieur de Bourmont and Monsieur de Polignac have paid him the compliment of asking him to join their ministry,* I do not wish so conspicuous a place for him. It would commit him too much; and I prefer the Audit Office because it is permanent. Our affairs here are in very good hands; so you need not fear; as soon as the steward has mastered the details, I will come and support Louis.

As for writing long letters nowadays, how can I. This one, in which I want to describe to you the daily routine of my life, will be a week on the stocks. Who can tell but Armand may lay hold of it to make caps for his regiments drawn up on my carpet, or vessels for the fleets which sail his bath! A single day will serve as a sample of the rest, for they are all exactly alike, and their characteristics reduce themselves to two—either the children are well, or they are not. For me, in this solitary grange, it is no exaggeration to say that hours become minutes, or minutes hours, according to the children's health.

If I have some delightful hours, it is when they are asleep and I am no longer needed to rock the one or soothe the other with stories. When I have them sleeping by my side, I say to myself, "Nothing can go wrong now." The fact is, my sweet, every mother spends her time, so soon as her children are out of her sight, in imagining dangers for them. Perhaps it is Armand seizing the razors to play with, or his coat taking fire, or a snake biting him, or he might tumble in running and start an abscess on his head, or he might drown himself in a pond. A mother's life, you see, is one long succession of dramas, now soft and tender, now terrible. Not an hour but has its joys and fears.

But at night, in my room, comes the hour for waking dreams, when I plan out their future, which shines brightly in the smile of the guardian angel, watching over their beds. Sometimes Armand calls me in his sleep; I kiss his forehead (without rousing him), then his sister's feet, and watch them both lying in their beauty. These are my merry-makings! Yesterday, it must have been our guardian angel who roused me in the middle of the night and summoned me in fear to Athénaïs's cradle. Her head was too low, and I found Armand all uncovered, his feet purple with cold.

"Darling mother!" he cried, rousing up and flinging his arms round me.

There, dear, is one of our night scenes for you.

How important it is for a mother to have her children by her side at night! It is not for a nurse, however careful she may be, to take them up, comfort them, and hush them to sleep again, when some horrid nightmare has disturbed them. For they have their dreams, and the task of explaining away one of those dread visions of the night is the more arduous because the child is scared, stupid, and only half awake. It is a mere interlude in the unconsciousness of slumber. In this way I have come to sleep so lightly, that I can see my little pair and see them stirring, through the veil of my eyelids. A sigh or a rustle wakens me. For me, the demon of convulsions is ever crouching by their beds.

So much for the nights; with the first twitter of the birds my babies begin to stir. Through the mists of dispersing sleep, their chatter blends with the warblings that fill the morning air, or with the swallows' noisy debates—little cries of joy or woe, which make their way to my heart rather than my ears. While Naïs struggles to get at me, making the passage from her cradle to my bed on all fours or with staggering steps, Armand climbs up with the agility of a monkey, and has his arms round me. Then the merry couple turn my bed into a playground, where mother lies at their mercy. The baby-girl pulls my hair, and would take to sucking again, while Armand stands guard over my breast, as though defending his property. Their funny ways, their peals of laughter, are too much for me, and put sleep fairly to flight.

Then we play the ogress game; mother ogress eats up the white, soft flesh with hugs, and rains kisses on those rosy shoulders and eyes brimming over with saucy mischief; we have little jealous tiffs too, so pretty to see. It has happened to me, dear, to take up my stockings at eight o'clock and be still bare-footed at nine!

Then comes the getting up. The operation of dressing begins. I slip on my dressing-gown, turn up my sleeves, and don the mackintosh apron; with Mary's assistance, I wash and scrub my two little blossoms. I am sole arbiter of the temperature of the bath, for a good half of children's crying and whimpering comes from mistakes here. The moment has arrived for paper fleets and glass ducks, since the only way to get children thoroughly washed is to keep them well amused. If you knew the diversions that have to be invented before these despotic sovereigns will permit a soft sponge to be passed over every nook and cranny, you would be awestruck at the amount of ingenuity and intelligence demanded by the maternal profession when one takes it seriously.

Prayers, scoldings, promises, are alike in requisition; above all, the jugglery must be so dexterous that it defies detection. The case would be desperate had not Providence to the cunning of the child matched that of the mother. A child is a diplomatist, only to be mastered, like the diplomatists of the great world, through his passions! Happily, it takes little to make these cherubs laugh; the fall of a brush, a piece of soap slipping from the hand, and what merry shouts! And if our triumphs are dearly bought, still triumphs they are, though hidden from mortal eye. Even the father knows nothing of it all. None but God and His angels—and perhaps you—can fathom the glances of satisfaction which Mary and I exchange when the little creatures' toilet is at last concluded, and they stand, spotless and shining, amid a chaos of soap, sponges, combs, basins, blotting-paper, flannel, and all the nameless litter of a true English "nursery."

For I am so far a convert as to admit that English women have a talent for this department. True, they look upon the child only from the point of view of material well-being; but where this is concerned, their arrangements are admirable. My children must always be bare-legged and wear woollen socks. There shall be no swaddling nor bandages; on the other hand, they shall never be left alone. The helplessness of the French infant in its swaddling-bands means the liberty of the nurse—that is the whole explanation. A mother, who is really a mother, is never free.

There is my answer to your question why I do not write. Besides the management of the estate, I have the upbringing of two children on my hands.

The art of motherhood involves much silent, unobtrusive self-denial, an hourly devotion which finds no detail too minute. The soup warming before the fire must be watched. Am I the kind of woman, do you suppose, to shirk such cares? The humblest task may earn a rich harvest of affection. How pretty is a child's laugh when he finds the food to his liking! Armand has a way of nodding his head when he is pleased that is worth a lifetime of adoration. How could I leave to any one else the privilege and delight, as well as the responsibility, of blowing on the spoonful of soup which is too hot for my little Naïs, my nursling of seven months ago, who still remembers my breast? When a nurse has allowed a child to burn its tongue and lips with scalding food, she tells the mother, who hurries up to see what is wrong, that the child cried from hunger. How could a mother sleep in peace with the thought that a breath, less pure than her own, has cooled her child's food—the mother whom Nature has made the direct vehicle of food to infant lips. To mince a chop for Naïs, who has just cut her last teeth, and mix the meat, cooked to a turn, with potatoes, is a work of patience, and there are times, indeed, when none but a mother could succeed in making an impatient child go through with its meal.

No number of servants, then, and no English nurse can dispense a mother from taking the field in person in that daily contest, where gentleness alone should grapple with the little griefs and pains of childhood. Louise, the care of these innocent darlings is a work to engage the whole soul. To whose hand and eyes, but one's own, intrust the task of feeding, dressing, and putting to bed? Broadly speaking, a crying child is the unanswerable condemnation of mother or nurse, except when the cry is the outcome of natural pain. Now that I have two to look after (and a third on the road), they occupy all my thoughts. Even you, whom I love so dearly, have become a memory to me.

My own dressing is not always completed by two o'clock. I have no faith in mothers whose rooms are in apple-pie order, and who themselves might have stepped out of a bandbox. Yesterday was one of those lovely days of early April, and I wanted to take my children for a walk, while I was still able—for the warning bell is in my ears. Such an expedition is quite an epic to a mother! One dreams of it the night before! Armand was for the first time to put on a little black velvet jacket, a new collar which I had worked, a Scotch cap with the Stuart colors and cock's feathers; Naïs was to be in white and pink, with one of those delicious little baby caps; for she is a baby still, though she will lose that pretty title on the arrival of the impatient youngster, whom I call my beggar, for he will have the portion of a younger son. (You see, Louise, the child has already appeared to me in a vision, so I know it is a boy.)

Well, caps, collars, jackets, socks, dainty little shoes, pink garters, the muslin frock with silk embroidery,—all was laid out on my bed. Then the little brown heads had to be brushed, twittering merrily all the time like birds, answering each other's call. Armand's hair is in curls, while Naïs's is brought forward softly on the forehead as a border to the pink-and-white cap. Then the shoes are buckled; and when the little bare legs and well-shod feet have trotted off to the nursery, while two shining faces (*clean*, Mary calls them) and eyes ablaze with life petition me to start, my heart beats fast. To look on the children whom one's own hand has arrayed, the pure skin brightly veined with blue, that one has bathed, laved, and sponged and decked with gay colors of silk or velvet—why, there is no poem comes near to it! With what eager, covetous longing one calls them back for one more kiss on those white necks, which, in their simple collars, the loveliest woman cannot rival. Even the coarsest lithograph of such a scene makes a mother pause, and I feast my eyes daily on the living picture!

Once out of doors, triumphant in the result of my labors, while I was admiring the princely air with which little Armand helped baby to totter along the path you know, I saw a carriage coming, and tried to get them out of the way. The children tumbled into a dirty puddle, and lo! my works of art are ruined! We had to take them back and change their things. I took the little one in my arms, never thinking of my own dress, which was ruined, while Mary seized Armand, and the cavalcade re-entered. With a crying baby and a soaked child, what mind has a mother left for herself?

Dinner time arrives, and as a rule I have done nothing. Now comes the problem which faces me twice every day—how to suffice in my own person for two children, put on their bibs, turn up their sleeves, and get them to eat. In the midst of these ever-recurring cares, joys, and catastrophes, the only person neglected in the house is myself. If the children have been naughty, often I don't get rid of my curl-papers all day. Their tempers rule my toilet. As the price of a few minutes in which I write you these half-dozen pages, I have had to let them cut pictures out of my novels, build castles with books, chessmen, or mother-of-pearl counters, and give Naïs my silks and wools to arrange in her own fashion, which, I assure you, is so complicated, that she is entirely absorbed in it, and has not uttered a word.

Yet I have nothing to complain of. My children are both strong and independent; they amuse themselves more easily then you would think. They find delight in everything; a guarded liberty is worth many toys. A few pebbles—pink, yellow, purple, and black, small shells, the mysteries of sand, are a world of pleasure to them. Their wealth consists in possessing a multitude of small things. I watch Armand and find him talking to the flowers, the flies, the chickens, and imitating them. He is on friendly terms with insects, and never wearies of admiring them. Everything which is on a minute scale interests them. Armand is beginning to ask the "why" of everything he sees. He has come to ask what I am saying to his godmother, whom he looks on as a fairy. Strange how children hit the mark!

Alas! my sweet, I would not sadden you with the tale of my joys. Let me give you some notion of your godson's character. The other day we were followed by a poor man begging—beggars soon find out that a mother with her child at her side can't resist them. Armand has no idea what hunger is, and money is a sealed book to him; but I have just bought him a trumpet which had long been the object of his desires. He held it out to the old man with a kingly air, saying:

"Here, take this!"

What joy the world can give would compare with such a moment?

"May I keep it?" said the poor man to me. "I too, madame, have had children," he added, hardly noticing the money I put into his hand.

I shudder when I think that Armand must go to school, and that I have only three years and a half more to keep him by me. The flowers that blossom in his sunny childhood will fall before the scythe of a public school system; his gracious ways and bewitching candor will lose their spontaneity. They will cut the curls that I have brushed and smoothed and kissed so often! What will they do with the thinking being that is Armand?

And what of you? You tell me nothing of your life. Are you still in love with Félipe? For, as regards the Saracen, I have no uneasiness. Good-bye; Naïs has just had a tumble, and if I run on like this, my letter will become a volume.

XLVI
MADAME DE MACUMER TO THE COMTESSE DE L'ESTORADE

Chantepleurs, 1829

My sweet, tender Renée, you will have learned from the papers the terrible calamity which has overwhelmed me. I have not been able to write you even a word. For twenty days I never left his bedside; I received his last breath and closed his eyes; I kept holy watch over him with the priests and repeated the prayers for the dead. The cruel pangs I suffered were accepted by me as a rightful punishment; and yet, when I saw on his calm lips the smile which was his last farewell to me, how was it possible to believe that I had caused his death! Be it so or not, he is gone, and I am left. To you, who have known us both so well, what more need I say? These words contain all.

Oh! I would give my share of Heaven to hear the flattering tale that my prayers have power to bring him back to life! To see him again, to have him once more mine, were it only for a second, would mean that I could draw breath again without mortal agony. Will you not come soon and soothe me with such promises? Is not your love strong enough to deceive me?

But stay! it was you who told me beforehand that he would suffer through me. Was it so indeed? Yes, it is true, I had no right to his love. Like a thief, I took what was not mine, and my frenzied grasp has crushed the life out of my bliss. The madness is over now, but I feel that I am alone. Merciful God! what torture of the damned can exceed the misery in that word?

When they took him away from me, I lay down on the same bed and hoped to die. There was but a door between us, and it seemed to me I had strength to force it! But, alas! I was too young for death; and after forty days, during which, with cruel care and all the sorry inventions of medical science, they slowly nursed me back to life, I find myself in the country, seated by my window, surrounded with lovely flowers, which he made to bloom for me, gazing on the same splendid view over which his eyes have so often wandered, and which he was so proud to have discovered, since it gave me pleasure. Ah! dear Renée, no words can tell how new surroundings hurt when the heart is dead. I shiver at the sight of the moist earth in my garden, for the earth is a vast tomb, and it is almost as though I walked on *him!* When I first went out, I trembled with fear and could not move. It was so sad to see *his* flowers, and *he* not there!

My father and mother are in Spain. You know what my brothers are, and you yourself are detained in the country. But you need not be uneasy about me; two angels of mercy flew to my side. The Duc and the Duchesse de Soria hastened to their brother in his illness, and have been everything that heart could wish. The last few nights before the end found the three of us gathered, in calm and wordless grief, round the bed where this great man was breathing his last, a man among a thousand, rare in any age, head and shoulders above the rest of us in everything. The patient resignation of my Félipe was angelic. The sight of his brother and Marie gave him a moment's pleasure and easing of his pain.

"Darling," he said to me with the simple frankness which never deserted him, "I had almost gone from life without leaving to Fernand the Barony of Macumer; I must make a new will. My brother will forgive me; he knows what it is to love!"

I owe my life to the care of my brother-in-law and his wife; they want to carry me off to Spain!

Ah! Renée, to no one but you can I speak freely of my grief. A sense of my own faults weighs me to the ground, and there is a bitter solace in pouring them out to you, poor, unheeded Cassandra. The exactions, the preposterous jealousy, the nagging unrest of my passion wore him to death. My love was the more fraught with danger for him because we had both the same exquisitely sensitive nature, we spoke the same language, nothing was lost on him, and often the mocking shaft, so carelessly discharged, went straight to his heart. You can have no idea of the point to which he carried submissiveness. I had only to tell him to go and leave me alone, and the caprice, however wounding to him, would be obeyed without a murmur. His last breath was spent in blessing me and in repeating that a single morning alone with me was more precious to him than a lifetime spent with another woman, were she even the Marie of his youth. My tears fall as I write the words.

This is the manner of my life now. I rise at midday and go to bed at seven; I linger absurdly long over meals; I saunter about slowly, standing motionless, an hour at a time, before a single plant; I gaze into the leafy trees; I take a sober and serious interest in mere nothings; I long for shade, silence, and night; in a word, I fight through each hour as it comes, and take a gloomy pleasure in adding it to the heap of the vanquished. My peaceful park gives me all the company I care for; everything there is full of glorious images of my vanished joy, invisible for others but eloquent to me.

"I cannot away with you Spaniards!" I exclaimed one morning, as my sister-in-law flung herself on my neck. "You have some nobility that we lack."

Ah! Renée, if I still live, it is doubtless because Heaven tempers the sense of affliction to the strength of those who have to bear it. Only a woman can know what it is to lose a love which sprang from the heart and was genuine throughout, a passion which was not ephemeral, and satisfied at once the spirit and the flesh. How rare it is to find a man so gifted that to worship him brings no sense of degradation! If such supreme fortune befall us once, we cannot hope for it a second time. Men of true greatness, whose strength and worth are veiled by poetic grace, and who charm by some high spiritual power, men made to be adored, beware of love! Love will ruin you, and ruin the woman of your heart. This is the burden of my cry as I pace my woodland walks.

And he has left me no child! That love so rich in smiles, which rained perpetual flowers and joy, has left no fruit. I am a thing accursed. Can it be that, even as the two extremes of polar ice and torrid sand are alike intolerant of life, so the very purity and vehemence of a single-hearted passion render it barren as hate? Is it only a marriage of reason, such as yours, which is blessed with a family? Can Heaven be jealous of our passions? There are wild words.

You are, I believe, the one person whose company I could endure. Come to me, then; none but Renée should be with Louise in her sombre garb. What a day when I first put on my widow's bonnet! When I saw myself all arrayed in black, I fell back on a seat and wept till night came; and I weep again as I recall that moment of anguish.

Good-bye. Writing tires me; thoughts crowd fast, but I have no heart to put them into words. Bring your children; you can nurse baby here without making me jealous; all that is gone, *he* is not here, and I shall be very glad to see my godson. Félipe used to wish for a child like little Armand. Come, then, come and help me to bear my woe.

XLVII

RENÉE TO LOUISE

1829

My darling,—When you hold this letter in your hands, I shall be already near, for I am starting a few minutes after it. We shall be alone together. Louis is obliged to remain in Provence because of the approaching elections. He wants to be elected again, and the Liberals are already plotting against his return.

I don't come to comfort you; I only bring you my heart to beat in sympathy with yours, and help you to bear with life. I come to bid you weep, for only with tears can you purchase the joy of meeting him again. Remember, he is traveling towards Heaven, and every step forward which you take brings you nearer to him. Every duty done breaks a link in the chain that keeps you apart.

Louise, in my arms you will once more raise your head and go on your way to him, pure, noble, washed of all those errors, which had no root in your heart, and bearing with you the harvest of good deeds which, in his name, you will accomplish here.

I scribble these hasty lines in all the bustle of preparation, and interrupted by the babies and by Armand, who keeps saying, "Godmother, godmother! I want to see her," till I am almost jealous. He might be your child!

SECOND PART

XLVIII

THE BARONNE DE MACUMER

TO THE COMTESSE DE L'ESTORADE

October 15, 1833

Yes, Renée, it is quite true; you have been correctly informed. I have sold my house, I have sold Chantepleurs, and the farms in Seine-et-Marne, but no more, please! I am neither mad nor ruined, I assure you.

Let us go into the matter. When everything was wound up, there remained to me of my poor Macumer's fortune about twelve hundred thousand francs. I will account, as to a practical sister, for every penny of this.

I put a million in the Three per Cents when they were at fifty, and so I have got an income for myself of sixty thousand francs, instead of the thirty thousand which the property yielded. Then, only think what my life was. Six months of the year in the country, renewing leases, listening to the grumbles of the farmers, who pay when it pleases them, and getting as bored as a sportsman in wet weather. There was produce to sell, and I always sold it at a loss. Then, in Paris, my house represented a rental of ten thousand francs; I had to invest my money at the notaries; I was kept waiting for the interest, and could only get the money back by prosecuting; in addition I had to study the law of mortgage. In short, there was business in Nivernais, in Seine-et-Marne, in Paris—and what a burden, what a nuisance, what a vexing and losing game for a widow of twenty-seven!

Whereas now my fortune is secured on the Budget. In place of paying taxes to the State, I receive from it, every half-year, in my own person, and free from cost, thirty thousand francs in thirty notes, handed over the counter to me by a dapper little clerk at the Treasury, who smiles when he sees me coming!

Supposing the nation went bankrupt? Well, to begin with: "'Tis not mine to see trouble so far from my door." At the worst, too, the nation would not dock me of more than half my income, so I should still be as well off as before my investment, and in the meantime I shall be drawing a double income until the catastrophe arrives. A nation doesn't become bankrupt more than once in a century, so I shall have plenty of time to amass a little capital out of my savings.

And finally, is not the Comte de l'Estorade a peer of this July semi-republic?* Is he not one of those pillars of royalty offered by the "people" to the King of the French? How can I have qualms with a friend at Court, a great financier, head of the Audit Department? I defy you to arraign my sanity! I am almost as good at sums as your citizen king.

Do you know what inspires a woman with all this arithmetic? Love, my dear!

Alas! the moment has come for unfolding to you the mysteries of my conduct, the motives of which have baffled even your keen sight, your prying affection, and your subtlety. I am to be married in a country village near Paris. I love and am loved. I love as much as a woman can who knows love well. I am loved as much as a woman ought to be by the man she adores.

Forgive me, Renée, for keeping this a secret from you and from every one. If your friend evades all spies and puts curiosity on a false track, you must admit that my feeling for poor Macumer justified some dissimulation. Besides, de l'Estorade and you would have deafened me with remonstrances, and plagued me to death with your misgivings, to which the facts might have lent some color. You know, if no one else does, to what pitch my jealousy can go, and all this would only have been useless torture to me. I was determined to carry out, on my own responsibility, what you, Renée, will call my insane project, and I would take counsel only with my own head and heart, for all the world like a schoolgirl giving the slip to her watchful parents.

The man I love possesses nothing but thirty thousand francs' worth of debts, which I have paid. What a theme for comment here! You would have tried to make Gaston out an adventurer; your husband would have set detectives on the dear boy. I preferred to sift him for myself. He has been wooing me now close on two years. I am twenty-seven, he is twenty-three. The difference, I admit, is huge when it is on the wrong side. Another source of lamentation!

Lastly, he is a poet, and has lived by his trade—that is to say, on next to nothing, as you will readily understand. Being a poet, he has spent more time weaving day-dreams, and basking, lizard-like, in the sun, than scribing in his dingy garret. Now, practical people have a way of tarring with the same brush of inconstancy authors, artists, and in general all men who live by their brains. Their nimble and fertile wit lays them open to the charge of a like agility in matters of the heart.

Spite of the debts, spite of the difference in age, spite of the poetry, an end is to be placed in a few days to a heroic resistance of more than nine months, during which he has not been allowed even to kiss my hand, and so also ends the season of our sweet, pure

339

love-making. This is not the mere surrender of a raw, ignorant, and curious girl, as it was eight years ago; the gift is deliberate, and my lover awaits it with such loyal patience that, if I pleased, I could postpone the marriage for a year. There is no servility in this; love's slave he may be, but the heart is not slavish. Never have I seen a man of nobler feeling, or one whose tenderness was more rich in fancy, whose love bore more the impress of his soul. Alas! my sweet one, the art of love is his by heritage. A few words will tell his story.

My friend has no other name than Marie Gaston. He is the illegitimate son of the beautiful Lady Brandon, whose fame must have reached you, and who died broken-hearted, a victim to the vengeance of Lady Dudley—a ghastly story of which the dear boy knows nothing. Marie Gaston was placed by his brother Louis in a boarding-school at Tours, where he remained till 1827. Louis, after settling his brother at school, sailed a few days later for foreign parts "to seek his fortune," to use the words of an old woman who had played the part of Providence to him. This brother turned sailor used to write him, at long intervals, letters quite father-ly in tone, and breathing a noble spirit; but a struggling life never allowed him to return home. His last letter told Marie that he had been appointed Captain in the navy of some American republic, and exhorted him to hope for better days.

Alas! since then three years have passed, and my poor poet has never heard again. So dearly did he love his brother, that he would have started to look for him but for Daniel d'Arthez, the well-known author, who took a generous interest in Marie Gaston, and prevented him carrying out his mad impulse. Nor was this all; often would he give him a crust and a corner, as the poet puts it in his graphic words.

For, in truth, the poor lad was in terrible straits; he was actually innocent enough to believe—incredible as it seems—that genius was the shortest road to fortune, and from 1828 to 1833 his one aim has been to make a name for himself in letters. Naturally his life was a frightful tissue of toil and hardships, alternating between hope and despair. The good advice of d'Arthez could not prevail against the allurements of ambition, and his debts went on growing like a snowball. Still he was beginning to come into notice when I happened to meet him at Madame d'Espard's. At first sight he inspired me, unconsciously to himself, with the most vivid sympathy. How did it come about that this virgin heart has been left for me? The fact is that my poet combines genius and cleverness, passion and pride, and women are always afraid of greatness which has no weak side to it. How many victories were needed before Josephine could see the great Napoleon in the little Bonaparte whom she had married.

Poor Gaston is innocent enough to think he knows the measure of my love! He simply has not an idea of it, but to you I must make it clear; for this letter, Renée, is something in the nature of a last will and testament. Weigh well what I am going to say, I beg of you.

At this moment I am confident of being loved as perhaps not another women on this earth, nor have I a shadow of doubt as to the perfect happiness of our wedded life, to which I bring a feeling hitherto unknown to me. Yes, for the first time in my life, I know the delight of being swayed by passion. That which every woman seeks in love will be mine in marriage. As poor Félipe once adored me, so do I now adore Gaston. I have lost control of myself, I tremble before this boy as the Arab hero used to tremble before me. In a word, the balance of love is now on my side, and this makes me timid. I am full of the most absurd terrors. I am afraid of being deserted, afraid of becoming old and ugly while Gaston still retains his youth and beauty, afraid of coming short of his hopes!

And yet I believe I have it in me, I believe I have sufficient devotion and ability, not only to keep alive the flame of his love in our solitary life, far from the world, but even to make it burn stronger and brighter. If I am mistaken, if this splendid idyl of love in hiding must come to an end—an end! what am I saying?—if I find Gaston's love less intense any day than it was the evening before, be sure of this, Renée, I should visit my failure only on myself; no blame should attach to him. I tell you now it would mean my death. Not even if I had children could I live on these terms, for I know myself, Renée, I know that my nature is the lover's rather than the mother's. Therefore before taking this vow upon my soul, I implore you, my Renée, if this disaster befall me, to take the place of mother to my children; let them be my legacy to you! All that I know of you, your blind attachment to duty, your rare gifts, your love of children, your affection for me, would help to make my death—I dare not say easy—but at least less bitter.

The compact I have thus made with myself adds a vague terror to the solemnity of my marriage ceremony. For this reason I wish to have no one whom I know present, and it will be performed in secret. Let my heart fail me if it will, at least I shall not read anxiety in your dear eyes, and I alone shall know that this new marriage-contract which I sign may be my death warrant.

I shall not refer again to this agreement entered into between my present self and the self I am to be. I have confided it to you in order that you might know the full extent of your responsibilities. In marrying I retain full control of my property; and Gaston, while aware that I have enough to secure a comfortable life for both of us, is ignorant of its amount. Within twenty-four hours I shall dispose of it as I please; and in order to save him from a humiliating position, I shall have stock, bringing in twelve thousand francs a year, assigned to him. He will find this in his desk on the eve of our wedding.

If he declined to accept, I should break off the whole thing. I had to threaten a rupture to get his permission to pay his debts.

This long confession has tired me. I shall finish it the day after to-morrow; I have to spend to-morrow in the country.

October 20th

I will tell you now the steps I have taken to insure secrecy. My object has been to ward off every possible incitement to my ever-wakeful jealousy, in imitation of the Italian princess, who, like a lioness rushing on her prey, carried it off to some Swiss town to devour in peace. And I confide my plans to you because I have another favor to beg; namely, that you will respect our solitude and never come to see us uninvited.

Two years ago I purchased a small property overlooking the ponds of Ville d'Avray,* on the road to Versailles. It consists of twenty acres of meadow land, the skirts of a wood, and a fine fruit garden. Below the meadows the land has been excavated so as to make a lakelet of about three acres in extent, with a charming little island in the middle. The small valley is shut in by two graceful, thickly-wooded slopes, where rise delicious springs that water my park by means of channels cleverly disposed by my architect. Finally, they fall into the royal ponds, glimpses of which can be seen here and there, gleaming in the distance. My little park has been admirably laid out by the architect, who has surrounded it by hedges, walls, or ha-has, according to the lie of the land, so that no possible point of view may be lost.

A chalet has been built for me half-way up the hillside, with a charming exposure, having the woods of the Ronce on either side, and in front a grassy slope running down to the lake. Externally the chalet is an exact copy of those which are so much admired by travelers on the road from Sion to Brieg,* and which fascinated me when I was returning from Italy. The internal decorations will bear comparison with those of the most celebrated buildings of the kind.

A hundred paces from this rustic dwelling stands a charming and ornamental house, communicating with it by a subterranean passage. This contains the kitchen, and other servants' rooms, stables, and coach-houses. Of all this series of brick buildings, the facade alone is seen, graceful in its simplicity, against a background of shrubbery. Another building serves to lodge the gardeners and masks the entrance to the orchards and kitchen-gardens.

The entrance gate to the property is so hidden in the wall dividing the park from the wood as almost to defy detection. The plantations, already well grown, will, in two or three years, completely hide the buildings, so that, except in winter, when the trees are bare, no trace of habitation will appear to the outside world, save only the smoke visible from the neighboring hills.

The surroundings of my chalet have been modeled on what is called the king's garden at Versailles, but it has an outlook on my lakelet and island. The hills on every side display their abundant foliage—those splendid trees for which your new civil list has so well cared. My gardeners have orders to cultivate new sweet-scented flowers to any extent, and no others, so that our home will be a fragrant emerald. The chalet, adorned with a wild vine which covers the roof, is literally embedded in climbing plants of all kinds—hops, clematis, jasmine, azalea, copæa. It will be a sharp eye which can descry our windows!

The chalet, my dear, is a good, solid house, with its heating system and all the conveniences of modern architecture, which can raise a palace in the compass of a hundred square feet. It contains a suite of rooms for Gaston and another for me. The ground-floor is occupied by an ante-room, a parlor, and a dining room.

Above our floor again are three rooms destined for the *nurseries*. I have five first-rate horses, a small light coupe, and a two-horse cabriolet. We are only forty-minutes' drive from Paris; so that, when the spirit moves us to hear an opera or see a new play, we can start after dinner and return the same night to our bower. The road is a good one, and passes under the shade of our green dividing wall.

My servants—cook, coachman, groom, and gardeners, in addition to my maid—are all very respectable people, whom I have spent the last six months in picking up, and they will be superintended by my old Philippe. Although confident of their loyalty and good faith, I have not neglected to cultivate self-interest; their wages are small, but will receive an annual addition in the shape of a New Year's Day present. They are all aware that the slightest fault, or a mere suspicion of gossiping, might lose them a capital place. Lovers are never troublesome to their servants; they are indulgent by disposition, and therefore I feel that I can reckon on my household.

All that is choice, pretty, or decorative in my house in the Rue du Bac has been transported to the chalet. The Rembrandt hangs on the staircase, as though it were a mere daub; the Hobbema faces the Rubens in *his* study; the Titian, which my sister-in-law Mary sent me from Madrid, adorns the boudoir. The beautiful furniture picked up by Félipe looks very well in the parlor, which the architect has decorated most tastefully. Everything at the chalet is charmingly simple, with the simplicity which can't be got under a hundred thousand francs. Our ground-floor rests on cellars, which are built of millstone and embedded in concrete; it is almost completely buried in flowers and shrubs, and is deliciously cool without a vestige of damp. To complete the picture, a fleet of white swans sail over my lake!

Oh! Renée, the silence which reigns in this valley

would bring joy to the dead! One is awakened by the birds singing or the breeze rustling in the poplars. A little spring, discovered by the architect in digging the foundations of the wall, trickles down the hillside over silvery sand to the lake, between two banks of water-cress, hugging the edge of the woods. I know nothing that money can buy to equal it.

May not Gaston come to loathe this too perfect bliss? I shudder to think how complete it is, for the ripest fruits harbor the worms, the most gorgeous flowers attract the insects. Is it not ever the monarch of the forest which is eaten away by the fatal brown grub, greedy as death? I have learned before now that an unseen and jealous power attacks happiness which has reached perfection. Besides, this is the moral of all your preaching, and you have been proved a prophet.

When I went, the day before yesterday, to see whether my last whim had been carried out, tears rose to my eyes; and, to the great surprise of my architect, I at once passed his account for payment.

"But, madame," he exclaimed, "your man of business will refuse to pay this; it is a matter of three hundred thousand francs." My only reply was to add the words, "To be paid without question," with the bearing of a seventeenth-century Chaulieu.

"But," I said, "there is one condition to my gratitude. No human being must hear from you of the park and buildings. Promise me, on your honor, to observe this article in our contract—not to breathe to a soul the proprietor's name."

Now, can you understand the meaning of my sudden journeys, my mysterious comings and goings? Now, do you know whither those beautiful things, which the world supposes to be sold, have flown? Do you perceive the ultimate motive of my change of investment? Love, my dear, is a vast business, and they who would succeed in it should have no other. Henceforth

I shall have no more trouble from money matters; I have taken all the thorns out of my life, and done my housekeeping work once for all with a vengeance, so as never to be troubled with it again, except during the daily ten minutes which I shall devote to my old major-domo Philippe. I have made a study of life and its sharp curves; there came a day when death also gave me harsh lessons. Now I want to turn all this to account. My one occupation will be to please *him* and love *him*, to brighten with variety what to common mortals is monotonously dull.

Gaston is still in complete ignorance. At my request he has, like myself, taken up his quarters at Ville d'Avray; to-morrow we start for the chalet. Our life there will cost but little; but if I told you the sum I am setting aside for my toilet, you would exclaim at my madness, and with reason. I intend to take as much trouble to make myself beautiful for him every day as other women do for society. My dress in the country, year in, year out, will cost twenty-four thousand francs, and the larger portion of this will not go in day costumes. As for him, he can wear a blouse if he pleases! Don't suppose that I am going to turn our life into an amorous duel and wear myself out in devices for feeding passion; all that I want is to have a conscience free from reproach. Thirteen years still lie before me as a pretty woman, and I am determined to be loved on the last day of the thirteenth even more fondly than on the morrow of our mysterious nuptials. This time no cutting words shall mar my lowly, grateful content. I will take the part of servant, since that of mistress throve so ill with me before.

Ah! Renée, if Gaston has sounded, as I have, the heights and depths of love, my happiness is assured! Nature at the chalet wears her fairest face. The woods are charming; each step opens up to you some fresh vista of cool greenery, which delights the soul by the sweet thoughts it wakens. They breathe of love. If only this be not the gorgeous theatre dressed by my hand for my own martyrdom!

In two days from now I shall be Madame Gaston. My God! is it fitting a Christian so to love mortal man?

"Well, at least you have the law with you," was the comment of my man of business, who is to be one of my witnesses, and who exclaimed, on discovering why my property was to be realized, "I am losing a client!"

And you, my sweetheart (whom I dare no longer call my loved one), may you not cry, "I am losing a sister?"

My sweet, address when you write in future to Madame Gaston, Poste Restante, Versailles. We shall send there every day for letters. I don't want to be known to the country people, and we shall get our provisions from Paris. In this way I hope we may guard the secret of our lives. Nobody has been seen in the place during the years spent in preparing our retreat; and the purchase was made in the troubled period which followed the revolution of July. The only person who has shown himself here is the architect; he alone is known, and he will not return.

Farewell. As I write this word, I know not whether my heart is fuller of grief or joy. That proves, does it not, that the pain of losing you equals my love for Gaston?

XLIX
MARIE GASTON TO DANIEL D'ARTHEZ

October 1833

MY DEAR DANIEL,—I need two witnesses for my marriage. I beg of you to come to-morrow evening for this purpose, bringing with you our worthy and honored friend, Joseph Bridau. She who is to be my wife, with an instinctive divination of my dearest wishes, has declared her intention of living far from the world in complete retirement. You, who have done so much to lighten my penury, have been left in ignorance of my love; but you will understand that absolute secrecy was essential.

This will explain to you why it is that, for the last year, we have seen so little of each other. On the morrow of my wedding we shall be parted for a long time; but, Daniel, you are of stuff to understand me. Friendship can subsist in the absence of the friend. There may be times when I shall want you badly, but I shall not see you, at least not in my own house. Here again *she* has forestalled our wishes. She has sacrificed to me her intimacy with a friend of her childhood, who has been a sister to her. For her sake, then, I also must relinquish my comrade!

From this fact alone you will divine that ours is no mere passing fancy, but love, absolute, perfect, godlike; love based upon the fullest knowledge that can bind two hearts in sympathy. To me it is a perpetual spring of purest delight.

Yet nature allows of no happiness without alloy; and deep down, in the innermost recess of my heart, I am conscious of a lurking thought, not shared with her, the pang of which is for me alone. You have too often come to the help of my inveterate poverty to be ignorant how desperate matters were with me. Where should I have found courage to keep up the struggle of life, after seeing my hopes so often blighted, but for your cheering words, your tactful aid, and the knowledge of what you had come through? Briefly, then, my friend, she freed me from that crushing load of debt, which was no secret to you. She is wealthy, I am penniless. Many a time have I exclaimed, in one of my fits of idleness, "Oh for some great heiress to cast her eye on me!" And now, in presence of this reality, the boy's careless jest, the unscrupulous cynicism of the outcast, have alike vanished, leaving in their place only a bitter sense of humiliation, which not the most considerate tenderness on her part, nor my own assurance of her noble nature, can remove. Nay, what better proof of my love could there exist, for her or for myself, than this shame, from which I have not recoiled, even when powerless to overcome it? The fact remains that there is a point where, far from protecting, I am the protected.

This is my pain which I confide to you.

Except in this one particular, dear Daniel, my fondest dreams are more than realized. Fairest and noblest among women, such a bride might indeed raise a man to giddy heights of bliss. Her gentle ways are seasoned with wit, her love comes with an ever-fresh grace and charm; her mind is well informed and quick to understand; in person, she is fair and lovely, with a rounded slimness, as though Raphael and Rubens had conspired to create a woman! I do not know whether I could have worshiped with such fervor at the shrine of a dark beauty; a brunette always strikes me as an unfinished boy. She is a widow, childless, and twenty-seven years of age. Though brimful of life and energy, she has her moods also of dreamy melancholy. These rare gifts go with a proud aristocratic bearing; she has a fine presence.

She belongs to one of those old families who make a fetich of rank, yet loves me enough to ignore the misfortune of my birth. Our secret passion is now of long standing; we have made trial, each of the other, and find that in the matter of jealousy we are twin spirits; our thoughts are the reverberation of the same thunderclap. We both love for the first time, and this bewitching springtime has filled its days for us with all the images of delight that fancy can paint in laughing, sweet, or musing mood. Our path has been strewn with the flowers of tender imaginings. Each hour brought its own wealth, and when we parted, it was to put our thoughts in verse. Not for a moment did I harbor the idea of sullying the brightness of such a time by giving the rein to sensual passion, however it might chafe within. She was a widow and free; intuitively, she realized all the homage implied in this constant self-restraint, which often moved her to tears. Can you not read in this, my friend, a soul of noble temper? In mutual fear we shunned even the first kiss of love.

"We have each a wrong to reproach ourselves with," she said one day.

"Where is yours?" I asked.

"My marriage," was her reply.

Daniel, you are a giant among us and you love one of the most gifted women of the aristocracy, which has produced my Armande; what need to tell you more? Such an answer lays bare to you a woman's heart and all the happiness which is in store for your friend,

MARIE GASTON

L

MADAME DE L'ESTORADE TO MADAME DE MACUMER

Louise, can it be that, with all your knowledge of the deep-seated mischief wrought by the indulgence of passion, even within the heart of marriage, you are planning a life of wedded solitude? Having sacrificed your first husband in the course of a fashionable career, would you now fly to the desert to consume a second? What stores of misery you are laying up for yourself!

But I see from the way you have set about it that there is no going back. The man who has overcome your aversion to a second marriage must indeed possess some magic of mind and heart; and you can only be left to your illusions. But have you forgotten your former criticism on young men? Not one, you would say, but has visited haunts of shame, and has besmirched his purity with the filth of the streets. Where is the change, pray— in them or in you?

You are a lucky woman to be able to believe in happiness. I have not the courage to blame you for it, though the instinct of affection urges me to dissuade you from this marriage. Yes, a thousand times, yes, it is true that nature and society are at one in making war on absolute happiness, because such a condition is opposed to the laws of both; possibly, also, because Heaven is jealous of its privileges. My love for you forebodes some disaster to which all my penetration can give no definite form. I know neither whence nor from whom it will arise; but one need be no prophet to foretell that the mere weight of a boundless happiness will overpower you. Excess of joy is harder to bear than any amount of sorrow.

Against him I have not a word to say. You love him, and in all probability I have never seen him; but some idle day I hope you will send me a sketch, however slight, of this rare, fine animal.

If you see me so resigned and cheerful, it is because I am convinced that, once the honeymoon is over you will both with one accord, fall back into the common track. Some day, two years hence, when we are walking along this famous road, you will exclaim, "Why, there is the chalet which was to be my home for ever!" And you will laugh your dear old laugh, which shows all your pretty teeth!

I have said nothing yet to Louis; it would be too good an opening for his ridicule. I shall tell him simply that you are going to be married, and that you wish it kept secret. Unluckily, you need neither mother nor sister for your bridal evening. We are in October now; like a brave woman, you are grappling with winter first. If it were not a question of marriage, I should say you were taking the bull by the horns. In any case, you will have in me the most discreet and intelligent of friends. That mysterious region, known as the centre of Africa, has swallowed up many travelers, and you seem to me to be launching on an expedition which, in the domain of sentiment, corresponds to those where so many explorers have perished, whether in the sands or at the hands of natives. Your desert is, happily, only two leagues from Paris, so I can wish you quite cheerfully, "A safe journey and speedy return."

LI

THE COMTESSE DE L'ESTORADE TO MADAME MARIE GASTON

1835

What has come to you, my dear? After a silence of two years, surely Renée has a right to feel anxious about Louise. So this is love! It brushes aside and scatters to the winds a friendship such as ours! You must admit that, devoted as I am to my children—more even perhaps than you to your Gaston—a mother's love has something expansive about it which does not allow it to steal from other affections, or interfere with the claims of friendship. I miss your letters, I long for a sight of your dear, sweet face. Oh! Louise, my heart has only conjecture to feed upon!

As regards ourselves, I will try and tell you everything as briefly as possible.

On reading your last letter but one, I find some stinging comments on our political situation. You mocked at us for keeping the post in the Audit Department, which, as well as the title of Comte, Louis owed to the favor of Charles X. But I should like to know, please, how it would be possible out of an income of forty thousand livres, thirty thousand of which go with the entail, to give a suitable start in life to Athénaïs and my poor little beggar René. Was it not a duty to live on our salary and prudently allow the income of the estate to accumulate? In this way we shall, in twenty years, have put together about six hundred thousand francs, which will provide portions for my daughter and for René, whom I destine for the navy. The poor little chap will have an income of ten thousand livres, and perhaps we may contrive to leave him in cash enough to bring his portion up to the amount of his sister's.

When he is Captain, my beggar will be able to make a wealthy marriage, and take a position in society as good as his elder brother's.

These considerations of prudence determined the acceptance in our family of the new order of things. The new dynasty, as was natural, raised Louis to the Peerage and made him a grand officer of the Legion of Honor. The oath once taken, l'Estorade could not be half-hearted in his services, and he has since then made himself very useful in the Chamber. The position he has now attained is one in which he can rest upon his oars till the end of his days. He has a good deal of adroitness in business matters; and though he can hardly be called an orator, speaks pleasantly and fluently, which is all that is necessary in politics. His shrewdness and the extent of his information in all matters of government and administration are fully appreciated, and all parties consider him indispensable. I may tell you that he was recently offered an embassy, but I would not let him accept it. I am tied to Paris by the education of Armand and Athénaïs—who are now respectively thirteen and nearly eleven—and I don't intend leaving till little René has completed his, which is just beginning.

We could not have remained faithful to the elder branch of the dynasty and returned to our country life without allowing the education and prospects of the three children to suffer. A mother, my sweet, is hardly called on to be a Decius, especially at a time when the type is rare. In fifteen years from now, l'Estorade will be able to retire to La Crampade on a good pension, having found a place as referendary for Armand in the Audit Department.

As for René, the navy will doubtless make a diplomatist of him. The little rogue, at seven years old, has all the cunning of an old Cardinal.

Oh! Louise, I am indeed a happy mother. My children

are an endless source of joy to me—*Senza brama sicura ricchezza*.

Armand is a day scholar at Henry IV's school. I made up my mind he should have a public-school training, yet could not reconcile myself to the thought of parting with him; so I compromised, as the Duc d'Orléans did before he became—or in order that he might become—Louis Philippe. Every morning Lucas, the old servant whom you will remember, takes Armand to school in time for the first lesson, and brings him home again at half-past four. In the house we have a private tutor, an admirable scholar, who helps Armand with his work in the evenings, and calls him in the morning at the school hour. Lucas takes him some lunch during the play hour at midday. In this way I am with my boy at dinner and until he goes to bed at night, and I see him off in the morning.

Armand is the same charming little fellow, full of feeling and unselfish impulse, whom you loved; and his tutor is quite pleased with him. I still have Naïs and the baby—two restless little mortals—but I am quite as much a child as they are. I could not bring myself to lose the darlings' sweet caresses. I could not live without the feeling that at any moment I can fly to Armand's bedside and watch his slumbers or snatch a kiss.

Yet home education is not without its drawbacks, to which I am fully alive. Society, like nature, is a jealous power, and will have not her rights encroached on, or her system set at naught. Thus, children who are brought up at home are exposed too early to the fire of the world; they see its passions and become at home with its subterfuges. The finer distinctions, which regulate the conduct of matured men and women, elude their perceptions, and they take feeling and passion for their guide instead of subordinating those to the code of society; whilst the gay trappings and tinsel which attract so much of the world's favor blind them to the importance of the more sober virtues. A child of fifteen with the assurance of a man of the world is a thing against all nature; at twenty-five he will be prematurely old, and his precocious knowledge only unfits him for the genuine study on which all solid ability must rest. Life in society is one long comedy, and those who take part in it, like other actors, reflect back impressions which never penetrate below the surface. A mother, therefore, who wishes not to part from her children, must resolutely determine that they shall not enter the gay world; she must have courage to resist their inclinations, as well as her own, and keep them in the background. Cornelia had to keep her jewels under lock and key. Shall I do less for the children who are all the world to me?

Now that I am thirty, the heat of the day is over, the hardest bit of the road lies behind me. In a few years I shall be an old woman, and the sense of duty done is an immense encouragement. It would almost seem as though my trio can read my thoughts and shape themselves accordingly. A mysterious bond of sympathy unites me to these children who have never left my side. If they knew the blank in my life which they have to fill, they could not be more lavish of the solace they bring.

Armand, who was dull and dreamy during his first three years at school, and caused me some uneasiness, has made a sudden start. Doubtless he realized, in a way most children never do, the aim of all this preparatory work, which is to sharpen the intelligence, to get them into habits of application and accustom them to that fundamental principle of all society—obedience. My dear, a few days ago I had the proud joy of seeing Armand crowned at the great interscholastic competition in the crowded Sorbonne, when your godson received the first prize for translation. At the school distribution he got two first prizes—one for verse, and one for an essay. I went quite white when his name was called out, and longed to shout aloud, "I am his mother!" Little Naïs squeezed my hand till it hurt, if at such a moment it were possible to feel pain. Ah! Louise, a day like this might outweigh many a dream of love!

His brother's triumphs have spurred on little René, who wants to go to school too. Sometimes the three children make such a racket, shouting and rushing about the house, that I wonder how my head stands it. I am always with them; no one else, not even Mary, is allowed to take care of my children. But the calling of a mother, if taxing, has so many compensating joys! To see a child leave its play and run to hug one, out of the fullness of its heart, what could be sweeter?

Then it is only in being constantly with them that one can study their characters. It is the duty of a mother, and one which she can depute to no hired teacher, to decipher the tastes, temper, and natural aptitudes of her children from their infancy. All home-bred children are distinguished by ease of manner and tact, two acquired qualities which may go far to supply the lack of natural ability, whereas no natural ability can atone for the loss of this early training. I have already learned to discriminate this difference of tone in the men whom I meet in society, and to trace the hand of a woman in the formation of a young man's manners. How could any woman defraud her children of such a possession? You see what rewards attend the performance of my tasks!

Armand, I feel certain, will make an admirable judge, the most upright of public servants, the most devoted of deputies. And where would you find a sailor bolder, more adventurous, more astute than my René will be a few years hence? The little rascal has already an iron will, whatever he wants he manages to get; he will try a thousand circuitous ways to reach his end, and if not successful then, will devise a thousand and first. Where dear Armand quietly resigns himself and tries to get at the reason of things, René will storm, and strive, and puzzle, chattering all the time, till at last he finds some chink in the obstacle; if there is room for the blade of a knife to pass, his little carriage will ride through in triumph.

And Naïs? Naïs is so completely a second self that I can hardly realize her as distinct from my own flesh and blood. What a darling she is, and how I love to make a little lady of her, to dress her curly hair, tender thoughts mingling the while with every touch! I must have her happy; I shall only give her to the man who loves her and whom she loves. But, Heavens! when I let her put on her little ornaments, or pass a cherry-colored ribbon through her hair, or fasten the shoes on her tiny feet, a sickening thought comes over me. How can one order the destiny of a girl? Who can say that she will not love a scoundrel or some man who is indifferent to her? Tears often spring to my eyes as I watch her. This lovely creature, this flower, this rosebud which has blossomed in one's heart, to be handed over to a man who will tear it from the stem and leave it bare! Louise, it is you—you, who in two years have not written three words to tell me of your welfare—it is you who have recalled to my mind the terrible possibilities of marriage, so full of anguish for a mother wrapped up, as I am, in her child. Farewell now, for in truth you don't deserve my friendship, and I hardly know how to write. Oh! answer me, dear Louise.

LII

MADAME GASTON TO MADAME DE L'ESTORADE

The Chalet

So, after a silence of two years, you are pricked by curiosity, and want to know why I have not written. My dear Renée, there are no words, no images, no language to express my happiness. That we have strength to bear it sums up all I could say. It costs us no effort, for we are in perfect sympathy. The whole two years have known no note of discord in the harmony, no jarring word in the interchange of feeling, no shade of difference in our lightest wish. Not one in this long succession of days has failed to bear its own peculiar fruit; not a moment has passed without being enriched by the play of fancy. So far are we from dreading the canker of monotony in our life, that our only fear is lest it should not be long enough to contain all the poetic creations of a love as rich and varied in its development as Nature herself. Of disappointment not a trace! We find more pleasure in being together than on the first day, and each hour as it goes by discloses fresh reason for our love. Every day as we take our evening stroll after dinner, we tell each other that we really must go and see what is doing in Paris, just as one might talk of going to Switzerland.

"Only think," Gaston will exclaim, "such and such a boulevard is being made, the Madeleine is finished.* We ought to see it. Let us go to-morrow."

And to-morrow comes, and we are in no hurry to get up, and we breakfast in our bedroom. Then midday is on us, and it is too hot; a siesta seems appropriate. Then Gaston wishes to look at me, and he gazes on my face as though it were a picture, losing himself in this contemplation, which, as you may suppose, is not one-sided. Tears rise to the eyes of both as we think of our love and tremble. I am still the mistress, pretending, that is, to give less than I receive, and I revel in this deception. To a woman what can be sweeter than to see passion ever held in check by tenderness, and the man who is her master stayed, like a timid suitor, by a word from her, within the limits that she chooses?

You asked me to describe him; but, Renée, it is not possible to make a portrait of the man we love. How could the heart be kept out of the work? Besides, to be frank between ourselves, we may admit that one of the dire effects of civilization on our manners is to make of man in society a being so utterly different from the natural man of strong feeling, that sometimes not a single point of likeness can be found between these two aspects of the same person. The man who falls into the most graceful operatic poses, as he pours sweet nothings into your ear by the fire at night, may be entirely destitute of those more intimate charms which a woman values. On the other hand, an ugly, boorish, badly-dressed figure may mark a man endowed with the very genius of love, and who has a perfect mastery over situations which might baffle us with our superficial graces. A man whose conventional aspect accords with his real nature, who, in the intimacy of wedded love, possesses that inborn grace which can be neither given nor acquired, but which Greek art has embodied in statuary, that careless innocence of the ancient poets which, even in frank undress, seems to clothe the soul as with a veil of modesty—this is our ideal, born of our own conceptions, and linked with the universal harmony which seems to be the reality underlying all created things. To find this ideal in life is the problem which haunts the imagination of every woman—in Gaston I have found it.

Ah! dear, I did not know what love could be, united to youth, talent, and beauty. Gaston has no affectations, he moves with an instinctive and unstudied grace. When we walk alone together in the woods, his arm round my waist, mine resting on his shoulder, body fitting to body, and head touching head, our step is so even, uniform, and gentle, that those who see us pass by night take the vision for a single figure gliding over the graveled walks, like one of Homer's immortals. A like harmony exists in our desires, our thoughts, our words. More than once on some evening when a passing shower has left the leaves glistening and the moist grass bright with a more vivid green, it has chanced that we ended our walk without uttering a word, as we listened to the patter of falling drops and feasted our eyes on the scarlet sunset, flaring on the hilltops or dyeing with a warmer tone the gray of the tree trunks.

Beyond a doubt our thoughts then rose to Heaven in silent prayer, pleading as it were, for our happiness. At times a cry would escape us at the moment when some sudden bend on the path opened up fresh beauties. What words can tell how honey-sweet, how full of meaning, is a kiss half-timidly exchanged within the sanctuary of nature—it is as though God had created us to worship in this fashion.

And we return home, each more deeply in love than ever.

A love so passionate between old married people would be an outrage on society in Paris; only in the heart of the woods, like lovers, can we give scope to it.

To come to particulars, Gaston is of middle height— the height proper to all men of purpose. Neither stout nor thin, his figure is admirably made, with ample fullness in the proportions, while every motion is agile; he leaps a ditch with the easy grace of a wild animal. Whatever his attitude, he seems to have an instinctive sense of balance, and this is very rare in men who are given to thought. Though a dark man, he has an extraordinarily fair complexion; his jet-black hair contrasts finely with the lustreless tints of the neck and forehead. He has the tragic head of Louis XIII. His moustache and tuft have been allowed to grow, but I made him shave the whiskers and beard, which were getting too common. An honorable poverty has been his safeguard, and handed him over to me, unsoiled by the loose life which ruins so many young men. His teeth are magnificent, and he has a constitution of iron. His keen blue eyes, for me full of tenderness, will flash like lightning at any rousing thought.

Like all men of strong character and powerful mind, he has an admirable temper; its evenness would surprise you, as it did me. I have listened to the tale of many a woman's home troubles; I have heard of the moods and depression of men dissatisfied with themselves, who either won't get old or age ungracefully, men who carry about through life the rankling memory of some youthful excess, whose veins run poison and whose eyes are never frankly happy, men who cloak suspicion under bad temper, and make their women pay for an hour's peace by a morning of annoyance, who take vengeance on us for a beauty which is hateful to them because they have ceased themselves to be attractive,—all these are horrors unknown to youth. They are the penalty of unequal unions. Oh! my dear, whatever you do, don't marry Athénaïs to an old man!

But his smile—how I feast on it! A smile which is always there, yet always fresh through the play of subtle fancy, a speaking smile which makes of the lips a storehouse for thoughts of love and unspoken gratitude, a smile which links present joys to past. For nothing is allowed to drop out of our common life. The smallest works of nature have become part and parcel of our joy. In these delightful woods everything is alive and eloquent of ourselves. An old moss-grown oak, near the woodsman's house on the roadside, reminds us how we sat there, wearied, under its shade, while Gaston taught me about the mosses at our feet and told me their story, till, gradually ascending from science to science, we touched the very confines of creation.

There is something so kindred in our minds that they seem to me like two editions of the same book. You see what a literary tendency I have developed! We both have the habit, or the gift, of looking at every subject broadly, of taking in all its points of view, and the proof we are constantly giving ourselves of the singleness of our inward vision is an ever-new pleasure. We have actually come to look on this community of mind as a pledge of love; and if it ever failed us, it would mean

as much to us as would a breach of fidelity in an ordinary home.

My life, full as it is of pleasures, would seem to you,
nevertheless, extremely laborious. To begin with, my
dear, you must know that Louise-Armande-Marie de
Chaulieu does her own room. I could not bear that a
hired menial, some woman or girl from the outside,
should become initiated—literary touch again!—into
the secrets of my bedroom. The veriest trifles connected with the worship of my heart partake of its sacred
character. This is not jealousy; it is self-respect. Thus
my room is done out with all the care a young girl in
love bestows on her person, and with the precision of
an old maid. My dressing-room is no chaos of litter; on
the contrary, it makes a charming boudoir. My keen eye
has foreseen all contingencies. At whatever hour the
lord and master enters, he will find nothing to distress,
surprise, or shock him; he is greeted by flowers, scents,
and everything that can please the eye.

I get up in the early dawn, while he is still sleeping,
and, without disturbing him, pass into the dressing-
room, where, profiting by my mother's experience, I
remove the traces of sleep by bathing in cold water. For
during sleep the skin, being less active, does not perform its functions adequately; it becomes warm and
covered with a sort of mist or atmosphere of sticky matter, visible to the eye. From a sponge-bath a woman
issues ten years younger, and this, perhaps, is the inter-
pretation of the myth of Venus rising from the sea. So
the cold water restores to me the saucy charm of dawn,
and, having combed and scented my hair and made a
most fastidious toilet, I glide back, snake-like, in order
that my master may find me, dainty as a spring morning, at his wakening. He is charmed with this freshness,
as of a newly-opened flower, without having the least
idea how it is produced.

The regular toilet of the day is a matter for my maid,

and this takes place later in a larger room, set aside for the purpose. As you may suppose, there is also a toilet for going to bed. Three times a day, you see, or it may be four, do I array myself for the delight of my husband; which, again, dear one, is suggestive of certain ancient myths.

But our work is not all play. We take a great deal of interest in our flowers, in the beauties of the hothouse, and in our trees. We give ourselves in all seriousness to horticulture, and embosom the chalet in flowers, of which we are passionately fond. Our lawns are always green, our shrubberies as well tended as those of a millionaire. And nothing I assure you, can match the beauty of our walled garden. We are regular gluttons over our fruit, and watch with tender interest our Montreuil peaches, our hotbeds, our laden trellises, and pyramidal pear-trees.

But lest these rural pursuits should fail to satisfy my beloved's mind, I have advised him to finish, in the quiet of this retreat, some plays which were begun in his starvation days, and which are really very fine. This is the only kind of literary work which can be done in odd moments, for it requires long intervals of reflection, and does not demand the elaborate pruning essential to a finished style. One can't make a task-work of dialogue; there must be biting touches, summings-up, and flashes of wit, which are the blossoms of the mind, and come rather by inspiration than reflection. This sort of intellectual sport is very much in my line. I assist Gaston in his work, and in this way manage to accompany him even in the boldest flights of his imagination. Do you see now how it is that my winter evenings never drag?

Our servants have such an easy time, that never once since we were married have we had to reprimand any of them. When questioned about us, they have had wit enough to draw on their imaginations, and have given us out as the companion and secretary of a lady and gentleman supposed to be traveling. They never go out without asking permission, which they know will not be refused; they are contented too, and see plainly that it will be their own fault if there is a change for the worse. The gardeners are allowed to sell the surplus of our fruits and vegetables. The dairymaid does the same with the milk, the cream, and the fresh butter, on condition that the best of the produce is reserved for us. They are well pleased with their profits, and we are delighted with an abundance which no money and no ingenuity can procure in that terrible Paris, where it costs a hundred francs to produce a single fine peach.

All this is not without its meaning, my dear. I wish to fill the place of society to my husband; now society is amusing, and therefore his solitude must not be allowed to pall on him. I believed myself jealous in the old days, when I merely allowed myself to be loved; now I know real jealousy, the jealousy of the lover. A single indifferent glance unnerves me. From time to time I say to myself, "Suppose he ceased to love me!" And a shudder goes through me. I tremble before him, as the Christian before his God.

Alas! Renée, I am still without a child. The time will surely come—it must come—when our hermitage will need a father's and a mother's care to brighten it, when we shall both pine to see the little frocks and pelisses, the brown or golden heads, leaping, running through our shrubberies and flowery paths. Oh! it is a cruel jest of Nature's, a flowering tree that bears no fruit. The thought of your lovely children goes through me like a knife. My life has grown narrower, while yours has expanded and shed its rays afar. The passion of love is essentially selfish, while motherhood widens the circle of our feelings. How well I felt this difference when I read your kind, tender letter! To see you thus living in three hearts roused my envy. Yes, you are happy; you have had wisdom to obey the laws of social life, whilst I stand outside, an alien.

Children, dear and loving children, can alone console a woman for the loss of her beauty. I shall soon be thirty, and at that age the dirge within begins. What though I am still beautiful, the limits of my woman's reign are none the less in sight. When they are reached, what then? I shall be forty before he is; I shall be old while he is still young. When this thought goes to my heart, I lie at his feet for an hour at a time, making him swear to tell me instantly if ever he feels his love diminishing.

But he is a child. He swears, as though the mere suggestion were an absurdity, and he is so beautiful that—Renée, you understand—I believe him.

Good-bye, sweet one. Shall we ever again let years pass without writing? Happiness is a monotonous theme, and that is, perhaps, the reason why, to souls who love, Dante appears even greater in the *Paradiso* than in the *Inferno*. I am not Dante; I am only your friend, and I don't want to bore you. You can write, for in your children you have an ever-growing, every-varying source of happiness, while mine . . . No more of this. A thousand loves.

LIII
MADAME DE L'ESTORADE TO MADAME GASTON

MY DEAR LOUISE,—I have read and re-read your letter, and the more deeply I enter into its spirit, the clearer does it become to me that it is the letter, not of a woman, but of a child. You are the same old Louise, and you forget, what I used to repeat over and over again to you, that the passion of love belongs rightly to a state of nature, and has only been purloined by civilization. So fleeting is its character, that the resources of society are powerless to modify its primitive condition, and it becomes the effort of all noble minds to make a man of the infant Cupid. But, as you yourself admit, such love ceases to be natural.

Society, my dear, abhors sterility; but substituting a lasting sentiment for the mere passing frenzy of nature, it has succeeded in creating that greatest of all human inventions—the family, which is the enduring basis of all organized society. To the accomplishment of this end, it has sacrificed the individual, man as well as woman; for we must not shut our eyes to the fact that a married man devotes his energy, his power, and all his possession to his wife. Is it not she who reaps the benefit of all his care? For whom, if not for her, are the luxury and wealth, the position and distinction, the comfort and the gaiety of the home?

Oh! my sweet, once again you have taken the wrong turning in life. To be adored is a young girl's dream, which may survive a few springtimes; it cannot be that of the mature woman, the wife and mother. To a woman's vanity it is, perhaps, enough to know that she can command adoration if she likes. If you would live the life of a wife and mother, return, I beg of you, to Paris. Let me repeat my warning: It is not misfortune which you have to dread, as others do—it is happiness.

Listen to me, my child! It is the simple things of life—bread, air, silence—of which we do not tire; they have no piquancy which can create distaste; it is highly-flavored dishes which irritate the palate, and in the end exhaust it. Were it possible that I should to-day be loved by a man for whom I could conceive a passion, such as yours for Gaston, I would still cling to the duties and the children, who are so dear to me. To a woman's heart the feelings of a mother are among the simple, natural, fruitful, and inexhaustible things of life. I can recall the day, now nearly fourteen years ago, when I embarked on a life of self-sacrifice with the despair of a shipwrecked mariner clinging to the mast of his vessel; now, as I invoke the memory of past years, I feel that I would make the same choice again. No other guiding principle is so safe, or leads to such rich reward. The spectacle of your life, which, for all the romance and poetry with which you invest it, still remains based on nothing but a ruthless selfishness, has helped to strengthen my convictions. This is the last time I shall speak to you in this way; but I could not refrain from once more pleading with you when I found that your happiness had been proof against the most searching of all trials.

And one more point I must urge on you, suggested by my meditations on your retirement. Life, whether of the body or the heart, consists in certain balanced movements. Any excess introduced into the working of this routine gives rise either to pain or to pleasure, both of which are a mere fever of the soul, bound to be fugitive because nature is not so framed as to support it long. But to make of life one long excess is surely to choose sickness for one's portion. You are sick because you maintain at the temperature of passion a feeling which marriage ought to convert into a steadying, purifying influence.

Yes, my sweet, I see it clearly now; the glory of a home consists in this very calm, this intimacy, this sharing alike of good and evil, which the vulgar ridicule. How noble was the reply of the Duchesse de Sully, the wife of the great Sully, to some one who remarked that her husband, for all his grave exterior, did not scruple to keep a mistress. "What of that?" she said. "I represent the honor of the house, and should decline to play the part of a courtesan there."

But you, Louise, who are naturally more passionate than tender, would be at once the wife and the mistress. With the soul of a Héloïse and the passions of a Saint Theresa, you slip the leash on all your impulses, so long as they are sanctioned by law; in a word, you degrade the marriage rite. Surely the tables are turned. The reproaches you once heaped on me for immorally, as you said, seizing the means of happiness from the very outset of my wedded life, might be directed against yourself for grasping at everything which may serve your passion. What! must nature and society alike be in bondage to your caprice? You are the old Louise; you have never acquired the qualities which ought to be a woman's; self-willed and unreasonable as a girl, you introduce withal into your love the keenest and most mercenary of calculations! Are you sure that, after all, the price you ask for your toilets is not too high? All these precautions are to my mind very suggestive of mistrust.

Oh, dear Louise, if only you knew the sweetness of a mother's efforts to discipline herself in kindness and gentleness to all about her! My proud, self-sufficing temper gradually dissolved into a soft melancholy, which in turn has been swallowed up by those delights of motherhood which have been its reward. If the early hours were toilsome, the evening will be tranquil and clear. My dread is lest the day of your life should take the opposite course.

When I had read your letter to a close, I prayed God to send you among us for a day, that you might see what family life really is, and learn the nature of those joys, which are lasting and sweeter than tongue can tell, because they are genuine, simple, and natural. But, alas! what chance have I with the best of arguments against a fallacy which makes you happy? As I write these words, my eyes fill with tears. I had felt so sure that some months of honeymoon would prove a surfeit and restore you to reason. But I see that there is no limit to your appetite, and that, having killed a man who loved you, you will not cease till you have killed love itself. Farewell, dear misguided friend. I am in despair that the letter which I hoped might reconcile you to society by its picture of my happiness should have brought forth only a paean of selfishness. Yes, your love

369

is selfish; you love Gaston far less for himself than for what he is to you.

LIV

MADAME GASTON TO THE COMTESSE DE L'ESTORADE

May 20th

Renée, calamity has come—no, that is no word for it— it has burst like a thunderbolt over your poor Louise. You know what that means; calamity for me is doubt; certainty would be death.

The day before yesterday, when I had finished my first toilet, I looked everywhere for Gaston to take a little turn with me before lunch, but in vain. I went to the stable, and there I saw his mare all in a lather, while the groom was removing the foam with a knife before rubbing her down.

"Who in the world has put Fedelta in such a state?" I asked.

"Master," replied the lad.

I saw the mud of Paris on the mare's legs, for country mud is quite different; and at once it flashed through me, "He has been to Paris."

This thought raised a swarm of others in my heart, and it seemed as though all the life in my body rushed there. To go to Paris without telling me, at the hour when I leave him alone, to hasten there and back at such speed as to distress Fedelta. Suspicion clutched me in its iron grip, till I could hardly breathe. I walked aside a few steps to a seat, where I tried to recover my self-command.

Here Gaston found me, apparently pale and fluttered, for he immediately exclaimed, "What is wrong?" in a tone of such alarm, that I rose and took his arm. But my muscles refused to move, and I was forced to sit down again. Then he took me in his arms and carried me to the parlor close by, where the frightened servants pressed after us, till Gaston motioned them away. Once left to ourselves, I refused to speak, but was able to reach my room, where I shut myself in, to weep my fill. Gaston remained something like two hours at my door, listening to my sobs and questioning with angelic patience his poor darling, who made no response.

At last I told him that I would see him when my eyes were less red and my voice was steady again.

My formal words drove him from the house. But by the time I had bathed my eyes in iced water and cooled my face, I found him in our room, the door into which was open, though I had heard no steps. He begged me to tell him what was wrong.

"Nothing," I said; "I saw the mud of Paris on Fedelta's trembling legs; it seemed strange that you should go there without telling me; but, of course, you are free."

"I shall punish you for such wicked thoughts by not giving any explanation till to-morrow," he replied.

"Look at me," I said.

My eyes met his; deep answered to deep. No, not a trace of the cloud of disloyalty which, rising from the soul, must dim the clearness of the eye. I feigned satisfaction, though really unconvinced. It is not women only who can lie and dissemble!

The whole of the day we spent together. Ever and again, as I looked at him, I realized how fast my heartstrings were bound to him. How I trembled and fluttered within when, after a moment's absence, he reappeared. I live in him, not in myself. My cruel sufferings gave the lie to your unkind letter. Did I ever feel my life thus bound up in the noble Spaniard, who adored me, as I adore this heartless boy? I hate that mare! Fool that I was to keep horses! But the next thing would have been to lame Gaston or imprison him in the cottage. Wild thoughts like these filled my brain; you see how near I was to madness! If love be not the cage, what power on earth can hold back the man who wants to be free?

I asked him point-blank, "Do I bore you?"

"What needless torture you give yourself!" was his reply, while he looked at me with tender, pitying eyes. "Never have I loved you so deeply."

"If that is true, my beloved, let me sell Fedelta," I answered.

"Sell her, by all means!"

The reply crushed me. Was it not a covert taunt at my wealth and his own nothingness in the house? This may never have occurred to him, but I thought it had, and once more I left him. It was night, and I would go to bed.

Oh! Renée, to be alone with a harrowing thought drives one to thoughts of death. These charming gardens, the starry night, the cool air, laden with incense from our wealth of flowers, our valley, our hills—all seemed to me gloomy, black, and desolate. It was as though I lay at the foot of a precipice, surrounded by serpents and poisonous plants, and saw no God in the sky. Such a night ages a woman.

Next morning I said:

"Take Fedelta and be off to Paris! Don't sell her; I love her. Does she not carry you?"

But he was not deceived; my tone betrayed the storm of feeling which I strove to conceal.

"Trust me!" he replied; and the gesture with which he held out his hand, the glance of his eye, were so full of loyalty that I was overcome.

"What petty creatures women are!" I exclaimed.

"No, you love me, that is all," he said, pressing me to his heart.

"Go to Paris without me," I said, and this time I made him understand that my suspicions were laid aside.

He went; I thought he would have stayed. I won't attempt to tell you what I suffered. I found a second self within, quite strange to me. A crisis like this has, for the woman who loves, a tragic solemnity that baffles words; the whole of life rises before you then, and you search in vain for any horizon to it; the veriest trifle is big with meaning, a glance contains a volume, icicles drift on uttered words, and the death sentence is read in a movement of the lips.

I thought he would have paid me back in kind; had I not been magnanimous? I climbed to the top of the chalet, and my eyes followed him on the road. Ah! my dear Renée, he vanished from my sight with an appalling swiftness.

"How keen he is to go!" was the thought that sprang of itself.

Once more alone, I fell back into the hell of possibilities, the maelstrom of mistrust. There were moments when I would have welcomed any certainty, even the worst, as a relief from the torture of suspense. Suspense is a duel carried on in the heart, and we give no quarter to ourselves.

I paced up and down the walks. I returned to the house, only to tear out again, like a mad woman. Gaston, who left at seven o'clock, did not return till eleven. Now, as it only takes half an hour to reach Paris through the park of St. Cloud and the Bois de Boulogne, it is plain that he must have spent three hours in town. He came back radiant, with a whip in his hand for me, an india-rubber whip with a gold handle.

For a fortnight I had been without a whip, my old one being worn and broken.

"Was it for this you tortured me?" I said, as I admired the workmanship of this beautiful ornament, which contains a little scent-box at one end.

Then it flashed on me that the present was a fresh artifice. Nevertheless I threw myself at once on his neck, not without reproaching him gently for having caused me so much pain for the sake of a trifle. He was greatly pleased with his ingenuity; his eyes and his whole bearing plainly showed the restrained triumph of the successful plotter; for there is a radiance of the soul which is reflected in every feature and turn of the body. While still examining the beauties of this work of art, I asked him at a moment when we happened to be looking each other in the face:

"Who is the artist?"

"A friend of mine."

"Ah! I see it has been mounted by Verdier," and I read the name of the shop printed on the handle.

Gaston is nothing but a child yet. He blushed, and I made much of him as a reward for the shame he felt in deceiving me. I pretended to notice nothing, and he may well have thought the incident was over.

May 25th

The next morning I was in my riding-habit by six o'clock, and by seven landed at Verdier's, where several whips of the same pattern were shown to me. One of the men serving recognized mine when I pointed it out to him.

"We sold that yesterday to a young gentleman," he said. And from the description I gave him of my traitor Gaston, not a doubt was left of his identity. I will spare you the palpitations which rent my heart during that journey to Paris and the little scene there, which marked the turning-point of my life.

By half-seven I was home again, and Gaston found me, fresh and blooming, in my morning dress, sauntering about with a make-believe nonchalance. I felt confident that old Philippe, who had been taken into my confidence, would not have betrayed my absence.

"Gaston," I said, as we walked by the side of the lake, "you cannot blind me to the difference between a work of art inspired by friendship and something which has been cast in a mould."

He turned white, and fixed his eyes on me rather than on the damaging piece of evidence I thrust before them.

"My dear," I went on, "this is not a whip; it is a screen behind which you are hiding something from me."

Thereupon I gave myself the gratification of watching his hopeless entanglement in the coverts and labyrinths of deceit and the desperate efforts he made to find some wall he might scale and thus escape. In vain; he had perforce to remain upon the field, face to face with an adversary, who at last laid down her arms in a feigned complacence. But it was too late. The fatal mistake, against which my mother had tried to warm me, was made. My jealousy, exposed in all its nakedness, had led to war and all its stratagems between Gaston and myself. Jealousy, dear, has neither sense nor decency.

I made up my mind now to suffer in silence, but to keep my eyes open, until my doubts were resolved one way or another. Then I would either break with Gaston or bow to my misfortune: no middle course is possible for a woman who respects herself.

What can he be concealing? For a secret there is, and the secret has to do with a woman. Is it some youthful escapade for which he still blushes? But if so, what? The word WHAT is written in letters of fire on all I see. I read it in the glassy water of my lake, in the shrubbery, in the clouds, on the ceilings, at table, in the flowers of the carpets. A voice cries to me WHAT? in my sleep. Dating from the morning of my discovery, a cruel interest has sprung into our lives, and I have become familiar with the bitterest thought that can corrode the heart—the thought of treachery in him one loves. Oh! my dear, there is heaven and hell together in such a life. Never had I felt this scorching flame, I to whom love had appeared only in the form of devoutest worship.

"So you wished to know the gloomy torture-chamber of pain!" I said to myself. Good, the spirits of evil have heard your prayer; go on your road, unhappy wretch!

May 30th

Since that fatal day Gaston no longer works with the careless ease of the wealthy artist, whose work is merely pastime; he sets himself tasks like a professional writer. Four hours a day he devotes to finishing his two plays.

"He wants money!"

A voice within whispered the thought. But why? He spends next to nothing; we have absolutely no secrets from each other; there is not a corner of his study which my eyes and my fingers may not explore. His yearly expenditure does not amount to two thousand francs, and I know that he has thirty thousand, I can hardly say laid by, but scattered loose in a drawer. You can guess what is coming. At midnight, while he was sleeping, I went to see if the money was still there. An icy shiver ran through me. The drawer was empty.

That same week I discovered that he went to Sèvres to fetch his letters, and these letters he must tear up immediately; for though I am a very Figaro in contrivances, I have never yet seen a trace of one. Alas! my sweet, despite the fine promises and vows by which I bound myself after the scene of the whip, an impulse, which I can only call madness, drove me to follow him in one of his rapid rides to the post-office. Gaston was appalled to be thus discovered on horseback, paying the postage of a letter which he held in his hand. He looked fixedly at me, and then put spurs to Fedelta. The pace was so hard that I felt shaken to bits when I reached the lodge gate, though my mental agony was such at the time that it might well have dulled all consciousness of bodily pain. Arrived at the gate, Gaston said nothing; he rang the bell and waited without a word. I was more dead than alive. I might be mistaken or I might not, but in neither case was it fitting for Armande-Louise-Marie de Chaulieu to play the spy. I had sunk to the level of the gutter, by the side of courtesans, opera-dancers, mere creatures of instinct; even the vulgar shop-girl or humble seamstress might look down on me.

What a moment! At last the door opened; he handed his horse to the groom, and I also dismounted, but into his arms, which were stretched out to receive me. I threw my skirt over my left arm, gave him my right, and we walked on—still in silence. The few steps we thus took might be reckoned to me for a hundred years of purgatory. A swarm of thoughts beset me as I walked, now seeming to take visible form in tongues of fire before my eyes, now assailing my mind, each with its own poisoned dart. When the groom and the horses were far away, I stopped Gaston, and, looking him in the face, said, as I pointed, with a gesture that you should have seen, to the fatal letter still in his right hand:

"May I read it?"

He gave it to me. I opened it and found a letter from Nathan, the dramatic author, informing Gaston that a play of his had been accepted, learned, rehearsed, and would be produced the following Saturday. He also enclosed a box ticket.

Though for me this was the opening of heaven's gates to the martyr, yet the fiend would not leave me in peace, but kept crying, "Where are the thirty thousand francs?" It was a question which self-respect, dignity, all my old self in fact, prevented me from uttering. If my thought became speech, I might as well throw myself into the lake at once, and yet I could hardly keep the words down. Dear friend, was not this a trial passing the strength of woman?

I returned the letter, saying:

"My poor Gaston, you are getting bored down here. Let us go back to Paris, won't you?"

"To Paris?" he said. "But why? I only wanted to find out if I had any gift, to taste the flowing bowl of success!"

Nothing would be easier than for me to ransack the

drawer sometime while he is working and pretend great surprise at finding the money gone. But that would be going half-way to meet the answer, "Oh! my friend So-and-So was hard up!" etc., which a man of Gaston's quick wit would not have far to seek.

The moral, my dear, is that the brilliant success of this play, which all Paris is crowding to see, is due to us, though the whole credit goes to Nathan. I am represented by one of the two stars in the legend: Et M **. I saw the first night from the depths of one of the stage boxes.

July 1st

Gaston's work and his visits to Paris shall continue. He is preparing new plays, partly because he wants a pretext for going to Paris, partly in order to make money. Three plays have been accepted, and two more are commissioned.

Oh! my dear, I am lost, all is darkness around me. I would set fire to the house in a moment if that would bring light. What does it all mean? Is he ashamed of taking money from me? He is too high-minded for so trumpery a matter to weigh with him. Besides, scruples of the kind could only be the outcome of some love affair. A man would take anything from his wife, but from the woman he has ceased to care for, or is thinking of deserting, it is different. If he needs such large sums, it must be to spend them on a woman. For himself, why should he hesitate to draw from my purse? Our savings amount to one hundred thousand francs!

In short, my sweetheart, I have explored a whole continent of possibilities, and after carefully weighing all the evidence, am convinced I have a rival. I am deserted—for whom? At all costs I must see the unknown.

July 10th

Light has come, and it is all over with me. Yes, Renée, at the age of thirty, in the perfection of my beauty, with all the resources of a ready wit and the seductive charms of dress at my command, I am betrayed—and for whom? A large-boned Englishwoman, with big feet and thick waist—a regular British cow! There is no longer room for doubt. I will tell you the history of the last few days.

Worn out with suspicions, which were fed by Gaston's guilty silence (for, if he had helped a friend, why keep it a secret from me?), his insatiable desire for money, and his frequent journeys to Paris; jealous too of the work from which he seemed unable to tear himself, I at last made up my mind to take certain steps, of such a degrading nature that I cannot tell you about them. Suffice it to say that three days ago I ascertained that Gaston, when in Paris, visits a house in the Rue de la Ville l'Evêque,* where he guards his mistress with jealous mystery, unexampled in Paris. The porter was surly, and I could get little out of him, but that little was enough to put an end to any lingering hope, and with hope to life. On this point my mind was resolved, and I only waited to learn the whole truth first.

With this object I went to Paris and took rooms in a house exactly opposite the one which Gaston visits. Thence I saw him with my own eyes enter the court-yard on horseback. Too soon a ghastly fact forced itself on me. This Englishwoman, who seems to me about thirty-six, is known as Madame Gaston. This discovery was my deathblow.

I saw him next walking to the Tuileries with a couple of children. Oh! my dear, two children, the living images of Gaston! The likeness is so strong that it bears scandal on the face of it. And what pretty children! in their handsome English costumes! She is the mother of his children. Here is the key to the whole mystery.

The woman herself might be a Greek statue, stepped down from some monument. Cold and white as marble, she moves sedately with a mother's pride. She is undeniably beautiful but heavy as a man-of-war. There is no breeding or distinction about her; nothing of the English lady. Probably she is a farmer's daughter from some wretched and remote country village, or, it may be, the eleventh child of some poor clergyman!

I reached home, after a miserable journey, during which all sorts of fiendish thoughts had me at their mercy, with hardly any life left in me. Was she married? Did he know her before our marriage? Had she been deserted by some rich man, whose mistress she was, and thus thrown back upon Gaston's hands? Conjectures without end flitted through my brain, as though conjecture were needed in the presence of the children.

The next day I returned to Paris, and by a free use of my purse extracted from the porter the information that Madame Gaston was legally married.

His reply to my question took the form, "Yes, *mademoiselle.*"

July 15th

My dear, my love for Gaston is stronger than ever since that morning, and he has every appearance of being still more deeply in love. He is so young! A score of times it has been on my lips, when we rise in the morning, to say, "Then you love me better than the lady of the Rue de la Ville l'Evêque?" But I dare not explain to myself why the words are checked on my tongue.

"Are you very fond of children?" I asked.

"Oh, yes!" was his reply; "but children will come!"

"What makes you think so?"

"I have consulted the best doctors, and they agree in advising me to travel for a couple of months."

"Gaston," I said, "if love in absence had been possible for me, do you suppose I should ever have left the convent?"

He laughed; but as for me, dear, the word "travel" pierced my heart. Rather, far rather, would I leap from the top of the house than be rolled down the staircase, step by step.—Farewell, my sweetheart. I have arranged for my death to be easy and without horrors, but certain. I made my will yesterday. You can come to me now, the prohibition is removed. Come, then, and receive my last farewell. I will not die by inches; my death, like my life, shall bear the impress of dignity and grace.

Good-bye, dear sister soul, whose affection has never wavered nor grown weary, but has been the constant tender moonlight of my soul. If the intensity of passion has not been ours, at least we have been spared its venomous bitterness. How rightly you have judged of life! Farewell.

LV

THE COMTESSE DE L'ESTORADE TO MADAME GASTON

July 16th

MY DEAR LOUISE,—I send this letter by an express before hastening to the chalet myself. Take courage. Your last letter seemed to me so frantic, that I thought myself justified, under the circumstances, in confiding all to Louis; it was a question of saving you from yourself. If the means we have employed have been, like yours, repulsive, yet the result is so satisfactory that I am certain you will approve. I went so far as to set the police to work, but the whole thing remains a secret between the prefect, ourselves and you.

In one word, Gaston is a jewel! But here are the facts. His brother, Louis Gaston, died at Calcutta, while in the service of a mercantile company, when he was on the very point of returning to France, a rich, prosperous, married man, having received a very large fortune with his wife, who was the widow of an English merchant. For ten years he had worked hard that he might be able to send home enough to support his brother, to whom he was devotedly attached, and from whom his letters generously concealed all his trials and disappointments.

Then came the failure of the great Halmer house; the widow was ruined, and the sudden shock affected Louis Gaston's brain. He had no mental energy left to resist the disease which attacked him, and he died in Bengal, whither he had gone to try and realize the remnants of his wife's property. The dear, good fellow had deposited with a banker a first sum of three hundred thousand francs, which was to go to his brother, but the banker was involved in the Halmer crash, and thus their last resource failed them.

Louis's widow, the handsome woman whom you took for your rival, arrived in Paris with two children—your nephews—and an empty purse, her mother's jewels having barely sufficed to pay for bringing them over. The instructions which Louis Gaston had given the banker for sending the money to his brother enabled the widow to find your husband's former home. As Gaston had disappeared without leaving any address, Madame Louis Gaston was directed to d'Arthez, the only person who could give any information about him.

D'Arthez was the more ready to relieve the young woman's pressing needs, because Louis Gaston, at the time of his marriage four years before, had written to make inquiries about his brother from the famous author, whom he knew to be one of his friends. The Captain had consulted d'Arthez as to the best means of getting the money safely transferred to Marie, and d'Arthez had replied, telling him that Gaston was now a rich man through his marriage with the Baronne de Macumer. The personal beauty, which was the mother's rich heritage to her sons, had saved them both—one in

India, the other in Paris—from destitution. A touching story, is it not?

D'Arthez naturally wrote, after a time, to tell your husband of the condition of his sister-in-law and her children, informing him, at the same time, of the generous intentions of the Indian Gaston towards his Paris brother, which an unhappy chance had frustrated. Gaston, as you may imagine, hurried off to Paris. Here is the first ride accounted for. During the last five years he had saved fifty thousand francs out of the income you forced him to accept, and this sum he invested in the public funds under the names of his two nephews, securing them each, in this way, an income of twelve hundred francs. Next he furnished his sister-in-law's rooms, and promised her a quarterly allowance of three thousand francs. Here you see the meaning of his dramatic labors and the pleasure caused him by the success of his first play.

Madame Gaston, therefore, is no rival of yours, and has every right to your name. A man of Gaston's sensitive delicacy was bound to keep the affair secret from you, knowing as he did, your generous nature. Nor does he look on what you give him as his own. D'Arthez read me the letter he had from your husband, asking him to be one of the witnesses at his marriage. Gaston in this declares that his happiness would have been perfect but for the one drawback of his poverty and indebtedness to you. A virgin soul is at the mercy of such scruples. Either they make themselves felt or they do not; and when they do, it is easy to imagine the conflict of feeling and embarrassment to which they give rise. Nothing is more natural than Gaston's wish to provide in secret a suitable maintenance for the woman who is his brother's widow, and who had herself set aside one hundred thousand francs for him from her own fortune. She is a handsome woman, warm-hearted, and extremely well-bred, but not clever. She is a mother; and, you may be sure, I lost my heart to her at first sight when I found her with one child in her arms, and the other dressed like a little lord. The children first! is written in every detail of her house.

Far from being angry, therefore, with your beloved husband, you should find in all this fresh reason for loving him. I have met him, and think him the most delightful young fellow in Paris. Yes! dear child, when I saw him, I had no difficulty in understanding that a woman might lose her head about him; his soul is mirrored in his countenance. If I were you, I should settle the widow and her children at the chalet, in a pretty little cottage which you could have built for them, and adopt the boys!

Be at peace, then, dear soul, and plan this little surprise, in your turn, for Gaston.

LVI

MADAME GASTON TO THE COMTESSE DE L'ESTORADE

Ah! my dear friend, what can I say in answer except the cruel "It is too late" of that fool Lafayette to his royal master? Oh! my life, my sweet life, what physician will give it back to me. My own hand has dealt the death-blow. Alas! have I not been a mere will-o'-the-wisp, whose twinkling spark was fated to perish before it reached a flame? My eyes rain torrents of tears—and yet they must not fall when I am with him. I fly to him, and he seeks me. My despair is all within. This torture Dante forgot to place in his *Inferno*. Come to see me die!

LVII

THE COMTESSE DE L'ESTORADE TO THE COMTE DE L'ESTORADE

The Chalet, August 7th

My love,—Take the children away to Provence without me; I remain with Louise, who has only a few days yet to live. I cannot leave either her or her husband, for whose reason I fear.

You know the scrap of letter which sent me flying to Ville d'Avray, picking up the doctors on my way. Since then I have not left my darling friend, and it has been impossible to write to you, for I have sat up every night for a fortnight.

When I arrived, I found her with Gaston, in full dress, beautiful, laughing, happy. It was a heroic falsehood! They were like two lovely children together in their restored confidence. For a moment I was deceived, like Gaston, by the effrontery; but Louise pressed my hand, whispering:

"He must not know; I am dying."

An icy chill fell over me as I felt her burning hand and saw the red spots on her cheeks. I congratulated myself on my prudence in leaving the doctors in the wood till they should be sent for.

"Leave us for a little," she said to Gaston. "Two women who have not met for five years have plenty of secrets to talk over, and Renée, I have no doubt, has things to confide in me."

Directly we were alone, she flung herself into my arms, unable longer to restrain her tears.

"Tell me about it," I said. "I have brought with me, in case of need, the best surgeon and the best physician from the hospital, and Bianchon as well; there are four altogether."

"Ah!" she cried, "have them in at once if they can save me, if there is still time. The passion which hurried me to death now cries for life!"

"But what have you done to yourself?"

"I have in a few days brought myself to the last stage of consumption."

"But how?"

"I got myself into a profuse perspiration in the night, and then ran out and lay down by the side of the lake in the dew. Gaston thinks I have a cold, and I am dying!"

"Send him to Paris; I will fetch the doctors myself,"
I said, as I rushed out wildly to the spot where I had
left them.

Alas! my love, after the consultation was over, not
one of the doctors gave me the least hope; they all believe that Louise will die with the fall of the leaves. The
dear child's constitution has wonderfully helped the
success of her plan. It seems she has a predisposition
to this complaint; and though, in the ordinary course,
she might have lived a long time, a few days' folly has
made the case desperate.

I cannot tell you what I felt on hearing this sentence,
based on such clear explanations. You know that I have
lived in Louise as much as in my own life. I was simply crushed, and could not stir to escort to the door
these harbingers of evil. I don't know how long I remained lost in bitter thoughts, the tears running down
my cheeks, when I was roused from my stupor by the
words:

"So there is no hope for me!" in a clear, angelic
voice.

It was Louise, with her hand on my shoulder. She
made me get up, and carried me off to her small drawing-room. With a beseeching glance, she went on:

"Stay with me to the end; I won't have doleful faces
round me. Above all, I must keep the truth from *him*. I
know that I have the strength to do it. I am full of youth
and spirit, and can die standing! For myself, I have no
regrets. I am dying as I wished to die, still young and
beautiful, in the perfection of my womanhood.

"As for him, I can see very well now that I should have
made his life miserable. Passion has me in its grips, like
a struggling fawn, impatient of the toils. My groundless jealousy has already wounded him sorely. When
the day came that my suspicions met only indifference—which in the long run is the rightful meed of all

jealousy—well, that would have been my death. I have had my share of life. There are people whose names on the muster-roll of the world show sixty years of service, and yet in all that time they have not had two years of real life, whilst my record of thirty is doubled by the intensity of my love.

"Thus for him, as well as for me, the close is a happy one. But between us, dear Renée, it is different. You lose a loving sister, and that is a loss which nothing can repair. You alone here have the right to mourn my death."

After a long pause, during which I could only see her through a mist of tears, she continued:

"The moral of my death is a cruel one. My dear doctor in petticoats was right; marriage cannot rest upon passion as its foundation, nor even upon love. How fine and noble is your life! keeping always to the one safe road, you give your husband an ever-growing affection; while the passionate eagerness with which I threw myself into wedded life was bound in nature to diminish. Twice have I gone astray, and twice has Death stretched forth his bony hand to strike my happiness. The first time, he robbed me of the noblest and most devoted of men; now it is my turn, the grinning monster tears me from the arms of my poet husband, with all his beauty and his grace.

"Yet I would not complain. Have I not known in turn two men, each the very pattern of nobility—one in mind, the other in outward form? In Félipe, the soul dominated and transformed the body; in Gaston, one could not say which was supreme—heart, mind, or grace of form. I die adored—what more could I wish for? Time, perhaps, in which to draw near the God of whom I may have too little thought. My spirit will take its flight towards Him, full of love, and with the prayer that some day, in the world above, He will unite me once more to the two who made a heaven of my life below. Without them, paradise would be a desert to me.

"To others, my example would be fatal, for mine was no common lot. To meet a Félipe or a Gaston is more than mortals can expect, and therefore the doctrine of society in regard to marriage accords with the natural law. Woman is weak, and in marrying she ought to make an entire sacrifice of her will to the man who, in return, should lay his selfishness at her feet. The stir which women of late years have created by their whining and insubordination is ridiculous, and only shows how well we deserve the epithet of children, bestowed by philosophers on our sex."

She continued talking thus in the gentle voice you know so well, uttering the gravest truths in the prettiest manner, until Gaston entered, bringing with him his sister-in-law, the two children, and the English nurse, whom, at Louise's request, he had been to fetch from Paris.

"Here are the pretty instruments of my torture," she said, as her nephews approached. "Was not the mistake excusable? What a wonderful likeness to their uncle!"

She was most friendly to Madame Gaston the elder and begged that she would look upon the chalet as her home; in short, she played the hostess to her in her best de Chaulieu manner, in which no one can rival her.

I wrote at once to the Duc and Duchesse de Chaulieu, the Duc de Rhétoré, and the Duc de Lenoncourt-Givry, as well as to Madeleine. It was time. Next day, Louise, worn out with so much exertion, was unable to go out; indeed, she only got up for dinner. In the course of the evening, Madeleine de Lenoncourt, her two brothers, and her mother arrived. The coolness which Louise's second marriage had caused between herself and her family disappeared. Every day since that evening, Louise's father and both her brothers have ridden over in the morning, and the two duchesses spend all their evenings at the chalet. Death unites as well as separates;

it silences all paltry feeling.

Louise is perfection in her charm, her grace, her good sense, her wit, and her tenderness. She has retained to the last that perfect tact for which she has been so famous, and she lavishes on us the treasures of her brilliant mind, which made her one of the queens of Paris.

"I should like to look well even in my coffin," she said with her matchless smile, as she lay down on the bed where she was to linger for a fortnight.

Her room has nothing of the sick-chamber in it; medicines, ointments, the whole apparatus of nursing, is carefully concealed.

"Is not my deathbed pretty!" she said to the Sèvres priest who came to confess her.

We gloated over her like misers. All this anxiety, and the terrible truths which dawned on him, have prepared Gaston for the worst. He is full of courage, but the blow has gone home. It would not surprise me to see him follow his wife in the natural course. Yesterday, as we were walking round the lake, he said to me:

"I must be a father to those two children," and he pointed to his sister-in-law, who was taking the boys for a walk. "But though I shall do nothing to hasten my end, I want your promise that you will be a second mother to them, and will persuade your husband to accept the office of guardian, which I shall depute to him in conjunction with my sister-in-law."

He said this quite simply, like a man who knows he is not long for this world. He has smiles on his face to meet Louise's, and it is only I whom he does not deceive. He is a mate for her in courage.

Louise has expressed a wish to see her godson, but I am not sorry he should be in Provence; she might want to remember him generously, and I should be in a great difficulty.

Good-bye, my love.

Elle avait exigé de moi que je lui lusse en français le **De Profundis**, pendant qu'elle serait ainsi face à face avec la belle nature qu'elle s'était créée.

MÉMOIRES DE DEUX JEUNES MARIÉS.

Plate VI: *The Comtesse Louis de l'Estorade at Madame Marie Gaston's bedside*
Illustration by Tony Johannot

August 25th (her birthday)

Yesterday evening Louise was delirious for a short time; but her delirium was the prettiest babbling, which shows that even the madness of gifted people is not that of fools or nobodies. In a mere thread of a voice she sang some Italian airs from *I Puritani*, *La Sonnambula*, *Moïse*,* while we stood round the bed in silence. Not one of us, not even the Duc de Rhétoré, had dry eyes, so clear was it to us all that her soul was in this fashion passing from us. She could no longer see us! Yet she was there still in the charm of the faint melody, with its sweetness not of this earth.

During the night the death agony began. It is now seven in the morning, and I have just myself raised her from bed. Some flicker of strength revived; she wished to sit by her window, and asked for Gaston's hand. And then, my love, the sweetest spirit whom we shall ever see on this earth departed, leaving us the empty shell.

The last sacrament had been administered the evening before, unknown to Gaston, who was taking a snatch of sleep during this agonizing ceremony; and after she was moved to the window, she asked me to read her the *De Profundis* in French, while she was thus face to face with the lovely scene, which was her handiwork. She repeated the words after me to herself, and pressed the hands of her husband, who knelt on the other side of the chair.

August 26th

My heart is broken. I have just seen her in her winding-sheet; her face is quite pale now with purple shadows. Oh! I want my children! my children! Bring me my children!

1838-41

Addendum to *Letters of Two Brides*
The following personages appear in other stories of
The Human Comedy.

Arthez, Daniel d'
Lost Illusions (A Distinguished Provincial at Paris)
The Deputy for Arcis
The Secrets of the Princesse de Cadignan

Beauseant, Marquise de
The Deserted Woman

Bianchon, Horace
Old Goriot
The Atheist's Mass
César Birotteau
The Interdiction
Lost Illusions (A Distinguished Provincial at Paris)
The Rabouilleuse
The Secrets of the Princesse de Cadignan
The Bureaucrats
Pierrette
A Study of Woman
Scenes from a Courtesan's Life
Honorine
The Brotherhood of Consolation
The Magic Skin
A Second Home
A Prince of Bohemia
The Muse of the Department
The Imaginary Mistress
The Petty Bourgeoisie
Cousin Bette
The Village Rector

In addition, Monsieur Bianchon narrated the following:
Another Study of Woman
La Grande Bretêche

Bridau, Joseph
The Purse
The Rabouilleuse
Lost Illusions (A Distinguished Provincial at Paris)
A Start in Life
Modeste Mignon
Another Study of Woman
Pierre Grassou
Cousin Bette
The Deputy for Arcis

Bruel, Claudine Chaffaroux, Madame du (Tullia)
The Rabouilleuse
A Prince of Bohemia
Lost Illusions (A Distinguished Provincial at Paris)
The Petty Bourgeoisie

Canalis, Constant-Cyr-Melchior, Baron de
Lost Illusions (A Distinguished Provincial at Paris)
Modeste Mignon
The Magic Skin
Another Study of Woman
A Start in Life
Béatrix
The Unconscious Humorists
The Deputy for Arcis

Chaulieu, Henri, Duc de
Modeste Mignon
The Rabouilleuse
Scenes from a Courtesan's Life
The Thirteen

393

Chaulieu, Eleonore, Duchesse de
Eugénie Grandet

Dudley, Lady Arabella
The Lily of the Valley
The Ball at Sceaux
The Magic Skin
The Secrets of the Princesse de Cadignan
A Daughter of Eve

Esgrignon, Victurnien, Comte (then Marquis d')
Jealousies of a Country Town
A Man of Business
The Secrets of the Princesse de Cadignan
Cousin Bette

Espard, Jeanne-Clementine-Athénaïs de Blamont-Chauvry,
Marquise d'
The Interdiction
Lost Illusions (A Distinguished Provincial at Paris)
Scenes from a Courtesan's Life
Another Study of Woman
A Shadowy Affair
The Secrets of the Princesse de Cadignan
A Daughter of Eve
Béatrix

Estorade, Louis, Chevalier, then Vicomte and Comte de l'
The Deputy for Arcis

Estorade, Madame de l'
The Deputy for Arcis
Ursule Mirouët

Estorade, Armand de l'
The Deputy for Arcis

Gaston, Louis
  La Grenadière

Gaston, Marie
  La Grenadière
  The Deputy for Arcis

Givry
  The Lily of the Valley
  Scenes from a Courtesan's Life

Lenoncourt-Givry, Duc de
  Cousin Bette
  The Deputy for Arcis

Lenoncourt-Givry, Duchesse de
  The Lily of the Valley
  Scenes from a Courtesan's Life

Marsay, Henri de
  The Thirteen
  The Unconscious Humorists
  Another Study of Woman
  The Lily of the Valley
  Old Goriot
  Jealousies of a Country Town
  Ursule Mirouët
  The Marriage Contract
  Lost Illusions (A Distinguished Provincial at Paris)
  The Ball at Sceaux
  Modeste Mignon
  The Secrets of the Princesse de Cadignan
  A Shadowy Affair
  A Daughter of Eve

Mary
The Deputy for Arcis

Maucombe, Comte de
Lost Illusions

Maufrigneuse, Duchesse de
The Secrets of the Princesse de Cadignan
Modeste Mignon
Jealousies of a Country Town
The Muse of the Department
Scenes from a Courtesan's Life
Another Study of Woman
A Shadowy Affair
The Deputy for Arcis

Mirbel, Madame de
Scenes from a Courtesan's Life
The Secrets of the Princesse de Cadignan

Montriveau, Général Marquis Armand de
The Thirteen
Old Goriot
Lost Illusions (A Distinguished Provincial at Paris)
Another Study of Woman
Pierrette
The Deputy for Arcis

Nathan, Raoul
Lost Illusions (A Distinguished Provincial at Paris)
Scenes from a Courtesan's Life
The Secrets of the Princesse de Cadignan
A Daughter of Eve
The Brotherhood of Consolation
The Muse of the Department
A Prince of Bohemia
A Man of Business
The Unconscious Humorists

Appendix
The Heron and *The Maid*,
two linked fables by Jean de La Fontaine
from Book Seven, Fables 4 and 5
Translated by Elizur Wright, Jr.

The Heron

One day,—no matter when or where,—
A long-legged heron chanced to fare
By a certain river's brink,
With his long, sharp beak
Helved on his slender neck;
It was a fish-spear, you might think.
The water was clear and still,
The carp and the pike there at will
Pursued their silent fun,
Turning up, ever and anon,
A golden side to the sun.
With ease might the heron have made
Great profits in his fishing trade.
So near came the scaly fry,
They might be caught by the passer-by.
But he thought he better might
Wait for a better appetite—
For he lived by rule, and could not eat,
Except at his hours, the best of meat.
Anon his appetite returned once more;
So, approaching again the shore,
He saw some tench taking their leaps,
Now and then, from their lowest deeps.
With as dainty a taste as Horace's rat,
He turned away from such food as that.
"What, tench for a heron! poh!
I scorn the thought, and let them go."
The tench refused, there came a gudgeon;
"For all that," said the bird, "I budge on.
I'll never open my beak, if the gods please,
For such mean little fishes as these."

401

He did it for less;
For it came to pass,
That not another fish could he see;
And, at last, so hungry was he,
That he thought it of some avail
To find on the bank a single snail.
Such is the sure result
Of being too difficult.
Would you be strong and great,
Learn to accommodate.
Get what you can, and trust for the rest;
The whole is often lost by seeking the best.
Above all things beware of disdain;
Where, at most, you have little to gain.
The people are many that make
Every day this sad mistake.
It's not for the herons I put this case,
You featherless people, of human race.
—List to another tale as true,
And you'll hear the lesson brought home to you.

The Maid

A certain maid, as proud as fair,
A husband thought to find
Exactly to her mind—
Well-formed and young, genteel in air,
Not cold nor jealous;—mark this well.
Whoever would wed this dainty belle
Must have, besides rank, wealth, and wit,
And all good qualities to fit—
A man it were difficult to get.
Kind Fate, however, took great care
To grant, if possible, her prayer.
There came a-wooing men of note;
The maiden thought them all,
By half, too mean and small.
"They marry me! the creatures dote:
Alas! poor souls! their case I pity."

(Here mark the bearing of the beauty.)
Some were less delicate than witty;
Some had the nose too short or long;
In others something else was wrong;
Which made each in the maiden's eyes
An altogether worthless prize.
Profound contempt is aye the vice
Which springs from being over-nice,
Thus were the great dismissed; and then
Came offers from inferior men.
The maid, more scornful than before,
Took credit to her tender heart
For giving then an open door.
"They think me much in haste to part
With independence! God be thanked
My lonely nights bring no regret;
Nor shall I pine, or greatly fret,
Should I with ancient maids be ranked."
Such were the thoughts that pleased the fair:
Age made them only thoughts that were.
Adieu to lovers: passing years
Awaken doubts and chilling fears.
Regret, at last, brings up the train.
Day after day she sees, with pain,
Some smile or charm take final flight,
And leave the features of a "fright."
Then came a hundred sorts of paint:
But still no trick, nor ruse, nor feint,
Availed to hide the cause of grief,
Or bar out Time, that graceless thief.
A house, when gone to wreck and ruin,
May be repaired and made a new one.
Alas! for ruins of the face
No such rebuilding ever takes place.
Her daintiness now changed its tune;
Her mirror told her, "Marry soon!"
So did a certain wish within,
With more of secrecy than sin,—
A wish that dwells with even prudes,
Annihilating solitudes.

This maiden's choice was past belief,
She soothing down her restless grief,
And smoothing it of every ripple,
By marrying a cripple.

*
Endnotes

References which can normally be found when consulting an unabridged dictionary of the English language, or are otherwise self-explanatory, are not included here unless they have some special significance to the text or the author.

Author's Introduction

the great dispute . . . between Cuvier and Geoffroi Saint-Hilaire . . . Unity of structure: Cuvier opposed the theory of evolution as set forth by Lamarck and elaborated upon by Étienne Geoffroy Saint-Hilaire (1772-1844). A French zoologist, Saint-Hilaire set forth the principle known as "unity of structure" or "unity of plan" which holds that all organisms in nature, despite their high levels of diversity, are all essentially of one basic design.

As a young man, Balzac attended at least one of Cuvier's lectures at the Natural History Museum in Paris and was so impressed after hearing him speak that, along with Napoleon and Irish politician Daniel O'Connell, he considered him to be one of the three greatest men who had ever lived (Balzac himself hoped to become the fourth).

Swedenborg, Saint-Martin: Balzac was first exposed to the Christian mysticism of Swedenborg through his mother, Anne-Charlotte-Laure Sallambier. Though there is no evidence that he actually read any of the mystic's works, their philosophy and vision informed a later part of the *Comédie Humaine* known as the *Philosophical Studies*: in particular the novels *Louis Lambert* and *Séraphita*.

Claude de *Saint-Martin* (1743-1803) was a French philosopher and mystic who took his inspiration from the Jewish Kabbalah.

407

xii   *Charles Bonnet,* organic molecules, *the* vegetative force *of Needham*: Charles Bonnet (1720-1793) was a Swiss naturalist who discovered what came to be known as parthenogenesis, a form of asexual reproduction, while observing the behavior of aphids.

       "Organic molecules," as conceived of by Buffon, were primary indivisible units that came together to create living organisms via an attractive force and were then guided to form the specific entity itself by means of an embryonic internal mold.

       John Turberville *Needham* (1713-1781) was an English naturalist and Catholic priest who believed that his experiments had proven the existence of spontaneous generation. He developed the theory of a "vegetative force," a process essential to all life, which was itself composed of two opposing forces: resistance and expansion.

xiv   *Abbé Barthélemy,* Le Jeune Anacharsis: Jean-Jacques Barthélemy (1716-1795) was the French author of *Voyage du jeune Anacharsis en Grèce dans le milieu du IVe siècle* (1788), a historical novel about Ancient Greece inspired by his archaeological work done in the ruins of Pompeii.

       Clarissa Harlowe is the title character of a novel by English writer Samuel Richardson. A tragic figure always striving for virtue, she is forced by her family to marry an undesirable older man for his money and social position. This causes her to come under the influence of the duplicitous *Robert Lovelace* who runs away with her, maltreats her, and continuously tries to destroy her virtue as a means of revenging himself against the Harlowe family who had earlier mistreated him.

       Julie d'Etanges is the female protagonist of Rousseau's best-selling epistolary novel *La Nouvelle Héloïse.*

       My Uncle Toby: one of the principal characters in *Tristram Shandy* by Laurence Sterne; he is an eccentric military veteran obsessed with recreating the battle where he sustained a groin injury.

Werther is the doomed hero of Johann Wolfgang von Goethe's *Die Leiden des Jungends Werthers*. Written in diary form, it recounts Werther's obsessive and unrequited love for a married woman and his resulting self-destruction. A very popular novel, it inspired many imitators and reportedly even a number of like-minded suicides.

René is the title character of an immensely popular novella by François-René de Chateaubriand. First published in 1802 as part of his *Génie du christianisme*, it is the story of a young distraught romantic who eventually finds solace with a Native American tribe.

Corinne is the exiled poetess in the romantic novel of the same name by Madame de Staël (see note for page xx).

Adolphe is the eponymous hero of a short novel by Benjamin Constant first published in 1816. Rather than pursue a hopeless love affair, Adolphe instead wishes to free himself from a relationship with Ellénore, a Count's mistress, which he had begun out of egotism rather than love.

Paul and Virginia are the title characters in a romantic novel by French writer and botanist Bernardin de Saint Pierre (1737-1814). Heavily influenced by Rousseau and written just prior to the French Revolution, it concerns the love of two children growing into adolescence far away from the corrupting influences of society on the idyllic Isle of France (now known as Mauritius). It was extremely popular in its day and spawned many similarly themed works.

Jeanie Deans is one of the principal characters in Sir Walter Scott's *Heart of Midlothian* and the half-sister of Effie Deans (see note for page xxi).

John Graham of *Claverhouse*, 1st Viscount of Dundee (c.1648-1689), also known as "Bonnie Dundee," was a hero of the first Jacobite Rebellion and the subject of a poem by Scott.

Manfred is the tormented title character of a supernatural dramatic poem by Lord Byron.

Another of Goethe's characters, *Mignon* is a young

Italian dancer rescued from servitude by Wilhelm in *Wilhelm Meisters Lehrjahre*.

xvi   Amans-Alexis *Monteil* (1769-1850) was a French historian who stressed the importance of studying people of different social classes in history rather than focusing solely on royal or military figures.

Louis Gabriel Ambroise de *Bonald* (1754-1840) was a French philosopher and conservative politician who opposed the Revolution and supported the return of the Bourbons. The idea that human language is divine in origin and ultimately the source of all truth is the basis for most of his works including *Theorie du pouvoir politique et religieux* (1796) and *La Législation Primitive* (1802). He was highly influential during the period of the Restoration.

xviii   *the* Corps Législatif: from the time of the Revolution through the Napoleonic era and up until it was dissolved by Louis XVIII in 1814 and replaced by the Chamber of Deputies, the lower legislative house of France.

xx   *Madame Necker*: Anne Louise Germaine Necker was the birth name of Swiss authoress Baronne Anne Louise Germaine de Staël-Holstein, better known simply as Madame de Staël. She authored the romances *Delphine* (1802) and *Corinne* (1807) and was renowned throughout Europe for her influential literary salons.

xxi   *the painter of Effie and Alice*: Effie Deans and Alice Bridgenorth are characters that appear, respectively, in Scott's *Heart of Midlothian* and *Peveril of the Peak*.

xxii   Franz Joseph *Gall* (1758-1828) was an Austrian neuroanatomist and pioneer in the field of cranioscopy, better known today as phrenology now considered to be a pseudoscience.

xxiii faits et gestes: "actions" or literally "deeds and gestures."

Félix Davin (1807-1836) was a young French novelist, poet, and journalist employed by Balzac to write an extensive introduction to his as yet unfinished complete works. Davin proceeded to do so despite Balzac's continuous meddling and rewriting. Filled with effusive praise, this introduction, though attributed to Davin, is really much more a product of Balzac's own pen.

xxv Pathology of Social Life, Anatomy of Educational Bodies, Monograph on Virtue: Balzac did not live to see any of these three works completed.

At the Sign of the Cat and Racket
Originally titled *Gloire et Malheur* (*Glory and Misfortune*), the story which opens *La Comédie Humaine* was inspired by the lucrative haberdashery business run by the Sallambier family on Balzac's maternal side.

1 *Mademoiselle Marie de Montheau*: some thirteen years after it was first completed, Balzac had the story dedicated to Mademoiselle de Montheau, the granddaughter of Madame Joséphine Delannoy, in time for the edition published by Charles Furne in 1842. Madame Delannoy was a friend of Balzac's family from whom the author borrowed money on more than one occasion, frequently to her detriment.

3 *the Rue Saint-Denis in Paris . . . the Rue du Petit-Lion*: one of the city's oldest streets dating back to the 1st century A.D., the Rue Saint-Denis is located on the Seine's right bank and runs from the 1st or *1er arrondissement* all the way to the Boulevard Saint-Denis in the 2nd *arrondissement* to the north. The street has a long history of being a center of prostitution, though Balzac makes no mention of this in the story. It was rendered in watercolor in 1802 by English painter Thomas Girtin (1775-1802) (see plate VII).

The Rue du Petit-Lion was located in the 6th

Plate VII: *The Rue Saint-Denis in Paris* by Thomas Girtin (1775-1802)

Plate VIII: *Tête de Vierge (d'après Girodet)* by Athenaïs Paulinier (1798-1889)

arrondissement, to the south of the 1st, and across the Seine on its left bank. Today it is known as the Rue Saint-Sulpice, taking its name from the second largest church in Paris.

10 *Provost of Merchants . . . Sentence of the Consuls*: before the position was abolished at the beginning of the Revolution (Jacques de Flesselles, the last to hold the post, was assassinated on 14 July 1789, the same day the Bastille was stormed), the Provost of Merchants was the office responsible for the Municipality of Paris.

The Consulate, comprised of Napoleon, Jean Jacques Régis de Cambacérès (1753-1824), and Charles-François Lebrun, duc de Plaisance (1739-1824), was the body that governed France from 1799 to 1804, after which Napoleon was given the title of Emperor by the Senate and a public referendum.

the law of maximum prices: in April 1793 during the Reign of Terror, the Committee of Public Safety instituted a law whereby a maximum price was set on goods; as a result, the maximum price was always charged. The existence of a thriving black market also served to undermine the law, and it was abandoned some eight months later.

11 *Louviers*: a commune of the Eure *département* in northern France.

12 *Mass at Saint-Leu*: Saint-Leu-Saint-Gilles, a church dating from the 13th century located at No. 92 on the Rue Saint-Denis.

15 *Le Ragois*: Claude Le Ragois (d. 1683) was a French abbot and the author of *Instruction sur l'histoire de France et sur l'histoire romaine*, a popular history text of dubious educational value.

17 Hippolyte Comte de Douglas, Le Comte de Comminges: the former, written in 1691, is the title of a popular

Plate IX: *The Transfiguration* by Raphael (1483-1520)

Plate X: *Ossian receiving the Ghosts of the French Heroes* by Girodet

historical romance set in the time of Henry VIII by Marie-Catherine Le Jumel de Barneville, Baronne d'Aulnoy (c.1651-1705), usually known simply as Madame d'Aulnoy; the latter is the title of a similarly themed novel penned by Claudine Guérin de Tencin (1682-1749), a former nun, in 1735.

18   *the first decree by which Napoleon drew in advance on the conscript classes*: a reference to the *Levée en masse* or policy of mass conscription instituted by Napoleon around the time of the French Revolutionary Wars wherein " . . . all Frenchmen are in permanent requisition for the services of the armies. The young men shall fight; the married men shall forge arms and transport provisions; the women shall make tents and clothes and shall serve in the hospitals; the children shall turn linen into lint; the old men shall betake themselves to the public squares in order to arouse the courage of the warriors and preach hatred of kings and the unity of the Republic."

20   *Anne-Louis Girodet de Roussy-Trioson* (1767-1824) was a French Romantic painter renowned for his portraits of Napoleon and Chateaubriand. Anne-Marie Meininger, in her introduction to a French edition of this story, finds a striking resemblance between Théodore's painting of Augustine and one by Girodet entitled *Étude de Vierge* that was exhibited at the Salon de Paris in 1812 (see plate VIII for a work done in imitation of Girodet's in 1834).

27   Cendrillon *at the Variétés*: respectively, the title of an opera (*Cinderella*) by Massenet, and the Théâtre des Variétés located on the boulevard Montmartre in Paris.

32   *devoted Céladons*: Céladon is the deeply romantic and sentimental hero of *L'Astrée*, a lengthy pastoral novel by French writer Honoré d'Urfé (1568-1625). The word is sometimes used to describe any lover of ardent feeling.

415

36   All French historical personages representing a wide array of artistic occupations: *Vernet* (presumably Monsieur Guillaume is referring to Joseph Vernet, 1714-1789, rather than his son Carle or his grandson Horace) was a painter; Henri Louis Cain, better known by his stage name *Lekain* (1728-1778) was an actor; Jean-Georges *Noverre* (1727-1810) was a celebrated dancer and ballet master; the *Chevalier de Saint-Georges* (1745-1799) was a famous composer, violin player, and swordsman sometimes known as "the Black Mozart" because of his African ancestry; François-André Danican *Philidor* (1726-1795) was a chess player and composer.

37   Génie du Christianisme (*The Genius of Christianity*, 1802): the title of a book by Chateaubriand that sets forth an impassioned defense of Christianity which at the time of its writing was under attack by the new-found ideals of the Enlightenment and the French Revolution (see note to page xiv, *René*)

Chevalier of the Legion of Honor: the *Ordre national de la Légion d'honneur*, founded by Napoleon in May 1802, was a decoration that could be awarded to soldiers and civilians alike based on their merits and service to France and did not hold nobility as a prerequisite for its bestowal. The Order is divided into five degrees: Chevalier (or Knight), Officer, Commander, Grand Officer, and Grand Cross; its motto is *Honneur et Patrie* (Honor and Fatherland). After the Restoration, Louis XVIII decided to keep the order, but changed the design of the medals so that images of Napoleon were no longer displayed. The award has gone through a number of subtle changes over the years, but to this day remains the highest honor France can grant to an individual.

Monsieur Dupont: Pierre Dupont de l'Étang (1765-1840) was a French general of the Revolutionary and Napoleonic Wars. He supported Napoleon's coup against the Directory in 1799.

41   *the Rue du Colombier,* located in the 6th *arrondissement* on the Seine's left bank, was named for the pigeon house (colombier is French for "dovecote") at Saint-Germain-des-Prés, a Benedictine abbey built in the 6th century.

42   *the Rue des Trois-Frères*: a street of the 18th *arrondissement* in the northern Montmartre district of Paris.

45   *Raphael's* Transfiguration: see plate IX

49   *a box at the Français:* the Comédie-Française or Théâtre Français, France's only state theater.

56   *Faubourg Saint-Germain*: an area around the Boulevard Saint-Germain located on the left bank of the Seine which takes its name from Saint-Germain-des-Prés.

58   the *Bois de Boulogne* is a park located in Paris's 16th *arrondissement* on the right bank of the Seine (bois is French for "wood").

The Ball at Sceaux

A story based upon two of La Fontaine's fables: *La Fille,* and, to a lesser extent, *Le Héron* (see Appendix). It originally bore the alternative title *"Ou le pair de France,"* but Balzac later decided against using it.

71   *The Bourbon cause*: the Restoration of Louis XVIII of the Bourbon dynasty to the French throne after the Revolution and the Napoleonic Wars.

       La Vendée, The Battle of Les Quatre Chemins, Vendéen: the Vendée is a French *département* located on the western coast just beneath the Loire river. Between 1793 and 1796 it was the site of a counterrevolutionary war (one of the battles of which was that of Les Quatre Chemins) between Royalist and Republican factions. The Royalists were eventually routed by Republican forces at Savenay on 23 December 1793, but the region was not completely pacified until 1796 after a bloody series of massacres. A veteran of this battle might be referred to as a Vendéen.

the second revolution: a reference to the Hundred Days (actually 111 days in total) when Napoleon returned to Paris from exile in an attempt to reclaim power on 20 March 1815. He was defeated by the combined armies of the Seventh Coalition at Waterloo on 28 June and finally surrendered on 15 July. Louis the XVIII was restored to the throne of France for a second time on 8 July bringing the period of the Hundred Days to an end.

the new Constitution: the Charter of 1814, a constitution required by the Congress of Vienna as a precondition for Louis XVIII's restoration to the throne. It guaranteed equality before the law and freedom of religion for all Frenchmen, but it also made Catholicism the country's official faith. In the role of constitutional monarch, Louis XVIII's powers were somewhat diminished, but the king still had the power to make war or peace and was the only one who could introduce legislation.

72   *the crosses of the Legion of Honor and of Saint-Louis*: for the former, see note to page 37, *Chevalier of the Legion of Honor*.

The *Ordre Royal et Militaire de Saint-Louis*, considered to be a precursor to the Legion of Honor, was established by Louis the XIV in 1693 as a means of honoring distinguished officers; it was the first decoration that could be awarded to men of common as well as of noble birth, though the bearer was required to be a Catholic. Its three degrees were Chevalier, Commander, and Grand Cross. It disappeared during the Revolution, was reinstated by Louis XVIII, and finally abolished by Louis-Philippe in 1830.

73   *the League and the day of the Barricades*: the Catholic League of France was created in 1584 by Duke Henry

of Guise as a means of wiping out Protestants during the French Wars of Religion.

The Day of the Barricades (12 May 1588) was a popular insurgency against Henry III and the Edict of Beaulieu which relaxed restrictions against Protestants, named for the makeshift fortifications of barrels, wagons, and loose timbers that were erected by militiamen throughout Paris to prevent troop movements. It was a reaction to a census ordered by the King for the purpose of identifying and capturing Catholic League members.

74 *Louis XVIII and Monsieur Beugnot spoiled everything at Saint Ouen*: Jacques Claude Beugnot (1761-1835) was a politician who had previously sided with Napoleon but later went on to serve the King in a number of important governmental positions. He drew up the Charter of 1814 on Louis XVIII's behalf, and on 2 May of that year the King gave the Declaration of Saint Ouen establishing a constitutional monarchy.

the wittiest and most successful of our diplomates . . . the Court at Ghent, etc.: Balzac probably means Chateaubriand, the French Romantic writer and politician, who fled to Ghent in Belgium with Louis XVIII during the Hundred Days.

76 *the affair of the Trocadéro*: the Battle of Trocadero, named for the fort on the *Isla del Trocadero* in the Bay of Cádiz in Andalusia, was the final conflict of the Spanish Civil War (1820-23) in which revolutionary forces led by constitutionalist General Rafael del Riego y Nuñez (1784-1823) were eventually overcome by French troops and Ferdinand VII was freed from captivity and restored to the throne.

sous-préfet: French for "sub-prefect," a sous-préfet is the official in charge of a particular *arrondissement* answerable to the prefect in charge of the larger *département*.

77   "Amicus Plato sed magis amica Natio" is a play on
       "*Amicus Plato, sed magis amica Veritas*" ("a friend of
       Plato, but a greater friend of Truth); here, the Latin word
       "*Natio*" (nation) has been substituted for "*Veritas.*"

79   *as Mascarille says*: Mascarille is a comedic stock charac-
       ter that originated in Italian stage comedies. He makes
       an appearance, perhaps most famously, in Molière's
       Les Précieuses as a valet impersonating his master so as
       to make a mockery of Magdelon and Cathos, the ridic-
       ulous women of the title.

       a fetfah of the Sultan by the Turks: a religious decree.

       Saint-Germain quarter: see note to page 56.

80   *the little word to which the throne owed so many partisans*:
       the preposition *de* used in some French names to indi-
       cate place of origin. It usually (but not always) denotes
       a person with some degree of royalty in their family.

81   *As far from Lafayette's party as he was from La
       Bourdonnaye's*: Lafayette was a member of the *Feuillants*,
       a group that had broken with the radical Jacobins and
       advocated a constitutional monarchy; François Régis
       de La Bourdonnaye (1767-1839) was Minister of the
       Interior under Charles X and leader of the reactionary
       ultra-royalist party.

       the Rohans: a historically significant French noble fam-
       ily that hailed from the Rohan commune of Brittany.

83   *the malady of which he was to die*: Louis XVIII was afflict-
       ed with gout for many years; his condition eventually
       became serious enough towards the end of his life
       that he was confined to a wheelchair. He died on 16
       September 1824.

84   *the House of Austria, which . . . threatens to pervade Europe*:
       the House of Hapsburg, a royal family that ruled much
       of Europe for more than six centuries.

this one's name was Durand: a typically French Protestant surname, belonging to figures such as the martyrs Pierre (1700-1732) and Marie Durand (1715-1776) as well as the minister David Durand (1680-1763), to which most of the Catholic nobility would likely be quite averse.

the part of Célimène: the name of a conceited female character in Molière's *Le Misanthrope* who flirts with Alceste, the misanthrope of the title.

87   *he must be a peer of France*: the *Pairie de France*, as it existed in the time of the Bourbon Restoration, was a rank of hereditary nobility established by a provision of the Charter of 1814 and appointed by the King. It was similar to the British Upper House of Lords, and was considered to be the very highest honor that a member of the French nobility could attain. Inherited peerages were later changed to lifetime appointments after the July Revolution of 1830, and after the revolution of 1848 the Chamber of Peers was permanently dissolved.

the days of Longchamps in Holy Week: during three consecutive days of the week before Easter Sunday known as "Holy Week" (Holy Wednesday, Maundy Thursday, and Good Friday) it was customary for members of French high society to visit the abbey of Longchamps in the Bois de Boulogne (see note to page 58) where opera singers would perform the *Tenebrae*. This custom survived despite the abbey's closure before the Revolution, its subsequent neglect, and eventual destruction.

89   *The Poitevin gentleman*: Poitevin is the masculine name for a resident of Poitiers, a town in west central France.

the official supporters of the Villèle Ministry: Jean-Baptiste de Villèle (1773-1854) was the ultra-royalist statesman made Prime Minister by Louis XVIII in 1822, a position he held until 1827 when he was succeeded by the more moderate Martignac (see note to page 323).

ailes de pigeon: French for "pigeon's wings," they are the curled earlocks that appear on some styles of powdered wigs.

91   Il Barbiere: *The Barber of Seville* (1816), an opera by Rossini.

pelerine à la neige: a fur cape "with snow."

95   Cara non dubitare *in the "Matrimonio Segreto:"* ("Dear, don't doubt it") a duet between the lovers Paolino and Carolina in Cimarosa's *The Secret Marriage*.

96   *Duc de Bordeaux*: Henri Charles Ferdinand Marie Dieudonné, Comte de Chambord (1820-1883), known to French legitimists as Henry V, was the grandson of Charles X and originally only bore the title of Duke of Bordeaux. He would later unsuccessfully try to claim the French throne. As implied, he would have been quite young at the time the story takes place.

98   *Aulnay, Antony, and Châtenay*: Aulnay-sous-Bois is a commune of the Le Raincy *arrondissement* which constitutes one-third of the Seine-Saint-Denis *département* that lies to the northeast of Paris. Antony and Châtenay-Malabry are both communes located in the Antony *arrondissement* which is itself part of the Hauts-de-Seine *département* in Paris's western suburbs.

The green seclusion of Sceaux: Sceaux, Hauts-de-Seine, is a commune located in Paris' southern suburbs.

the flats of La Beauce, the valley of the Bièvre: the Beauce region is a large plateau to the southwest of Paris devoted mainly to agriculture. The Bièvre is a river that flows from the commune of Guyancourt in the southwestern suburbs of Paris into the Seine.

101 *the Lovelaces of the counting-house*: see note to page xiv, *Clarissa, Lovelace*.

102 *Girodet . . . French Warriors received by Ossian*: see note to page 20 and Plate X.

107 La Belle-Poule: several ships in the French Navy have borne the name *Belle-Poule*; Balzac is probably referring to the warship that began service in 1802 and was part of the fleet sent to take back French colonies in the Indian Ocean that had been relinquished to the English as part of the short-lived Peace of Amiens. She was captured by the British some four years later and inducted into the Royal Navy.

108 *Rue du Sentier*: a street of the 2nd *arrondissement* that has traditionally been a home to textile wholesalers (a detail significant to what will take place later in the story).

109 *Chevreuse*: a commune of the Yvelines *département* located in the midst of the Parc Naturel Régional de la Haute Vallée de Chevreuse to the south of Paris.

111 *no Guimard, no Duthé*: Marie-Madeleine Guimard (1743-1816) was a French ballerina known as much for her many love affairs as for her dancing; Rosalie Duthé (1752-1820) was a French courtesan, dancer, and artist's model.

112 *École Polytechnique*: to this day considered to be one of the finest schools of its type in the world, the *École Polytechnique* is a French engineering school founded in 1794.

124 *Chevalier de Saint-Georges*: see note to page 36.

126 The *Rue de la Paix* is a street of Paris's 2nd *arrondissement* formerly known as the Rue Napoléon; it was renamed after the second restoration and still boasts some of the most stylish and expensive shops in the world.

129   Padrona della casa: "lady of the house."

133   *the lash of an illustrious writer*: another reference to Chateaubriand.

134   La Quotidienne: an ultra-royalist newspaper. After merging with two other papers it became known as the *Union monarchique*, and in 1847 Balzac had his novel *L'Élection*, later to be known as *Le Député d'Arcis*, serialized in its pages.

    Monsieur de Suffren's first expedition: Comte Pierre André de Suffren de Saint Tropez, bailli de Suffren (1729 -1788), was a French admiral best known for his battles against Vice Admiral Sir Edward Hughes in the Indian Ocean. As a young cadet he survived plague and shipwreck during the Duc d'Anville's failed attempt to recapture Cape Breton in Nova Scotia from the English.

Letters of Two Brides

This epistolary novel evolved from two earlier unfinished stories: *Mémoires d'un jeune femme* (1834) and *Sœur Marie des Anges* (c. 1835). Serialized in an abbreviated form by the conservative *La Presse*, it was then revised twice more before reaching this final version. The *Mémoires* were generally not well received by the public. Balzac, however, had great hopes for it. In a letter to Madame Hańska, a Polish noblewoman whom he would eventually marry in 1850, he wrote of his great hopes for the *Mémoires*: "I desire to mark the termination of my youth . . . by a work different from all my other works; a book apart which may be put into the hands of all women, be placed upon every table; a book in which I shall describe all the insensate fears, all the groundless jealousies, and all the sublimity of the gift of one's own being . . ."

141   *To George Sand*: George Sand was the pen-name of French writer Amandine Aurore Lucile Dupin, Baroness Dudevant (1804-1876). She is today remembered for her novels *Indiana*, *Lélia*, and *Consuelo*, as well

as her affairs with many prominent artistic figures of her day, her feminist views, and her penchant for dressing in men's clothing.

144   *Beauvisage*: "handsome face."

       a Mademoiselle de la Vallière: Louise de La Vallière (1644-1710) was one of Louis XIV's mistresses. She bore him many children (possibly as many as seven), but eventually fell out of favor and was replaced by the more artful Marquise de Montespan. La Vallière became a Carmelite nun, taking her final vows in 1675. Ironically, Montespan would later consult her old rival, who by then had forgiven her, on matters of religious piety.

145   *Gémenos valley*: Gémenos is a commune located to the east of Marseilles on France's southern coast.

146   *Beaugency*: a commune on the right bank of the Loire river in the Loiret *département* of central France.

       the Bois de Boulogne: see note to page 58.

148   *on the side of the Invalides*: the Hôtel des Invalides, located in Paris' 7th *arrondissement*, is a hospital and retirement home for war veterans as well as the final resting place for many of France's greatest military heroes.

149   *the Maréchal de Richelieu*: Louis François Armand du Plessis, duc de Richelieu (1696-1788), was a French ambassador, general, and philanderer not to be confused with his great uncle, Cardinal Richelieu.

153   *Return of the Bourbons*: see note to page 71, *The Bourbon cause*.

161   Corinne, Adolphe: see note to page xiv, *Corinne, Adolphe*

167   *The Place Louis XV*: a square located in Paris's eighth
       arrondissement adorned with many fountains and stat-
       ues built in honor of the monarch whose name it bears.
       Today it is more commonly known as the Place de la
       Concorde.

171   *After Leipsic no more was heard of him*: the Battle of
       Leipzig took place from 16-19 October 1813 and end-
       ed in Napoleon's defeat by the forces of the Sixth
       Coalition.

172   *a code which will drive as many girls of good family into
       convents as it will find husbands for*: like most other
       European countries at that time, the Napoleonic Code
       granted complete authority to the husband in matters
       of marriage, but differed by making it relatively easy
       to obtain a divorce.

174   *the Knight of the Sorrowful Countenance*: an epithet be-
       stowed upon Don Quixote by Sancho Panza.

176   *the Court of Lions*: the name of the royal court located at
       the center of the Palace of the Lions which itself forms
       part of the great Alhambra citadel in Granada, Spain.
       It was built by the Nasrids, Spain's last Muslim dynas-
       ty, in the late 14th century.

       the blood of the Abencerrages: an eminent family of un-
       certain historicity in 15th century Moorish Grenada
       mentioned in the Spanish romance *Guerras civiles de
       Granada* by Ginés Perez de Hita (1544-1619).
          Interestingly, one member of this family is said to
       have wooed a lady of the Spanish royal family by ven-
       turing up to her window as Don Félipe Hénarez, the
       Baron de Macumer, will do later in the story to gain
       the attentions of Louise.

177   *Valdez actually believed in his protestations:* Cayetano
       Valdés y Flores (1767-1834) was a Spanish admiral. He
       returned to Spain after being shipwrecked in England

and fought in the Spanish War of Independence (1808-1814) against the French. He was the Captain General in charge of Cádiz until the restoration of King Ferdinand VII in 1814. He briefly served as minister of war during the Spanish Civil War of 1820-1823 but was again forced to flee after the King was restored for a second time.

178   *I heard of Riego's end:* Rafael del Riego y Nuñez (1784-1823) was a Spanish general who led a revolt in 1820 against Ferdinand VII in the hopes of restoring the liberal 1812 Constitution. The King was forced to accept the constitution, and a period known as the *Trienio Liberal* or the Three Liberal Years ensued. However, in 1823 France intervened on the side of the King and Riego was captured, found guilty of treason, and executed.

rey netto: absolute king.

179   *the Duc d'Angoulême*: Louis-Antoine, Dauphin of France and Duke of Angoulême (1775-1844), was the eldest son of Charles X and Legitimist pretender to the throne of France from 1836-1844. He fought for the reinstatement of his cousin Ferdinand VII during the Spanish War of Independence.

180   *Galignani*: Giovanni Antonio Galignani (1757-1821) was the Italian-born publisher of Galignani's *Messenger,* an English-language newspaper printed in Paris with the expressed aim of trying to promote friendship between England and France.

the Rue Hillerin-Bertin: between the Rue de Grenelle and the Rue de Varenne, the Rue Hillerin-Bertin formed part of the Rue de Bellechasse in Paris's 7th *arrondissement* on the left bank of the Seine.

after the fashion of Dionysius at Corinth: a bishop of the second century known only through the writings of

Eusebius of Caesarea (263-c.339), the "Father of Church History."

181 *no longing to try the game again like Napoleon*: see note to page 71, *the second revolution*.

183 *one evening at the Italiens, another at the Grand Opera*: the Théâtre-Lyrique Italien or Opéra-Italien and the Théâtre de l'Académie Royale de Musique, both located in Paris.

184 *Garcia in his splendid duet with Pellegrini in* Otello: Manuel del Pópulo Vicente García (1775-1832) was considered to be the finest Spanish tenor of his day; Felice Pellegrini (1774-1832) was an Italian bass-baritone who appeared in many of Rossini's operas.
  What a cry in "Il mio cor si divide!": "My heart is divided!"

189 *Chimène in the* Cid: in Corneille's *Le Cid*, Chimène is the lover of Don Rodrigue.

  as though he were Gonsalvo di Cordova: Gonzalo Fernández de Córdoba (1453-1515), also known as *El Gran Capitán*, was a Spanish general largely responsible for Spain's status as a world power in the 15th and 16th centuries.

196 *an imitation* Nouvelle Héloïse: see note to page xiv, *Julie d'Etanges*.

  Clarissa also is much too pleased with herself and her long, little letter . . . Richardson's work, etc.: see note to page xiv, *Clarissa*.

199 *the party of Marius and the party of Sulla*: Gaius Marius was a member of the *populares*: a faction that wanted to give a greater degree of power to the plebeians; Lucius Cornelius Sulla Felix was head of the rival *optimates* who wanted to increase the influence of the pro-aristocratic senate.

203　*following the King of Spain to Valençay:* on 6 May 1808 Ferdinand VII was forced by Napoleon to abdicate his throne. The Emperor took him into his protection, sending him to a comfortable imprisonment in Valençay, a commune in central France. Napoleon then installed his elder brother Joseph Bonaparte as King of Spain, but this led to a popular uprising amongst the people which became the War of Spanish Independence. Napoleon would later agree to recognize Ferdinand VII as King as part of the Treaty of Valençay, though the armistice it promulgated did not hold and the war continued.

217　*a member of the Council General of the Department:* the *conseil général* is an elected assembly that manages each of France's many *départements*.

219　*Chamber of Peers*: see note to page 87, *Peer of France.*

228　*Saint-Preux*: Julie d'Etanges's tutor and lover in Rousseau's *Nouvelle Héloïse.*

230　Cyrus *and* Astræa: *Artamène, or Cyrus the Great* (1648-53) by Madeleine de Scudéry is a massive historical novel of seemingly endless plot twists and digressive stories based around the Persian Emperor and his beloved Mandane. *Astræa* or *L' Astrée* (1607-1628) by Honoré d'Urfé (1568-1625) is a pastoral romance set in 5th century Gaul concerning the heroine of the title and her troubled relationship with the devoted but misunderstood Céladon (see note to page 32).

236　*While you were reading* Corinne, *I conned Bonald*: see notes to pages xiv, *Corinne*, and xx. See also note to page xvi, *Bonald.*

237　*Madame de Mirbel*: Lizinska Aimée Zoé de Mirbel (1796-1849) was a famous miniaturist painter known for her delicate and colorful portraits of royal and noble figures.

238   *an Italian* cavaliere servente: literally an "obliging knight," a swain who is openly in love with a married woman and attends to her every whim.

240   *the vote of the Cortes*: the *Cortes Generales* is the name for the Spanish national legislature. During the Spanish War of Independence when French troops occupied much of the country, the *Cortes* was able to hold its sessions in the heavily fortified port city of Cádiz in southern Spain, functioning as a government in exile. The Cádiz *Cortes* was responsible for the liberal Spanish Constitution of 1812 which placed sovereignty in the hands of the populace but also recognized Ferdinand VII as the legitimate King of Spain. Despite the King's pledge to honor the new constitution, he soon came to reject it after being reinstated in 1814 and moved to quash liberal elements that had supported its ratification. He would later relent and accept the constitution for a period of three years after an army revolt, but this did not prevent the eventual outbreak of the Spanish Civil War in 1820.

242   *the sage of Aveyron*: presumably a reference to Bonald who was born near Millau in the Aveyron *département* in 1754.

251   *Racine's* Bérénice: a tragedy first performed in 1670 concerning the Roman emperor Titus whose love for Bérénice, the Queen of Palestine, meets with disapproval from the populace forcing them to part ways.

253   Senza brama, sicura ricchezza!: as translated from the Italian by Mark Musa: "O wealth unfailing, that can never want!" The line is from Canto XXVII of Dante's *Paradisio* and not from the *Inferno* as implied.

267   *the great "Perhaps" of Rabelais*: a reference to what may have been the satirist's last words: "I am off in search of a great perhaps."

272   *at the* Mairie: town hall.

the Church of Sainte-Valère: the Sainte-Clotilde et Sainte-Valère Basilica on the Rue Las Cases in Paris's 7th *arrondissement*, known for its impressive twin spires.

273   *Montargis*: a commune located to the south of Paris that forms part of the Loiret *département* in north-central France.

274   *Briare*: a commune located on the right bank of the Loire river, also part of the Loiret *département*.

277   *Rue du Bac*: a Paris street located in the 7th *arrondissement* on the left bank of the Seine.

279   *get him elected deputy . . . the Chamber*: at the time of the Restoration and the July Monarchy, the Chamber of Deputies, which by this time had replaced the *Corps législatif* (see note to page xviii), was the lower legislative house of government; its members were elected to five year terms by census suffrage.

283   *Obermann, "roots slake their thirst in the foulest streams"*: the quote is from Letter LXXV of *Obermann* (1804), a melancholy epistolary novel by French essayist Étienne Pivert de Senancour (1770-1846).

296   *Célimène in Molière's* Le Misanthrope: see note to page 84, *the part of Célimène.*

297   Faciem semper monstramus: "We always show the face."

300   *I am writing in the presence of the Keeper of the Seals*: the Keeper of the Great Seals of France was a title held by the royally appointed *Chancelier de France* or Minister of Justice who also presided over the Chamber of Peers.

301   *the Bouches-du-Rhône*: literally, "the mouths of the Rhône," the Bouches-du-Rhône is a *département* on the coast of southern France named for Rhône river.

313   *the cross of the Legion of Honor*: see note to page 37, *Chevalier of the Legion of Honor*.

      in the days of King René: René I of Naples (1409-1480), also known as René d'Anjou.

319   *a* capo d'opera *or a* bel quadro: respectively, a "chief work," or "masterpiece," and "beautiful picture."

322   *Gessner's or Florian's sheepfolds, which Rivarol longed to see invaded by a wolf*: Solomon Gessner (1730-1788) was a Swiss poet known for his charming and bucolic pastorals; Jean-Pierre Claris de Florian (1755-1794) was a French poet and dramatist who largely based his style on that of Gessner's. Antoine de Rivarol (1753-1801) was a French epigrammatist notorious for attacking and ridiculing many of the popular writers of his day, Gessner and Florian being only two of his many literary targets. The exact work in which the two poets are parodied is unknown.

323   *Numa was not so far removed from his Egeria*: Numa Pompilius was a Roman king of legend said to be the successor to Romulus; Egeria was his wife and royal advisor, a nymph who taught the king great wisdom.

      you terrible mother Gigogne: "*gigogne*" is a French adjective meaning "nesting." Russian Matryoshka dolls which consist of a series of small wooden figures that nest inside one another are sometimes known in France as *poupées gigognes* (nesting dolls); the name is also a reference to la Mère Gigogne, a character from puppet theater who was a symbol of strength and fertility as well as the mother of many children.

      Martignac: Jean Baptiste Gay, Vicomte de Martignac (1778-1832), was a moderate royalist statesman. As Prime Minister of France under Charles X from 1828-9, he tried to steer a middle course between right and left factions, but was ultimately ineffectual. He was succeeded by the reactionary Prince de Polignac (1780-1847).

325   *Monsieur de Bourmont and Monsieur de Polignac*: Louis-Auguste-Victor, Count de Bourmont (1773-1846), was a French marshal and minister of war under Charles X.

Jules Auguste Armande Marie, Prince de Polignac (1780-1847), succeeded Martignac to become the 8th Prime Minister of France. An ultra-royalist, he was responsible for issuing the July Ordinances which, among other things, ended freedom of the press and dissolved the elected Chamber of Deputies. The July Revolution was a direct result of Polignac's actions.

338   *this July semi-republic*: the final years of Louis XVIII's life and the succession of Charles X saw the gradual erosion of liberties gained from the Charter of 1814 (see note to page 71, *the new Constitution*) as well as attempts to restore the old pre-revolutionary order. The July Monarchy of Louis-Philippe, a more moderate constitutional monarchy than that of Louis XVIII, began with the July Revolution of 1830 and lasted until 1848.

343   *Ville d'Avray*: a commune located in the westernmost suburbs of Paris.

Brieg: also known as Brig or Brigue, it is a Swiss town in the canton of Valais.

359   *the Madeleine is finished*: the Église de la Madeleine is a church situated in the 8th *arrondissement* of Paris designed after a Roman temple and constructed in the Neo-Classical style. It was unfinished at the time of the Revolution and there were disagreements as to its purpose. Napoleon had it turned into a grand memorial to the French army in 1806, but it was overshadowed by the Arc de Triomphe completed two years later. Louis-Philippe had the building serve as a monument

to national reconciliation before it was finally conse-
crated and utilized as a church in 1842.

379   *Rue de la Ville l'Évêque*: a street located in Paris's 8th *arrondissement* on the right bank of the Seine.

391   I Puritani, La Sonnambula, Moïse: The first two are
operas by the Italian composer Vincenzo Bellini: *The
Puritans* and *The Sleepwalker*; the third is *Moses and
Pharaoh* by Rossini.

Bibliography
and Further Reading

Floyd, Juanita Helm, *Women in the Life of Balzac* (Austin: Holt, Rinehart & Winston, 1921).

Gerson, Noel B., *The Prodigal Genius: The Life and Times of Honoré de Balzac* (New York: Doubleday, 1972).

Keim, Albert and Louis Lumet, *Honoré de Balzac* (New York: Frederick A. Stokes Company, 1914).

Lawton, Frederick, *Balzac* (New York: Wessels, 1910).

Robb, Graham, *Balzac: A Biography* (New York: W.W. Norton & Company, 1994).

Sandars, Mary F., *Honoré de Balzac, His Life and Writings* (London: J. Murray, 1904).

Wettlaufer, Alexandra K., *Pen Vs. Paintbrush: Girodet, Balzac, and the Myth of Pygmalion in Post-Revolutionary France* (New York: Palgrave, 2001).

Zweig, Stefan, *Balzac* (New York: The Viking Press, 1946).

CPSIA information can be obtained
at www.ICGtesting.com
Printed in the USA
BVHW041414240519
549223BV00001B/10/P

9 780976 706205